ALSO BY CHARLOTTE BACON

There Is Room for You
Lost Geography
A Private State

SPLIT ESTATE

SPLIT ESTATE

·

Charlotte Bacon

·

Farrar, Straus and Giroux

New York

Farrar, Straus and Giroux
18 West 18th Street, New York 10011

Copyright © 2008 by Charlotte Bacon
Distributed in Canada by Douglas & McIntyre Ltd.
Printed in the United States of America
First edition, 2008

Grateful acknowledgment is made for permission to reprint the following material:

"What the Living Do," from *What the Living Do* by Marie Howe. Copyright © 1997 by Marie Howe. Used by permission of W. W. Norton & Company, Inc.

"A Brief for the Defense," from *Refusing Heaven: Poems* by Jack Gilbert. Copyright © 2005 by Jack Gilbert. Used by permission of Alfred A. Knopf, a division of Random House, Inc.

Library of Congress Cataloging-in-Publication Data
Bacon, Charlotte.
  Split estate / Charlotte Bacon.—1st ed.
    p. cm.
  ISBN-13: 978-0-374-28183-0 (hardcover : alk. paper)
  ISBN-10: 0-374-28183-1 (hardcover : alk. paper)
  1. Loss (Psychology)—Fiction. 2. Bereavement—Fiction. 3. Domestic fiction. I. Title.

PS3552.A27S55 2008
813'.54—dc22

2007042856

Designed by Jonathan D. Lippincott

www.fsgbooks.com

1 3 5 7 9 10 8 6 4 2

*For Rachel and for Nick
and for
John Charles Smith*

Everything only connected by "and" and "and."

—Elizabeth Bishop, "Over 2000 Illustrations
and a Complete Concordance"

PART I

. . . we want the spring to come and the winter to

pass. We want

whoever to call or not call, a letter, a kiss—we want more and more

and more and

then more of it.

But there are moments, walking, when I catch a glimpse of myself in the

window glass,

say the window of the corner video store, and I'm gripped by a

cherishing so deep

for my own blowing hair, chapped face, and unbuttoned coat that I'm

speechless:

I am living, I remember you.

—Marie Howe, "What the Living Do"

ARTHUR

In April, the second woman jumped. "It happened again," was all Cam told Arthur.

"Oh God," Arthur said into the receiver. He had his palm on his forehead; the light angled in a golden wedge across his desk, his papers. Dust sharpened to particles of gray diamond. The news about Laura had created the same terrible brilliance. He'd also found out by phone, and again the day, which had been pressing steadily forward, had snapped as inevitably as bad rope.

"Mrs. Van Buren," his son said. "The mother of this kid in eighth grade." He was trying hard to school his voice to calmness. "We knew her." A face swam into Arthur's mind. Someone in a plaid taffeta shirt at Christmas parties. Cheeks round as plates. "I'll be right there, I'll leave now," Arthur said, gathering pens, fumbling at the lock on his briefcase.

As he swayed uptown on the subway with all the other darkjacketed men, New York seemed a failed, grimy detour. Arthur had rarely felt more than lightly tethered here. Laura, another transplant, had also appeared bemused to find herself in the city, surrounded by its particular abundance. "The Philharmonic," she'd say. "We could go to the symphony," as if it were a slight surprise that this resource existed so close by.

New York had merely been the setting in which Arthur tended his family and earned the money that kept them housed, fed, sustained. A stage, while the real life, the secret life amid his wife and children unfolded in a maze of jokes and dinners, moods and arguments, a life tied not so much to location as to gesture, scraps of memory, the shape of the kitchen taps, and the quality of light in the bedroom.

But then Laura had jumped, and the one part of the city about which he'd claimed intimate knowledge proved to be fatally unfamiliar. He never said "after Laura died": "jump" was the verb his mind selected, as if the soft exhalation of "died" were too tranquil or passive. "Jump" was all decisive, smashing action.

New York, city of water, was in the end a bad match for a person raised in a desert. But in Wyoming, where he was born, he'd be able to keep an eye on his children. They would need to be driven to and from school. In Callendar, they'd be unable to slip out of his grasp below the city's surface, lost in its knots of tunnels. They'd have no use for cell phones out there where towers stood miles from one another. Lucy, his mother, a consummate watcher, would join him in this dry vigilance. Despite weather dedicated to extremes, its guns and rattlesnakes, the West at that moment seemed a safer place to raise children. Mostly, it was a spot that held less of Laura and more of Lucy, who had chosen to wind her life into one small town. It was not that Wyoming hadn't changed, but it was where what was left of his family had decided to be a known and visible part. His name scratched the dirt there.

Arthur had lived in Callendar until he was fourteen and went back every August to visit Lucy, who still owned a house among the miles of fence parceling the rounded land to squares, amid falcons and meadowlarks, elk and sky. He knew this was at best a partial image. Golf courses now carpeted scrubland, condominiums and box stores bulked into the narrow valleys. Even so, he had been edging his way toward a return since Laura's death. He would take his children back this summer; they would stay for at least the fall. An advertisement offered him a chance to repair a torn earlobe. The doors sprang open at Lexington and Eighty-sixth Street, and he and all the other whites leaped to the platform.

Aboveground, the light was full, wet, soft, far greener than the day in October, near Halloween, when his wife had launched herself from a tenth-story window and landed on the canopy before finishing her fall to the sidewalk. She'd left no note. Again and again, he raked through the details of that morning. He could picture Laura flicking a match to make the unreliable pilot light burn steady. The bones of her wrist pressed like triangular pearls against the skin as she poured orange juice. Nothing different. Nothing as it had not been for month after month. He'd allowed himself to think her well. Some balance for the moment achieved. There'd been no special look the day she died, no extra pressure to her touch. As if the thought to leave had struck her for the first time a little later that day, as casually arrived at as a choice of shoes. But little was casual with Laura, not shoes, not notes, not anything.

At the apartment, he found Cam balled on the sofa, his long body nearly swallowed in velvet. A piece of furniture that Laura used to say ate change, magazines, cats. "But we don't have cats," their daughter, Celia, would say, insisting on literal truth to a mother who preferred the curve of story over bald accuracy. Now, with Laura gone, Cam said from the cave of the cushions, "They're going to think she started it. People will think it's her fault."

Arthur sat on the arm of the sofa and noticed how worn the treads of his son's sneakers were. He would take him this weekend and buy three new pairs. Arthur touched his son's ankle and its breadth and hair surprised him. When had Cam developed the foot of a man? "Buddy, can I get you something?" Cam shook his head. Arthur saw that lint had gathered in a fine pelt below the coffee table. The apartment smelled as if they had already left, as if it were already empty. Nearby, perhaps across the hall, a neighbor started to fry an onion. A radio was switched to news, and voices spoke above the static of the day's events.

Celia would be home any moment, and soon they heard the click of the elevator in the hall, the sound of her feet. The light slicing the blinds caught her glasses and reflected a pair of burning disks. She jerked back from the doorknob; she hadn't expected them. Always alert to any indication of change, she'd told Arthur nothing had appeared strange to her either, the morning Laura died. She'd seemed the same as always, a little tired, a little distracted, Celia said. Arthur had understood. You never knew. There was a great deal he hadn't known about. Opening the bathroom cabinet in early November to find aspirin, he'd found himself fumbling instead among his wife's medicines. The pills made cheerful clicks in their plastic tubes. She hadn't taken any in weeks. He could not have determined the precise ratio of rage to sadness as he crushed the vials to orange fragments beneath his heel. She had seemed well, he kept telling himself. Her hands smelled of fixer, a sign she was working, a sign that she was fine. She had bought new lenses. There'd been no need for special vigilance. But apparently there had.

"What happened, Dad?" Celia asked now. "Why isn't Cam at practice? Why are you home?"

"This woman jumped," Cam said. "Mrs. Van Buren." His voice was rough, as if from disuse. Celia dropped her book bag. The impact made the aglets of Arthur's laces jump and tap the tooled leather of his shoes. Laura had taught him that word years ago. She had enjoyed how specifically names attached themselves to things. It seemed incredible to him that someone could care that much about a slender bit of language, a piece of inconsequential metal, and then decide to leave. "Arthur," his mother had told him one bad night, "you have to remember that when Laura was happy, she loved the world."

"Jesus," Celia said, moving out of the banded light. "It's catching, I knew it was catching." Out of the sun, her eyes were huge below her glasses. She refused contacts. Her father worried no one would ever ask her to dance. "But I'm not a good dancer," Celia had said.

As the day faded, Arthur ordered Chinese food. Laura had been frugal, hating the waste of plastic forks and wads of napkins that arrived with takeout. When she could be coaxed into it, she saved the duck sauce in a corner of a kitchen drawer, which was crackling now with the packets. Since Laura's death, nothing prevented them from eating like this most nights. It was one of their more obvious betrayals. Arthur used the novelty as a bribe. He could lure his children to dinners during which he could watch them for signs of despair. Calzones, he would say. Thai tonight, and they would abandon friends and schoolwork and the computer and sit with him at the table and eat greasy, delicious food and talk of very little.

The cartons left damp squares on the white cloth, and the humidity might have damaged the wood below. The children spooned heaps of fragrant rice onto their plates. They were silent as they ate, Cam and Celia deft with chopsticks. Arthur's resolve to leave New York wavered as he watched them at their familiar places at the table. But as he began to talk, the spell he wanted to cast on them netted his own imagination instead. The blunt, unpeopled land. The single area code. Animals and wind. He knew he was leaving out a great deal. And they were less susceptible to western dreams than those who had tried in part to live them. His voice was the voice he hoped for in opposing counsel, one of hollow, ringing confidence. His argument was thin as well. Still, he could feel unwinding in himself a fiery thread of desire to be done with city life, looped instead around something fierce and open.

The children stopped eating. He always thought of them this way, as "the children," in a brace, inseparable, the word he and

Laura had always used, lumping them together. They'd arrived only a year and half apart and looked so much alike, hazel-eyed and lanky, their mother's genes stamping them more firmly than his own. But Arthur had seemed to miss the interval between their childhood and this new stage. They had learned to hold their height. At fifteen and seventeen, they were on the brink of a self-possession most adults did not have. Yet they were still learning to conjugate verbs for languages used in countries they had never visited.

"Have you talked to Lucy?" Celia asked. When the children were little, Lucy had asked that they call her by her first name; "Grandma," she said, made her feel prematurely withered, and soon Arthur, too, was on a first-name basis with his mother. Celia nudged a noodle around her plate. Cam was churning a plastic sack of soy sauce to brown froth.

"Not yet," Arthur admitted. He had no idea what Lucy would say. She had come when Laura died, and it was clear as always that she had no patience for New York, for its urgencies and glossy surfaces. She had stayed three weeks, been effortlessly competent. Cam and Celia had followed her like anxious cats. But living with Lucy, not just for part of the summer, but living with her rules, her chores, would be something else entirely. "She'll be glad to have us. We can start with her. We can see how it goes." He felt none of the casualness his words aimed to capture.

Cam leaned back in his chair, squeezing the soy sauce as he did so. "You think that's going to solve it, Dad?" he said, though he obviously expected no response. He pressed the packet so tightly that it burst with a soft gush on the white tablecloth. "That is one lousy idea." He made no attempt to arrest the stain. He sat there holding the small empty sack. Celia looked down, at the table, at her food.

Arthur watched the dark spot assume first the shape of a ragged quarter moon and then a hand with missing fingers. His

son's rejection rang in the air. He thought, I must remain calm.
He had had to for so long—the compromise arrived at in his
marriage, vestigial wildness traded because reliability was what
Laura required. But now something scandalously direct and un-
parental emerged, as if a feral dog were loose inside him. He
said, "You know why I want to go? Because I can't stand walking
past that part of the sidewalk. And now there's another one. I
cannot watch that all over again." It didn't matter that he'd spoken slowly and not in anger. He'd spoken in raw wonder at the
extent and tenacity of his own pain, which he had tried to mask
from his children—fruitlessly, it turned out.

Cam sprang from the table and knocked his chair over. Celia
closed her eyes.

"I'm so sorry," Arthur said.

Celia didn't move for a moment and then said, "Me, neither.
I can't stand it, either."

She reached across the table; her hand in his was firm and
long and man-size. It seemed like months since he had touched
his daughter. They'd lost that habit when the children became
teenagers and wrapped in the mysteries of their suddenly adult
bones. The thinness to her fingers felt familiar, and he knew it
was because she reminded him of Laura, of what it had felt like
to hold Laura's hand.

Celia released her grip on him. She did not bother to right
her brother's chair. "That's never going to come out," she said,
tilting her chin toward the stain. From Cam's room, they heard
the thud of darts hitting cork again and again, the sound of his
precise and muffled rage. "He'd hate it out there," Celia said. Of
the family, he had had the hardest time on their annual trips
west. He always looked slightly awkward under the high, empty
blue. Someone suited for ocean, not for sky.

"Maybe," Arthur said, seeing he'd once again ordered twice
as much as they needed. He started to tuck the flaps back into
the cartons, to ready himself for the cleaning up and then the

call to Lucy. "It's too soon to tell. He's just so sad. It's normal," he said to Celia.

"It's not normal at all," Celia said, stacking the plates, which she put to one side. She pulled the tablecloth off and mashed it to a wrinkled lump. She was preparing, he knew, to take it to the washing machine. Without a word, Celia had taken over the laundry since her mother died. "There is not one thing that's normal about this," she added, holding the cloth tight.

Lucy was reading when he called. For years she had indulged a taste for tales of extreme climates, roaming from polar explorations to rain forests. This season she was committed to desert narratives, stories in which nomads in the Empty Quarter ate lizards. Cam and Celia were both in bed, and Arthur thought they were asleep. No lights or sounds came from their rooms, at least. Cam had not emerged again, though Arthur had knocked and asked if he wanted more food. Later, he would creep in and check that they were still in bed, still alive. He had done this every night since Laura died, a habit from their infancies, reasserted now that their mother had shown them that suicide was a possibility. He had had to steel himself against locking windows the way he locked doors. Lucy answered on the first ring.

They always began with weather, but never New York weather, which was largely inconsequential in terms of its impact on daily life. Umbrellas could be raised, taxis sought for cover. But twenty minutes of storm in Wyoming could compress ten years' worth of bad luck and financial disaster. Once you had seen wheat fields thrashed by hail or a pasture heaped with lightning-struck cows, you rarely thought of weather in the city as anything but girlish and simple. Tonight Lucy was saying that two feet of snow had fallen in the Bighorns. The road was shut between Lovell and Greybull again. People were worried about their lambs.

Days could go past and Arthur never thought of livestock,

the stark fact of animals with their need to be husbanded and their scheduled deaths in hopes of profit. But he had grown up surrounded by creatures. Horses and Black Angus, chickens, pigs, cats, and dogs. Surrounded, too, by the commerce and drama that attended the presence of those that could be eaten. How much Kozlowski's beef had sold for; the ravages of coyotes on someone's sheep. Lucy no longer ran cattle on their land: she'd sold off too much acreage to sustain even a few head, but she still had a taste for ranching and the operatic news its economics gave rise to. She kept a border collie and pigs, all named after a president or a scientist she admired—Edison, Roosevelt, Einstein, Lincoln. No president since Kennedy had made it onto the list. Her politics were resolutely mired in the New Deal, which made her, as she said, about as rare as a jackalope in her home state. It was an issue best left undiscussed between them. Arthur's vague but reflexively conservative views aroused in her thin-lipped disgust.

He also never mentioned to Lucy, since she knew it too completely, that even the gossip of the sort they traded would be gone in ten, twenty years. No one was making it on small ranches anymore, if they ever really had. The scrappy single-family operations of the sort people had fallen for had been doomed romances from the start. It was no wonder the animals' names were stalled in the 1960s.

Arthur listened to details of the storm's path. Lucy was the fourth generation of her family to expose itself to Wyoming weather, an old lineage for whites in the state. A scattering of nieces and nephews were left, but all of her siblings were gone and now their children were moving on, wanting to live in a place where the wind didn't blow the paint from the houses. They were tired of such scoured land and uncertain prospects. The real-estate peddlers, the titanium miners, the idiot hunters from California—they could have it. Her students, too, were keen to leave; Lucy had taught school for thirty-eight years and could remember where almost every one of them had fled to.

His mother's news always inspired a grave intentness in Arthur, which might have seemed sham but wasn't. He was still interested, though the concern felt foolish. There was nothing in him that knew anymore how to manage a cattle sale or a saddle-shy colt. He had lost those skills, if he'd ever had them, in the thirty years he'd been away, lawyering, as Lucy put it, back East. Not all those years were lawyer years, he pointed out. There had been boarding school and college. To which you sent me, he might have added but did not. To which you insisted I go. "But it ended in lawyering," Lucy would say, as if that hadn't been her plan all along, to save him from the ragged, chancy world of ranches.

There had also been the unfortunate fact that not one piece of Wyoming life came naturally to him: ham-fisted with tools, stiff with horses, more unlucky with rope than a man set to be hanged, as his father, Sean, once commented. "You are one large scar," Laura said to him when they first met, touching the bubbled skin on his arm where a piece of barbed wire had wound round it. Arthur had answered that she should see what he did to metal detectors. By the time he was fourteen, both radii were studded with metal pins and his right knee had developed a permanent ache. His doctor had called him a boy with an old man's bones.

Lawyering had its drawbacks, but it had at least foiled another shattered pelvis and a part-time job wasting away in an ER. Lawyering was what had stuck and what he rather grudgingly excelled at. He'd learned for the first time at his eastern school that he did not have to stow away his mental agility. He had also learned that girls would approach him, talk to him, touch him. He developed a stronger sense of confidence, but one built from materials most people in Wyoming wouldn't particularly value—striking looks and a brain good at puzzles done indoors. Gifts that wouldn't have gotten him through a Wyoming winter had been more than enough to provide for a life in New York.

He looked at the arm of the chair where he sat in the room they'd called the library and let his mind wander further as his mother talked about the operations of acquaintances and this year's tax assessment. Lucy knew better than to ask how he was. The answer was darkly, laughably the same, day after day. Her own husband had died, not by his own choice but just as abruptly. She understood that kind of experience left you with little but the husk of yourself and the harshest part was, the refurnishing of that self was left entirely up to you. The person who might have helped was gone, and worse, her loss had caused the desolation. Laura had thought his cowboy scars were signs of woundedness, a trait they might share. But Arthur's kind—physical, medically reparable—was nothing compared to what she had lived with inside her mind. A surface like silk, an inner life of total, sudden breakages.

Books were piled about the floor, on the shelves. A television teetered on top of a covered radiator and next to that sat a stereo and a scattering of CDs. Laura's music, mostly Laura's books. They'd been a specific sort of fuel for her. Brazilian songs one year, Spanish poets the next. But she didn't like to travel; too much sensation all at once, she said, and she'd moved so much as a child. This, she'd say, tapping a book cover or an album case with a short fingernail, this I can measure out. She had liked to sit next to the window so she could read in natural light.

It started to rain. If they moved out to Callendar, he knew he would not bring one of those sad books, a single one of those haunting albums. He had stopped reading or listening to music since she died; he needed to strip from his mind anything that stirred up too much feeling. He sought no chance to conjure up his wife, since the memories came anyway and he hadn't found a way to stop them. They arrived at night, tenacious, unprovoked. He woke most mornings thick with salt and exhaustion. "Lucy," he said inside a pause, "I've got an idea." He told her what he hoped to do: find a tenant for the apartment; talk to Dwight Higgins about getting some work at his firm; bring the kids out for at least the summer and fall. He did not explain then about Susan Van Buren's suicide and the suddenness of the need to leave the city.

"They don't deliver pizza out my way," Lucy finally said. "You might do better to start in town. The children could meet more people." What she was saying was that there was no cure for being motherless and he ought to keep his expectations in check, despite the grandness of the change. She was warning him not to lean too hard on geography. She was reminding him that after Sean died, she had stayed put and that turned out to be a choice that yielded something she could live with. But she hesitated. He guessed she was thinking of Cam and Celia, of what it cost them to manage in public with how thoroughly their mother had exposed their private lives. Finally, she said that Franklin, the dog, would be glad of company that was not exclusively that of an old woman.

If his mother accepted their possible return with less ready pleasure than he'd wished for, she had still agreed. She had seen the plan's appeal, even without knowing that another woman had jumped. Now he had the children to convince. Arthur turned off the lamp. Wide veins of silver water flowed on the pane. The window was open and through it came the smell of city spring: damp and sooty; wedged below that, the hint of earth. A headache gathered and pulsed at the root of his brain. It was almost always there; he just had to sit still long enough for it to find him. He was too tired to search for aspirin and he wasn't drinking. Whiskey made the memories start to swing like a set of sharp-toothed keys hurled at a hook.

He picked up the pillow that Laura had always propped behind her head for reading. After she died, it still held the scent of her hair. He'd discovered that by chance and had made a sound he did not like to think about. Now he lifted it tentatively to his face. Nothing but dampness on one side, dust on the other. Ordinary, uninflected with association. Instead of liquor, he allowed himself one cigarette a day, indulging again in his only childhood vice. He'd started when his father died, as if smoking meant that there was a man around the house. Lucy's punishments were real and fierce, but nothing she did or said had stopped him until one day, about ten years ago, he'd quit and not once been tempted to start again. Then, the day after Laura jumped, he started again and although the nicotine made him dizzy, he stubbornly continued. He lit up now, aiming the smoke out the open window. Done, he tossed the stub to the sidewalk, imagined its quick tumble downward, and settled back in the chair, unable or unwilling to move further. When he woke near dawn, the rain had stopped. His back ached. But dreams and sweat had not jolted him awake as they had the past few months. It was the light, gray and uncertain. His body was dry.

That morning, he watched Cam and Celia, trying to gauge their reactions, and saw only aggrieved alignment as they passed each other the jam. He knew that they understood why departure might be helpful, but that they would also resist it.

Especially Cam, though he was the one who might benefit most from the change. "Not working to potential" became a phrase he and Laura had seen since the earliest report cards. A dreamer, other teachers put it, more charitably. Silent, an athlete, a beautiful draftsman, a beautiful boy, very much like his mother. When he was a baby, people had stopped to tousle his dark curls and admire his face. Now they merely stared— girls, women, men. Cam appeared not to notice the attention he attracted and never mentioned his looks. He wasn't sullen, but he also wasn't tempted by speech and the achievements it could bring.

Arthur had insisted on tests, measurements, concrete information they could act on. He couldn't believe he'd produced a son resistant to school. The professionals shrugged; some suggested special routines, different curricula. Laura had said, "Leave him be. He's got talents. They're just not yours." Implying, I wasn't unlike him, be gentle. It was true that when Arthur cajoled and scolded less, Cam was happier and filled notebooks with sketches for elaborate tree houses. And he could fix or build anything with speedy, intuitive grace. Wyoming had room for quiet boys who were competent with their hands. If they could find him a job, he might find purchase out there.

Celia, Arthur allowed, would be a harder fit, though she loved and admired Lucy. Nervy, precocious, all brain and skinny legs—it was hard to see how exactly she'd manage the transition. But she would, because that's how she was. Learning for her was the kind of drug it had been for Arthur: the source of reliable satisfaction.

For now, however, both of them would rage and resist and make it as difficult as they could. He could see the moping gather around Cam, settle between his shoulders as he hoisted his backpack and set off for the day. My asshole father. Celia would need to place the blame less categorically, but there would eventually be scenes, slammed doors.

When they left for school, he changed his shirt for one that was less wrinkled. He shaved. "He shaved," Arthur said out loud. "He took a leave from his job. He arranged a sublet. His children hated him. He hoped it was temporary. He suspected it might not be. They have doubts about his competence that seem justified. How will the failed cowboy improve their lives out there in the New West?" He had taken to narrating his life in the third person and seeing in it its extreme paltriness.

Despite the stumbling of his confidence, he set the move in motion. He explained to their teachers that they would be gone for at least six months. He endured the skeptical appraisals of his judgment. He talked to Dwight Higgins, the first lawyer he'd ever known. Arthur remembered when Dwight became an attorney, after he'd washed out as a rancher. He had come to see him and Lucy when Sean died. Arthur had thought Dwight strange, and then realized it was only because the man's fingers were pink and clean. He was a person who looked more comfortable inside, which made him seem almost foreign in Wyoming, until he started to talk. His voice was all battered pickup.

Dwight interrupted after Arthur's third sentence. "Arthur, shut your mouth. I'll find you something. The deal is, I can't promise you'll like it. Re-read your mining law: split estate, eminent domain. Learn your mining law in the first place, for Christ's sake." Pity, Arthur thought. The pity of men for men, unexpressed but potent, made him feel both grateful and enraged. He could imagine Dwight going home to his beautiful wife, Denise, and shaking his head at Arthur's plight. "I had to offer the poor cocksucker a job, honey," he'd say. "After what that woman, that Democrat, did to him? What else could I do?" Arthur looked out at the great clear panels that covered the office building opposite: they blazed orange in the sun, and he grew giddy thinking about how high he was in the air to be able to see the effects of light on glass from this perspective.

At the apartment, he fought the battles he'd anticipated with his children until one night late in May when the first of the city's summer heat was on them. They were in the kitchen drinking iced tea from a mix, another betrayal. Laura had always made theirs from steeped Irish Breakfast, fresh lemons, stalks of mint. The way Virginians make it, she would say. "You're from D.C.," Arthur would retort. The Virginia side, she'd answer. Via Bucharest and Tehran, he'd add, Taipei and Beirut. Foreign service brat. Never made it yourself. Hard words, to lighten adoration so thick it embarrassed him. Political splits, families so unlike each other they might have been of different species, none of it mattered. Even when he knew her to be dangerously fragile, he never did not want to touch her. Still, even soon after her death, certain traditions she'd insisted on hadn't lasted. Cam brought a tin of the fake stuff from the store one day and they'd been drinking it since. In honesty, Arthur liked it better than his wife's. It tasted like tea someone on TV had imagined, tea from a planet where they didn't have it. Chemical and deadly sweet.

Suddenly Cam said, "Callendar. Callendar, Wyoming. You want to go?" he asked his sister.

Celia considered her brother. It registered for all of them that he was really asking her. He was waiting to see what she would say. As if her opinion could tilt his own. A link between them when they'd all grown used to chronic separation.

"Yes," she said. Celia was looking at something outside the window, and Arthur wondered what was running through her mind. Perhaps her school, perhaps her classmates, girls who frightened off boys with their passion for math and French. Girls who gathered in pizza parlors where strings of cheese laced their braces. Laura had photographed Celia like this once. Otherwise, Arthur would not have seen this fragment of his daughter's life, an expression on her face, eager and wry, that she never wore at home. Talking to her hunched and laughing friends, slices drooping in their hands. Laura had taken the picture through the restaurant window. Celia hadn't seen her mother, who'd merely happened to pass by. "It's weird," his daughter said now, still not looking at Arthur. "I wouldn't mind it for a while." She might have been imagining New York's plane trees in cages or its constant night sirens. The melting tar of streets in August. Or none of those at all.

"Cam?" Arthur asked and felt a tightness gather in his chest. Celia had taken in his gratitude for her response, but they both knew a decision couldn't be reached without Cam's consent. Like his mother, he had the power to roughen or to console.

"Maybe," said Cam in such a way as to mean yes. The short word was heavy with regret, and their old life, with Laura its uncertain center, filled the room. The weeks when taking her sad, elegant pictures had made her happy. The Sundays when they had to be quiet because she was sleeping and she slept so rarely. The visits from her parents and brother, the house filled with handsome, dark, drinking DeVrieses, and cutting boards littered with the rinds of limes. Or maybe not, thought Arthur. It was impossible to know what happened in other people's versions of their years with Laura. He felt all at once the weight of taking Celia and Cam so far from the familiar. He knew how partially prepared he was to be their guide out there.

"We'll be freaks. The school mascot is a buffalo," Celia said to no one in particular.

"Go Bison," Cam commented, a response that constituted the final piece of his agreement. Arthur tried not to draw attention to his astonishment. He'd been waiting for his son to stalk off, sulk, slam a door. Cam so often spoke in absences. Arthur was frayed with relief and bubbled up too quickly with chatter. "We'll see the soccer coach when we get out there. Meet some teachers."

"Whatever, Dad," Cam said. "I'm going to take a shower." But he didn't move, as if he, too, was stunned at his willingness to be transplanted.

Celia picked up Laura's camera then. Arthur hadn't seen it; she must have had it stashed on the floor. Since April, she had been taking roll after roll of terrible pictures with her mother's Pentax. Laura to the end had resisted the ease of the digital age. "Smile," she told her brother and father. The shutter clicked too slowly. She had no flash. It would be another awful photograph. Cam had turned just as she gave her command; all she'd capture was the back of his curly head. Arthur grinned reflexively and knew he'd probably look like a drunk who'd won a fight. "What are you going to call it?" he asked, so tired he felt he could fall asleep on his feet. Even at their worst, Celia named the photographs and glued them into bulky journals. She was kind enough, mostly, not to insist that he look at every one.

"*Iced Tea,*" his daughter said.

They said goodbye to friends, who had seemed alternately confused or appalled by what they were doing, Wyoming as distant to most New Yorkers as Ukraine. Arthur had always presented his ties to the state in semicomic self-deprecation—he'd learned quickly that most easterners saw the West as a place where the fashion and the politics were equally benighted, and he'd painted life there in broad, shallow strokes. To have it emerge as a serious destination that could reabsorb his family bewildered most people. "Didn't you get that out of your system?" a colleague asked, as if Wyoming were some stubborn virus. Others at Arthur's firm were more openly displeased but reluctant to be seen punishing a man who had experienced his sort of misfortune; the senior partners grudgingly approved his leave. The subletter, a seedy banker, had been apprised of everything from where to put recycling to the moods of the super, but appeared to be only half-listening. He might be planning to use the apartment for a brothel or a base of operations for a drug ring. In truth, Arthur cared about none of it. He was frantic to be on his way. He couldn't stand another moment of covert sympathy from the circle of onlookers that defined his community. This sense of exposure gave rise to an ugly cousin: rage at these people for not knowing what it was like to lose your wife with such complete and sudden meanness. At times he burned with hatred of the unafflicted and he wanted to be as far away as possible from witnesses, even if it meant returning to a town whose ideas of mastery he had never achieved.

It was finally time to go, and all that was left was a thorough cleaning of the apartment. He'd sent the children off for the afternoon, a Saturday, humid and bright. He could have paid someone to do the scrubbing, but he'd often taken on domestic chores himself, too much Lucy's son to rely on someone else, Laura would have said. Actually, he was good at housecleaning and needful of any reminder of proficiency. "But why did Arthur send his children away?" he heard himself ask aloud and knew the answer. In this last scouring, he entertained the dubious, unworthy hope that he would uncover a note.

One November night, when Cam and Celia were safe with neighbors, he had torn through the apartment. His anger at Laura and her silence caught and spread, his bones its kindling. He'd thrown drawers into the middle of rooms as he scavenged for a reason. Finally, he sat on the bed he had slept in with his wife and pounded the headboard until he bruised the meat of his palms. He had sweat and cursed, and it was like watching a film about a deranged man, shaggy with rage, someone he wouldn't encounter otherwise.

The anger returned with slightly less force as he mopped the kitchen floor, noticing the scars on the blue linoleum. It diminished almost entirely when he scrubbed the bathroom sink and wrestled with the hot-water tap that they had never managed to repair. On the brink of abandoning this apartment, he'd never felt so attached to its balky fixtures and its tarnished, slanted light. This set of rooms, with its banging radiators and inadequate closets, its soft dust, this perch on the tenth floor that had held his family. He had put silver and books and paintings into storage, but he noticed that both Cam and Celia were bringing things they didn't dare abandon. Cam had packed his dartboard and his soccer balls. Celia had Laura's cameras and her own blighted photographs. He had selected essential files and some clothes. Now, as he cleaned, he found only paper clips and pennies. Not a scrap of admissible evidence.

During the drive west in the days to come, he was to remember with shame the way he'd investigated the backs of drawers, the corners of the linen closet. If she'd wanted to leave me a note, he kept telling himself, she would have put it where I could find it. It would have been held down with a rock she'd pulled from a river. A wine bottle. She wouldn't have resorted to secrecy. She just didn't want to talk about it. There was, in the end, probably nothing to say. The idea of suicide had likely lurked in her mind for years. Her past was studded with abrupt departures: a grandmother and an uncle had both killed themselves. Her brother had been hospitalized several times for depression and now he might well feel that his sister had cleared the way for him. Over the years, Arthur had cautiousy revealed these jagged fragments of Laura's history to his mother and he'd sensed Lucy's sharp questions, though she never voiced them. Why did you choose someone who needed such delicate care? Someone with so many fault lines in her character?

You could give a thousand different versions of why you married the person you did. The reason could be as slight as admiring how light outlined her ankles when she wore summer dresses. You could just as easily ground an answer inside the pinched, sterile language of pathology: how you complemented each other's neurotic habits so that together you created a seamless knot of dysfunction. You could concoct another that emphasized practicality, another that stressed chance. Not even fifty conversations with a sensitive listener could come close to describing the weird continuity of marriage. Now, thinking of Lucy's stern wonder at the extent of Laura's failures, he was tempted to respond, I liked looking after someone who, for once, needed me. I liked caring for a person who appreciated my strengths. Saying merely that he loved Laura was too mawkish, stark, and incomplete.

He repeated these lines only at low moments and only in his

own head. It was unnerving to hear them return with such force in the motels where he and Cam and Celia slept on the drive out. Still, he would finish this imagined dialogue with the conclusion that there were no excuses for what she had done. The least she could have attempted was an explanation.

Lying awake so much at night made him tired during the day, and he often needed to pull over at rest stops. "Just a quick nap," he'd say. "But they're not naps, Dad," Celia told him in Ohio. "They're mini-comas. Semis roar past and you don't move. Cam blasts the radio and you don't move." Pulling back onto the road, he was often still tangled inside the remnants of a dream. He felt only half-conscious, as if black fragments of nightmare were floating in front of him as he steered into the right lane. He saw Celia look at him then and averted his eyes, as though, when their glances met, she'd be able to glimpse the detached limbs he was seeing, the stairways that ended in air.

Cam and Celia fought often: too many long bodies crammed into too small a space. Laura had argued for years against a car—too expensive, not used enough in city life—and Arthur had just as stubbornly insisted on one, sensing that it was critical to plan for escape from New York. The compromise had been in its size, which Arthur regretted when he saw what it took for Cam and Celia to fold themselves into the backseat of the Toyota. Sullen peace held for a few hours in the morning, each of them lost in music or books, but then arguments broke out about where and when they'd eat lunch and gathered to stormy intensity in the last hour before they stopped for the night. At least, Arthur thought, I know exactly where they are. At least we don't have to dicker about directions. They headed north, then straight west on the wide, wide highways.

The open skies of the plains usually unknotted his chest. He felt safer for no clearly discernible reason as they traveled toward the mountains, though the speeds on the roads were punishingly dangerous and gun ownership in the surrounding towns higher than one might feel comfortable with. But relaxation did not come this time. Where Laura should have sat, one of the children now did. If they were getting along well enough to share the back, then the cooler, with its waterlogged cheese and beaded bottles of soda, occupied her place. Also, Celia would not stop taking pictures with Laura's Pentax. He had given it to his wife fifteen years ago, when photography first snared her, and she'd said that as lumpy and old-fashioned as it was, she still loved the Pentax best. She had said that only a week before she killed herself. Love of anything, even a complicated piece of metal and glass, should have been enough to keep Laura from the edge of the sill. Celia couldn't have known that the Pentax was the very thing he would have liked to hurl out a window, to hear it shatter on pavement, but he said nothing. Taking pictures had opened in Laura an arena of competence. She was effortlessly good at it, intuitively fluid with its apparatus and its timing. A gift you might not have expected in someone who so often hesitated. Photos were nothing if not examples of small, decisive moments.

It pained Arthur to see how careful his daughter was with his wife's favorite camera. Cleaning the lens, swabbing the interior, a delicacy not reflected in the actual images she captured. She was adept only at framing rectangles of sky above people's heads. Retinas flared red. Bodies were chopped in half. Her pictures looked like stills from frightening movies. She shifted to black and white on the drive west and made Cam and Arthur pose against diner signs and billboards. They'd emerge, Arthur guessed, as squint-eyed fugitives.

When they crossed the border from South Dakota, Celia wanted a shot of the WYOMING WELCOMES YOU sign, with its images of Devil's Tower and the cowboy on the back of the bronco, hat in hand, both flung to the sky. She loved the arch of the animal's back, a shape that didn't seem possible for a horse to make.

She'd wanted to frame it just so, she said, to make sure she caught the way the sun glanced off the sign and the slender, glittering aspens, their leaves in the wind flashing like coins.

In Arthur's dreams of Laura, she always wore her camera, the strap slung across her chest like a bandolier. Sometimes he took the camera from her and found that it had managed to turn into a gun. He shot his wife back. The picture was absurd, the usual warping in which dreams specialized, but what was utterly true about the act was the rage he felt as he aimed the lens toward her and saw her fall.

Yet Laura never died in those dreams; she was just grievously wounded. Always the first in their family to notice damage, she'd been the one to see the new roads that scored the land as they approached Lucy's ranch two years before. "What's that horrible road?" she had asked. "And that one." Once you started looking, you saw them everywhere, scraped into the sides of the hills and valleys surrounding Callendar. What made the roads worse was that they didn't creep slowly outward as Callendar's city limits had, but leaped straight, red, and unabashed across land that had never seen even the threat of construction. They led, all of them, to coalbed methane pumps, which were sprouting throughout the county. They were especially numerous near the scrap of land Lucy still owned.

No one talked about exactly how many acres his mother had hung on to. "Seventy-two and not a square foot more," she said when the children were still too young to realize westerners would rather talk about their sex lives than about how much land they possessed or how many head they ran. Lucy's parcel wasn't quite that small, yet it was nothing compared with the hundreds and thousands of acres held by neighboring ranchers and energy companies. But as far as Arthur knew, Lucy owned her land to the roots, and she was probably the only one up Coal Creek draw to be able to say that. She hadn't let anyone test for methane on her land. She also hadn't mentioned the roads. "No point," she'd said. "I knew you'd see them. Why bother gracing something uglier than Casper with conversation? What's new about Wyoming and mining, anyway?" She was the daughter and granddaughter of coal men, but Arthur suspected that this new surge of extraction depressed her too much to talk about.

Around his mother's fields spread the usual pointillist canvas of western ownership. Maps showed blue dots for state land, red for Forest Service, yellow for Bureau of Land Management, pink for reservations, purple for private, little of it more than dabs of color, except for ragged splotches of green that indicated the national forests to the west and south. But even in the small violet patches, the owned tracts, the layers of what constituted personal property kept lawyers in business. You could have deeds for acres of sagebrush and alkali flats and possess all the right in the world to go deeply into debt pursuing your dream of raising pedigreed alpacas, but just feet below your thin grass, someone else had the option to rake the earth for coal, uranium, or diamonds. Split estate. In New York you could buy and sell the air above buildings; here it was stratum after stratum of soil and rock and fossils. Then you added leasing arrangements for water, minerals, and grazing and you had plastered on the landscape a net of relationships more complicated than the genealogy of the Hapsburgs. Next you had to factor in history, since of course it had all once been the territory of the Cheyenne, Shoshone, Crow, Arapaho, or Lakota. For them, the idea that these hills and valleys might be fenced, farmed, drilled, or anything other than hunted on or carefully observed would have been an absurdity.

Arthur looked left and right as they drove north, almost there now. BLM properties to the south, spiked with mines for bentonite and trona and now methane. Across the road, the Flaxmans had a long, narrow stretch of land made valuable by its ready access to water. Snake Ranch, Lucy called it, because it unfurled in a green line along the creek. Not, Arthur had said to her, because the Flaxmans charge you twice what the Masons do for water. Not because for some unknown reason you have always liked sparring with Ted Flaxman about anything from what time it is at noon to politics.

But he hadn't heard his mother disparage the Flaxmans in some time. Not since one of the methane companies had come in to set up their wells, dig their plastic-lined containment ponds, and tear gravel paths across hillsides parallel to the creek. Not since the Flaxman boys had stopped entering rodeos and riding snowmobiles because they now spent their days ferrying paper from one courthouse to the next.

Fields were openly pocked with wells now, almost as if the establishment of one had magically spawned another, like a disease vector out of human control. Lucy had said nothing about the pumps since the last summer, but even in the fading light it was obvious that dozens more had gone in. Arthur wondered at what point Callendar would stop looking like itself. When would you become more conscious of what was on the land than of what it simply was?

By early evening they drove across the last cattle grid, and he felt the thrum through his body of the car passing over the twelve lengths of steel and that, at least, reminded him that he was home. The porch light was on, but the house, built of roughly dressed silex, was dark. Lucy had told them that she would be on her way to town and there was no way to reach her. Cell phones were useless to her, given that the mountains scattered reception like pollen. Wednesdays were bridge nights and their arrival wouldn't alter that. Sticking to her routine was a sign of Lucy's odd courtliness; she hadn't wanted to draw attention to anything unusual in this year's visit. The dog barked, not catching their scent.

Arthur opened the car door. Cam and Celia got out and

stretched themselves back to their full height. They'd driven three hundred miles that day. At first that was why Arthur thought he couldn't lift his other hand from the steering wheel—a total yet temporary paralysis, as if he'd been shot with a dart, a rogue animal in the wrong environment, a moose in the middle of a street. He tried again to unclench his fingers, but the muscles were still locked. He knew the children were watching him. Franklin continued to bark. Heated sage spiced the air.

Cam and Celia stared at him. His pulse thudded unevenly. It was eerie that his children weren't frightened, that they were simply waiting to see what would happen next. The attitude of refugees, cautious and strangely patient, husbanding their strength for whatever was to come. He had to move. The children would be hungry. It was time to make a meal, unpack, wash. He'd been driving with the windows down; his left arm was furred with dust. He heard the whirring rattle of grasshoppers. Sounds and sensations from childhood of which he was acutely conscious, as if he were stuck between time frames, mind one place, body another, both frozen by the split.

Arthur tried again to loosen his grip. That was all he had to do, and his muscles would remember what should happen next, of that he was certain. All he had to do was to seep back into his own bones. Slowly, his fingers unwound. The action appeared to revive him. Then, as he eased himself out, his ankle gave way.

He came to with his head ringing, his eyes facing the sky, which swirled as if it had been turned to meteors imagined by animators. "Dad?" It was Celia. Her face was shadowed by long hair and behind her the stars starting to come out in the darkening sky. The pricks of light settled into piercing white stability. Cam stood next to her. Arthur was sprawled on the ground, the stones of his mother's driveway pressing sharply into his spine. He felt a wet, aching hurt at the back of his skull and pain ringed his ankle. How he managed to inaugurate their stay with self-injury, one of his Wyoming specialties, he did not want to know. "I'm not dying," he said, and knew at once it was just the wrong thing to say. "I promise," he said, making it worse. Mental insta-bility, verbal ineptitude, the forcible removal of his children. They would be taken from him. The authorities would say, You didn't even get them into counseling when she died. But I tried! he'd plead. I went myself and all I did was sit there with my head between my knees. I eat dinner with them every night. I check their homework even though they are too old for that. I sit in the dark and I watch them breathe. A slow panic started to work in his chest. He couldn't get up. Cam stood behind Celia. "I'll be fine," Arthur told them, still supine. He thought he heard Cam sigh. The dog kept barking. He closed his eyes. He realized then that it wasn't only Lucy's collie howling, but a coyote. The sound was more unchained than any dog could make.

Cam had to drive them to the hospital, which he did with alarming competence. Arthur was bleeding and his head pounded. Celia had fetched a cloth and some ice from the house. She had brought Lucy's note: "Back at eleven. Make yourselves comfortable."

They went to Callendar Memorial, the place where he was born, though the maternity wing had since burned down and another—far spiffier—had been added, complete with a cancer-care unit and a plastic-surgery center. "This is where I was born," he said to his children as they walked into the ER. He had the dish towel clamped with one hand on his wound.

"You've told us, Dad. We know that," Cam said and Arthur felt disgust for himself settling more deeply into his joints. He wanted to smoke but was too tired to stand. It was being in a hospital: it drained you of whatever health and initiative you had left by the time you got there. He remembered it from the many occasions when he'd been towed in for the stitches and casts that came with the way his father introduced him to ranching. He remembered, too, how disappointment cramped Sean's face after some accident. His expression implied that they shouldn't have had to spend as much time in the ER as they had. Arthur ought to have held tighter to the rope or the pommel or been less clumsy with the wire cutters. Past a certain point, injury was no longer an initiation but an embarrassment, especially if it hadn't helped to hone a skill. Although the rest of the hospital had been renovated, this department didn't seem to have changed much since he last visited. The deadly lights, the pale tiles, the nurses in their sensible shoes—these rooms were the mildest of variations on one another. Geography should make an impact on something as important as a place you went when ill or hurt.

"No car wrecks tonight at least," the charge nurse said cheerfully. The only way you could really tell you were in Wyoming, apart from the number of Indians, were the hats and cowboy boots. Not even the sign that said to leave your weapons outside distinguished this setting. New York had that, too. He'd seen it at the hospital where they'd taken Laura. He hadn't quite understood why she had to be transported there. She was so obviously past repair. Now he and the children had been waiting an hour, beaten out by a man with viral pneumonia and a diabetic in a near coma. At least he'd been registered. He toyed with the band around his wrist.

Laura, too, had had a tag dangling there. She'd never worn a watch or bracelets and the twist of plastic had looked entirely wrong on the delicate lump of her wrist. Her fingernails were unpolished, as always. Nothing prepared him for the grief of seeing his wife's ringless hand; her wedding band had disappeared. Even unadorned, her hand was as familiar to him as the belt buckle he tugged into place every day. That was when something critical slid inside him and forced open an awful gap. On one edge, he'd been alive, and on the other he wasn't quite. He hadn't looked at her face. He hadn't been able to.

There wasn't much left to look at. She had landed on her side. Past her neck, through her brown hair, he saw a flash of bone where there should not have been. That face. Widely spaced eyes, dark hazel. Starting finally to grow traced with lines. She'd always looked young until the last year, when, abruptly, she'd become her age. Marred, she felt, but she never said it with strain, as if it was something of a relief. He'd felt guiltily pleased, as if it were now less likely that he'd lose her to someone else. He wondered now, his skull aching, if she cared about the change more than she'd let on. He shook his head, which made it hurt more. He had never been able to pry memories loose and let them float off and attach elsewhere. His were hardheaded and insisted on being spliced into the present.

He suspected this was the case as well with Celia, who'd also inherited the painful faculty of remembering in great detail. She was sitting next to him reading an ancient *Discover* magazine. "Tell me something," he said. Cam had gone to get them coffee. To easterners, they would have seemed too young for it, but they'd started drinking the stuff in October. Death brought out hot food, hot drinks. You adapted. He himself had begun on coffee at eight, which had amazed his wife. He'd shrugged and said that if she'd had to get up at four in the morning to herd cattle, she would have appreciated the caffeine, too. Arthur's body throbbed. He saw his torn shirtsleeve and was glad. None of his city finery would make sense here, although changing clothes would be the least of the shifts necessary.

"Wombats are the size of a grain of rice when they're born," his daughter said, not looking up. "This is taking forever."

"A grain of rice." He nodded. His own children weren't much bigger than that at birth, it had seemed. The thought of dropping Cam from his clumsy grip so terrified him, he barely held the baby. He stood over him instead, stared at his son's scowl, and felt unmoored by responsibility, completely unclear as to how he was supposed to conduct himself in the face of this screaming red-ness, his child. Laura, too, had shared his uncertainty, though he'd wanted to see her anxiety as the normal jitters of a new mother. Understandable, finite, bound up in overwhelming love. The love was real, that he knew. But so was the fear that she'd get it all wrong. No edges to that, either. And still, it hadn't kept her from wanting another baby; nor him—being an only son had early on felt like a large burden. For Laura, he'd also seen the children as ballast. Cam and Celia the two biggest reasons to stay well. As an experiment, however, motherhood had failed: family turned out not to have weighed enough after all. "What's keeping Cam?" he asked sharply.

"He's probably met some girl in the cafeteria," Celia answered, flashing the picture of the animals at her father. Arthur stared at a mass of glistening pink and black, something taken at night inside a den. Without a caption, you'd have no idea what was going on.

Arthur shifted around to face her more squarely. The movement, slight as it was, opened the cut again. He could feel blood welling down the tendons of his neck and reached for the dish towel Celia had wrung out twice already. "Cam has girlfriends?"

"All the time," Celia said, flipping the magazine closed. Sighing. She felt guilty, he sensed, for having revealed something Cam had chosen not to.

"Serious?" Arthur inquired cautiously. He was ashamed that this news came as such a surprise. He had been watching so carefully. He had been listening for hints. He had the impossible conversation about sex and had provided a paper bag full of condoms and an offer, unaccepted, for further talk. He had no experience with this kind of discussion; he hoped but did not trust that Laura had managed it with Celia. His father had died before he would have had reason for such inquiries, and his mother had decided not to let herself know about her son's private activities. Despite his vigilance, Arthur didn't want to know everything about his children's lives, either. The other possibility—that Cam was secretive and wily—was unpleasant but also had to be entertained.

"Serious?" Celia scoffed. "With Cam it's never serious. There are just always girls around." She told him something he'd never known: that older girls at her school had tried to be friends with her to get to know beautiful Cam. "Your brother is so gorgeous." He was known all over the neighborhood. He saw on her face then that Wyoming was meant to release her of the obligation of being a plain sister to a handsome boy, and that she already feared it wasn't going to work.

He continued to feel the blood working like a warm finger down his back. The *Discover* fell to the floor. It cracked open at a picture of an alarmingly verdant forest. "Do you remember when I sprained my ankle?" Celia asked. "Yes," he told her, reaching for the magazine, shutting away the green. "I remember."

She had hurt herself roller-skating. She was ten, hair in a skinny, crooked braid down her back, teeth too big for her small face. Laura had called him from the hospital, speaking with elaborate precision. She couldn't manage the forms, she said. An attentive mother for birthdays, treats, flights of whimsy, but at unpredictable moments the course of daily life could stun her temporarily. Paperwork could do it, or unexpected pain, and if they were combined, as in a trip to the ER, she could freeze altogether. She needed Arthur that afternoon, her incompetence on display for everyone to see. A daughter who knew that, too, her face bright with tears, her ankle wound inside a bandage. "Mom couldn't fill out the forms," Celia said. "Why couldn't she just fill out the stupid forms?" Why, Celia was asking now, had it been so hard for her? His daughter was also saying that he had damn well better pull himself together. She needed at least one parent intact. So far, her slouch implied, he was off to a rather poor start. There was no way to get up and hold Celia without smearing her in blood.

Cam walked in with the coffee and a tray filled with sugar and cream. Steam swam upward from the hot drinks. The nurse arrived and said, "Your turn, Mr. King. Looks like it's my job. Doc's got a baby to deliver."

"What have you been talking about?" Cam asked, pivoting away from the nurse, who stood there with her curly hair and open smile, a person whose cheerfulness was close to unimaginable to them all. "Why we're here," Celia said.

Cam put down the drinks and began to make the coffees sweet and milky, stirring each with a long red straw. "Sure had a smooth beginning," he said softly.

Arthur stood. He was shorter than his son. He had been watching the disparity grow, but its permanence now struck him. Cam had at least three inches on him. "I will not have that," he said. "I will not." I am the parent who paid your tuition. I am the one who filled out the forms. I am the one who stayed, he was telling them.

"There's blood all over your back," Celia said. "Your shirt's ruined. And I know what I want. I want to learn to drive."

"Yeah, right," said Cam, sipping. "That's a plan. You behind the wheel." Arthur silently agreed with his son's skeptical assessment of Celia's abilities as a driver. It was one of the reasons they'd come: Arthur was going to be the chauffeur for the first few months. He had counted on their cooperation and then recalled Cam's lazy, unearned confidence as he handled the Toyota. "Shut up," Celia hissed.

Arthur saw the nurse looking at them. He saw them all from her perspective. A pair of sulky teenagers, a damaged father, mother nowhere in sight. Blood speckling the tiles. Lights that flickered. Burned, steaming coffee. All of them in the wrong clothes, with at least two decidedly eastern voices. It had been months since he'd felt so close to his children. "Stop," he told them both. "Stop it. I need you to make sure they stitch me up right." To his amazement, they shook themselves out of their anger and followed him. A miracle of minor proportions: they were right there. Arthur wondered if it was fair to call any miracle minor.

The nurse was competent and measured, and he found himself curious to know if nurses were this way before they entered their profession or if it was a mantle conferred upon them with experience and enough exposure to trauma.

"Are you allowed to stitch him up?" Celia asked a little menacingly. "Aren't doctors supposed to do that?"

The woman looked at her. "I'm a nurse-practitioner. And that makes a difference. And this is a small town. So people usually take the help that's offered. Bad fall," she added, and in the following pause, during which all of them were too embarrassed to explain, she continued, "I'm assuming neither of you took a kitchen knife or a hammer to your dad's head." She paused in her threading of the curved needle. As if she wouldn't complete the procedure unless they explained. The children gawked at her. Even as New Yorkers, this possibility struck them as grotesque. What kind of environment had their father brought them to?

"Oh, for God's sake, no," Arthur interrupted. "No, it was my own fault. I tripped getting out of the car. I must have hit myself on a rock. My own stupid fault." He couldn't bring himself to say what had really happened. His voice was tight with shame. The children glanced away.

The nurse was shaving his head. The razor's blade scraped softly. Feathery bits of dark, matted hair fell to his lap. "This is one wide cut," she said speculatively.

Arthur heard Celia walk up behind him. Cam, too. "How many stitches?" Celia asked, mollified now.

"He'll need twenty or so," the nurse said. "Lidocaine now," she told Arthur, and he felt the bite of the needle and then a spreading warmth. A thickness soon enveloped the back of his head and the nurse chatted as they waited for the drug to work its numbing wonder. By the time she started to sew, the heaviness was nearly pleasant, though he didn't like the tugging of the thread against the lips of the wound. "Arthur King," the nurse said as she worked. "You related to Sean and Lucy?"

"My parents," Arthur admitted, darting a look at his children. They were alert for the revelation of information he hadn't told them, an indication of where they stood in this territory where you could be asked if you'd taken a blunt instrument to your father.

"My aunt and uncle had the ranch next to theirs. The Emmerichs." A world of questions vibrated quietly below her statement: Why are you out here so early in the summer? Your mother planning to hold on to that land she's been paying taxes on all these years? Going to renovate the old house? He knew how language worked out here. From the barest fragments of talk, people sensed decisions to cash out, move to Vegas, the advent of divorce. It was like predicting the entire shape of a dinosaur on the remnant of a shinbone. You could get a lot wrong, but still, you engaged in the reconstruction.

As nurses learn unflappability, lawyers cultivate evasion. Arthur was not sure if he acquired indirection from his parents, his profession, or in his old role as Laura's protector, but it was ingrained enough now to be a reflex. "Yes, the Emmerichs," he said. "Polled Herefords." His voice was false and full. His back was caked with his own dried blood.

She kept sewing. "That's right. Sold off years ago."

"You've got a black eye, Dad," Celia said.

"That happens sometimes with a mild concussion," the nurse said, knotting and snipping her last stitch. "Well, keep tabs on him, kids. He's a man who needs watching."

Loneliness struck him then. Since his teens, women had looked at him. Muscular and broad, wide-jawed, he had none of Cam's loose grace received directly from Laura. Arthur saw beauty in height, slimness, social ease. His own handsomeness startled and eluded him, though he knew it preceded him and crafted impressions of talent and power that he felt were not accurate. He saw the children register the nurse's knowledge of his widower status and wondered if they'd realized that all the stews, the offers of help, the notes on heavy paper that arrived in the wake of Laura's death were the same kind of signal. Women had no idea how shy he was, how hard it was for him to accept assistance or even recognition. How bad he was at domestic conversation and, worse, flirtation.

It was ten by the time they got back to Lucy's. They sat in the moon-filled kitchen waiting for her. Franklin had growled, recognized them, allowed his ears to be fondled, then settled with a clatter of nails at their feet. Arthur was grateful for the old table, the dog's scent of hay. His head started to pound more deeply. But they all wanted to stay up to see Lucy, as if to certify the start of their summer, as if she opened the gate to their arrival.

Celia said, "Did you know Wyoming has more subscribers to *Playboy* than almost any other state?" Arthur laughed and said no, but should they get it for Lucy as a Christmas present?

Along with their memories, he and Celia shared this ability to be in charge of facts. They didn't compete with each other about who knew more or who got a piece of information right. They liked expanding each other's range of knowledge. They were aware that facts couldn't help you become close to a thing, a landscape. But there was comfort in detail, too. Pleasure in the storing of news. Decoration for talk. Facts, used correctly, could make you seem more at ease in conversation than you really were. The veins in his scalp hammered as if they might burst his stitches. Arthur's reliance on scraps of information was all that kept him from screaming sometimes when people talked to him. He had no idea if it was good for them to stay here, but what he'd said to Cam and Celia in New York was true. He couldn't stand to see that sidewalk right now.

The phone rang. It was Lucy, saying her truck was having

trouble and she didn't trust it to last all the way back. Arthur had noticed she had more or less stopped using the word "ranch" about five years ago when she sold the last large parcel to the Flaxmans. Now she wouldn't hear of his coming to get her. She was going to stay in town tonight with friends. "How is everyone?" she asked. "Are you settling in all right?"

"Just fine," Arthur said. "Nothing to worry about."

Neither of his children asked why he'd said nothing about his accident. Lucy would see the bandage soon enough. She'd give it a critical glance, ask what had happened, then divert the topic of discussion elsewhere. No one had died or been permanently disfigured. To Lucy, only events that changed a person's life were worth giving fuller comment on. But she'd been nearly silent in the aftermath of Laura's dying. She'd seen it as close to inevitable. Then why didn't she tell me that? he'd thought. Why was I so surprised?

Arthur saw Cam and Celia yawn, seized with total fatigue. He helped his children to bed. Hoping to spare them the ambush of memory, Lucy had taken the guest room where he and Laura had usually stayed. She'd given Cam her room, on the first floor, so he could start prowling outside as early as he liked. Celia was sleeping in what they called the sewing room. Thoughtful. Designed to minimize the shock of no Laura, but this house held fewer traces of her than anywhere else.

Once the children were asleep, he went onto the porch with the dog and his palmed cigarette. The air was so much drier here, even harder on his lungs, but he kept on smoking. He stamped out the butt with elaborate care, fire the greatest fear of anyone who lived in semipermanent drought. Every conflagration originated in a single lick of flame, even if it seemed its only intention was to provide heat or the consolation of cooked food. When Arthur was ten, the Donovans' entire barn had been turned to ash in an hour from a hand too drunk to smash out a

Winston. His father had taken him to see the ruin the next day. They drove forty miles out of their way and smelled the charred wreck from twenty miles off. Other families had done the same, coming with meat and casseroles, lending horses, their boys witnessing the effect of small and careless actions—the assumption being that boys were the ones both to mend and to cause trouble on a ranch. Every time Arthur had dragged on a cigarette in the confines of an empty horse stall, he experienced a mix of enjoyment and guilt, until that feeling accompanied him every time he lit up, even in places like the Mint Bar in Sheridan, which were unlikely to burn.

Lucy had caught him in the barn the summer after his sophomore year of high school, and it was one of the only times she had ever cuffed him in the face. "After what we've done for you," she said, her voice low, her hand as wide as the scoop of a shovel, thick as the front door. "After what we've given up for you, you risk my land and house for a stick of tobacco. I am ashamed, I have never been so ashamed." Her arm raised, her hair in a wiry halo around her face where it had escaped from her braid. Breathing so her chest rose and fell behind the dense cotton of her nightgown. It wasn't his lungs she was worried about, but the possibility of fire. Risk what, he'd thought then. I was the one taking the risks. I got the scholarship. I left the state. I was the one who hit those boys when they tried to haze me, hit ones bigger and older, hit them so I could survive not having a father, and being poor, and you so far away. He knew now all she'd been at bottom was scared.

She had had to discipline him hard all by herself. His care had landed fully in her lap. And not just care for him, but for the barn, the animals, her land, none of it with ready access to creeks. Enough moisture seeped from springs to keep their acreage from total aridity, and they'd dotted their fields with bathtubs and tanks when they owned enough to run cattle. Lucy had three tanks behind the barn, filled with water she had to buy from ranchers with drainage on Coal Creek, her well just vital enough to provide for careful use in the house. Arthur had never seen anyone so miserly with moisture as his mother. She still took baths by dipping a washcloth in a saucepan, he suspected. She had been raised during the droughts of the 1930s and had lived to see her father, a coal miner, turned into a man in a uniform repairing engines at TJ's Lube and Filter, a job he'd been lucky to have, though he hated it with every morsel of his body. In honor of that town-bound frustration, Lucy had preserved what measure of independence she could. In the process, she had turned into a ranch widow, a harsh breed, and become among the harshest. No one messed with her, not hunters, not neighbors, not even assessors. They had never had a fire on the ranch, not even by lightning, as if fire knew better than to start on Lucy King's land.

But no one was exempt; no one even pretended to be, not even his mother. To do so was to express an arrogance that would almost invite calamity. Still, it was a remarkable fact of living with Lucy, and Arthur wasn't going to be the one to cause the disaster. He pocketed the butt and stirred on the porch. Franklin groaned in his sleep.

Arthur went inside and found himself, almost against his will, crouched in front of the cupboard below the sink. This was where Lucy kept the whiskey, nestled among cleaning products and sponges, as if liquor were as utilitarian a tool as these. Tonight he permitted himself the lie that alcohol might help him to sleep. He also allowed himself the self-indulgent thought that everyone had a couple of soft spots on their character, like coins of rot on even the best peach. Weakness somehow turning him back into a human. He felt oddly alert, enlivened by pain. He poured himself a drink, took one of the pills the nurse had given him, and settled back outside in the cool, dry night.

He knew he would have to wait for the precise moment

when exhaustion settled into his bones before he could go to his room. Lucy had put him in the attic, where he had slept as a boy, a room she now used to store linen and force seeds. It smelled of starch and potting soil. He had seen the bed, as white and narrow as an empty envelope, and had come immediately back downstairs.

Closing his eyes, he tried to identify what was happening on the ranch purely from sound. It amazed him how distorting this sense was, though he admitted his hearing might be wavering from the long drive, pain, drugs, whiskey. One night when he was fifteen, he'd woken to what he was sure was the smack of feet coming up the road. He could have sworn that a man was coming closer and closer, and his heart had swelled in fear. It had taken all his courage and the dog by his side to investigate. But the sound had been only the latigo of a saddle that he had laid on a sawhorse; the wind had stirred it, made it slap the wood at sharp, even intervals. He'd been so angry at himself he'd kicked the saddle and made the stirrup smack the sawhorse. You couldn't trust anything you didn't see in front of you and even then you couldn't be sure of what you saw. Roscoe, the horse his father died on, had been a beautiful animal. And not only well proportioned; you would have said he was gentle to his bones. But Arthur had seen what his hooves had done to the skull. Panic could strike any animal or human, and once it sparked its way along the veins, anything might happen.

In May, over lunch, a friend had asked him if he was making too rash a decision in moving back to Wyoming. Arthur had given a thoughtful answer, lawyer's words, but the friend was not appeased. "It just seems out of character, Arthur," the man had said. At that moment, Arthur had felt like a perforated card—a renewal, say, to a magazine—that had been ripped from the spine of what held it tight, the eastern piece of his life, those associations, links, memories, rendered as flimsy as paper, as easily dispensed with. More than thirty years, scrapped. Arthur rose and walked toward the car. He wanted to see if he could find what he'd hit his head on. The dog followed at his heels.

Since Laura died, he'd discovered that he was not very clear on what his character was or might become. It appeared to be built of spiky, disparate parts that had clumped together depending on what those around him needed. For his mother, he'd endured the shock of being a scholarship boy at fancy schools. He'd seen how she wanted the West drummed out of him and how frightened she was at his ending as Sean had, and he'd done exactly as she asked. For his dead father, he'd needed to prove his competence and had engaged and succeeded in violent competition first at law school and then at his firm. For his beautiful, damaged wife and his children, he reliably provided shelter and support, and all of that had shaped what he'd come to think of as himself. He was used to needing to appear substantial. It surprised him, now that the family was severely altered, that the appearance was all he had. He'd counted on Laura to help shore up the illusion that he actually was what he seemed.

Now she was gone, and so to a degree was he, both of them having slipped away, as Lucy's ranch would one day soon. Arthur hadn't foreseen his wife's death, but everyone, including Lucy, acknowledged that the ranch would dissolve in a matter of time. Lucy wouldn't let him help prevent that outcome, though he offered to every year. The land wasn't interesting enough ecologically to put an easement on—thorny, stubborn acres, the most valuable of which had been sold off as stingily as Sean and Sean's father had amassed them. Lucy would turn away discussion of her future with a mixture of disdain and astonishment and the same stern gesture with which she refused invitations for travel to the Caribbean. Did he think she could be so easily bought? That money had that kind of sway with her? She would not be seen needing anyone so overtly, much less the son she'd raised to such strict independence. Even though he wanted to, Arthur would not be able to forestall the loss. By the time she died, he expected almost all of her land would be gone, knowledge that was sad but manageable.

But other losses were impossible to corral; they had their own ferocious energy. That he hadn't been able to prevent Laura's death stunned him daily. He'd had no notion she was so close to despair. She'd hidden it carefully, as he read that suicides often do. Sitting on the gravel, his head loose from the whiskey and medicine, he thought about how his father had also come unknotted from his hold. People were harder to hold on to even than acreage. He wanted to go and check on his children but couldn't bring himself to move. He crouched by the car and guessed that a slightly blacker spot on the driveway was where his head had smacked. A low lump of rock sat there. The dog sniffed and licked at it with a dog's primal awareness of blood.

When his father died, he was fourteen, slightly younger than his children now. Lucy had found him at school. The other children had seen her first and gone silent with a stillness that meant an unexpected arrival—a visiting superintendent, another parent—had come because bad news could not wait. He just never expected to see his mother there. She must have needed to find some other child, to give someone else a message. It was early spring, and the mud was deep. She had risked getting stuck in the gumbo by coming out to get him. He felt the gaze of the other children following him like a panicked shadow and felt his own fear rise. She did not speak until they were in the truck. Then she said, "Rick Skinner found your dad this morning. His horse fell, then dragged him. Rick was driving on Coal Creek Road when he saw Roscoe."

Arthur rolled down the window. "Goddamn," he kept saying. The wind that blew in was cold and wet. Snow was on the way from the mountains.

"That won't help a thing," his mother said, and he stopped. He went back to school the day after next, once they'd sorted out which hands could help with the work his father would have done. He got the letter about his scholarship that week, too, the other piece of childhood that tilted his later years in such a strange direction. Within a week, he'd gone from being a rancher's son to a boy with no father heading east by fall. Within a year, he didn't recognize himself, and the slow reshaping of his life had started.

They buried his father near the top of the meadow Sean had liked for its broom snakeweed. Arthur and Rick Skinner dug the grave, work that took an entire day because the ground was still so cold. They had to dig it deep to discourage animals. Arthur blistered his fingers so that they bled through the gloves. On the way back, Rick noticed and was angry. "Why didn't you say anything, Arthur? How do you think your mother's going to feel, me bringing you home all banged up? Don't you think she's got enough to worry about?"

"Yes, sir," Arthur said. "I didn't notice, sir." But raw hands seemed like the least he could offer. His father had died badly. Wire, reins, hooves. They made for an awful combination: a lot of pain, administered slowly. One leg had been crushed, his skull had been smashed. His mother hadn't tried to make him believe it had been quick or that Sean hadn't known what happened. It looked as if he might even have tied himself to the reins, knowing Roscoe would drag him along a familiar trail or to water. A place where someone would find him before the ravens did. Sean had loved that animal. Lucy sold him within days to a Jackson man who was not aware of his local history.

Arthur heard an eddy of whinnying from the draw on the other side of the house. A spring allowed more than leafy spurge to grow there, and Lucy now let neighbors graze a few sheep and horses in that pasture. He hadn't ridden a horse in years. The feeling that he might want to again flickered out almost as soon as it was born. A horse with any sense of pride would try to run him off. His mother told him he looked like a sack of feed in a saddle, and about as misplaced. He'd never had much of a seat, and it seemed lawyers lost theirs entirely when they traded horses for chairs. He stood and leaned back against the car. The whiskey was almost gone and his head was still throbbing.

Laura had loved to ride, one of the only delights that chased the shadow from her. But as soon as the thought of his wife's long legs on a horse flashed across his mind, a picture of her in their kitchen filled it instead—sitting there, her fingers wrapped around a cup of coffee, lost. What, baby, he would ask, as he always did, what is it? And she would dip her chin and try to smile, a sliver of spirit summoned to quiet his worry. During one of those moments, she'd been plotting how to close the gap between her body and that windowsill. That image must have seeped from a closed box in her brain and out, a pulse of energy or even of light that she couldn't close down. Then his own brain slipped again and pushed toward the white wing of bone he'd glimpsed at the hospital. The face he had not been able to look at, evidence now only of collision. The grief came on in a fit as abrupt as a seizure. The longing for his wife made him gasp. The dog whined. The horses stopped their nickering. Everything alive near him was aware of him, as animals are aware of the net of other animals with whom they share terrain. He could not breathe straight.

Laura would not have liked it that he plucked the children from school, from New York. She mistrusted sudden change, though that was exactly what she had inflicted on all of them. "But you're not here to stop me," he said aloud, and picked up a piece of gravel and chucked it hard into the sage. That was what he'd really been wanting: the chance to talk aloud to his wife, to fight with her as they had never learned or dared to fight, with venom and abandon. He'd always been so frightened of upsetting her. "You'd hate all of this," he said in a voice that was only just below a normal tone. "All of it." Especially his working for Dwight, for whom he'd have to represent mining companies, the very interests eating up the land of his neighbors. "You'd have told me to chase the buzzards out of town."

Laura had gone to school in the Middle East with the sons and daughters of oil executives. More American than Coke, she'd say. As if she wasn't. As if her father's work in the foreign service improved the quality of her own nationality. That had changed when she died. Her parents, Peter and Evie, shrank in importance, and he could see them as the embittered snobs they were. They lived now in Charlottesville, where they nursed gin and a muted anger that flared occasionally in his direction. They were not happy about what they called the "relocation of our grandchildren." But they had done nothing. "I still hate your parents," Arthur said aloud. The field was silent. He finished his drink.

He had disliked them from the start, but nothing could have stopped him from wanting their daughter. Even at her worst, he had felt nothing but the thickest kind of love. They met when he was twenty-five, just out of law school and in Washington to start his first job. His hair was wet, combed in wide ridges, his shoes newly buffed. A friend from college invited him to a cocktail party in Georgetown given in a town house with an overgrown yard. The air was tropical, blurred with insects. On the brink of entering the yard, he stood at the threshold of the garden and was visited with suffocating shyness, wondering suddenly if his clothes were wrong. His jacket felt hot, his shirt of too dense a material. Then he saw Laura. She was standing in the center of the garden. She was talking to no one and was holding nothing. She wore a white dress and sandals. She looked at him and said, "I need a drink." He got her a gin and tonic. "Thank you," she said, and eased the ice cubes over the lip of the glass and onto the heavy grass, where they shimmered near her toes.

The terrible sounds came out of him again. The dog licked his wrist. He threw the whiskey glass over the fence and expected to hear it shatter. But it must have landed in a clump of sage or broom. Because he had brought his children safely back, because he was so tired, because the dog refused to leave him, he said to the moon, to the field, to the horses he could hear but not see, "You bitch." He said it again, he called her a bitch, he called her a cunt, he heard the ugly words land in the air and felt them stick to her. He meant them. Then he sank against the car, where the dog lay panting by the front tire, apparently no longer willing to try to provide comfort. He'd been judged beyond hope. The house stayed dark. An owl creaked overhead.

He would never tell anyone what he'd done when he finished cleaning the apartment in New York. Mop rinsed, soap and sponges put away, he stood in the middle of the bedroom and looked at the window from which Laura had jumped. He walked over to it and placed his hand on the sill. This was as close as he'd gotten to it since she died. Sometimes, they made love propped against its hard lip, as if they were still young, as if the children weren't sleeping only yards away. Yet she had chosen to leave through this exact space. He had refused to open it again, and now it rose awkwardly after months of being sealed. He hoisted the sash as high as it would go and then climbed out on the ledge and let his legs dangle from there, half his body scraping brick, the other still wedged in the room. Then he caught a glimmer of motion across the street: someone had glimpsed him and frozen. It was a woman in the apartment just opposite theirs, across the avenue. He had never seen her before. A stranger with stiff brown hair. She spotted him, and her mouth slowly opened. No, she shouted. Though he couldn't hear her, he could tell. She couldn't believe it was happening again, at the same window. Her fingers were working, fumbling for a latch. He pulled his legs back into the apartment and slammed the sash shut. He yanked the blind down and curled up on the floor. He told himself he didn't want to die, that he'd just needed to see what it was like, to know what she had seen. But that wasn't true. He had wanted to die. He had felt the pull of the air and the density of his body and had yearned in that moment to feel himself lashed into another shape by the current of wind that traveled like a transparent hand along the rough bricks. To be as light as that, and as flexible. He would have preferred it to the wreckage with which he lived now, a life that felt as if shards of glass had been sewn into the seams of his clothes, glinting there below dark fabric. She had hurt so many people. That woman, Arthur knew, had seen it all, had been unable to stop it, and she would never be the same. And she had never lived with Laura. "But we did," he told the dog, still turned away from him, staring, it seemed, at the hubcap. The owl flew past again, something in its claws. "We were right next to her."

CELIA

Celia thought the birds knew first. Meadowlarks and ravens lifted off of streetlamps and telephone wires and settled onto other perches. Otherwise, everything looked perfectly normal: one side of Main Street lay in shade, the other was washed in slanted copper. Clouds like towers of hollowed stone hovered in the sky, and the shops were closed or nearly closing. Celia could see bunches of keys in people's hands, to lock storefronts or start cars, and she imagined the metal warm in their palms, ready for the front door. A day stitched tight.

They'd spent the morning and afternoon with Lucy, eating at the diner, getting Lucy's truck fixed, chatting with friends and neighbors they ran into. Everyone aware of her and Cam, not as Celia and Cam, but as Arthur's suddenly motherless children. Yet Laura's absence sat differently out here. Celia wasn't sure why, but it seemed that death might be less of an affront or an embarrassment in Wyoming. One of her facts sprang to mind: the state had the third highest rate of suicide in the country, which might make people either more callous or more sympathetic, depending on their perspective.

Then, heading back to the truck, Celia felt the sidewalk tremble. Cam sensed it, too, glancing at his feet, then up again at the road. At that moment, she saw them—horses, lathered, at a run, striking blue fire from macadam striped in double yellow.

Sorrels and grullos, two bays, some paints, twelve altogether. They kept their pace as they raced down the center of the street. Two shoes flung clear, another sang a crack along the post-office window. Bunched muscles caught in plate glass, squares holding fractions of curves. Lights flicked from red to green, the few trucks on the road braking fast, elbows, heads, close to whole bodies hanging from windows, hats tilted back, drivers' mouths lively with curses. But the cars all stopped. To move was to hit or be hit. The horses unfurled like a crazed flag. Black manes, socked feet, blazes, separate horses in a way, but also not. The tail of one grazed the forelock of another, as if they were feathers, overlapping, enough to make a wing. They were flying, that intent on putting air between themselves and the road, between themselves and the earth.

"Good Lord," said Lucy. "What was that about?" She stared after the horses, her hand a shelf over her eyes as she peered down the street.

"They could have killed someone," Arthur said. He wore sunglasses to hide the black eye and his tiredness. You could see it anyway, it seemed to Celia, in the set of his shoulders and his empty, cupped hands. He still looked like someone who'd been attacked by hoodlums, even though he'd created the damage all by himself.

"They were airborne," said Cam. People gathered at the post office to inspect the cracks. Shopkeepers stood in front of their stores, blinking at the quickly receding curtain of dust that signaled the horses. Trucks rolled cautiously forward.

They were free, thought Celia. Riding terrified her, but something in the animals' total commitment to escape had thrilled Celia. Maybe it would be different this year. Maybe she could be horseback and not panic. But she doubted it; horses had strength, size, speed, and instinct on their side. It was laughably clear who was in charge.

She voiced none of this aloud. Lucy was busy shepherding

them back to the truck: it had been repaired and Arthur had left his car at the garage for a tune-up.

Lucy had been glad to see Celia and Cam that morning at the diner, turning them around as she always did to inspect them for signs of change. "When will either of you stop growing? Kings are never this tall." She glanced at Arthur, who stood by sheepishly, his bruises and bandage there for all to witness. Lucy had seemed somewhat appalled that he'd managed to start their stay so calamitously.

"But you're taller than I am," Celia said.

"I am not a King," said Lucy.

They went to fill up the truck with gas before returning home, and Celia heard other customers trade theories about the horses as heat made the fumes rising from the nozzle shimmer in a wide, distorting band. Her finger lay on the trigger, the tank clicking full. She watched the numbers roll past and tapped her toes whenever the device clocked a double zero. It was getting worse, this need to frame small events. Habits of terrible, private precision, rituals of order that served no practical purpose. She hoped that Lucy and Callendar might make a difference, but she admitted the problem was probably a little larger than geography. She forced herself to listen to the other customers. The horses were from the pound, someone said, some ragtag mustangs rounded up north of Sheridan. A worker left the corral open by accident. Someone else said that one had managed to jump, and the others, inspired, followed. Another person suggested that the gate had been ajar on purpose, the horses riled and sent packing. Celia screwed the gas cap back and slid behind Lucy in the truck's large cab. She watched her grandmother's hands, settled like two brown books one atop the other in her wide lap. "Why," asked Celia, "would anyone do that?"

Lucy looked out the window into a sky shot with clouds the shape of lean purple fish. She started the truck. A low buzz pulled at the backs of Celia's thighs as the engine chuffed to life.

"Oh, baby, who knows?" her grandmother said, aiming the truck back toward the road. "Someone with a peculiar sense of drama." Men were riding the hills, they heard. "They'll get tired, those horses," she said. "They'll get thirsty or go lame. They'll round them up."

"What happens then?" Celia pressed, though she could guess.

"Dog food," said Lucy. "Glue. That's where they were headed anyway."

Arthur shifted in his seat and with sudden sharpness pressed Lucy for details about summer plans. As if he could protect us from bad endings, Celia thought. As if the future somehow had the corner on safety. As if the first thing he hadn't done out here was to land himself in a hospital. In spite of herself, she watched Lucy's odometer and clicked her molars each time a new mile turned over. She stopped for a moment to listen to her grandmother's plans; as always Lucy was on top of things and could be counted on to make the day march forward at proper intervals. With her usual resourcefulness, she had already lined up jobs for both Celia and Cam. She steered their way out of town and said Celia could start as early as Monday at the C Bar C. As for Cam, an old neighbor of theirs, Mac Barlow, needed help with everything at the condo community he managed now his ranch had gone bust. "You'll need your permit pretty soon," Lucy added, glancing at Cam in the rearview mirror. Cam brightened in spite of himself, even with his knees bent up under his chin. Lucy had used the essential bait: the promise of driving. But Arthur slumped further; he was not a fan of independence based on access to vehicles. He himself was to start at Dwight's on the first of the week as well. "Hope the shiner will be gone by then," he said. He dropped pronouns the moment he got out here, Celia noticed, and she couldn't say if it was because that was what he'd done when he was a boy or because he was hoping to fit in again.

"It won't be," said Lucy, staring balefully through the windshield.

"Not a chance," said Cam, who often had black eyes from contact with soccer balls.

"You never know," Celia wanted to add, since someone clearly needed to be on her father's side, but she couldn't summon the generosity, as if it were a commodity in short supply here, as tightly regulated as water.

Back at Lucy's, Celia watched her father and grandmother usher her and Cam toward their old routines, like cattle down a chute. Hoping chores would make them forget that Laura, too, had had jobs before dinner. And I am a lot smarter than a cow, she told herself. I would never let myself believe that the chute meant anything but bad news, an evil end. But she said nothing and took on her mother's old task of setting the table in silence. If she could have ironed the place mats without calling attention to herself, she would have. The wrinkles stared up at her in brazen, miniature ridges. Lucy, reassured that everyone had their hands around some work, went off to prepare the meat. Cam washed vegetables, Arthur watered the animals, and Celia, when she was done with the table, swept the porch. Lucy believed in chores with a kind of fervor most people reserved for Jesus, horses, or football, her father once said. But her appetite for activity was more basic than faith, Celia thought. Work kept you roped to a place and gave your body a way to belong there. A purpose. Wyoming, so weathered where Lucy lived, made you feel that an articulated reason to stay was a good thing to develop. Lucy lived alone. Work kept her sane, Celia sensed, though it was the most ferocious sanity she'd ever seen. It needed policing and had the strictest of boundaries.

When Celia was first told to sweep the porch, she'd liked the job for its echo of *Little House on the Prairie.* Then she realized that the porch really did need sweeping every night and she enjoyed not only the steady piles of dirt she created, but the chance to watch the meadow just beyond Lucy's fence as it grew fluid with birds and animals, the grass stirring with the silkiness of a river. She liked this reminder that another order, older and more primal than Lucy's, existed right at the doorstep to her fiercely kept home. A whole other realm of insects and things with wings and claws and beaks clicking away at being alive, gathering food, protecting their young. Laura had loved to watch the meadow at this time of day, when the heat lowered and the animals, in reprieve, uncoiled into action. Both Celia and her mother had liked the feeling of dipping a ladle into this bigger world and then heading back in to eat Lucy's careful, balanced cooking, her starched curtains stirring in the wind.

After dinner, there would be more chores, and Celia thought she would also volunteer for Laura's task of drying dishes. Lucy doesn't trust your profligate eastern way with water, Arthur had teased his wife; you're not allowed to wash them. Celia cautiously let the image of her mother's face crowd back into her mind. The large eyes that took on the color of the clothes she wore. The brown hair threaded with silver. The chipped front tooth that should not have improved her smile but somehow did. All of it outlined in the banked light of memory: real but not tangible. Right now, the picture didn't hurt, but you could never tell when it might, when something would slip and she'd be hostage to a sliding gallery of visions that her brain pieced seamlessly together in order, it seemed, to test her precise sensitivity to pain. Celia stowed the broom and went inside, following the smell of browning beef.

At supper, they hesitated before the four chairs set at the kitchen table and the air tightened as Arthur settled in what had been her mother's regular chair. Lucy pressed forward with the dinner, she spooned out peas, passed the meat, and insisted so on habit that they had no choice but to bend to her will and eat. Afterward, Arthur put the dishes in the sink, Cam slipped out to the barn, Lucy and Celia did the dishes and then hunkered in to read. Another assertion of long practice. There was no television at Lucy's, though satellites were readily available. Arthur had tried to coax her to get one, to stay in touch, he said. "To stay in touch with what? Girls in bikinis eating mealworms? *CSI* here, there, and everywhere?" Celia knew that when Lucy went to town to see friends and play bridge, she watched the Weather Channel and stock sales and probably some *CSI*. But she drew a circle around her own house when it came to the hectic entertainments of television. It made for quiet, hemmed with the noise of grasshoppers and passing trains. It made for early nights, and if you couldn't sleep, there were acres of Lucy's books to pull from: she'd spent years collecting and reading literature about Africa, South American rivers, the tribes of the Himalaya. No one could say Lucy hadn't tried to invite the larger world inside her own. Even though she hated planes, she was the sharpest investigator of places Celia had ever met. Lucy had loved it when she could get Laura to talk about her life as a child in Tehran and Beirut. She wanted to know what the dates tasted like and how high the palms grew, and it was always a wonder to Celia how mere words, just conversation, could make you taste the fruit and see the swaying trees even as the Wyoming hills spread out all around you.

Although she'd taken a book about the Hindu Kush to bed, Celia couldn't lose herself in the cold mountains. Instead, she found herself listening to coyotes singing in disheveled patterns. Low yips, croons, a round of sharp barks, sounds that thrilled and agitated, a scattered music, notes thrown by joyous throatfuls down the fencelines. Stalks of light rose through the register set in the pine floorboards. Her father and grandmother talked in the kitchen, their words rising with the downstairs glow. Pipes shuddered as someone closed and opened a tap. Lucy, probably, having found a last plate to wash. Celia could sense her care with the water. Another drought year.

For some reason a scrap of Latin, lines from the *Aeneid*, rose in her mind. They'd finished the first book by the end of the school year. Leaping ahead because they'd raced through Cicero.

"An appetite for Latin," her mother had said wonderingly. "Where did that come from?" *"Arma virumque cano,"* Celia recited, lying in bed below the thin coverlet. *"Troiae qui primus ab oris / Italiam fato profugus Laviniaque venit litora."* It was still there, a whole month later. She had gotten the best grades of her life this past year. Teachers had been astounded, but she wanted to tell them that school was easy compared with your mother dying. No contest. And Latin scanned. It was a language whose poetry sprang from a tight syntactical order. You could practically graph it. She listened to the coyotes and the gathering force of their howls. "I sing of arms and the man, the first who came, compelled by fate, an exile out of Troy, to Italy and the Lavinian coast." She whispered the last part. But the coyotes made the verse seem small and old and feeble.

It was odd how bits of an epic written twenty-five hundred years ago could emerge in Lucy's house, near her creaking barn and in air that smelled of pine and sage. A place where the supermarket was decorated with the heads of elk and bighorn sheep mounted above the freezers. Odd, too, how a few thousand miles away, the city where she was born continued on with its own existence, with its taxis and lawyers wearing fat ties and, in the spring, tulips like cups of yellow satin that swayed on their stems in the window boxes of brownstones. Where women in pastel dresses pushed children in strollers, where trash rolled down the street and buildings scissored the sky into bits of blue. She couldn't tell if she missed it or not.

Celia shifted in her bed. Her father and grandmother were still talking. Probably about her and Cam now. Something had darkened in their tone, gone more whispery. That was what happened when adults discussed how they were doing; voices deepened and thinned at once, as if bad news cast you into permanent shadow and diminished you. Celia could guess at the contours of the conversation. Whether or not they'd adapt. Whether they'd find their way where the buffalo roamed before they were killed off along with the Indians. They taught Latin at Callendar High, her father had told her. And they wouldn't have to wear uniforms. Celia was surprised to feel that she would mind that change slightly. Lack of choice had made getting dressed each morning so much easier. Hers had announced to the world exactly where she fit in.

Uniforms belonged to schoolchildren and to doormen in hats glinting with short lengths of gold braid. Garbagemen, janitors. Maids in white, pink, or mint-green dresses, wedges of rubber holding up their laced shoes. Soldiers, whom she saw in smeared photographs in the *Times* or in dizzy, moving clusters on the television screen. If uniforms were intended to mask people, they made Celia notice them more clearly. The necks, legs, faces were that much more remarkable for the bodies being cloaked. The soldiers she remembered in particular. Sharp noses or rounded, guns slack or upright, shoulders hunched against a wind the helicopter blades kicked up.

She turned over again in bed and groped in her memory for the next fragment of the poem. It came more slowly, as if dissuaded by the coyotes. Maybe clearing out the apartment, the long drive, and the running horses had been enough to start erasing whatever kind of hold New York had on her mind. "*Multum ille et terris iactatus et alto / vi superum, saevae memorem Iunonis ob iram, multa quoque et bello passus, dum conderet urbem inferretque deos Latio,*" she told the blankets.

Why reciting the first lines of the *Aeneid* made her hungry, she didn't know. It would be easy to go downstairs and ask for something to eat. Lucy's refrigerator was always full of good, rich food. Potato salad made, thankfully, without onions. Slices of roast beef. The lids to the condiment jars never crusted with old mayonnaise or mustard. Sheets of waxed paper separating the cookies she baked, in tins kept in the pantry.

It made no sense to miss the way her mother had kept their kitchen, since when she'd been alive, her slack habits had been a reliable point of contention. Almost always Celia could count on there being little more than canned bouillon, a picked-over chicken whose ribs were translucent pink slats, a head of celery gone to rubber, a quart of last week's milk. Often Celia had stopped at a deli on the way to school for a Danish and juice. "Much buffeted on the land and on the deep by the violence of the gods, through that long rage and that lasting hate of Juno's. And he suffered much also in war until he built his city and brought his gods from Latium." It had been rough for Aeneas, all those stirred-up deities, that violent departure from home, bullied by his fate.

Celia put on her glasses and went to the window. She looked at the moon, close to full, the wrong shade of yellow, a dented golden apple. Particles from the new sulfur mine near Gillette were changing the colors of things, Lucy had said at the table. The residue was making for strange moons and generously dappled sunsets. The talk and clanking continued below. Wood gave with her father's heavy steps. The same sounds each year, the density of the place settling around her like one of Lucy's old coats that she wore if the weather turned cold. But not the same, either.

Celia counted the eight steps it took to reach the bureau and in the top drawer found the velvet box among the tidy balls of her socks. She had brought a dozen pairs and it had taken her exactly four minutes to match and roll them. In between two pairs, she found the box that held her mother's wedding ring. The *Aeneid* was gone for now. So was her hunger. The ring swung loose on all her fingers. Along with her jewelry, Laura's shoes had been forced off in the fall. One landed on the hood of a car, the other hung by its heel from the limb of a pear tree. Celia knew this. She had glimpsed the tree but had not known whose shoe it was. She had thought, how weird, a shoe on a tree. Then she'd seen the thick belt of people gathered around something on the sidewalk. A woman from the building had seen her, turned gray, and said, "Oh my God, it's the daughter." The daugh-

ter. They saw Vivian Allen at least twice a week. She had a corgi
called Fergus. Why doesn't she know my name, Celia said to
herself, annoyed, and that was the last clear recollection she had
of the day.

The coyotes had stopped. Quieted themselves as they went
off to find food or a place to rest in a nest of black-tipped fur,
their voices stowed for now. In ten years of summers here, she
saw them only rarely. Invisible against a rock face or a road, until one flicked its tail. So small, she'd said to Lucy once, to make
such noise. They don't sing alone, her grandmother said. They
have a chorus. They need each other's company.

Lucy was the only landowner on the draw who did not shoot
them on sight, set out snares, or leave mounds of poisoned meat
for them. Even after she came out of the house one dawn to find
that most of the chickens in her coop had been reduced to yellow claws and bloodied mounds of feathers. No one had heard
them come, kill, go. The pig hadn't grunted, the horses in the
pasture had stayed quiet, and the chickens themselves had perhaps been too stunned to make a sound. The coyotes' stealth was
remarkable for its speed and completeness. Celia had helped
her grandmother soothe the few birds left and sweep the heads
and wings into a sack. That night, a neighbor came by and argued again for wiping them out and Lucy had said mildly, no, not
that. It was hard, she said, not to respect a creature who could
gnaw off its own paws, leave the stubs in traps, and still make its
living with only one real foot left intact. Coyotes were smarter
than chickens, not to mention most humans. It was in the order
of things that chickens should get eaten. "It's what we do to
them," she said, her knife and fork making a steeple above her
plate. "The coyotes got there first this time. Besides, it is hard to
be sentimental about a creature that can drown itself at a tap." The
utensils descended, set to work cutting the pork chop that came
from the hog she'd raised the year before, coddled and scratched
between his eyes until she had his throat slit. Jefferson.

Celia took off her glasses. Not being able to see what was right ahead of you blurred old memories. Lucy faded, as did the bits of chickens, the large pig. The window sash, the bookcase corner, too: furred edges now, her eyesight that bad. The ring, even, when she held it above her head so it could glow in the moonlight, looked softer, a band of ribbon.

Celia had found it two days after her mother jumped, eyes trained on the sidewalk to avoid neighbors. She was returning from a trip to the corner store for bread and milk and jam. Her first trip outside, the world jagged and impossibly bright. She'd glimpsed the ring in the gutter, a small C of light. She took it because it was shining and valuable and there to be taken, the way magpies in fairy tales steal sparkling things. She took it because it was a way for her to be back inside her body, to feel it bend and shift after two days of weightlessness. Then, in the elevator, she pulled it from her pocket and saw at once the familiar pits and scratches in the gold. Her lungs pinched tight. The elevator continued ticking upward. She pushed the ring back into her jacket. She'd forgotten the jam. Celia said nothing about what she'd found and couldn't have said why. Heat knocked at a radiator. Someone—a relative, a friend—was crying in the living room.

She still hadn't told anyone. What was the point? If she mentioned it now, her father's face would turn into a terrible shape and he would ask to hold the ring. Cam would say something caustic or accuse her of weirdness for not confessing right away. Lucy would try to comfort her, and that might be the worst of all, since Lucy had never quite seen the worth in their mother. Celia knew that the way she knew her hair was brown: a flat, undeniable fact. Celia held the ring more tightly. When she was little, her mother sat with her before she slept and stroked her hair. The curve of the ring had run a slim, warm river along her scalp. Without her mother's touch, the day could not be over. She could not yield to rest. It seemed like a terrible violation that she could sleep now without that touch, but she could. She slept like the dead. Celia went back to the bureau, the world still blurred, and found the box by feel. She slid the ring back in, shut the drawer.

She stood in the center of the sewing room, as Lucy called it, though it held mostly forty-five years of *National Geographics*, hacked to shreds as she, Cam, and their father before them had cut out pictures of pandas and polar bears, baobab trees and Masai tribesmen. When she was six, she'd discovered a story about the lost tribe in the Venezuelan rain forest and made her mother read it to her. In the pictures, men hung one-armed from trees against a veil of green light. The warriors had ragged bangs and carried spearheads bound to shafts with strips of tapir fur. She had found her mother on the porch, her hand held like a piece of shell against her forehead, shielding her from the Wyoming sun. She'd been about to go help Lucy fold sheets, but sat back down with Celia and the magazine. Laura rubbed Celia's back as she read about the jungle, the scientists. The smell of baked linen rose from the yard. Lucy's shadow wavered on a wall of white cloth. "I wish I slept in trees," Celia said. "You'd have ants itching you all night long," Laura said, "not to mention those jaguars. And worst of all, the three-toed sloth." Her mother's fingers danced slowly in imitation of the arched claws, crawling up Celia's back. "What would you do about the three-toed sloth?" "You would be there, Mom," Celia said. "You would light a torch and scare it away." "Of course," said Laura, fingers stalled on a knob of Celia's spine. "I forgot that part."

The pipes stopped shaking downstairs. The talk had slowed, too. Still without her glasses, Celia went to the register in the floor and lay down beside it. Each room on the second story had one, best sited to catch the heat from the stove below. When she was younger, she used it to watch her parents and grandmother as they talked and played cards, loving the chance to hear what

they said when they weren't arranging their words to accommo-
date the presence of children. We always knew you were listening, her father told her later. We could hear you breathing.
Tonight she didn't care if they heard her. She didn't even care if
she recorded the exact content of their conversation. She didn't
need to see them in focus, either. It was enough to feel the
slightly warmer air rising from below as if buoyed by light. To
know that the dishes were being placed in the walnut cupboard.
That her father would leave a crumpled towel on the counter
and Lucy would quietly retrieve it. Celia closed her eyes, felt the
cool grate bite into her arm, relishing the sharpness.

The next day, she and Lucy went back to town, first to see
Lucy's old friend the bank manager at his house and then to
meet the owner of the C Bar C. They were quiet as they drove
to Callendar, twelve miles off. Celia held the Pentax at her side
and ignored Lucy's glance at it. Lucy said only, "You're old
enough in a few months to get your license, you know. We're an
agricultural state. You can start younger out here." The same
lure she'd offered Cam. Celia had told her father at the hospital
that she wanted to learn to drive, but now she wasn't so sure.
She'd forgotten how fast cars went in Wyoming, even on dirt
roads, and how stunningly large most of them were. She'd fallen
asleep on the grate the night before, and the metal had stamped
a dent deep in her arm.

"Sure," Celia said, not wanting to talk. What she really
wanted to do was watch the mountains, the pine-ridged triangular masses of rock that eased up on the land with apparent reluc-
tance, snowcapped almost all year. She thought even Aeneas
might have had a hard time in a town like this. Latium's climate
must have been less formidable.

Weather rubbed against Callendar at every turn, even
though the town sat in a broad cleft between two steep hills.
Celia rolled the window down as soon as they reached the outskirts and the wind wouldn't whip them quite so badly. The smell

of hot sage pressed down the street, chalky dust settled in new patterns on the sidewalk, and sunlight dropped in a clear, wide knife from the sky. It was not a place where you could imagine horses running, but they had.

Celia sat on the porch as Lucy held open the screen door to go and visit her banker friend. "No fun for you, baby. Won't be long. Just wait here," and Celia nodded, doubting it was simple gossip the two old people were trading, but happy to be left alone. The bright light appeared to broaden sounds, and Celia wanted to listen to the noises weaving the day on the street: women calling children, children calling women. Crying. Phones. Doors slapping shut on wooden jambs. Mixed breeds that barked with intent and threw themselves at chain-link fences, making them ring like a wall of falling coins. She heard advertisements for cars, rodeos, insurance. Television laughter. Then the wind bore in again and blunted the noise of humans, stories, dogs.

Sitting on the porch, she thought of another reason why their father had moved them out here. It wasn't the spiked bite of the sage. It wasn't the pronghorns springing with vertical intensity across the hills. He'd claimed landscape and animals as benefits of leaving New York and ignored the less appealing aspects of life in Callendar that Laura had always noted—regular methamphetamine busts, frequent hunting accidents, discord about teaching evolution. Celia had spent enough time here to know his picture was biased, but he hadn't mentioned the most obvious advantage: most of the houses were only one story tall. No one could jump from a high window.

She lifted her camera, focused, and took a picture of the satellite dish hiding behind cottonwoods next door. It wouldn't come out, and worse, the subject wasn't worth commemorating. Yet the click of the shutter confirmed that she was still here. This was the frame of mind in which she took most of her pictures. She knew they were awful, but the thought of the film advancing inexorably along the roll, the steadiness of shots taken one after another was a small way to measure and feel part of the passing of time. Maybe this was why her mother had loved the camera: its frank ability to keep a record of the fact that you had picked it up, aimed it, and witnessed whatever was there to witness. Her mother had not often truly known or believed in the simple fact of her existence. But Laura also wanted to extract beauty, mood, and sensibility in the process. Her subjects had angles. She wanted to press their simple being into art. It was never enough for Laura, never enough just to be.

A thin voice in Celia's mind, its origins vague, said, and we weren't enough for her, either. Below that rose a coil of anger. Why was that so? What had she and Cam and their father lacked? What had robbed their family of its ability to console? Worse, shouldn't her mother have been ashamed to leave like that?

In these moods, Celia found she needed math, a subject she had never really loved until after Laura died, when it snared her with its cool precision. She recited the number of steps between the porch and Lucy's truck. She multiplied it in her head by three. She calculated the frames left on the roll. She would have stopped to count the leaves on the aspen in front of the bank manager's house if it helped to shake off this impossible set of feelings that could freeze you to ferocious inertia with their unanswerability. She walked fifteen paces down the street. An hour had passed, and Celia had seen three people, all men in pickups, whom she had surreptitiously photographed. That was one way to get back at her mother.

Laura had rules about pictures of people. She'd been scrupulous about that, at least. Ask, always ask, she said. Just before she died, she'd done a series of people and their scars. Men lifting shirts to reveal a line of puckered flesh on the belly. Fingers tracing the arc of a knife high on a cheekbone. Accompanied by short interviews about the origin and meaning of the scar. That should have told us something. Why didn't we pay attention to that? Celia wondered as she looked at her feet marking off the paces.

But Laura had been cheerful making those portraits of drastic damage. None of the usual alarms had flickered. She'd had a haircut. She watched the news without deflating into the sofa. The level of red in the wine bottles descended slowly. When Laura was bad, the recycling bin was heavy with clinking glass. If Celia had been asked—which she hadn't been—she would have said her mother was as well as she had ever seen her. But it was also true that she had wearied of inspecting Laura for signs of trouble. Celia's vigilance had slipped. She hadn't wanted to keep track anymore. And look what happened.

Celia played with the f-stop, the shutter speed, and the focus, then looked through the viewfinder and clicked. She captured one man in a torn T-shirt for a second time and still hadn't asked him for permission. She didn't think he'd give a rat's ass about a girl with glasses and her camera. She'd been right out there in the open and he hadn't noticed her. The Pentax, heavy, unsleek, bumped against her chest. Its black lens cupped the day's heat. Rat's ass. She liked the expression. Cam had brought it home one day from school a few years ago and she used it frequently.

She thought again about the possibility for jumpers out here. Even from the roof of Lucy's, it would be hard to kill yourself. From twenty feet, if you were lucky or simply cursed with survival, you might suffer no more than bad bruises or a concussion. But past a third story, your chances of living were minimal. Just ten or twelve extra feet, and the body couldn't deal with it. It was terrible that you could find out things like this on the Internet. She had wanted, when the screen burned blue, for someone, any adult, to come in, loom over the computer, and tell her, stop that, you should not know that. But they hadn't, and she'd learned a lot more that now permanently resided in her brain.

She was relieved that Lucy lived in relentless denial of the significance of the Web and refused attempts to get her house wired. Whenever her father tried to persuade his mother to join the modern world, it never worked. Lucy didn't welcome change. It didn't offer respite. But Arthur saw it as his only way out. He was trying, in some essential way, to remodel both himself and his children, and he would take the most obvious steps on his own behalf first. He would stop wearing ties and maybe, horribly, he'd change to a bolo. She thought it likely he would trade the Toyota for a behemoth vehicle; he'd gotten the old car tuned up in preparation for its sale. But not wearing ties and buying a new truck would not be enough. He'd forgotten to bring the household gods.

Lucy came out looking pinched around the eyes, but Celia knew better than to ask what she and the bank manager had talked about. "What were you doing down there?" Lucy asked.

"Looking around," Celia told her. "Investigating."

"Investigating?" Lucy said. "Any good clues?"

"Not a one," Celia said.

They went then to a coffee shop to meet Mr. Starmer, the dude ranch owner, who told Celia she could start in the kitchen. She would be paid five dollars an hour. "Do I get to wear a uniform?" she asked and startled him by smiling when he said yes.

Lucy drove her there the next day and as they went, they listened to a book on tape about an Englishman who'd spent five years in Arabia in the 1940s. It was odd to hear words like "crescent dunes" and "oryx" while driving past Hereford cattle and the crushed remains of rattlesnakes. "Is this your first job, missy?" Lucy inquired, turning the volume down.

"Do you count babysitting?" Celia replied, meticulous with truth around Lucy. If Lucy had been a goddess, she would have been Athena, ruthless in her justice, punitive when roused. She was terrifying to most people, yet Celia adored her. It was just that the love was mixed with a great deal of awe.

"Absolutely. One of the hardest around."

"Well then, I've been a babysitter." She didn't feel compelled to add she hadn't been much at ease around the pair of helter-skelter boys, their noise, and the violent rules for games invented and changed at a moment's whim.

Dishwashing might be better suited to her temperament. She liked cloaking her hands in mitts of fine bubbles as she scrubbed pans and baking tins. A dripping pile of washed pitchers was satisfyingly concrete. She liked the large, dim kitchen with its oversize equipment: baking sheets for a hundred cookies, pots large enough to boil six chickens. The shelves gleamed with tools whose names she did not know, and she was glad she was going to have so much to occupy her inside this busy space. She was happy, too, to have a job that would keep her indoors for most of the summer, away from the stark heat, the snakes. Close to water and the smells of clean, steady industry.

But she wasn't used to the shuffle of so many people, and all of them new. She felt embarrassed for the dudes, obvious easterners in their snappy outfits, brazenly walking around in clean chaps. She respected the waitresses and their quick, muscled arms, obvious westerners in their ease with work and dumb easterners. It was satisfying, too, to watch the wranglers stomping around in boots with heels worn down to the thinness of dominoes. A lot of hustle went into whooping up this cowboy fun. Mr. Starmer was everywhere at once, steady and focused, attentive to detail. When Celia learned how much it cost to enjoy a week of this rustic simplicity, she understood why. But it was a good place, she could see that. People cared about what they did and tried to do it well. The horsemen were tactful about matching horses to guests. They saved the half donkey–half Percheron for what they called the larger guests, and gave girls who said they rode all winter animals only slightly less wild than the ones they said they wanted.

It would have been easy to make friends, since many of the employees were in their late teens and early twenties, but a crippling bout of silent shyness set in. Moving it off was like prying a boulder from the mouth of a cave. She had learned it would roll away when she least expected, and then there'd be a torrent of words and sociability waiting to be used up.

The third day, the kitchen manager let her off early. There was nothing left to clean. He had caught her wiping grime from high on a range hood and said, "Get out, Celia. Wander around. We'll pay you," and shooed her out the door. She didn't know quite what to do. First, she walked down to the pool, loud and bright with girls she might have gone to school with in New York—blond, sleek, fully parented. She couldn't stay there long, and found her way to the corral.

Soon this became a habit. When her shift was done, she would wait there for Arthur or Lucy to pick her up. She liked to watch the cowboys bring the horses over the lip of the hill and down toward the barn to prepare them for the evening rides. It was thrillingly real: the charged animals, the hollering men. They all loved it, the wranglers, the guests, maybe even the horses. But it also frightened Celia, and she wondered if the spectacle bothered anyone but her. The hill was so steep, the hooves so sharp. It would have been so easy for someone to stumble and be crushed.

One afternoon, too early for the roundup, Celia saw that the corral was empty except for a black-and-white paint standing near the fence. The horse whuffed and shook its tangled mane. These Wyoming horses were raw compared with ones she knew from home. Though she longed to feel comfortable on one, her heart pounded and her breath grew fast when she rode. Laura had always made her try, but the results were the same, summer after summer. Nervousness always outweighed the pleasure of touching the animal's skin and admiring its obvious beauty.

Horses were radically larger than girls. It was far easier to watch one and approach with caution, her feet still on the ground. She was glancing down at her fingers, the skin still puckered from so much immersion, when she heard, "His name's One-Eyed Jack." Celia nearly turned and ran. It would be easier to flee than talk. Her voice was caught somewhere in her chest, densely wound under her ribs, but suddenly her feet were leaden.

The boy who'd spoken had lush red hair and was skinny and knobbed as a cottonwood twig, yet his voice was deep and broad. It seemed strange that a body so meager could produce a noise so sonorous. He spoke like a judge, a skilled attorney, a doctor, someone used to passing on difficult news with authority. His jeans were loose enough to fit another tall, slim person inside them and stayed on only because his belt, anchored with a buckle the size of a small platter, cinched his waist. The leather of his boots was pleated like old-lady skin at the ankles.

"Why One-Eyed Jack?" she asked. Her voice sounded as if she'd been breathing earth.

"That's some famous quarter horse. This one's just part mustang, part barbed wire. He can't stand a saddle. My dad bought him at auction near Billings; they're letting me keep him here, see if I can make him reasonable." The horse wandered closer as the boy started to talk. He smacked a triangle of shit from his heel and stood next to Celia in an entirely neutral way. As if she were a shingle fallen from a roof, a shock of weed in a field.

"Can I touch him?" she asked. Even though horses frightened her, Celia was never uninterested in them. Her mother had so badly wanted her to like the animals.

"He bites. Take a piece of your ass if you let him," the boy said.

Celia took that as permission. The horse was looking sideways at them—one wet, dark eye fringed with flies. He banged a hoof on the ground. Celia reached toward his neck. His ears pressed back. The boy said nothing. The horse's patchwork skin felt like heated silk. He snorted, but did not flinch. Her fingers were on a wide vein that rivered its way down toward his cheek when he ducked his head to nip with tough yellow teeth. She yanked her hand back, curving it to her chest as if it were a bird.

"Nearly got you," the boy said, still neutral.

After only a few days, people here seemed to know her story and to lean toward her with a muted sympathy. With few words, no words at all, actually, but a gaze filled with awareness. The kid with the dead mother, the jumper. Lucy King's granddaughter, from back East. But this boy projected nothing toward her. He either had no idea what had happened or, more interestingly, didn't care.

"I'm Celia," she said.

"I know it," he answered. The horse drifted toward the center of the corral. The day was growing cool. Celia closed her eyes and listened to the rough swish of the pinto's tail. The boy still hadn't offered his name. The scent of heated pine traveled on air descending from the mountains. "You know how to drive?" he asked.

"I'm fifteen," she said, opening her eyes. She could have added, I'm from New York. I don't even know how to turn a car on.

"You better learn," he said. The horse whinnied. She wanted to say, I don't need to learn, we're not staying for good, but she was aware that both she and the boy knew this was probably not true. "You ride?"

She had to say no, not really. He sighed, apparently amazed at finding himself next to someone so skilless. Nonetheless, he said, "I'm Carson. I'm gonna take Jack for a walk, teach him some trails. Want to come?"

Carson was seventeen, a wrangler. His father had worked at the C Bar C, too, but he'd hurt his knee in a bad fall and was now "between employments." Carson announced this with weary love. He'd clipped a halter rope on Jack, and the horse stamped a back hoof. Carson talked to him in his strong, man's voice, telling him things like this girl was coming along and Cheyenne was the capital of Wyoming and the highest mountain in the state was Gannett Peak, 13,804 feet over in the Wind River Range. Told him his name shouldn't be Jack, it should be Lucky Son of a Bitch because he had the good fortune to land in a place with a stubborn person. "Undo the gate," Carson told Celia. She didn't think he was much for pleases or thank-yous. But he seemed to be treating her as an equal, which was its own form of politeness given her newness to the ranch and her inexperience.

As they walked up the mountain, Carson kept a careful eye on Jack, who was, he said, behaving because it suited him to. "When he wants to get mean," he said, "he'll get mean. He just won't bother to send you a letter before it happens." Carson had learned that early about horses. His first memory was of nearly being trampled to death because he'd wandered into the stall of a nasty bay named Skipper. Celia was silent as the boy steered Jack through a stand of ponderosas. Her first memory, of her mother giving her a present crackling with ribbon one Christmas, was at once too painful and too ordinary to mention.

They moved quietly upward through a narrow canyon that widened gradually as they climbed. Abruptly, the land opened out and Celia saw they'd reached a meadow, a bowl of wild wheat, knee-high and pale gold, flashing. They followed a faint track through the field, which rose along a fold of earth and appeared to be edged on one side, down a cleft, by a creek banked in box elder. She knew the names of the plants. Laura had learned them from Lucy and taught them to her. Plants matter, names of plants matter, her mother had said. Not enough, Celia thought. Not quite enough. But she realized she wasn't counting steps, she was simply walking.

They kept to the trail, red dirt rising. The horse was still performing his piece as a tractable animal. They stopped by a low boulder. The wheat bowed and chattered with birds and wind. It gleamed, and Celia, moving off the path to stand in it, felt as if caught in dry water, surging and tidal. "Down there are sheep," Carson said. "Watch for snakes." He was acting as if the meadow didn't affect him. He needed to say something blunt and practical that would make sure she knew he was a boy. But she'd seen his face when they'd arrived at its crest and found the shining slope unfolding before them. He'd chosen this spot. It was necessary to him. Indian paintbrush. Aster. Ponderosa. Too many names, too much to watch. She wanted something warm to steady her and leaned, for a moment, on Jack's piebald side. He reared instantly. Front hooves blocked the sky near her head. She saw sliced cloud, the glint of shoes, mane, foreleg, her own hand rising as a shield.

Carson wasn't a boy, he was a flash of motion. His sheaf of hair a blaze. "Goddamn fool," he shouted, at Jack, at Celia. He threw his jacket over the horse's head and the animal settled below the dark comfort of cotton that smelled like Carson, though his withers and hindquarters shivered and twitched. His nostrils released air in short, hot huffs.

"I wasn't thinking," Celia whispered.

"That doesn't need mentioning," said Carson and spat, his back to her. He had already told her Jack was a spooky horse, so badly beaten he was close to useless when near most humans. Anything could set him off, he'd explained, the slightest pressure in a place he hadn't expected it.

The wind blew harder. It was time to go. But Celia stood there, trying to remember something. She hadn't been surprised when Jack shied and came so close to connecting his hoof with her skull. There was no prying beauty from danger. There never was. Carson knew it, too, which accounted for his speed and accuracy. The two twined together, the way the meadow held snakes, the breath of the earth, a horse that could kill you, grass like stalks of gold.

Celia walked back carefully with Carson and Jack, who quieted as Carson told him more about his new state. The name of the bronc on the license plate was either Steamboat or Deadman; about that point there was controversy. Wolves were back in the Lamar Valley in Yellowstone. Leafy spurge was taking over rangeland in Sheridan County. Filling in the horse's education, acquainting him with his place. It wasn't until Jack was safely back in the corral and they were standing at the fence that Carson spoke to her directly. "Next time he won't miss. That was his warning shot."

Celia nodded. They watched Jack munch hay, tail flicking. The sun was fading under a wash of blackened clouds. Twilight crept in. She shivered and hoped Carson didn't see and judge her soft.

He asked if she had a lift and she said yes, her dad was coming to pick her up. Carson said he was on his way home, too. Tomorrow was his day off. He was going to visit his dad. Celia waited, sensing more. His father, he went on, was living at the Motel 8 for the time being. Guests at the ranch started to gather for the evening meal. "My parents are bound and determined to kill each other," he said, watching the families walk to their dinners. He was telling her this because he knew about her mother.

"Who's going to get there first?" Celia asked. She was watching a woman bend to take her small son's elbow and steer him toward the dining room.

Carson didn't answer for a moment. "That's not at all clear. Not clear at all," he said at last. She thought about warning him. He might want to think about the fact that people could take death on themselves and avoid murder altogether. Looking at him as his eyes followed the mother, Celia thought he probably knew this already, though it didn't necessarily make it any easier to live with. Such information just gave you that many more

chances to experience confusion. Jack pricked his ears at something only he had noted as a possible threat. Fear that could
have stemmed from anything at all.

Her father drove up soon after and she said thanks for the
walk and good night. "You bet. See ya," Carson answered, two
fingers lifted in salute.

"Who's the cowboy?" her father asked as she got in the car.
Celia wished he wouldn't try to sound so proprietary. As if Carson were someone he might have to protect her from, when they
both knew that girls as skinny as Celia, with glasses as big as hers,
didn't need much defending from boys. She also let herself
have the narrow idea that her father might not be as adept as he
hoped at protection.

"His name's Carson," she said. "I'm not so sure he's a
cowboy."

"He had a rodeo buckle the size of Lake DeSmet," her father said. In the sunset light, the bruise around his eye was mottled green. It was healing slowly. "You don't get those faking your
cowboy credentials."

"Oh, I'm sure he can ride. I know he knows horses. That's
just not all he does," Celia said, and they were quiet for a time.

"Was it a good day?" her father asked after a few minutes.
She'd decided almost instantly she wouldn't tell him about what
happened in the meadow. He needed no stories of close calls.
When she was little, she had loved coaxing him to tell her about
all the times he'd fallen from a horse or been bucked from a
steer at a rodeo. But it had been some time since she wanted to
know about the origins of his weak knee, his scars.

"Yes," she said. "Chef saw me washing dishes and said I was
a natural." Arthur smiled then, a rare, real one. He was still so
tired. A few miles later they stopped to help a woman change a
flat on her station wagon. By the time they neared Lucy's, the sky
was quite dark. They passed horses in a field, one of them a paint
like Jack. If the night were moonless, you wouldn't be able to say

for certain it was even a horse. If you weren't paying attention, all you might notice were the lobes of white on the coat. You might be tempted to believe all you'd seen were floating pieces of a jigsaw puzzle. Unconnected, on the move. She touched her father's arm. "Hi, Dad," she said. "I'm here."

He glanced at her. "I know, honey," he said. "I know."

When the telephone rang at Lucy's, it sounded as ferocious as an alarm and provoked the same kind of response: they all leaped up, ready for bad news. Usually it was just a friend calling for Lucy or Dwight needing Arthur. It was never for Celia or Cam. Still, they always responded as if something drastic were about to happen. Mail, real mail, was even more infrequent, but fetching it became something Celia grew feverish about, even when the box held only circulars for Albertsons. Lucy didn't understand this need to run all the way down the long drive. "Rattlers on the way there, bills inside. That is all there is to a mailbox. What are you expecting?" she would ask her granddaughter. "A round-trip ticket to Shanghai? Expenses paid by the People's Republic?" In fact the mail itself did not concern Celia; she was keeping track of exactly how long it took to get there and back. Then, a couple of weeks into their stay, Celia returned from work to find that Lucy had beaten her to the punch. A letter waited for her on the kitchen table. Lucy was appropriately apologetic. "Of course you've got friends who would write, baby," she said. "Naturally."

Celia didn't tell her that she recognized neither the name nor the writing, and she darted upstairs, fingers working at the envelope. At first she'd thought the letter was from Ellie, her oldest friend. In her room, still wearing her C Bar C uniform, Celia sat on the bed and noticed the moons of grime below her fingernails. Something crumpled in her pocket—her first paycheck, for $308, which seemed to represent some enormous step toward competence and independence, though what she might buy with it other than film or hamburgers was unclear.

But Ellie had yet to be in touch, and Celia guessed that the depth of the friendship had been sounded and been found less important than expected. It hadn't always been that way. The summer and fall before her mother died, she and Ellie had been visited with a brief, radiant sensitivity to the near future, when—for reasons they had not determined—they could often predict what was about to happen. Mostly their clairvoyance operated at a low frequency. They would pick up phones just before they rang. Guess which classmate was about to come down a hallway. The incidents could often be explained by their keen awareness of habits and preferences, the deeply sched-uled way the lives around them seemed to operate. People thought they were acting out of free will, they often said to each other—it was the semester they were reading *Paradise Lost*—when it was clear that much of what they did was conditioned: when they arrived, when they left, what they wore or bought or ate.

Still, it was unusual how often they were right about which bracelet a student would wear or how a teacher's hair would be done, which flowers would be in the vase in the entryway of El-lie's building. Their accuracy lent the air around them a small, constant echo. Still, their gift had the scope of a walkie-talkie: short-ranged, with specific targets.

Celia folded the paycheck and put it in her drawer. She would have to ask her father about getting a bank account. He would be home soon, with Cam riding shotgun in his new truck. She'd been right. The Toyota had only lasted a week and last Tuesday he'd returned with a blue Ford F-150, which Cam im-mediately called the Whale. "Extended cab," her father said, ig-noring his son, his hand on the hood.

Celia thought that her prediction of this new acquisition did not really count as evidence of her psychic acumen. She just knew her father well. She didn't like to think about it, and as with her mother's ring, she never talked with her family about this small, weird talent. She wondered if Laura had had it, too, and had also kept it hidden.

Celia almost hoped that the clairvoyance would work only with Ellie or on the island of Manhattan, bound by old friendships or by water. But it was already happening at the ranch and at Lucy's. Her brain would fuzz over, then everything would grow so sharp it seemed almost distorted, and a picture in her mind would appear and then vanish. She'd known, for instance, that Dwight was going to invite them to a barbecue. She'd glimpsed three German shepherds with tragic expressions because they were in the split-second image, too. But what good did it do anyone to have visions of dogs or to intuit you were going to eat short ribs?

She opened the letter, which was from someone named Courtney Van Buren. Celia heard Lucy banging around in the kitchen the way she did when she wanted someone to help her make dinner, but Celia ignored her. Lucy had not had faith that people beyond her family would see fit to write to Celia. She could dice carrots on her own.

Courtney was a ninth grader at Chapin, the letter explained, and she was the daughter of Susan Van Buren. She'd seen Celia and her family at Christmas parties sometimes. She'd gotten Celia's address from a mutual friend of both families. She was sorry to bring up bad memories, but it was obvious she and Celia had something in common, something really bad, and there weren't many people to talk to about it. She hoped Celia was having a good summer in Wyoming, where she had never been. Just once to Colorado to see cousins. She had one question. The worst one, she added. But something about people dying made you ask it. Did she know why her mother had done it? She would understand, she ended, if Celia didn't want to write back, and signed it yours truly, Courtney Van Buren.

Lucy called her down to supper. Cam and her father were back. Celia had heard the scrape of the Whale's tires on the gravel, but she was so absorbed in Courtney's letter that she'd missed the sound of boots moving across the floor downstairs. She would write Courtney back and it struck her then how lonely she had been. As she washed, she was aware that she didn't let herself really feel things like that until a possibility existed of not feeling them. Until someone arrived who suggested that your particular experience, even the worst of it, might be something worth knowing about.

At supper, Lucy asked, "Enjoy your mail?" and Celia said she had. A friend had written. Arthur and Lucy looked relieved, and Cam seemed mildly surprised. "What?" said Celia. "Is it so weird—someone wanting to be my friend?" As she heard her voice ring on the hot air, she understood her family's concern. She was so shorn of frippery and lip gloss. None of the girls she knew cared as much about scansion as she did. With knowledge based in gloomy social awareness, not the ability to glimpse what was coming next, she was certain it was going to be even harder to make friends out here. There were cheerleaders. There were rodeo queens. There were girls at the ranch who were seventeen, married, and mothers. A couple of them even had their pilot's licenses. These people were a whole other order of business.

"No, honey," her father said. "It's not that. It's just that we're glad you have people to talk to." His stitches were out. The hair was beginning to grow back. He was getting brown on the face and left arm from the trips back and forth to town with the window rolled down. He looked more content than he had since Laura died. Celia wouldn't have called it happy, just not quite so completely ruined. Something was righting itself in him. Cam, too, she saw, and knew with a flash that he must have a girlfriend. He had that creamy, satisfied look he got when he was touching girls.

"Well, I do," she said. But what she wanted to tell her family, sitting there eating steak and carrots, is, I've found my mother's ring. I have no idea why I've kept it from you. I also want to tell you I can see things that are slightly in the future, like knowing what's around a corner. She wanted to talk with them, not with Courtney Van Buren, about why her mother had killed herself. It was almost nine months later, and the topic was fenced off, a compound that no one dared enter from a public road.

But there were things to say. Theories could be discussed. Hadn't they all seen that melancholy had snagged Laura a long time ago? Hadn't they all known how she'd lived in open-eyed knowledge of disaster? You had only to look at the way she read the newspaper and at the photographs she took to understand that. There had never been any assuaging of her grief, so what had gotten so bad in the fall of 2003 that she couldn't stand it anymore? Can I tell you, she wanted to add, that I stopped watching? That I just didn't want to anymore, and part of me thinks she knew that and found a way to slip off? Notice! she wanted to yell at Lucy, Cam, her father. Notice I've stopped eating, and my plate is still full. That I am whispering a string of numbers under my breath all the time. That my toe is tapping out square roots below the table. But they didn't. They were hungry. Cam was grimy, Arthur and Lucy tired with their own day's work. They kept sawing at their meat and pouring water. They didn't see her give the steak to the dog or even hear his teeth cracking at the porous bone right at their feet.

Going to work had become a blunt necessity: its routines grew critical and her responsibilities expanded. Her talent for order was visible there. She was sorry it took Lucy or her father forty minutes to drive her to and from the C Bar C, but thought it was the least they could do if they couldn't see her openly giving a porterhouse to the dog.

Now and then, Carson stopped and talked to her on his way

to and from the kitchen for the multiple sandwiches he needed to sustain himself. She asked after Jack, who was still in the corral looking as mean-spirited as ever. "Cussed. I would even say wounded," Carson said, "but he's waking up to the fact I don't intend to whip him." "Is that progress?" Celia asked. "You bet," said Carson.

One afternoon he asked her if she would like to try a trail ride, and she surprised herself by agreeing, aware she must be pretty desperate to expose herself so directly to a horse. For her, Carson picked an aged gelding misnamed Rocket, while he rode a nervous horse called Floyd. He watched Celia the whole time and midway through permitted himself a scathing critique of everything from the way she held the reins to her posture. It amazed her she was able to correct her mistakes and almost enjoy herself. But when a pair of rabbits jumped from the scrub and the horses startled and leaped, she thought her heart would burst. She prayed he couldn't see how her arms went wooden or smell the fear rising like smoke off her back. At the barn, pulling burrs from Floyd's mane, Carson said, "You're no natural, but you could learn."

After that, Celia thought he might leave her alone, but a couple of days later he asked if he could drive her back to Lucy's. The invitation made her breath catch, as if she were horseback again. He talked the whole way there, then stopped his truck abruptly at the base of the driveway. He watched her walk up toward the house for a minute or two before turning his ancient Chevy around.

Lucy said she'd known him as a seventh grader. "He understood comma splices the first time I explained them. Smart boy, though it might have killed him to reveal that." Sometimes Celia forgot that Lucy had only recently retired from teaching English, social studies, and almost everything else at one time or another at the Callendar Middle School. Naturally, her reputation had been fearsome, but no one at the ranch wanted to embarrass Celia with stories about her grandmother. Maybe they were scared. Even if she was retired, you never knew what a woman was capable of who could stop class, come to your house, and drag you straight from your bed to school.

Still, Lucy was tractable when she met Carson again at the C Bar C one evening. "Carson Novak, have you grown three feet since I last saw you? And did I read in the paper that you had taken time off from that growth spurt to get high honors last year?" He said "Yes, ma'am," and "yes, ma'am," and mashed his straw hat, which he did only when he was very happy.

Carson liked to point out landmarks around town, different people's cattle, the fields that were especially fertile. He knew all the brands, the talk at the saddle shop, who was borrowing more money for a new tractor or better bull semen. He could say words like bull semen and not make her feel embarrassed. Talking to Carson was like gossiping with a girl. "I thought cowboys were supposed to be taciturn," Celia said one day when he was particularly chatty—though he pried for news about Lucy, their ranch, and Cam, whom he'd met at the Albertsons, he hadn't asked her a single personal question. He'd been stung, which she hadn't quite expected. "Think I didn't take my SATs, Miss Manhattan?" and after that she let him talk.

Although he was discursive on many topics, he would not, to her chagrin, tell her much about the high school. He shrugged off mention of it like a gnat on his arm, saying, "It's just school, like school anywhere," and Celia knew he was willfully, stubbornly wrong. It seemed a fact that her city school with its anorexic heiresses and high-pitched hymn singing would bear little resemblance to this place in the mountains with boys who'd been calf riding since they were five.

Nor did kids their age drive trucks where Celia was from, much less trucks like Carson's. He told her that he carried no insurance on it and it had not been inspected in several years. Though Celia did not quite know what these details meant, she grasped the implied warning. Carson might be reliable; he had areas of deeply established knowledge—he understood horses, the weather, and marital discord. But most teenagers couldn't be trusted with a can opener much less a car.

And his vehicle might lose a critical element at any time. Its fenders were as bent as old pine boughs and the sound it made when the engine was turned on was something between a hiccup and a bomb going off. Carson drove it, however, with the same fluency that he used to fork hay and flip shut the blade of a knife. He maintained an impeccable economy of gesture. Everyone from the dudes to Mr. Starmer came out to watch him rope the horses. He could stand in their midst, slapping rumps, dodging hooves, and calmly, quickly, and with the sheerest grace sort one from the other. The horses, too, seemed to acknowledge his mastery. Celia swore they just dipped their heads and let the lariat tighten around their rough, hot necks.

Celia always strapped herself in with a seat belt; Carson didn't, but he made no comment about her choice. The floor of the truck was littered with plastic caps that snapped on Styrofoam coffee cups. Carson alternated between coffee and Dr Pepper, but he must have had the bladder of a cow. He never excused himself to go to the bathroom.

"Are you and Carson Novak friends?" Lucy asked one night at dinner and Celia said, instantly, yes. They were. It wasn't a friendship like any she'd had before, but she recognized it as one. It had that sort of heft. That she cared about it more than he did was a problem. She didn't like it that seeing Carson made her feet start drawing patterns in the dust. Still, she was unduly pleased when, one afternoon in late July, he tilted his hat, strode up to her, and said, "I got something I want to show you. You free Sunday?"

Celia's stomach jolted. He'd asked her somewhere. Then she forced herself to listen to his tone, to look at him. He was staring right at her, not sidelong, the way boys apparently did when they liked you and feared rejection. This was in his usual, uninflected way. He had no interest, no real interest, the sort that would lead to touching, and Celia was mad that she experienced this as quite a blow. She said then, no, she didn't have plans, but he'd have to come and pick her up. Her dad and Lucy would want to say hello and know where they were going.

"It's not that kind of getting together," Carson said, clearly alarmed.

"Believe me," said Celia, looking not at him but at the shadows gathering in the eastern valley, "I know that."

Carson wore his better hat when he came to get Celia, which meant the one without the frayed rim and the stained band. "Hi, ma'am," Carson said to Lucy, hat off his head. He was wearing sneakers, the first time Celia had seen him without boots. He appeared, oddly, younger.

Celia noticed him looking around the house, at the neat displays of books and photographs, peering down the hall to the tidy kitchen and its full pantry. He shook hands with her father, then with Cam. He couldn't stop staring at her relatives, their house. Celia wished her father and brother weren't there. She could show Carson all the pictures she had taken. She could even show him pictures of her mother and the few of Laura's that Lucy had framed. She wanted to sit there and talk to him about all that.

But her father was pressing forward with the afternoon. He was insisting on treating this like a date, although Carson didn't appear to grasp that, too busy glancing covetously around him.

It's just a house and not a fancy one at that, Celia wanted to tell him. It was old for the area, built in 1920, two asphalt-shingled stories, plunked straight on the side of a hill that gave it a view of the rolling, speckled grazing land in front of it. The rooms had high ceilings and the porch had a partial view of the valley. You could hear the trains from Callendar if the wind blew in the right direction. But there were no mountaintops to be spotted, no rushing brook in the yard. To Celia, it looked vulnerable on its plot, with its two rickety cottonwoods threatening to topple anytime, its distance from real water. "You like the house?" Celia asked as they got into Carson's truck. She had brought her camera with her, hoping she would have the courage to ask if she could take a picture of him.

"Your great-grandfather built it," he said. He explained that when Lucy was his teacher, she had told them the story about how the whole population of Callendar had come to build it. "You own that land." Celia had heard it, too; it was one of dozens of tales Lucy told, wrapped in the names and occupations of those who had helped out, the kinds of food they'd brought, the state of the weather. As if Lucy herself had been there. She might have invented the details, for all Celia knew. She told the story often enough to have polished it to a high gloss. Made it familiar as wallpaper, as her father might have said.

They drove slowly along the road to town. Carson had yet to say where they were going and Celia knew better than to ask. His truck banged along the washboard. For once, he was silent. It was the owning. It was the relative oldness that got him. It was having the stories to tell at all. Celia reminded herself that his father lived at a Motel 8. She had learned from Lucy that his mother, Teresa Novak, was something of a terror, the only woman at the entire Bureau of Fish and Game. Unless you were extremely nice to her, you had no hope of getting a chance to blow something's head off. Celia had seen her driving. A small, blond woman whom you could barely spot behind the wheel of her powder-blue Buick, frowning as she steered through town. Exhaust streamed in a straight, fierce plume behind her shiny car. Carson had noted that his mother was one of those people with long memories. He slumped slightly as he said this, as if he had suffered at her excellent recall.

"Lucy owns it," she said to him now.

He shrugged. "Same difference. It's in your family. It'll go to your dad, then you, if you want it. The point is, it's there. You'll get to make a choice about it." It did not seem kind to mention that there was a lot less of it than there had been and she tried to figure out where they were headed. He turned off on a road that was unfamiliar to her and soon they were in a neighborhood on the outskirts of Callendar that Celia had never seen before. The houses were low ranches set on treeless lawns fried to brown. Harvard Street crossed Princeton at Yale. "Carson," Celia asked, "where are we going?" Even if this wasn't a date, he could act a little less as if he were entirely by himself.

"Kelso, the ghost town," he said. "This is a shortcut." Celia had never heard of a ghost town so close to Callendar and was about to ask more when Carson tilted his head toward a house a few hundred yards away and said, "My mother lives there." Then he pulled his truck up shortly and killed the engine, as if sudden silence would mask the racket it had been making. Just then a man in a dented Ford sedan stopped in front of a house down the street, got out, and walked toward the door. Celia said, "That's got to be your father." The man had a shock of red hair and was ropy with muscle, but his body went slack as he stood in front of the house. He played with the brim of his hat, returned to his car, sat on the hood for a moment, his arms crossed on his lean body, then rose again to go and knock. He raised his hand this time. The air was in one of its lulls. The flag in the front yard hung limp as a sock on its pole. The man turned from the door, got into his car, and reversed all the way down the street.

"He tries this every couple of weeks or so, I think. He has bouts of regret for his bad behavior, in between wanting to shoot her." Carson had his right fingers balled up on the dashboard.

His voice was quiet. Celia knew better than to say anything. Little made you feel more exposed than having your family revealed in all its frailty. Her mind stirred and the hazy weight that preceded mild clairvoyance filled her head. She saw small trophies featuring a gold cowboy on a bucking horse, their electroplating worn off somewhere vital like the horse's mane or the cowboy's hat, the dull gleam of the alloy showing through. Someone in the family had touched the trophies quite often. She knew they were Carson's. She blinked and the picture left. Carson started the truck again. "Let's go," he said, as if she'd been the one keeping them there.

He steered the truck through the neighborhood, then down Main Street, past Cody's Bar and the saddlery, the Red Hawk Barber Shop, a realtor's, then over the creek and up a road Celia had never seen before. "Carson," she finally asked, "what's in Kelso?"

"Not much," he told her. Some mining company had built a few houses, a school, and a little church and had tried to get at some uranium. But the lode gave out quickly and all that was left were a few old houses and a cemetery. The church had burned down years ago. That still didn't explain why they were going, but she wasn't going to ask him more right now. His face was closed off from conversation and she guessed he was stuck about five miles back, thinking about his father and his two dejected trips up the street to Teresa's door.

At times, Celia could not fathom that her mother's death had brought them to this town where you could buy chaps, boots, and Stetsons, where people used and wore them and looked normal doing so. Where there were ghost towns and grandstands. Rodeos and highways littered with the haunches of mule deer and antelope. She had not done much traveling, but this was the most separate, self-contained place she'd ever been. So much land, so relentless, wide, and blunt in its colors and shapes. She didn't know why, but its sparseness made it feel more real than New York, which operated within a shimmer of exhaust. Carson had been only to Montana and Colorado, and she decided this did not mean he hadn't been much of anywhere.

"Here," he said now. They rose up the last incline and Celia saw eight shells of stucco houses, roofless, the glass of their windows shattered into a sparkling field. But "field," a word that conjured something burgeoning, wasn't quite right. As they climbed out of the truck, Celia saw smoke rising from what was left of the road and smelled the bitterness of scorched rubber. "Come on," Carson said, motioning her past an abandoned tractor. Their feet crunched below them and the glass winked like mottled, dangerous mica. Green and brown bottle fragments, mixed with clear. People came up here to drink. Everything near the houses—a washing machine here, a car there—was scored with bullet holes. Beer and .22s: my least favorite combination, Lucy used to say. Every year, she had students lose eyes, cheeks, fingers.

"You want to show me the fire?" Celia asked now, following Carson as he strode down the pitted tarmac. Empty potato-chip bags spun in the wind and Celia's shoe banged against a crushed can of root beer. Celia tried to imagine what it had been like to live and work in Kelso, how the wives managed and what winters were like on top of the ridge. She saw the cemetery, still carefully fenced, and wondered if it held headstones for children who died of snakebite and if their relatives were the ones who kept the fence intact. Her mother would have loved this place and come with her camera and stayed and stayed and stayed.

Carson still wasn't talking, just heading grimly on toward the column of smoke. Finally Celia spotted what he wanted her to see: a mass of smoldering rubber that appeared to be a careful arrangement of radials doused with gas or kerosene and ignited.

Firefighters or other officials had stamped a damp ring around the melted tires, but no one was around to prevent further mischief. It seemed to Celia that they should be, that some adult ought to be monitoring for flares. In New York, they would have needed cops to keep out the gawkers or the even crazier people. America seemed less policed here. Not just more open, but less supervised because people liked it that way. To be sighted only occasionally appeared the goal of many people near Callendar. But whoever had made this mess must have been caught in the middle, eager to be vividly recognized in some capacity, totally unknown in another.

"What is it?" Celia asked. "And who did it?" She snapped a picture and got part of Carson's hat in it.

"Some nutbag," Carson said. "How should I know?" His hands were in his pockets, but his thumbs were fiddling with his belt loops. The wind blew harder, and she bent to peel off the silvery skin of a chip bag from her ankle.

Carson settled back on his heels, as if he were sitting a horse, then said, "Every three weeks or so, someone's been hauling a mess of tires out here to make a word with them. Just three letters. Then he sprays the whole shebang with gasoline and torches it. No one's got any notion why." He explained that so far the tire man, as Carson called him, had gotten away with this two times and that he'd spelled MAT and CAR. Celia could vaguely see that they were standing near the legs of the R.

"MAT and CAR," Celia said. "How did they know they were letters?" It was incredibly hard to tell, now that they were burned and mostly melted. People said New York was weird, but she couldn't imagine New Yorkers being tempted to set fire to tires in the shape of words. She took several pictures.

Carson explained that a pilot had seen the MAT on the morning flight from Sheridan to Denver. Celia imagined the glowing orange letters as they might have appeared in the gray

morning and how tempting it would be for those who'd witnessed it to want to interpret it as a sign. "Why is the West so
doomed and epic?" she asked crossly. "Does anything plain or
simple happen out here?" He stared at her for a moment. She
knew she'd been found ungenerous. All he had to do was gesture
toward the mountains, the arch of blue sky, or the smudge by
the clouds they both knew to be a falcon. Only dumb people
couldn't see beyond the raggedness, slag heaps, scalded tires,
and greed. It struck her then how far gone he was on being a
cowboy and she nearly said something, but a gloom akin to the
arrival of a cold front had wrapped itself around him. She
wanted to go home.

As they walked back to the truck, which looked in the harsh
light like a small dinosaur sculpted from metal, she realized that
the word "home" now meant Lucy's ranch and that there was no
true comfort there. Worse, even if she were really home, in New
York, among the familiar lights and smells, near her bookcase
and chairs, she still would not feel complete—that was over, it
seemed.

Something crackled in her chest, as if a tide had heaved her
bones and tried to rearrange them. Laura had always made it
hard to believe in the safety of knowing that one moment was
woven to the next in a pattern you could more or less predict.
She had crept from day to day, picture to picture, as if they were
no more trustworthy than a hand-knotted bridge. But she was
the mother that Celia had had. She held back, steadying the
camera swaying on her chest, hoping that Carson, striding on
toward the truck, wouldn't see her. There was still the widest of
canyons between Laura alive and Laura dead. Celia was taking
pictures so she could show them to her mother.

She stopped walking. The wind swirled dust to Carson's
waist. He turned, looked at her. "Get in the truck, Celia," he
called. "Get in or you'll get blown off to Billings and I'd have to

come find you. And I hate Billings." He continued on to the truck and opened the door for her.

She came after him and sat on the worn seat, staring at the windshield. It was spidered with cracks in the corner and she saw that the mirror on her side was finally gone. It was the first time he'd used her name. That was why she followed. It wasn't even the nice thing he said about going all the way to Montana. It was the curve he gave her name when he said it, as if it were a place where he found momentary rest.

"You need a new truck, Carson."

"My vehicle is a model of perfection," he said, also staring out the windshield, which in addition to its cracks featured the messy funerals of hundreds of bugs. "You're the one getting snot all over its fine upholstery." She was, too. Her nose had been dripping and she had no Kleenex. He passed her a bandanna he kept stuffed in his back pocket. "Apart from the horseshit, it's clean."

She blew her nose in it. It smelled like horse, but not like shit.

When he started the truck, it made its usual sound of spectacular combustion. Carson shifted into drive. The truck rattled, rolled forward. Celia was astonished it did not shake a door loose. "My brother died two years ago," he said, looking not at her but at the ruts through which the pickup was jolting. "He got killed in an explosion on the pipeline in Alaska." She waited, but he said nothing more. He was, she realized, telling her he wished he didn't know what that was like, but that he did.

Neither of them spoke until he angled the car back up Main Street. Celia took the camera from around her neck and put it on the seat between them. She thought about the stealth required to haul all those tires to the field in the middle of the night, the desperation involved in the strangeness of the act. Someone driven by grief or craziness. Or passion—that was possible, too. To be seized by unholy love that spilled out in dark and complicated ways.

Just before they returned to the highway, Celia told Carson that she was going to be OK.

"I know that," Carson said with disgust. "Put the case back on that damn thing before it gets all dirty." He was at the end of their driveway. That was as far as he would go.

"Bye," she told him, taking the camera, being careful not to slam the door too hard.

"It won't break," he said, leaning out his window.

"Never know," Celia answered. She walked to the house and did not look back. I was strange before, she thought, but I'm worse now. He hadn't turned the truck around yet and was letting the engine idle, watching her. He was important to her because he was the first friend made after having been irrevocably damaged. Carson, SATs under his rodeo belt, knew what "irrevocably" meant. One day she would tell him that Courtney was partly wrong. Why someone killed herself wasn't the worst question. Had her mother been in pain and for how long? Those were worse. How long had her mother lain there alive and what had she felt? Lucy's house was coming closer. That meant she must be walking toward it, but she could barely sense her feet, even though her brain religiously recorded the number of steps it was taking to transport her body there. Carson would nod and take the questions seriously. She knew that because he had let her blow her nose in his bandanna, then stuffed it back in his pants pocket and had not thought about it for a single moment. She also knew she could keep counting and counting and no number would ever mask what wasn't there, the open zero of no mother.

She might even tell him that she looked at the sky wherever she walked, as if searching out leaves, birds, airplanes. But leaves, birds, and airplanes tend to move upward or glide parallel to the horizon. When they drop, when they really drop, not just yielding to a controlled move downward, it's an indication of the wrong kind of descent. People obey the same laws as stones—they plummet in a line that is startling for its directness, its intent. Now Celia knew the sky could contain a woman, and she would tell Carson that when she looked upward, she always had the same impossible thought: if she noticed in time, she might just be able to catch her.

LUCY

Lucy hadn't known what Arthur would look like as a widower once he'd had some practice at it and the change in him was sobering. He was worse than she expected, as if he'd been hit on the head by a truck, she said on the phone to her friend Janet Pardo.

When she saw her son in late October, the shock hadn't worked itself off his body yet. It took time for joints to release their locked disbelief and the damage to fully assert itself. She'd arrived in New York to help him with the children, the memorial service. It was the first time she'd been to the city in years and she found it more irksome than ever: the traffic, the voices, the air that smelled of diesel and spoiled milk. It hadn't been an option not to come, of course. She had to deal with the tasks impossible for those too close, the ones that involved touching what had been most familiar to Laura. Tightening the lids on jars of face cream and removing them from the medicine cabinet. Fishing change from the pockets of winter coats. Laura's parents were too distraught, they said, and her only brother lived in England. It was understood that Lucy's hands, separate enough, on franker terms with loss, could manage.

When the children were out, she packed up drawers of clothing, strings of beads. Half-used flasks of perfume and shoes that seemed small enough for birds. Early November, cramped city light, only brick and taxis and overdressed women to watch, nothing she was used to, she woke every morning not quite certain where she was. She'd always been surprised Arthur had adapted so completely to urban life. How could he not miss sky and seeing animals other than pigeons and squirrels? She cleaned and sorted, saving what she thought the children might want or be ready to see in a few years. Linen and necklaces. Silver pitchers and a college diploma unearthed at the back of a closet. Guesswork, all of it, mixed with the slow burn of wonder. How could a woman with children like Celia and Cam grow distant enough from having made them to want to die? Folding gauzy sweaters, reducing scarves to tidy packages of silk, she kept asking herself why the things of the world hadn't called Laura back from the window. How could you pat that cream on your cheekbones and not be glad for the tug of your fingers on skin? Celia came into Lucy's room every morning and curled herself like a pebble in bed. Cam brewed her strong, perfect tea. The day she left, they gripped her as tightly as lichen on rock. Those children are emptied out, Arthur, she said when she called him that night to let him know she was safely home in Wyoming. And Arthur, are you eating? I know, he said, and no, I'm not.

Lucy was thinking about her son and his tall, sad children as she drove along one of the new roads to a compressor well that had just gone in on the Flaxmans' land, which had once been hers and Sean's. A beautiful rise blanketed in silver sage and an abundance of pheasant and fences in good repair, it was the last piece she had parted with and she had bargained about it, Ted Flaxman said, like a dog defending a side of beef. The Flaxmans couldn't see her truck from their house and couldn't tell how greedy she felt as she steered her way below the ridge. Ownership was hard to yield. My sage, my fence. Someone's let the wire sag on that gate. My gate. But not my cow: that poor, scaly

Angus, perhaps down with a case of hyperkeratosis, would have been seen to on my land. The surrendering had stalled, even as Lucy often told herself, it was never your land in the first place. The proprietary feeling was spawned from only a few years of proximity, memories of storms you'd survived, a sheaf of deeds that the wind would have blown to California, and mornings that had offered a view you allowed yourself to find indispensable. That's how deep ownership ran.

Lucy stopped just below the top of the rise and listened to the dog's panting. He had turned into an old animal all of a sudden, wheezing like an asthmatic as he slept, his muzzle notched with gray. "When did that happen to you, Franklin?" she asked him. He yawned at her and she saw the sculpted pink ridges of his mouth, perfect as sand dunes. "Yesterday? Did you turn into an old dog just yesterday?" She eased herself out of the truck. Her friend Janet had announced the week before from her new home in Portland, Oregon, that she'd discovered she was old. "I looked in the mirror and just said, Oh, hell. That's it. I'm old. It was probably in the newspaper ten years ago, but I missed it."

When it comes to land, Lucy thought, I'm just as bad as Janet is about her face. The road she stood on was made of coarse red gravel. These roads were created in just hours, it seemed. A backhoe, a dump truck, a grader: that was all it took, plus two to four workers. Very little manpower to fashion this searing ugliness and the containment pond behind it. Very little time, too, compared to, say, WYDOT, the state road builders. What a difference it made when money and the lure of making more of it came into the equation. The installment of the pad itself was equally brisk: within days, a compact beige cube studded with pressure gauges would appear—a thing that looked as harmless as a box of doughnuts. Lucy sighed and let the dog make his way over to the well on which he peed in a desultory fashion. All this to pull out paltry amounts of a mostly useless fuel: the amount of methane yanked from all of Wyoming was enough to provide American families with only a single year's worth of natural gas. The dog walked three times in a circle, then settled himself bonily on a patch of scrub grass.

Coalbed methane mining was disheartening, with its excessive water use, its toxic salts, but hardly unprecedented in Wyoming's dark waltz with energy. Lucy's family had extracted coal near Gillette, and she remembered the black webs of grime radiating across her father's palms even after his immersion in the showers. One uncle had died in a cave-in in 1936 and another had gasped his way to death from a combination of Marlboros and soft coal. It stopped none of their children from tunneling on and on in mines all over Wyoming, Arizona, Montana, Canada. Or not doing much at all, depending on how much the fuel sold for in New York and Chicago. Half your father's working life was spent filling out forms at the unemployment office, her mother had said. Marrying into a ranching family, Lucy had hoped to escape that kind of hardship—but only for about ten minutes. Ranching was just as chancy a way to make a living, almost as brutal on the land, and certainly as interwoven with the government, as mining was. You simply braved your bad luck aboveground, amid grass and cows.

"It's a dumb life," she said neutrally to the dog. She reached below her seat and pulled out a canvas bag that advertised a convention for big-game hunters in Cheyenne. She had no idea where it came from. Inside was a large canister of blue spray paint. "Get yourself over here, Franklin," she said to the dog. "I don't want you turning blue and going state's evidence on me." He creaked back toward the truck. She pulled out as well a copy of Emily Dickinson's collected poems, the creased and greasy version she had used when teaching ninth graders. She flipped through some of her favorites. "As imperceptibly as grief." "Dare you see a Soul at the white heat?" Then she thought it would be a good idea to let chance select one, the way old-fashioned Christians liked to pick a name for a newborn with a finger stuck in the Bible. She'd had a cousin named Herod for that reason.

The wind was blowing hard, and skirts of dust were flowing across the draw below her. Seven years of poor rain. The lingering drought was one reason why the area had seized on coalbed methane mining. Every week in the *Callendar Post-Tribune*, people wrote letters defending themselves against accusations of doing bad things to watersheds and tearing up hillsides. I'm sending my kid to college with those tax credits; I'm paying my grandmother's nursing-home bill. This is the Wyoming way. Minerals and meat. Every single one had his justification. Lucy tested the paint on a corner of the well and made a dripping blue circle; it came out faster than she'd expected. There wasn't much call for spray paint at her house.

The dog looked at her. "So you don't approve of my taking to vandalism? Well, I don't much myself." She opened the volume of poetry and it fell to "Wild Nights." There wouldn't be room on the well for more than a few lines, but it would be just right. "Wild Nights! Wild Nights / Were I with thee / Wild nights should be / Our luxury!" She had to keep shaking the can. It was hard to control the amount of paint coming out. She wondered how graffiti artists managed to keep the borders of their swirls and crescents so sharp. As it was, the can almost ran out at "luxury." She slung the empty thing and the Dickinson back into the canvas bag and hurled it all in the truck. She wished she could be here when the driver came up to check on the well. No rough scrawl of obscenity, no crude drawing accompanied the quotation, but the writing managed to convey an air of desecration, even lewdness. "Wild Nights" was dripping slightly and looking rather more lurid than she'd expected; she was glad she hadn't chosen red paint.

"I should know better," she said aloud. Her heart banged unsteadily. She felt furtive and sweaty. "I really should." She heaved the dog back into the cab and started the truck. Although she knew that Ted Flaxman couldn't see her, he might, since the wind was blowing now from the west, be able to hear her engine. It was like the Arabs she'd been reading about, discerning conversations, arguments, and recent purchases of camels from the hieroglyphics of tracks and footsteps at an oasis. Here, news traveled through the timbre of mufflers, the glint of a fender from half a mile away. She imagined herself on the stand of the courthouse in Sheridan, her old friend Judge Watkins staring at her with the disappointment he usually reserved for someone who beat a horse. Did you or did you not, Lucille King, spray-paint a poem by Emily Dickinson on the side of compressor well number 481? Shit, yes, Alan—I mean Your Honor—I did, and I would happily do it again. I would also bring more paint to finish off my crime. It wouldn't come to that, probably. Ted had no love for coalbed methane and if he did confront her, she would manage to mention the antler gathering he'd engaged in last year near Owl Creek, which she'd caught him at just before the season opened. Her grip relaxed slightly on the wheel. These transgressions could easily cancel each other out without anyone needing to get themselves involved with something as public as a law.

She turned back down the road leading to her house. She had beans to look after and the whole garden could stand a good weeding. Ted and the truck driver would have no idea what the lines meant, but that was true of 98 percent of Americans. It was nothing to hold against the people of Wyoming in particular. A ridiculous English teacher named Miss Walton had been the first person to read that poem out loud to her. You could never tell who would introduce you to something as indispensable as Emily Dickinson; it didn't much matter that the source was someone insubstantial. Miss Walton was a San Franciscan, briefly misty-eyed about the Old West, and she'd come to teach Wyoming high schoolers about what she insisted on calling fine literature. What an unequivocal disaster she had been. Her hair flew in all directions as she recited the lines of "Wild Nights," trying to convince the class that the verse wasn't only about sexual passion but about union with a spiritual force. When she finished, a boy behind Lucy said, quite loudly, "Well, that's as obvious as piss," and the class dissolved in whoops and smacked desktops. The students were a mixture of kids—smart alecks, studious ones, indifferent ones, a scrum of boys in ninth grade for the third time. She thought the remark had come from one of them, but it hadn't. Sean King, a rancher's son from Dayton, a boy who was already bowlegged from being horseback so much, a boy who spelled better than anyone else, had had the audacity to make that comment. He's right, she thought, it is as obvious as piss. It was the first time she'd taken real notice of Sean King, and she didn't speak to him for nearly three years, until she and Ray Fontaine had broken up. But she remembered what his voice sounded like. He hadn't been entirely disrespectful. He just hadn't liked the teacher forcing it on them like that. Poetry, his tone implied, might not be necessary—it couldn't keep your head from getting kicked in by a bull—but it could be interesting.

Naturally, Sean was sent from the class. Lucy remembered the deliberate way he angled himself out the door, accompanied by shrill whistles. By the next week, the principal had coaxed Miss Walton on to Nathaniel Hawthorne. Her hair lost its energy after that and by January she had returned to her befogged city.

Lucy pulled into her yard and sat in the truck for a moment, listening to the chickens' gossipy squawk. The wind was making something bang on the far side of the house. On the front porch stood an array of boots and sneakers. That many feet hadn't walked through her house since Sean's father had moved in when Arthur was a baby, when neither the oldest nor youngest inhabitant had worn shoes. She put on the emergency brake, an old habit even on flat ground, in honor of the one time she hadn't and the truck had slipped into neutral and the wind had rolled it into the corner of the barn.

She paused on the porch to restore order to the tangle of laces. Still bent, noticing the vast size of Cam's and Celia's feet, she considered whether the desire to spray-paint poetry on compressor wells was a sign of impending dementia. It would have been if I had just found myself up there with a book and the paint in my hand, but I didn't, she told herself. She straightened and felt her back click slowly upright. She had unearthed the canister while cleaning out the barn and awoken the next morning with the idea. But why, Lucy King, does mining bother you so much now? You grew up with miners. Why haven't you taken to environmental activism in a more positive way, and why have you waited till your sixties to behave like a brigand? It was nothing but the purest childishness.

She poured herself some tar-flavored coffee. Arthur had made it and as usual it was so bad it could be used as a substitute for kerosene. She would have to tell him he could buy ground espresso at Jumpin' Java in town. Good coffee had come to Callendar the year before and she had never looked back. She couldn't answer the questions she had posed. She had called to ask Janet, and Janet, too, had expressed surprise at Lucy's behavior. She filled the dog's water bowl and listened to him slurp and sigh his way to his lair beneath the kitchen table.

She forced herself to move and took a cloth with her as she went toward the living room—the parlor, her mother had called it, another old word now dispensed with. In the wedding picture that Lucy picked up, she saw for the thousandth time how shocked Sean looked, as if he could not fathom how he managed to wind up in a bolo tie and polished boots, next to a smiling young woman in a white dress. A justice of the peace had married them at a Callendar restaurant called the T Bone. She wished those early years was all the picture brought back, but it didn't.

She had spotted Rick Skinner's truck heading up the draw while she was washing windows one morning. Rick never drove up here this time of day. Ammonia glazed the room and she guessed Rick had news about Sean. His truck got closer. She saw Rick's hat was off, and she'd known for sure that her husband was dead. He had fallen from his horse, gotten tangled in the reins, and been dragged to the edge of Coal Creek Road, where Rick found him below a chokecherry. As she listened, her bones turned to buckled iron, splintered wood. But it took months for the darkest part of the desolation to catch her. She sent Arthur on errands at the other side of the ranch when she felt the worst of it billowing up late that summer. It was then the coyote pack had settled on her land. The descendants had stayed for thirty years. That was where Arthur was living right now, Lucy suspected. Square in the center of his grief. People forgot you six months in. The rip in their day your sadness opened had closed for them long since, just when you were discovering its exact outline.

No more photographs; they tugged you into memory like a bog. She hadn't touched one of Laura in weeks. Arthur had stashed some of their family pictures in the crowd that already cluttered the top of the bookcase, sandwiched behind the photos of those alive and others long dead. Laura was still caught somewhere in between. She might stay in that purgatorial spot, as suicides often did. They were gone, but in such a fog of sadness and question, a harsh wonder that conferred a kind of pulse. Suicides persisted with a spectral intensity, as if they might be glimpsed in the corners of rooms, among roof beams, in little-used hallways. Lucy flicked the cloth at the sink. Sun gleamed on her watch. It was time to get outside.

Several years before, she'd attended a workshop in Laramie on permaculture and had installed a drip system in the garden. The plants thrived on their measured sips of water. Beans curled luxuriantly up their poles, their emerald vines twining like the hair of a princess in a story. She grew almost all the vegetables she ate, refusing except in the coldest segment of winter to supplement her horde. She was especially proud of her tomatoes—Early Girls, not even distant cousins to the mealy pink rocks trucked in from California. Even canned and frozen, her vegetables had more flavor than the entire produce section of Albertsons. My vegetables have *terroir* she once told Janet, who had snorted so hard she choked on her coffee. It was the year she was reading about France, in a departure from climatically dramatic places, and she'd been unbearable. Touching the leaves now, she felt righted and planned the day. She would weed until noon, stop to make coleslaw, feed the dog his medicine, the afternoon parceled into chores.

Then she found her fingers locked around the base of a bean plant and discovered she was ripping the roots from the earth, one after the other, scattering the poles, clumps of soil flying into the corners of her eyes and lips. She attacked five of them, almost half her crop, before she stopped and covered her mouth with her hand. "Good Lord, good Jesus Lord," she said. Arms still starred with dirt, she rose and went straight to the pickup.

She wanted only to go and find Janet and confess what she had done. Janet would open a beer, they would sit on her porch and listen to her cockatiel natter on. Lucy would admit her bout of craziness and Janet would coax her back toward something she recognized as manageably human. But Janet wasn't there. Janet had gone. Still, Lucy had to move.

The truck banged down the ruts; if she wasn't careful, she could crack an axle. Why don't I care about that right now, she wondered and realized she was thinking about Laura. She couldn't stop thinking about her daughter-in-law, here in the place where she had been least at home. In New York for the service, she'd been furious at Laura for giving in to her most despairing impulses, for letting terror take advantage. It happened to everyone, but when you had the biggest kind of responsibilities, you let those fears tear through you. They could shake your joints and snap your nights like panes of glass, but there was no excuse for an early departure when there were children involved. No amount of pain justified it.

She had not loved Laura enough, that she knew. She had judged her soft. Too pretty, too tender, too easily upset. An upbringing that had not given her character a chance to become sturdy. But I acknowledged her gifts, Lucy told herself. I truly did. Laura's photographs, the least disturbing ones, anyway, were all over her house. They had written, they had talked. Laura had confided. And she had loved Arthur with an intensity and generosity that astonished and pleased Lucy. She watched as that attention both settled and amplified her child, as if Laura were an anchor and a sun. In the early years, they gave off such a gleam.

But Laura had those parents and their depressive pull to alcohol. Spells of frozen grief, too, that Lucy learned of not only from Arthur but from Laura herself, who talked to her as they folded sheets or washed lettuce. She wouldn't say much, but, clothespins in her teeth, she'd allude to hard times. It showed in any case in her photographs, full of harrowing angles and people captured at terrible moments. A funeral series. One of drug addicts. She had been good, Lucy allowed, but she had courted sadness. At bottom, that struck Lucy as self-indulgent. The world had far too much misery, offered entirely for free, without needing to usher it into your life like a dark, primal tide.

Lucy was halfway to Callendar when she realized she was going in the opposite direction from the one she should to pick up Celia; she'd never be at the C Bar C in time. At the Kum and Go she stopped to call Arthur to ask him to fetch his daughter. At the tail end of the conversation, he asked, "Mom? You OK?"

"Of course I'm OK. Just got behind, and I don't like Celia to have to wait." She couldn't stop staring at the treats offered on the shelves of the convenience store. Six rows of potato chips, or at least products based in a distant past on a potato but rendered now into manila coated in chemicals, spice, and fat. Jesus, Lucille. Since when has snack food started to offend you? But there was no point whatsoever in telling the truth to her only child. She had never developed a habit of sharing the intimate details of her life with Arthur, much less an old woman's meanderings. She'd be back by six, cook a dinner organized solidly around meat, and the only one who would be the wiser about her episodes on the Flaxmans' hill and in the garden would be the dog.

She drove slowly through town. Ray Fontaine was the only cop around, and he had too few tourists to bust, so he was taking after locals. Even old girlfriends, if he suspected they hadn't voted for his brother, a creationist, for the school board. Small towns could just kill you sometimes.

In spite of her intention to settle down, Lucy found herself heading at fifteen miles an hour toward Janet's. Janet had been director of the local girls' home for years and had sung in the choir of the Methodist church. Lucy had admired her appealing combination of sweetness and elemental cussedness since they were in school together. Janet had also divorced three husbands. "The true crime," she liked to say, "is not to be a bad man, but a dull one." She played chess online and sponsored about seven monks in Tibet.

She had, as well, an ability to mind her own business. Janet was the only person, apart from Dr. Sturgis, now deep into a late phase of senility, who knew that Lucy had had five miscarriages.

Arthur had been the third of her pregnancies and she had felt no different with him than any of the others. The same catch of life, the quickening, the old, right word for it. With all of them, there'd been the same surge of fullness, the nausea. But even at seven months, she had worn Sean's old shirts instead of buying maternity clothes. She refused to discuss names. She rejected plans for a shower. She lived for nine months almost entirely suspended from her body until the pains came when they should have, and even then she didn't believe there would actually be a baby until he was there, a steaming lump with perfect fingers, lying on her chest. The star of love and relief that had burst from her chest had astonished her with its force, a searing brightness like an archangel, menacing with its intensity. Oh my God, she kept gasping, and hoped that Dr. Sturgis and Sean would think only that she was relieved to be done with labor.

But it was more than that. It was finally closing the gap between what she wanted and what she had. She had cultivated such separation, a necessary degree of distance, ever since the second miscarriage, which had occurred in the fifth month when suddenly, the blood and cramps had started. It had been a boy. He would have been two years older than Arthur and she would have called him David, for her father. Arthur had been Sean's choice, for his favorite uncle, a gnarled Irishman good with sheep. The next one, Sean said, you can name the next one. She'd been young through all this, in her twenties, perfectly healthy. "Why," she asked the doctor. "Why? My sister has six kids; my mother had five." As if fertility were entirely a family matter. As if what happened to your relatives would by rights happen to you. Dr. Sturgis wagged his glasses by a stem and said, "More women go through this than you know, Lucy. It's not that simple, making a baby."

But it looked that way, given how people in Callendar popped them out. "Is it Sean?" she asked the doctor once, after what turned out to be the last miscarriage, when Arthur was five. "I doubt it," he said. "You get pregnant; everything works fine. You're normal."

"Just unlucky," she said.

"Just unlucky," he agreed. "Lucy, don't go blaming yourself." He paused then and blew out his cheeks, which he did as a preamble to a pronouncement.

She sat there in his bare little office with his diplomas and memberships hung askew and cut him off before he could speak: "If you tell me it's up to God or that I am lucky to have even one, Doc, I will do something harmful to you." She had been gripping her schoolbag, which was full of surprisingly long reports on George Washington and the Continental Congress. To use discussion of the seeds of democracy as a possible weapon was a pleasing thought.

"I wasn't going to say that, Lucy. I was going to suggest you go to Denver to talk to a specialist." But he was partly lying. It was true he'd wanted to make some bland, useless statement such as life is a journey, and she'd robbed him of the opportunity for philosophy. She wasn't, however, going to be lectured about how to manage her specific pain. She devised her own way through. You purged your memory of prospective due dates. You made every effort to stop hating pregnant women and the mothers with their arms spread wide to sweep their band of children toward them. You plunged into work with a vigor others found a little intimidating, even ranch-hardened hands. You forced your brain away from visions involving the death of your one remaining child. You tried not to let the fierceness of your love for that child overwhelm the love itself.

Many people might have made such obstetric misfortune an obvious part of their personality, like a vivid geographical feature. Something to mention and observe. But in her case, that would have made it all the worse. Talking revealed how thin most people's reserves were for difficulties, even in a state as pockmarked with bad luck as Wyoming. Invocation of a personal disaster made others feel awful and then the ruin was doubled. There was nothing noble about such self-containment; you developed it because it kept you upright, able to raise your child and hold down your job.

What got lost in her case was the husband and then the land: after Sean's death, there was too much of it to run by herself. She missed making choices with him—when to get a new tractor, how or if to buy a bull. She missed making the land work with Sean. If she couldn't do it well, it seemed better to sell it off and own and manage the little she had left as best she could. To own it deep. And it seemed to work. Arthur had been successful. Arthur had lovely children, a life. And now it had changed again. You knew disaster could arrive any moment, she told herself. You knew better than almost anyone that no long stretch of peace goes untorn by misfortune. Despite all that hard schooling, little prepared you for seeing your grown son grapple with his own grief. Is that why I've taken to petty acts of vandalism? Because just when the world seemed to run out of ugly things that might happen in a lifetime, a new way to get hurt came flying past? Am I just sad and too dumb to see it? There was never a good moment to take to crime and self-destructiveness, but this was certainly about the worst. How strange that years of cool self-sufficiency could be dispensed with as easily as grains of rice wiped off the counter.

She turned down Janet's street. Her friend had lived in one of the first houses to be built in town, near Colonel August Callendar's original homestead. He had been one of Sheridan's men, known for his bloodlust for the Shoshone, which took something, given whom he'd worked for and how hard the Shoshone were to stir to war. A man with a Roman nose and pale eyes that glittered with a targeted form of western madness—a desire to possess land that was not his to possess in any technical or spiritual sense—Callendar had acquired this valley and the surrounding hills in a grab for which Lucy, Sean, and hundreds of other whites who came later should have been grateful. Callendar's rapacity and murderousness had enabled thousands of ranchers, miners, and prospectors to prod at the valley and the hills and make it yield them a living. The Indians, smarter, older, had never resorted to such foolishness, but still wound up with the worst of the deal. They got shipped to the parcel with no water, no trees, no rights worth buying, because there really was nothing there but beautiful views, tremendous sunsets, and other Indians.

Good Christ, this country could make you mournful. If you looked only at its printed history, the only picture that arose was of bleakness, bleakness, and more bleakness, with unattractive racial skirmishing and environmental degradation thrown in. If you took in only the riots against the Chinese in Green River, Matthew Shepard, the treatment of the Shoshone, and the mines sprouting all through the Powder River Basin, you'd pack up. If you looked only at lists of statistics about anyplace, you'd go crazy with grief. What those accounts left out was sky, sky, and more sky, animals, high mountains, and air spun through with winter light. It left out friends who would drive eighty miles to check on you after a blizzard. It left out drinking margaritas with Janet. You had to live with both sides, the excellence and the ugliness mixed, and be willing to be suspended in the contradiction, making your way through it one slow, conscious step at a time. You left that out and you lost everything. Why couldn't Laura bear the blend? Laura, whose face she could not stop thinking about.

Lucy pulled up in front of Janet's small Victorian house and stopped. The new owners—a computer salesman and an insurance agent—had removed the faded Tibetan prayer flags draped across the porch. A gleaming Chevy SUV instead of Janet's Nissan Maxima was in the driveway. "Oh, shit, Janet, couldn't you just be there?" But of course she wasn't. She was handling her own complicated, individual experience in a new state, a new town. The problem with needing other people was exactly that.

Lucy put the truck into reverse and went on without thinking to Ace Hardware. Jake Atkins, the assistant manager and a student of hers from the class of 1980, stiffened when he saw her. She'd given him a D in English and he still hadn't gotten over it. Not enough has happened to him, she thought. He's one of the lucky ones. But he wasn't, Lucy remembered. His wife, Danielle, known as Danny, had run off the year before with a man also called Danny, and Danny and Danny were having a high time of it over in Sheridan. That kind of hurt could make you hang on to other injustices, old, small ones, and mean you up. Now she'd give him something else to hold to. "I'd like spray paint, Jake."

"Aisle five, Mrs. King," he said. Former students never called her Lucy. There is something wrong with me if I can also remember all those goddamn grades, she thought. Her fingers caught lint on the edges of the shelves.

"Got a painting job going on at your place?" Jake asked, ringing up the six cans she selected—gold, black, orange, aqua, tan, and crimson. Lucy could imagine his narrow mouth as he gave testimony in Judge Watkins's courtroom. "Yes, sir," he'd say. "Mrs. King came in and bought all this paint. I noted the time and date because, to be honest, sir, it struck me as peculiar." Then he'd smirk at Lucy, recalling his D.

"Yes," Lucy answered. "A little redecorating." She was feeling better, even without talking to Janet. For reasons that weren't clear to her, committing actions whose motives remained obscure was something of a tonic. It felt lively to be moving and not merely stuck in woolgathering, an antidote to the maundering ways of some old people. Tonight she would look through more poetry and find samples for other wells along the draw.

At the entrance to her ranch, she thought of how Sean had repainted the sign every spring. He traced the letters—white on red—with the help of a stencil, a K with an R imposed on top of it, his father's brand, a knot made of the long legs of the K and the bulb of the R. Sean had been careful with his hands, and Cam had his easy feel with wood, wire, leather, nails, although Cam was a murkier character, full of secret life, Laura's son. Sean had been, simply, good. An uncomplicated kind of good. Was that possible? Lucy had staked her marriage on that belief: the clean grain of her husband's personality, the sharp edges to the reality he lived in. He had mostly fulfilled that intuition. He had been unflappable and loyal and he drank to excess only four times in their entire marriage. This alone qualified him for sainthood in Wyoming, according to Janet.

But you could wind up needing something broader in a husband, a hitch in his character that made him vulnerable to you. Sean had taken emotional continence to a fresh level. Nights when she would wake from the middle of a nightmare without details, a dream of pure feeling, a dream, always, about the lost babies, he did little more than pat her leg or say, "That was a long time ago, Lucy girl." She would sob and he would soon go back to sleep as she lay there awake, yards of old grief climbing through her like air released from underground: stale and cold and blown by some wind known only to caves. The next day, Lucy would apologize for waking him. Incredible, she thought, how people are animals of longing at night, then wake up sewn inside their human skins by morning. And then it starts all over again.

Sean never answered her when she said she was sorry. Instead, he would nod, pull on his boots, go and light the stove, then brew a pot of coffee. When Arthur was old enough to help with morning chores, Sean would wake his son not with words, but by jiggling his ankle through the blanket. To Sean, conversation seemed a disturbance to the air. It was as if he'd had a quota for the number of syllables he allowed himself to utter in a day, Lucy told Janet. He had been the kind of husband who made you cultivate excellent women friends. He'd been the reason she needed a teaching job: it gave her lots of people to talk to. And then he died, suddenly and quite young, and his memory had grown burnished, becoming perhaps larger than he had been, and she had to entertain her less-than-charitable thoughts alone or with Janet, who was not entirely sympathetic. What kind of standards do you have, Lucy, Janet would ask when she sounded bitter. What was a good husband anyway? Were you always a good wife?

Maybe goodness was plenty to ask for when people lived and worked in such close quarters with each other at such muddy, shit-spattered labors. Maybe you were lucky if goodness persisted in even one area of your life and you had a chance to see a talent flourish even mildly. Lucy stood in the middle of her garden and held the paint in its crackling paper bag. The tomatoes were ripening. The afternoon light had fattened to a rich gold. She rocked back on her heels. The pig was growing well. She could still please herself with jolts of love for this place and for how she had cared for it, and then she saw with shame the ruined beans. Bending to see if she might salvage them, she spied a flash of gray fur. The she-coyote was prowling near the chicken coop. "Git, git, git," she called and chucked a stone at the animal, which twitched its tail and stayed put.

That coyote ran that pack, moving them from boulder to boulder, den to den, producing her litters of wily kits. She pretended to nothing more than being a good coyote, competence proven in her mauled face and damaged paw. She'd been clever enough to wrestle herself out of inevitable trouble; her scars were badges marking that success.

Lucy eased herself up and saw the rise of dust at the end of the driveway that meant Celia, Cam, and Arthur were coming home. It frightened her a little how much she looked forward to seeing them all at the end of the day. She had lived alone so steadily, with her books and her chores. She had caulked the open spaces, or at least arranged a truce with them. But even the dog was happier. It was better not to be entirely alone. It was better. And what was she supposed to do with that knowledge? What would she do now if they moved back to New York?

Celia came into the garden with two glasses of water. "How you doing, baby?" Lucy asked and relished, again, Celia's appetite for shared days, for stories saved to be told to someone near sunset. Celia said that one of the dudes got bucked off a horse and had to go to the hospital, but since the man weighed a good 250 pounds, they were more worried about what he'd done to the horse.

"Help me with supper," Lucy said, smiling, but it was too beautiful in the garden to move and they stood there admiring the rows of vegetables. Celia was five feet eight or nine, her father's height, Sean's height, and still growing. All bone and smarts, right there in her face. How could a mother leave that face? How could she not want to see them every day, these two she'd been lucky enough to make? Simply to breathe in air that was close to them.

But Lucy herself had forced her son away when he was fourteen. You had reasons, Lucy, you had reasons, Janet would tell her. And he still loves you. And he came back.

Yes, she would say to her friend. I know those reasons. All that breakage of bone. Those splints. The doctor warning her that his pelvis wasn't going to make it the next time he cracked it. "Talk to Sean, Lucy," Janet had said. But they both knew there was no talking to Sean. Talk was not the medium he trafficked in, and Arthur, obstinate to the marrow, wouldn't stop trying to make his father proud. But Lucy had her sway over him, too. The quickening of their minds when they read and talked. Arthur, born for thinking. So Lucy sent away in secret for the brochures to boarding schools and collected them at a P.O. box one town over so Sean wouldn't find out. She had read through them at work and been surprised to feel the seeping of envy as she looked at the glossy pictures of the students and the cavernous libraries, the dorms that looked suited to well-heeled English children. The tuition made her teeth rattle. But she had helped Arthur with his applications and they hadn't told his father. They filled in the lines that asked where the parents had gone to college—Sheridan Community for Sean and University of Wyoming for Lucy, institutions that admissions officers no doubt rarely saw in that section. What's going to happen if I get in, Arthur had asked her. We'll think about that when we have to, she said. And then they hadn't needed to guard the secret. Sean had died and Arthur won a full scholarship that catapulted him off to the East Coast. She had missed him more than Sean that winter. She had ached so hard with it, she thought she had cancer of the stomach. Cut down on coffee, Lucy, and go see your son, Dr. Sturgis said.

She did and saw that he was happy at the snow-crusted, falsely Gothic campus. He had friends, mostly other boys who'd been sent from the West and for whom New England's cold barely represented a dip in the temperature. Ranch-roughened, some of them, but smart, too, and able to hold their own with the sleek easterners. Arthur had been proud to give her a tour of the library and his dorm. The pain in her stomach went away. She started her reading tour of jungles and deserts then. When Arthur returned that summer, he wasn't limping as badly. He showed her his lacrosse stick, as if it were an artifact brought back from a foreign war. He helped her on the ranch, but for the first time since he was six he watched the rodeo from the grandstand. He watched and seemed not to mind that that was all he did.

He'd proved adaptable. He'd proved himself competitive.

He wasn't a braggart, but he prevailed. My son goes to Harvard, she would say to herself and the coyotes while walking fence-lines, because she couldn't boast in town. My son. And then law school, and Washington, and still they recognized each other. They wrote and talked and visited. Arthur was better than most daughters at being a daughter, as Janet put it. Is he gay?

I don't think so, Lucy mused. There weren't many mentions of girlfriends, but then there was Laura. And that was it. It's all right, Lucy told herself, it will be all right. She is lovely, she is smart, she loves him to the core. But she knew she was merely trying to soothe herself. Laura would need far more minding than a ranch. She'd seemed better in the last months than she had in a long time, Arthur kept insisting. She had been calm, she had been working, she was drinking less. All those acres of un-spoken experience inside people. But it didn't surprise me, Lucy thought. I knew she was vulnerable to despair of that depth. Laura had one arm out the window. She was open to the allure of not being here. And why didn't you mention that to anyone, Lucy? What made you think it was all right to stay silent on that issue? Why was a part of you relieved to have her gone?

Celia was staring at her over the rim of her glass. "Where are you?" she asked and Lucy was startled. She wasn't used to hav-ing her face and feelings scanned. She wasn't accustomed to schooling her features to unreadability anymore—a teacher's habit that she'd lost, apparently. So she said bluntly, not meaning to, "I'm thinking about your mother," and wished instantly she hadn't.

"Don't. It won't get you anywhere," her granddaughter said, not looking at her. "We were always thinking about her. It didn't make any difference." Celia leaned down and carefully poured the rest of her water on the carrots.

Lucy stood there watching Celia and saw, too, how the wind twisted the tomatoes slightly on their vines. The earth around the beans was black where Lucy had pulled it up and tamped it

down again. You could almost see that the air was hazed in a veil
of brown near your ankles, soil that insisted on turning into dust
no matter how you tried to make it hold on to moisture.

Three nights later, Cam, Celia, and Arthur went off to a barbecue in town, the kids complaining, Arthur cajoling, another
lumpy episode in the drama between parents and teenagers.
Arthur dealt with it quite well, not rising to provocation, usher-
ing them all patiently to the door. Lucy waved them off in his absurd new truck. She had been invited, too, but declined. She was
planning to go to the top of Antelope Draw and decorate a compressor well or two. She was still thinking often of Laura, more
frequently than she had when Laura was alive, and with more
sharpness. "Epitaph" was a word running through her mind,
connecting the poems she chose to her daughter-in-law, who
had also loved poetry. Preparing for her night of graffiti making
filled her with a curious sorrow and a rakish merriment, as if
readying herself for a tryst she knew would lead nowhere. She
still didn't know why she was risking this complication, but she
also did not stop herself. No one had mentioned seeing the
Emily Dickinson and she was ashamed to be disappointed by
this. She had Elizabeth Bishop with her tonight, as well as the
black paint and the memory of Jake Atkins's smirking face.

Antelope Draw led off a road behind the high school, along
a steep hill that abruptly became a bluff, stubbed with wind-
flattened sage and an occasional chokecherry that tapped into a
thin spring. Kids liked the protection of the boulders there, which
a glacier had scattered one receding ice age, and they used to
come to smoke and drink after school or on weekends. But in
the 1970s the land was sold to a man named Hoffman whose
Baptist beliefs gave him what he felt was justification for shooting at young men sipping beer. Sometimes a Coors can would fly
straight out of the grasp of a sophomore's clammy fingers. Lucy

imagined the golden foam spiraling over faces and jeans. That was kind of amazing to witness, a student allowed once to Lucy. But the kids got tired of dodging bullets—it seemed Hoffman spent more nights out there waiting for them to sin than he did with his wife, which probably accounted for why she left him. He got meaner after that, even shooting at people who came to his door to tell him his cattle had strayed. He sold out to a hippie named Arnie and stumped off, people said, to eastern Montana, where all he'd have to shoot at were ravens and other Christians.

The hippie couldn't have cared less about the carousing, though he didn't appreciate the broken glass. Using a gun to dissuade the visitors never crossed his mind. But kids found less-exposed places for their naughtiness, and Antelope Draw now attracted only the occasional couple looking for a private spot or someone engaging in target practice. The boulders were nicked with white dents in patterns that, from a distance, could look as elegant as petroglyphs.

These days, the draw had also pulled in the methane people. A deep seam of low-quality coal that looked promising had been found along the bluff and neither Hoffman nor Arnie had owned a scrap of mineral rights. Lucy counted seven wells as she drove up the switchbacks. The moon reflected in the small ponds, a tight white ball bobbing on each rippled surface.

To Lucy's surprise, a Nova was parked just behind the well she hoped to annotate. Her surprise deepened when she saw it was Ray Fontaine in an unmarked car, meaning his own and not the town's sole cruiser. It flummoxed Lucy that her pulse still leaped when she saw Ray even in profile. How appalling that she still found him attractive after acquiring such intimate knowledge of his character. They'd been together for three years in high school when she decided her brain hurt too much when she was with him. It wasn't that he was unintelligent, just that he was aggressively unlearned. "You don't like to think, Ray," she told him. "It's not that you can't. It's that you don't want to." And she

flounced down the hall, swaying her hips the way she knew
drove him crazy. What a tart, she thought now. What kind of
horizons had she imagined for herself? What made her so much
better than that horny cowboy? Going off to Laramie for four
years and kissing other cowboys?

Spurned and furious, Ray had married Jeannie Knox, who
had significant breasts and had immediately conceived twins.
For fifteen years, Lucy and Ray stalked around each other at
rodeos, town meetings, parades. Sometimes, watching Ray with
a beer, his long, fine arms exposed to the elbow, his nose a lean
angle in the air below his Stetson, she wondered, more than was
helpful, if he could have given her the babies she apparently
couldn't have with Sean. He and Jeannie, though palpably
unhappy, had five children—handsome, sassy, wild. Everyone
thought Ray had become a cop so he could spring his kids from
trouble before Judge Watkins got hold of them.

The engine of her truck ticked cool. Ray had probably recognized its sound half a mile away, but he was still sitting in what
he insisted on calling his "vehicle." From the light of the moon,
she could see he had a pair of binoculars fitted with some in-
frared gizmo on the dashboard. He'd always had vaguely military
aspirations, but an interest in technology available at the army-
navy store in Cheyenne was as close as he had gotten to satisfying them. A bad astigmatism had kept him out of the service for
Korea, the only war for which he'd been just the right age.

She put her keys in her bag and made a fuss with the seat
belt, giving herself time to prepare. After those fifteen years of
giving each other a wide berth, Sean had died and soon after that
Jeannie had hightailed it to Vegas, a desert with gambling apparently more appealing than one without. Ray's kids were grown or
gone, Arthur was off at school, and all obstacles between their
bodies had been removed.

"It's good to see you, Lucy," Ray had said after one of those
reencounters. He was draped over her, his long leg pinning hers,

his hands cupping her breasts, all of it a sweaty, familiar, delicious tangle. "'See me'?" she said, propping herself up on an elbow. "That's what you call what just happened, Ray?" He was, as ever, a disappointment as a conversational partner, but that hadn't prevented quite a lot of energetic coupling for the next ten years. Eventually they stopped making it regular, because, as Lucy told Janet, it was just too hard to have sex with someone you didn't really like.

Still, the same thing happened every six months or so. One of them would show up at the other's house on some pretext—extra zucchini from the garden, rumors of feral dogs near Lucy's land—and they'd go through another spate of zesty fornication. Finally, Ray had a bout of prostate cancer, and that, Lucy thought with a combination of regret and relief, would be the end of that. And it was, since, on top of the prostate cancer, Ray had become serious about Jesus. His commitment was probably made more pressing given the presence of a blonde with no kids in the same congregation. Deep into her forties, she still gave off a pinkish light, a cushioned femininity. She looked like a woman who said often and aloud how much safer she felt with the police around.

Ray, as always, was himself. "What the hell are you doing here, Lucy?" He was still handsome at sixty-eight, with his white hair, straight nose, and hazel eyes. His flesh hadn't blurred. He was one of those men who turn with age into teak instead of baggy leather. Lucy heard that Nancy Baum the blonde was keeping him healthy.

"Taking in the night air, Ray."

"Not enough of that at your place?" he said, glancing at her bag. She walked to the passenger side of his Nova. They had had several passionate sessions in its appealingly wide backseat well into their fifties. As she settled in, Lucy felt a hint of the old tingle. When did a body just give that up? It was tiresome. Ray probably couldn't manage these days without a lot of encouragement and Viagra followed by repentance, and that kind of effort was just not within her scope of interest anymore. A loss, that was; he'd always been so boundingly enthusiastic.

Ray shifted his shoulders and pulled his body more tightly toward the driver's-side door. "Don't worry. I'll stay right where I belong," she said.

"Who said anything about wanting you anywhere else, Lucy? I'm just making sure I'm not sitting on my binoculars." Which were still where he had left them: on the dashboard. Janet had thought Ray Fontaine a terrible choice. Narrow as a pencil, Janet would crow. A dummy with a gun. How on earth, Lucy, I just don't understand.

I don't either, Janet, Lucy would say. It is one of the mysteries of my life why I like sleeping with Ray Fontaine. He never met a book he didn't want to burn; he is alive with the darkest of suspicions; he doesn't believe in global warming; and now he's claiming a relationship with Jesus.

But the night was too beautiful to waste on trying to have coherent ideas about attraction and sex. It would be much better just to have it, she thought impurely. The stars were a dazzle of diamond-sharp light, luscious and cold. A wind that carried the hum of autumn came through the crack in Ray's windows. Her spray paint and flashlight and volume of Elizabeth Bishop were lying next to her leg in her bag. "Have some whiskey on you, Ray?"

He looked offended again and lifted his eyebrows for emphasis. Whiskey had been smacked into the garbage along with all the other sins. She tried again. "What in God's name are you doing out here?" When you could be making Miss Nancy Baum feel safe in her water bed, was the part of the sentence left unsaid.

Ray swallowed. That, Lucy knew, implied the delivery of an official reason. "You know those horses that run down Main Street? It looks like someone did that on purpose. Banged the padlock off the gate of the corral and sent them packing. They still haven't found all of them yet and they're messing with the fences on Drew Ferguson's land. Now somebody's taken to violating some compressor wells." Lucy felt a thrill run up the front of her shins. Finally someone had reported the poetry.

But it turned out that Ray was talking about something else. Some son of a bitch had taken a wrench to six wells and whacked up the valves so badly they needed what Ray called "specialized repairs." Engineers with serious equipment. Two companies got hit—Mountain View Energy and Cloud Peak Methane—and while they were getting people on board to do some security detail, Ray was keeping watch on his own time. "Things are getting bad, Lucy. Mustangs gone loose, vandalism, some crazy man setting tires on fire. Callendar isn't the town where we grew up." He chewed mournfully on his gum, which he kept in a slick wad in his cheek now that cigarettes had joined the whiskey.

"No, now they actually sell books and most of the population can read," she said. She hated little more than old people getting nostalgic about the Commie- and bomb-spooked 1950s, when a black man or a Mexican couldn't walk down the street without everyone stopping to offer him directions out of town. Ray tucked in his chin the way he did when she contradicted him— he hated that in a woman—but she had to admit he was partly right. Callendar was different and not all those differences had benefited the town or the people. Still, there was no call for rheumy, apocalyptic musings. Her leg brushed the bag that held her paint. Wasn't what she was doing with poetry much along the same lines as Ray's self-imposed surveillance? Weren't both a stance against change? An assertion of old orders, old beliefs. Two people saying, rather feebly it had to be admitted, that they were not happy with how things were going. Conservative. Their backs up against the past, turning down the future as if it were some outlandish new dish at a restaurant.

Ray sighed an old-man sigh, the kind that gave off a whiff of something mentholated. She had not smelled that on him before. She felt oddly grateful for his vigilance and refusal to be anyone but himself. Not that he would ever want to be anyone else, but still. He'd remained loyal to what he recognized as the boundaries of his own character.

She stretched out her legs and he, more sensitive than she had realized to her presence, tucked his body more firmly in his seat. "Don't worry, you old goat. It's not that," and he surprised her further by looking full at her, his eyes black in the dim light, and saying, "Then what is it?"

History, she wanted to say, pulling her legs ostentatiously back toward her body. In spite of everything, you are someone I have known most of my life. But he would have snorted at any suggestion of earnestness. Even with Jesus and Nancy Baum in his life, he wasn't all that sentimental. "It's a nice night," she finally said. "It's just a lovely night."

He cleared his throat. He was deciding whether he was going to pierce that fragment of insincerity with a question, whether he was going to behave like a real police officer and not like Ray. Then he muttered, "See something moving down there?" and grabbed for the binoculars. "Nope," he announced after scanning the velvet-black draw. "Just a pronghorn."

"I'm going to get going," she said when he finished his inspection of the animal. "Nice to run into you." She reached for her bag.

"Why'd you come up here, Lucy?" Ray asked again as she eased herself out of the car, her keys scratching against the cylinder of paint.

"Have a good evening. Round up some ruffians. Stretch that taxpayer dollar," she said, closing the door.

He didn't respond and she knew he was watching her walk back to her truck. "Do I need to keep an eye on you, Lucy King?" he called.

"You usually do," she said, not turning around, knowing the air would carry her words right back to him, it was that clean, the sky that open to sound. He knew how to catch the cadence in her voice. He had always, in his own ignorant way, been a good listener.

The last week in July was a fine time for well decoration. The children were working and Arthur, too, had been busy. She put some Stevie Smith on a well near Clearwater Creek and William Blake on a pump near the landfill in Sheridan. She picked times quite casually, and if one pump had people or trucks near it, she didn't linger, but simply went on to the next; there were plenty to choose from. She waved to neighbors and friends she passed on the road. The dog panted beside her. A volume of whatever poetry she had chosen sat on the seat. Her secret task jounced around with them inside the truck. She was feeling fine. Finally, a picture got in the paper. Janet, who still subscribed from Portland, called her and said, "I see your shenanigans made page nine—Local News."

"Trust Lloyd not to have a sense of humor and stash it inside," Lucy said. Lloyd Jenks was the notoriously sober-sided editor. Coverage of religious life in the Callendar Valley had expanded in an ominous way during his tenure. Lucy had seen the picture; the photo made her crime look much less impressive than it was. The well appeared blocky and dull and defaced, far more squalid than she'd been prepared for. It was irritating. The shot did not capture the neatness of her lettering. She was finally mastering the paint; it just took some practice. The one the newspaper had chosen was the Blake quotation and all that could be seen was the word "fire." The caption said that at least three other wells had been spray-painted with what appeared to be poems, and that an English teacher at the high school had identified this one as several lines from Wilfred Blake. "I can't believe they called him Wilfred," she added. Other acts of vandalism concerning the wells might be connected. Investigations were ongoing, the caption continued, which meant basically that Ray was in his office with his boots on his desk, wondering whom he could pin it on.

"Lucy, I have not once told you what to do," Janet said, making a statement they both knew to be an utter lie, "but I wouldn't push this one too far." Healthy disrespect for convention Janet would always encourage. Wildness, even. But Lucy was skirting something else: the possibility of humiliation. The newspaper picture made the spray-painting look not impassioned or spirited but crazed. Six months ago, living alone, she could have withstood any amount of ridicule. It would have slid off her like sleet off a sheep. With Arthur and the children here, her behavior echoed differently; it influenced more layers. Laura's being dead changed it all.

"You're right, you're right," Lucy said testily to Janet. "Does it ever get boring being right all the time?"

"No, it does not. My opponent's responded. Gotta go." Janet often phoned in the middle of a chess match, which made for unpredictable rhythms in their conversations.

Lucy hung up and stood at the kitchen window. Celia was in the garden plucking tomatoes, finally ripe, for dinner. Cam was in the barn feeding animals and Arthur had called to say he would be late. They weren't talking much about his work—he was maintaining an owlish silence, which meant he was on cases she would not approve of. She was suspicious of his neutrality in politics, the way his legal mind treated every situation as no more than a problem to be solved, sheared clean of moral particulars. He was probably in the thick of tricky land deals involving methane or uranium claims or ways to develop near riverbanks. She'd seen him several times at lunch in town with men in perfectly shaped Resistols and Ray-Bans. The men who loved chrome. Wyoming had always attracted its fair share of swaggerers, but these men were emptier than most, all hat and brag and paunch. Packagers of land into ranchettes, probably Lucy's least favorite word of the last ten years. It sounded like something orange you stuck in onion dip.

She would stop, she told herself. She would roll this unexpected part of her character off her like a ball of wool off a sweater and she would be reasonable again. She would not search out Ray Fontaine as she wanted to do, both to confess and to touch him, even if it did take a lot of Viagra. Celia came in with her arms full of tomatoes and a story about how Carson had killed two rattlesnakes while leading a pair of dudes up to the high meadows above the C Bar C. A story with lots of voices, Lucy noted appreciatively—the shrieking dudes, Carson, whinnying horses, Mr. Starmer calming the hysterical women, who had probably never stumbled across a toad much less an amorous pair of four-foot rattlers. Celia did all the characters, complete with lots of hand waving. Where were Arthur and Cam, thought Lucy, watching her granddaughter's face, listening to her deepen her voice like Starmer's as he tried to ward off threats of legal action. They should see this. Laura should see this. Lucy almost clapped when Celia was done, as if to make up for the absent members of her audience.

Later that week, Celia called to tell Lucy she'd be staying at the C Bar C for a fancy western-dress dance at the ranch. Cam was home, but planning on going out that night with Amber Barlow, the daughter of his new boss. He'd only recently begun talking about her at the house, though it was clear to Lucy right from the first that Amber had caught Cam hard. His voice thickened and he couldn't look Lucy in the face when he spoke about her. She'd mentioned their attachment to Arthur, who wasn't pleased. Keeping Cam close to home under watchful adult eyes had been the plan for the summer. Distractions such as Amber hadn't been taken into account. Lucy counseled relative lenience. "She makes him happy, Arthur. Can't you see that?" Besides, they weren't seeing each other that frequently. Lucy had

had enough experience with teenagers to know they would find the sliest of paths away from you and it was often wiser to let them feel they were getting away with something. Arthur reluctantly agreed, but expressed discomfort about Amber's father. "Mac is meaner than he used to be, rougher." Lucy had to admit that. But Cam said he liked his job. Cam had made the connection on his own and, Lucy and Arthur agreed, that should be honored.

Lucy had taught Amber American history in a trailer her sixth-grade year, the fall the new middle school was being built. She remembered the shy persistence with which the girl volunteered her correct responses. Now she worked at the Albertsons, a job not in keeping with her quiet intelligence. Lucy wondered why she wasn't going to college. Over time, she'd become both blonder and darker: her hair grew lighter and lighter as more and more of her skin disappeared beneath tattoos. She would not have thought Amber and Cam a likely couple, but then again no one had ever figured on her and Ray. Lucy had come within three seconds of asking Cam if they were sleeping together and then within another three of offering birth control, but reminded herself that timing was of the essence; broaching such topics too quickly might clam her grandson up entirely. In any case, no one wanted to talk about contraception with his grandmother.

"Don't drive on Route 76," she gave as an alternate warning as he left. Route 76 had a few notorious curves, and dozens of people had died there. Over the last few years, white crosses draped in plastic yellow roses had become the memorial fashion and the road was now studded with them.

"Don't worry," he said. "We'll be careful"—a phrase to which he gave a slight extra push, as if he sensed her earlier desire to offer protection. His sensitivity to tones always took her aback. He always paid attention. But the way a cat did, Lucy thought—languidly, and with a degree of self-containment. He was harder to love, Cam was, but you craved his affection more because he seemed so hard to interest. It wasn't that he wasn't passionate but that he masked his passions, raking ash over coals.

As Lucy went in to make dinner, she realized she'd need only half of what she'd prepared since only she and Arthur would be eating. Arthur was looking better now that he'd healed from the fall and his hair had grown back in, but he worried her the most. He claimed to like working with Dwight Higgins and to be getting himself ready for the Wyoming bar. He gave every appearance of keeping his pain at a distance, but it lashed at him, Lucy suspected. It kept his smile tight and his voice narrow. He did not sleep well. He stalked the house at night. Everything creaked in the dry air and living alone for so long had accustomed her to waking frequently. A snap in the night could easily be a shutter being blown off, someone's bison tearing through a fence. Most sounds needed investigating. Now Arthur was adding to that nocturnal noise. He was slowly polishing off the whiskey, too. Slowly enough, she guessed, to pretend to himself and her that it wasn't really happening.

He came in that evening with a briefcase clenched in both fists. Work for the weekend, he explained. When, Lucy wondered, would he dare go on a date, free up time away from either children or law to allow himself to be a person relaxing? He was straining for a supernatural vigilance: creating a wall of fatherhood around his children. But they are on the move, Arthur. They do not need a fortress and there's no containing teenagers past a certain point. Instead, she asked if he wanted chutney with the roast chicken. She'd made it from some of Janet's peaches last year. Her friend had had one of the only trees in the valley that grew edible fruit. Lucy would never have access to it again; the new owners had pruned it down to a near stump.

She watched her son in the fading light. He gnawed a chicken leg, he drank water, he asked about her day. They talked of Dwight's partners, houses for sale, and other manner of local chat. It was like a phone conversation they were having in person. They mentioned methane as well, but cautiously, each giving the other about ten acres of space. But even as Arthur talked and forked vegetables into his mouth, he was snagged somewhere else. You are not here, she wanted to tell him. Arthur, you are at least an arm's length away from what you're saying and you have no idea that I am aware of this. She was on the brink of marring the evening with cold directness, when they heard the scream.

It was a horse. If you didn't know about horses, you would be tempted to think it was a person. Horses can stretch their voices to a human register but only when they are desperate. Lucy and Arthur looked at each other, utensils suspended above their plates. Lucy wiped her mouth with her napkin, Arthur did the same, and they both stood up. "How far up the draw?" he asked.

"I don't know. Bring flashlights and the big wire clippers. He's probably tangled in a fence. Running fast and didn't see it till too late." Lucy went to the room where she was sleeping this summer and got her Winchester rifle, old, clean, solid, a present from Sean's father when they were first married. She kept it stashed under her bed behind wrapping paper and a box of mittens. She did not want Cam anywhere near a gun, or, to be honest, Arthur either. She took it to pieces and oiled it once a month late at night when no one risked bothering her. It was a chore she did with displeasure, sliding the case shut, making sure to put distance between the bullets and the weapon itself.

When she was a girl, her father had gotten drunk one night after being laid off from the mines three times in a year. It was understandable. No one begrudged him a good binge. It didn't happen often and when it did, he was mostly loud and cheerful and prone to singing Polish folk songs. He sat in a grainy funk in the one upholstered chair and within two days sobered up. He never hit anyone. The sweetest drunk I know, her mother would say. But on the occasion of the third layoff, his mood soured. They'd had a dog who liked to bark. Given the right circumstances—cottonwoods rattling in a storm, trucks driving past—the animal would yelp intermittently all night long. Everyone complained about the barking, but given the amount of worry in that household on any given day, it barely registered as a problem. On the last day of his bender, Lucy's father loaded his shotgun, went into the yard, and in full sight of Lucy and her siblings blew the dog's head off. "Why?" Lucy's youngest brother asked her as he sobbed in his sister's arms. "Why did he kill Sammy?"

"So he wouldn't kill us," Lucy said, patting her brother's back. "No," said their mother. Immediately after the incident, she had driven off in the truck with the dog and the gun; when she came back, she had neither. Her hair was still disordered with the wind. "He shot him because he could," she said. They didn't see their father that night. No one ever mentioned the dog, though the chain to which his collar had been attached was still clipped to the pole in the yard and stayed there until they moved the next spring to Callendar, where her father had resigned himself to life aboveground, in a mechanic's uniform. She hadn't thought of the dog's name in years.

The sunset was flaring to a finish when she and Arthur set out. Red and purple bands of light shot through with a bolt of lemon. They walked up their fenceline toward the land she'd sold to the Flaxmans and at a post that divided Lucy's acres from theirs they saw the horse. One of the mustangs that had escaped the day Arthur and the children arrived. Shaggy, partially shod, unbranded, misproportioned. Suited for hardscrabble wildness, unlucky enough to be roped one day. A grullo, stocky in the chest but so starved the hide was pulled like a taut sail over the ribs. His tail had fought a duel with a bushful of burrs and turned into a weird brown broom.

"Shit," said Arthur when the sun revealed that the bottom string of barbed wire had snapped and wrapped itself around the animal's right knee and lashed deep into the joint. The gash was raw, the wire sunk tight. Glints of steel flickered from their sunken places in the sweaty hide. This was a wound that would lead to a slow, gangrenous death. Lucy saw, too, that the horse had suffered another wide cut on a rear leg; he might have been the one that had been tearing up Drew Ferguson's fences. In any case, he stood no chance. Even if they managed to get a rope on him and haul him into the corral, he'd be dead within a day. He'd ruined fence; he'd run crazy; he was too ugly and too old to be tamed. He was dispensable.

The animal screamed again. Red froth lined his mouth and teeth. Clouds banked like stacks of folded blue quilts were darkening in the east. The wind was rising and the horse's mane and forelock caught in it, lifted, and revealed eyes dense with pain. Arthur started to talk to the animal, which lunged at him. "Calm down, boy, whoa, we'll get you out of here."

Lucy held the rifle slack at her side. He didn't understand or, worse, wasn't willing to admit to the obvious. Arthur, she wanted to warn him, don't do this to yourself. This one is lost. There's no bringing him back. Speed, she wanted to counsel, speed. What matters is doing this in the last of the light so the bullets don't go flying into something else.

"Arthur," she said quite flatly and loudly in the voice she re-served for the truly delinquent boys in her ninth-grade classes. The ones who were fathers at fifteen, the ones who ran away on Greyhound buses. "Arthur, I am going to kill this horse now. You need to step away from it so I can do it in one shot."

There were about three ounces of sunset left; the light was red and liquid. She'd need all of it to keep the horse in her sights.

She hadn't used the rifle since last winter, when she'd seen a pack of boys on snowmobiles tearing after an elk. On the rise behind her house, she shot off four rounds, one for every boy. They probably recognized her; she was tall, her hair was unbound and long, and they would know they were on her property. Boys around here knew land the way city boys knew bars, though these boys knew bars, too. When the shots rang into the sky, they turned tail in an angry swerve that led them back to Callendar, while the elk breasted the snow back toward the valley from which it had strayed. A young bull, maybe swept away from its small herd by a blizzard.

"Arthur, move away." She had the horse's head in focus, the stock of the gun cold on her shoulder. Arthur was still too close. "Get back now. I am going to count to three." The horse neighed in frenzy again. They both knew that the animal's life would be worse if it lived. It would be maimed if it survived, corral-bound and tortured—a lone, injured male: nothing got picked on more. When she was a girl, she'd seen one animal with bite marks the size of steaks taken out of its ass. "Better off killing an animal like that," her father had said and he didn't even know his way around horses. "No waste of a bullet there."

Arthur always hated this. Even culling the cows each year. It was a hard, unsayable truth, but his hesitancy around death had angered Sean more than his clumsiness. Lucy had known it when Sean tossed his boots sharply to the floor after a day on the ranch with his son that he thought Arthur a failure. Weak. Unsuited to the kind of work his father admired. Just not strong enough at any level for it. Which was why, even after Sean died and Arthur was free from any obvious pressure to run the ranch, she still sent him off to school. She knew as well as her husband did that Arthur was no rancher; she was just surprised how much this disappointed her as well.

"One, two, three," Lucy counted and he was still too close. Laura was mixed into this, and the children, too. "Arthur," she said again. "Move back." He retreated slightly, she felt her finger on the cold curve of the trigger, saw the broad expanse of the horse's head and pulled. The rifle jerked back against her shoulder. It always hurt. Maybe when you used a gun more often, the report lessened in severity. But for her, a shooter who practiced three to five times a year, its strength never failed to rock her. And she'd missed. Goddamn it, she'd missed. She'd brought only three shells.

"Jesus, Arthur, stand back." She'd been so frightened of hurting him, she had gone wide by several feet, she guessed. She slid another shell into the cartridge, aimed, felt the hard press of the stock on her shoulder. The screaming stopped almost instantly. In its place was a heavy thud as the horse collapsed and, past that, Arthur's breathing.

The light had almost entirely faded from the sky. She could barely see the horse, its full weight slumped against the barbed wire and threatening to pull the posts from the ground. She'd have to call Ted, too, and tell him that part of the fence on his side was damaged. Wind blew the matted forelock; that she could just make out. She was glad she didn't have the light by which to see the size of the wound. She would have to wait until tomorrow to move it off the land. And by then coyotes or maybe even a wolf would have found it, an easy meal. They'd need a hoist, Ted's new truck, big enough for the body, a morning spent on dealing with the destruction it had wrought. More work. She remembered the animals on Main Street, the blur of them, their speed and intent, but she could not single this one out. She had no particular memory of him.

Absorbed in the details, the gun by her side, Lucy felt the ache in her shoulder and the knots of pain in her joints that meant a flare of arthritis was on its way. It was getting cooler; it had snowed in the Bighorns the week before and a foot and a half had dumped itself in the Absarokas. Lucy became aware then she did not know where Arthur was and she called for him.

There was no answer. The night was deepening, the flashlight close to ineffectual. She hurried toward the house.

He was sitting on the porch, fingers dangling around a drink he had placed on the floor. "What happened?" she said. "Why did you leave like that?" Her arm was painful. Her body was clenched with cold though the temperature hadn't descended that drastically. She wanted only to go and put the gun away.

He just looked at her. She saw terrible blankness on his face, life refusing to register on his features. She summoned her firmest voice. She rapped the stock on the hard ground and heard the settling squawks of the chickens in their coop. "Pull yourself together, Arthur. You're tired. You've been working hard."

"No, Mom," he said, his eyes trained on his hand. The porch light threw the veins, prominent as thin snakes, into relief. "That's not it." He finished his drink. "I just hate this," he said and waved at the yard. Lucy knew the gesture encompassed Wyoming, her, dislocation, the thinness of institutions such as marriage, the lack of Laura. He had no idea what he was doing. He had no vision for what was next. It was a terrible thing to be a man entirely deprived of orientation.

But she did not go to comfort him. She needed to clean the rifle and stash it safely away, this time in the locked closet at the back of her bedroom where no one would think to look for it. She needed to preserve a wide space between her son and a firearm. She thought she could stand anything and she had, mostly. But not that.

"I'll be right back," she told him. "Don't move." When she returned, it was clear he had listened to her advice. He was slumped in his chair, slumped as the horse had been, and for an awful moment she thought he was dead. The desolation this would have caused sliced her briefly, and then the rage came. "Stand up, Arthur. Do not give in to this." She remembered his stiff voice earlier that evening and knew the gap had closed between what he showed the world and what he felt.

He lifted his head. "I can't, Mom. I just can't." It was enough to make Lucy go up to him, thinking she was going to fold him to her, offer comfort, let him know she understood his vulnerability, that he could lay it out for her to see. But instead she found her fist balled into a scroll of bone heading toward her son's jaw. The impact hurt them both. They sucked in air, yelped, pushed away from each other. The dog whined at the door. "Even if you can't, you have to," Lucy hissed. "Even if it kills you." She was filled for a moment with what she suspected Sean had harbored toward their son: a stab of disrespect for the twist of passivity in him. She strode past Arthur. His head had drooped and the empty glass was still on the floorboards. She went into the house, which seemed bountifully filled with warmth. In the kitchen, she placed the kettle on the stove and noticed for the thousandth time how the flames were like slender blue teeth when they first caught until they melded to make their general, dangerous orange. In the light the fire cast, she saw that her knuckle was swelling from where she had connected with the sharp plane of Arthur's cheekbone. The flesh on her hand was brushed with tiny pits of powder the gunshot had spread.

She heard Arthur pacing the porch. Lucy wondered then if she had not been given more children because she'd been judged too narrow a human to mother more than one. She had come up against a settled, internal boundary past which she could not go to soothe her boy, and it involved ideas as stupid as pride and manliness. She had found the ugliest corner of her stony heart. Worse than a salty well. Strict as Wyoming. If she had loved him properly, with the lush abundance children required, he would not have married a woman just because she needed him so badly.

When her tea was ready, she sat at the table and blew until it was cool enough to drink. She readied herself to name the chores she'd have to deal with the next day. She listened to Arthur stalk the porch and swear with hushed ferocity. She heard the scratch of the pencil tip as her unpoetical list marched down the paper. Remove dead horse from fence, it began.

CAM

Cam met Amber the third day after they arrived, at the Albert-sons, where she had a job stocking produce. He'd gone in with a list his father and grandmother had jotted down on the back of an ATM slip from Nebraska. Lucy's print first: teacherly, straight, no ambiguity. Twine. Matches. Lightbulbs. Then his father's scrawl, the assumption being that someone—a secretary, his son—would be able to translate it. Batteries and candles. Band-Aids. Peanut butter. They sounded like emergency supplies, or ones for camping. Country songs streamed from the pie-shaped speakers on the ceiling. His body was still uncramping from the long time in the car, the fights with Celia about air-conditioning and music, the flat stretches of no conversation as they crossed the plains, their father grim-jawed at the wheel. That was what he was thinking about as Lucy spoke, telling him they'd meet in half an hour. She'd be across the road, at the post office. Did he need stamps? Sounds good, he'd said, and no, no stamps. It was such an optimistic idea, a stamp, a letter sent to someone waiting for your news. He couldn't remember the last time he had written more than a thank-you note and then he did: to his mother, from camp, telling her about mosquitoes and how much he missed her.

He'd wondered if the distance from home would make a difference, but it hadn't. He aimed the cart toward the tiers of vegetables. His mother was always there: her voice, her preferences, her habits. Anything she might have touched—a grocery cart, a doorknob, a bedpost—made her walk into his mind. Even inhaling brought her back, because there'd been a time when she'd done what people do, which is to breathe.

Right after she died, he'd spin around on the street, certain she was right behind him. Sometimes it was another woman, sometimes no one at all. He'd hear a sound in the apartment, charge toward it, find the slat of a blind tapping on a windowsill. After moments like those, his hands would start to shake, as they did on that first trip to the supermarket. He steered toward the citrus section and picked up far more oranges and lemons than his family would ever use. They weren't on the list, but touching the rough rinds masked the jitter. He started to do the same with apples. The bottom of the cart grew bumpy with fruit. Then he saw Amber. She was holding heads of iceberg lettuce in her arms. The plastic sheaths on the large heads crackled as she tried to stack them, working hard to make the arrangement attractive or at least stable. She dropped one and bent to fetch it, looking around to be sure no shoppers were looking. She blushed as she leaned over.

He retrieved the lettuce for her. His mother came with him. Unaccountably, iceberg had been the only kind she liked, cut in wedges with a dribble of French dressing. He walked toward Amber. She swam into view. The red, yellow, and orange fruit rolled along with him. Amber stood looking at him, nothing but soft, ample body, ears bristling with silver studs, forearms swirled with tattoos. Then his mother moved off, just a bit. He was still thinking of her, but she'd given him room. All that lingered was how she never cleaned pennies out of her bag, which meant it released the smell of tarnishing copper when opened.

Instead of talking to Amber—he knew her name from the tag on her Albertsons shirt—Cam placed the stray lettuce in his cart and began to balance the others. He was good at this kind of task, usually. Another memory: he was stacking cards in pyramids on a table in his room, his mother passing in her blue dress—Nice work, Cammy, keep it up—and the cards immediately started to slip, as if they'd heard doubt instead of encouragement. He kept building. Kings on queens, nines on tens. He had a system. But every time she passed, though she didn't speak, the cards collapsed. "Hi," he said to Amber. "You lost one."

She didn't answer. Shy, he guessed. He was to learn that in public or around others Amber was nearly mute. Then she said, "I know who you are. You're Mrs. King's family. Aren't you working for my dad this summer?"

For once, he hadn't been defined in reference to Laura. Amber probably knew about that, too, but said nothing. "Yeah," he said, "that's right. My name is Cam." He heard in his own voice an urgent need to prop himself above his parents and Lucy, to be someone separate, someone for Amber to see.

"Cam," said Amber, moving to adjust tomatoes, fingers pressing their red skins. "You must like lemonade or juice or pie or something," she added, looking at his cart.

"I couldn't find matches, so I started here." That was how it began, with a mild lie. She took his list and abandoned leafy greens. Then he remembered he had met her one year when she came along on an errand her father had run at Lucy's. "You didn't have so many tattoos then." They were quite recent, she agreed. She slowly told him more. She'd worked at the grocery store since graduating from high school last year, to save money for college. Her parents wanted to send her to some evangelical place, but she wanted to study interior design. Cam listened, watched her pass him a package of seventy-five-watt bulbs. His mother everywhere, but less dangerously. He remembered when she'd tried to unscrew a bulb in the front hall and it shattered at the neck. Flakes of frosted glass scattered on the floor. Sometimes this memory pulled along another picture of falling, of breaking: his mother on the canopy before her body bounced to the sidewalk. But it didn't happen this time. Amber guided him through the store, which seemed to him to have been entirely reorganized since his last visit. The tremor, like a slight electric current, was switched off.

From the moment he saw Amber lean down for the rolling head of lettuce, he sensed he was going to sleep with her. This specific knowledge was new to him, grasping not only that a girl liked him, but that she would open her body to him. Sex was mostly new to him, too. He had no ease with it, just dense thoughts, treasured moments of release. Last year, at a soccer camp, a counselor named Ellen, older, confident, had pulled him from time to time into the woods. He was amazed when he returned home that his parents seemed not to notice that desire radiated from him like a hot shield. They went on as before: his father out the door at seven, a blur of briefcase and black hair; his mother guessing, but not knowing what to say, and looking at him sidelong, if she looked at him at all.

In the end, late summer and early fall, he would find her sitting at the kitchen table as if stunned, and he'd know from a glance that she'd been locked there for hours, unable to drag her gaze away from something: the pepper mill or coffeepot. She usually pulled herself together for Celia and Arthur, who required action of her, who were critical of what Arthur called her moods. As if they were as airy and petulant as that word implied, instead of something nearly solid. Wood bound by metal, as if she were caught inside an old, stiff lock. Yet for her husband and daughter, she knew how to look industrious, how to look well. She would make breakfast, read the paper, plump pillows. But she let Cam see her as she was. When he was younger, he accepted these moments and his mother's strangeness. They shared an ability to get stranded.

But then the atmosphere changed. It terrified him to see something so dark pooling in her, and he told himself that it wasn't what it seemed, which was that she had sunk or drifted fur-

ther and further away. She was still taking photographs, which
he knew was enough for Celia and his father; she was being productive, wasn't she? He would pour water or get her a Tab. She
would say, "Tell me about your day, Cammy. Tell me a story." He
would talk to her about soccer practice or experiments in chem-
istry class in which a white liquid turned smoking purple. The
preposterous tie Mr. Arlen wore. The cafeteria worker with the
huge nose. It would almost always work. She had always loved
artifacts of the outside world: scraps of life that proved events
had happened beyond the pepper mill, the coffeepot. She would
straighten her skirt, finish the drink. "Thank you, sweetheart.
Thanks for talking," she would say. He would go to his room and
lie on his bed to stare out the window for a while, tired in a way
he couldn't explain. He loved no one more.

Cam tried something then. He brushed his hand on Amber's. She turned and gave him a slight smile. His mother, her
brown hair and tired face, faded. He asked, amazed at the con-
viction in his voice, "Are you free? After work?"

Amber was near the end of her shift and said she could drive
him home. He found Lucy at the post office, told her he'd manage the groceries on his own. His grandmother looked at him a
little thinly and said, "Amber Barlow. Be home by seven for supper." Cam found, to his surprise, that he could withstand Lucy's
disapproval. Maybe this was another aspect of Amber's apparent
magic. When he returned, the girl was waiting for him, wearing
a pair of oversize shades and a pink T-shirt instead of the green
Albertsons polo. She loaded his groceries onto the rear seat of
her Malibu wagon. "Let's go to my house first."

He didn't agree or disagree, he just went. It felt luxurious to
be riding in a car with a person close to his own age. The windows were rolled down. He let his hand flap in the wind and he
could almost feel the cool light streaming through the V's
between his fingers, like golden silk or fine wool. Amber said her
parents were still at work, her father at the condo complex,

her mother at the elementary school. Their house was a gambrel-roofed building on the edge of town in a neighborhood Cam had not visited. Frankly suburban except for the corrals with horses out back, the tumbleweeds, and the sign at the head of the street that warned of mountain lions. Inside, Amber stopped briefly to put a couple of sacks of his groceries that might spoil—butter and milk and frozen juice—in a refrigerator nearly twice the size of Lucy's. The house smelled of cooked bacon and melted wax. On the walls hung formal photographs of Amber and her brother, their fists below their chins, their faces in three-quarter profile. GOD BLESS THIS HOME stated a sign wreathed in braided straw that hung above the stairs. But Cam didn't have time to look around; Amber led him immediately to her room, which was carpeted in yellow and featured a canopy bed.

She pulled off her T-shirt and then her bra and sat below the frill of the canopy. "I'm on the Pill, but I have condoms, too," was all she said, her breasts spreading in the warm air. She smelled of fruity perfume and sweat and on her fingers the cleanser they used to swab floors at the market. She had a boyfriend, she added, but he didn't mind that she saw other guys sometimes. He went to school in Montana. He was studying to be an accountant. They were going to get married. She spoke more as Cam touched her, her voice never varying, as if they were sitting down to eat pizza after a movie, as if they were drinking Coke and looking at her scrapbooks. But there'd been none of those intermediary steps. She hadn't even let him kiss her, had even turned her head shyly away as if this, the mildest of intimacies, was too much to allow someone she had just met.

It was dizzying to be one moment in a grocery store, supervised by a grandparent, stalked by memories, then almost the next to find himself in the arms of a girl with a red dragon tattooed on her hip. To have barreled across the humid reaches of the Midwest and within days be naked on a strange bed, touching the breasts of a girl he barely knew. As his hands sank into the generous flesh around Amber's waist, he realized that the closer he got, the more their bodies touched, the less Laura interfered. Amber could absorb all his attention.

She tasted like gum. "Do you like my tattoos?" she asked. She had them all over her body, dragons and flowers, mostly on her hips and shoulders. The edges were clear now, but he imagined what would happen as she aged. The black lines would fade to brown and the dragons' slim tails and crisp scales would fatten and blur. In forty years her skin would be a muddied sea—if she were still alive.

With a directness that startled him, he said, "No, I don't," and then stripped off her shorts.

She was brisk after sex, glancing at her watch and saying, "Get off me, Cam, you gotta get out of here." She went to the kitchen and returned with his cool sacks of groceries and two apples, the one for herself already in her mouth. In the car, she ate it quickly then tossed the core with a flick of her left wrist into an irrigation ditch, right palm still on the steering wheel, eyes trained on the road. As if this were a ritual enacted after every sexual encounter: the devouring of some fruit, the starting of the ignition, the hustling of the lover away from the scene. Only once on the long trip to Lucy's did she look at him. "Well," she said, and that was it.

Amber drove with un-self-conscious ease. They raced by alfalfa fields and cattle staring accusingly at them, as if to say, so that's how you've been spending your afternoon. Meadowlarks darted past. Cam tested to see if his mother would walk near him now, and she didn't. He looked out at the broad, strong light that lay above the tan hills and felt pleasantly numb, his body heavy—rather close to what he recognized, as if from a great distance, as being happy.

Back at Lucy's, Celia was waiting. The first thing he thought when he saw his sister was that her glasses needed cleaning. Her hair was flying out of her braids. She needs to stop wearing pigtails was his next thought. She peered suspiciously into the car and scowled when introduced to Amber. Lucy and Arthur weren't home yet, she told Cam, and where have you been? She pulled the bags from Amber's car and stomped off to the kitchen to unpack them. Through the dust she left behind, Cam said to Amber, "See you," and then, "Thanks," because it seemed like the polite thing to do. He wanted to say more. He had fully intended to.

"See you, Cam," she said.

In the kitchen, Celia was slamming around and saying, "Lemons. Lemons and apples. About a thousand oranges. And iceberg lettuce. What am I supposed to do with that? Who's that girl? Why are you so late?" She'd been alone for a long time.

Cam couldn't answer her. The questions and accusations were sensible, on the money. "What are we going to do with all those lemons?" Celia shouted at him as he went out the back door to sit in the yard. "What am I supposed to do?"

Cam lay down on the crabgrass. He spread his legs into it, the short stems spiking into calves. He could smell Amber on him still and the memory wasn't so much arousing as comforting. The other girls he'd lured into sex were tense city creatures who needed quantities of vodka to coax the clothes off their stringy bodies, who, once naked, turned into fierce, sometimes tearful embracers, full of choked protestations of long-suppressed love. They provoked in him both longing and embarrassment. Amber created only an unusually pleasant sense of calm. She had asked for absolutely nothing.

Then it happened. Laura came back. He couldn't shake from his brain the picture of his mother on a sofa in her bedroom, reading in her peculiar fashion, flat on her back, hands holding her book straight above her head. He lay there even as the wind began to blow and Celia started to throw lemons at him from the door, even as they bounced off his stomach and landed with dull thuds in the grass. He heard crickets. A crescent moon was rising. The air held seven different striations of blue. He could count them.

Lucy asked about the lemons. Prepped by his mother and Celia, Arthur asked about Amber. Cam knew he was the one they worried about most in the wake of Laura's death. They had been so close, Arthur used to say with a measure of envy. But it was more than that. He was like her. They shared habits and tastes. They had laughed at the same things, things no one else thought were funny. When she died, he was the one who couldn't move from his bed, who almost stopped talking, the one for whom his father consulted psychologists. He was, he suspected, the real reason they were in Wyoming. He could be observed here: Callendar was small and Lucy sharp-eyed. Maybe that was why he felt nearly relaxed as he stretched at the table and watched their worried faces. He'd already found a way to sneak past them and it had taken only the flicker of a lie.

He was unusually cooperative and positive, at least from his father's perspective, when Arthur suggested a trip to the DMV. Arthur had grown used to dissension, truculence, but after Amber, Cam felt no immediate need to reject his father's offers. A summer and fall spent under the arch of sky. He was thinking he might try to like it out here.

At the DMV, there were boys two years younger than he was, boys with braces and buck teeth, barely taller than he'd been at ten, although they'd probably been driving since they were nine, just out of sight of the highways. These kids could also most likely operate complicated farm machinery and rope stubborn calves. They had probably bagged their first deer. They were treating this stop at the DMV as if it were a courtesy to their mothers and the State of Wyoming. Cam, who towered above them and had lost his virginity, felt shy next to these scrappy kids. It took ten minutes to take the test and sign a paper that said he'd finish driver's ed within the month.

On their way back to the car, Arthur said, clearly pleased, "You've got a learner's permit and a job. What do you think of that?" His black eye was purple. "Excited?"

No, Cam thought, I am not excited. I'm not feeling much of anything, but that is an improvement over feeling awful. He was, he admitted, curious about Mac Barlow, who apparently didn't have much influence on his daughter's behavior.

It was a sharply lighted day. Clouds were stacking in the west, offering a faint promise of rain. "Yeah, Dad, I'm excited," he said to preserve politeness with his father. Cam had learned the last few months that if he wanted his privacy, he had to yield more in conversation than he had before. Words now meant the world to Arthur. His father appeared satisfied, and Cam went back to thinking about a boy at the DMV whose right arm was in a cast. He'd taken the written test with his left hand, scribbling with supple fluency. "He's broken both so many times," his mother confided to Arthur, "he's turned himself ambidextrous."

Cam had never cracked a bone or held a gun. But in a blurred memory, he remembered seeing Mac Barlow with a rifle, once, many summers before. One of his cows had wandered onto Lucy's land, and it was unclear whether it could be pulled from the ditch where it had fallen and sunk. Mac had owned a small ranch adjacent to Lucy's and run cattle on it, though he hadn't lived there. She let him use her pasture. He helped her out on occasion, and when he started to have trouble on his property, Cam guessed Lucy had tried to assist him. Finally, he'd sold out, but the obligation remained. That was the origin of the offer of summer work.

"We'll practice driving tonight," Arthur said. "But we've got to distract Lucy a little. Can't let her in on this." Cam knew the story. When his father was ten, they'd needed him to drive so he

could move the truck between the barn and the far field to help
with haying. He wore boots with the tallest heels they could find
and sat on the absolute edge of the seat. But reaching the gears
wasn't the real problem; the real problem was that on his second
trip, the truck got stuck in reverse. The pigsty had been damaged, as had the pig. The year of lean bacon, Lucy called it.

Arthur dropped Cam at Pheasant Run, the condos Mac Barlow managed, announced with a barrel of marigolds and a
carved sign with its name and a picture of a pheasant that was
not convincing. The bird, in fact, looked more like a streamlined
rooster. "Be good. I'll be back around five-thirty." His father
waved with stern firmness. His gestures hardened out here, as if
to align himself better within Wyoming's sense of manhood.
Cam waved back. If he'd been with his mother, they would have
talked about the absurdity of living on this stretch of desert between highway and mall, no pheasants or any other creatures in
sight. Laura would have photographed the sturdy marigolds
then removed the candy wrappers and bottle tops littering the
soil. Arthur wouldn't have noticed them, wouldn't have seen
even the bullet holes in the sign. He just doesn't get affected by
things, Celia said about Arthur. He's impervious. That wasn't it,
exactly, Cam thought. He got badly affected, but once wounded,
he didn't know what to do with himself except keep moving.

Cam looked around. He was early. Mac might not even be
in. The development had twenty town houses, each with a lawn
the size of a large rug. The grass was going to be one of his responsibilities. Some of the lawns were emerald, as if they had access to a secret stash of chemicals. Some were being copiously
sprinkled. His mother wouldn't have approved. "At its best, all
this land wants to be is prairie," she'd say, and sweep her arm out
and you'd see the high grass, the buffalo, the miles of sky. There
she was again, persistent as a burr. He wandered toward the
town houses. They looked like the result of a forced marriage
between a Tudor cottage and a log cabin, with rawly dressed logs

and imitation half-timbered fronts. He'd seen a dog once that was half basset, half dalmatian. Dogs are supposed to lack self-consciousness, but this one had seemed cowed, ashamed of its low, long-backed spottedness. These houses looked similarly appalled at themselves.

A woman with a cigarette in her mouth was staring at him. He hadn't seen her at first; she was standing on her front porch behind two enormous hanging baskets of petunias. She appeared to be about fifty, at least her face did. Her body, strapped into pink leggings and a paler pink T-shirt, looked supple. "Who are you?" she asked through a cloud of smoke, her lips not moving around the cigarette. She was watering the plants and her voice came through a narrow cascade of overflow that had breached the lip of the basket. Her lawn was one of the emerald ones, its sprinkler sending out rainbowed arcs.

"Cam King," he answered. "I'm going to be working with Mac Barlow."

"You mean working *for* Mac Barlow," she said. The water siphoning off her petunias was slowing to drips. She put her arm below the stream and her skin, tanned to caramel, caught drops in perfect, clear jewels.

"That's what I mean," said Cam.

"I'm Nancy Baum," she said. "Mac and I go to the same church." She ground out her cigarette in an ashtray. "Do you have a relationship with Jesus?"

Lucy had mentioned a spike in the number of evangelical churches in and around Callendar. "At least none of the nuts have bought up great big tracts of land and tried to turn them into communes," she'd said once. "The ones in Callendar are poor as dirt, thank God." She also told them a story about a time when a proselytizer had approached her outside the courthouse and posed the same question Nancy Baum had just asked him. "No," Lucy had said, "but I won't hold it against you if *you* do."

"I don't have a relationship with anybody," Cam heard himself say, which surprised him on several levels. It was not strictly true; he had his family. He had the almost omnipresent conversation with his mother. He was starting some kind of relationship with Amber. And he had plenty of ties to plenty of other people—boys at school, teammates. So what was he saying to this water-spattered woman? Blond past reality, in high-heeled sandals at ten in the morning, closer to Victoria's Secret than to Jesus. She looked straight at me, thought Cam. She didn't stare past me at my father, my grandmother, my mother. She looked at me.

"Well then, come this Sunday to church," Nancy Baum said.

"OK," he said, but his mind scurried off to fashion a plausible excuse for not going. The idea of telling Lucy produced such anxiety he knew he'd find a way to break the engagement. He already felt bad about letting Nancy down, which also surprised him; it meant that he would like to go.

He heard footsteps behind him: it was Mac Barlow, as broad as a white bison, Arthur used to say. Mac was huge and wore sunglasses with lenses so dark you forgot his milky skin and found yourself wondering what color eyes he had. What color had Amber's been? Cam had no idea. She had pulled the shades in her room. She had worn sunglasses while driving. But these were all excuses. He had been focused on her breasts, her mouth. He hadn't cared at all about her eyes. She had made his mother go away.

"You've met Mrs. Baum," Mac said as he shook Cam's hand, grinding it around in his own. It took presence of mind not to examine it for injury afterward. A flicker of more than unease passed through Cam. Had Mr. Barlow—he would never call him Mac—seen him leaving with Amber, or did Amber have some kind of weird, almost unimaginable openness with her parents and let on that she had slept with Cam? "She needs her lawn trimmed," Mac added, nodding at Nancy's house, and took Cam by the shoulder and led him to a door marked OFFICE. Inside was a desk with a phone, a stuffed pronghorn head, a calendar from 2002. Coffee with a skin of old milk filled a mug that said EAT BEEF: THE WEST WASN'T WON ON SALAD. Mac took the more comfortable of the two available chairs. His long jaw glowed with the closeness of his shave. He gave Cam a sudden smile. His teeth were startlingly even.

"Your duties, Cam, will include lawn mowing and general maintenance: putting out the trash, stocking the laundry room, sweeping the walkways. There are a few elderly residents who might need help with their garbage cans." Mac continued to talk about the values that underlay how he managed Pheasant Run. The need for order in the toolshed. The proper disposal of clippings. The rules about getting rid of pet waste and the necessity of informing him of violations of policy. Cam nodded, asked questions when it seemed he should, and mostly let his mind wander. He decided Amber wouldn't say anything to her parents. "Fornication" would be the word they would have chosen for what Cam and Amber had engaged in. If she was even remotely accurate in her depiction of her plight—wanting to be an interior designer while her family foresaw a life of early marriage, long skirts, piety, casseroles, and the removal of all her tattoos—she would stay quiet about how she spent her time after work. Mac flexed his long, pale fingers as he talked. He did not remove his sunglasses, though he had taken off his hat to reveal an inch-high dent in his hair just above his ear, crimped there almost permanently, Cam guessed. Once Cam had his license, Mac said, they might add some work with the truck, and Cam felt something his father must have experienced thousands of times: the Wyoming scorn for city greenness, the assertion of ranch-hand pride, the view that a way of life tied to large vehicles and physical labor was preferable to any other, even if the job was connected to condos instead of cattle.

"Ready to get started, then?" the older man said. When he

rose to his full height, he blocked half of the pronghorn head, his bulk covering one of its shiny eyes. Mac showed Cam the lawn mower, the rakes, the boxes of garbage bags, the herbicides. He described with ominous attention to detail the habits of the residents. The widow who needed to be reminded to unplug appliances. The trucker who yelled at his TV. Which tenant had good credit, which didn't. Cam began to appreciate Lucy's isolation from town. Mac's preoccupation with sins small and large might have alarmed Cam enough to swear off Amber instantly, but he didn't. He looked at his fingers; they were still. He cast in his mind for thoughts of Laura and found none.

Mac was continuing to talk: he suspected that recent move-ins, a woman and her daughter, were harboring a cat. Tenants who had been here since 1999 had been grandfathered in; as of July 2003, new arrivals were strictly prohibited from keeping domestic animals in their residences. Cam was to stay on the lookout for illegal creatures. "Including ferrets," Mac said darkly. The rules did not seem to prevent Mac from staking three of his own horses out in the scrubby pasture behind the development.

Cam had no idea why Amber and Mac, these two rather menacing people, had the power to keep his mother distant, and he did not care. He knew only that he would see them as often as he could. "Ready?" Mac asked, settling his hat back on.

"Absolutely," Cam said.

He spent the morning wrestling with the lawn mower. It was simple once he learned its trick: you needed to start it with a two-layered yank, one long, one short, and it kicked right up. He had never operated a lawn mower before, but immediately liked its abrupt production of noise, the satisfying piles of sliced grass, the neatness of the squares of lawn that he reduced to military shortness. A few residents peered at him from their windows. One or two came out to introduce themselves. They seemed to have no idea who he was, except for the old lady with the hound dog who said she knew Lucy from the Historical Society and didn't seem to hold it against Cam for being related to her. He squared off the corner of the second-to-last lawn.

Cam headed to Nancy Baum's house. Her place looked more lived-in—not broken-down, but occupied—than several of the other units. He wondered how long she had been a resident. Pheasant Run operated with six-month leases and Mac had stern words for those who broke them early, as happened, he allowed, "from time to time." Pheasant Run, Cam realized, was slightly upgraded transient housing. Cam also suspected that for some tenants its proximity to the highway was one of its more appealing aspects.

Nancy was waiting for him. "When you're done with the lawn, Cam, I want you to see something out back." She was waiting for him in the fenced-in yard and pointing with her cigarette at a hole in the wire. "Can you fix that?" she asked. "I've been after Mac for weeks about it and he keeps saying it has been noted, but I'm tired of being noted and not acted upon."

Cam kneeled by the gap, made by someone on the inside of the fence with clippers or a hacksaw. But why? It wasn't large enough for a person. It was barely big enough for a cat. "Animals are using it," Nancy said. "I hear them at night and it just scares me," though she didn't look frightened. She was right, however. Red and tan fur was twined on the spiked ends. A dog, maybe, or a coyote, the texture too rough to be a house cat's. He could fix the hole with a few lengths from a spool of wire he'd seen in the toolshed. Knowing Mac would not approve of his taking on the task, he went straight to the shed for the supplies he'd need.

He unwrapped the wire in smooth lengths, notched and cut it after measuring. Then he wove the strips into open diamonds, leaving enough at each end to graft, with the help of needle-nose pliers, the new piece onto the old. He felt solid and smooth, the way he did when playing soccer, running, or throwing darts. He had the touch with tools, Lucy said. You'd be good on a horse, Cam, she'd said. You and your mother have the feel for hardware and animals. It's rarer than you think. He noticed Lucy had hesitated about putting the verb "have" into the past or present tense.

Nancy, in jeans now, along with the pink top and spiky sandals, had crouched down beside him to watch—she smelled of soap and tobacco. Silent until the repair was entirely finished, she said, "Looks like it never happened. Looks like it's been darned. You're good at this, Cam." It would have been easy to let her words slide in a more suggestive direction, but she spoke so flatly, like a bored actress who'd long ago dispensed with intonation. "Thanks," she said. "I appreciate your help. Go check in now with Mac. He'll have something else for you to do." Using words a grandmother could have spoken was when she sounded most seductive, as if she were inviting a more lurid interpretation.

Mac was in the office, staring at the calendar. He was still wearing his sunglasses and his hat. It was not clear he was doing anything at all or had been engaged in any activity all morning. He seemed to rotate between a state close to active violence and another akin to total inertia. Cam had difficulty seeing him as a serious Christian. The mug with the skin of old milk still sat on the desk. He smiled at Cam. "Progress report?"

Cam gave his boss the update, another phrase he suspected would appeal to Mac. The lawns mowed, the clippings bagged, the trash hauled to the truck so Mac could take it to the transfer station later on. "Transfer station" was a phrase that drove Lucy crazy. "What's wrong with calling it the dump? They haven't changed the name of the road, have they?" It was true that on maps and by everyone in town it was still called Old Dump Road. But naturally Mac Barlow used only the sanitized term.

Cam found that he didn't mention the repair to Nancy's fence, though that was what he was proudest of. The only way to tell there'd been a repair was that the wire was still shiny; it gleamed silver against gray. The delicacy it had required and the strangeness of the hole appealed to him. How had the damage come about in the first place? And why had Mac been reluctant to fix it? Instead, he said, though it was absolutely a lie, that he had spotted no evidence of cats in Unit 18. In fact, he had seen a large tabby perched in the front window and had knocked on the door and warned the skinny girl who answered that she should pull the curtains and move the cat. She had nodded slowly and whispered a thank-you. As they spoke, the cat had wound its plump body around the stalks of her ankles and made nearly silent peeps.

"You're off to a good start, Cam," Mac said. "Nice work." As if Cam were a new recruit to an armed service, given a warning behind the praise: it was only going to get tougher from here on in.

"Thanks, sir," Cam said, and wondered why he had known from the moment he met Mac Barlow that he would lie to him. The "sir" was also calculated, its military ring false and heavy.

"Off to the next task, then," Mac said. What Mac really enjoyed, Cam thought, was having someone nearby to order around. He held the screen door open for Cam to leave and asked, through the mesh, "Are you enjoying yourself?"

"Yes, I am, sir," Cam answered, but that wasn't a lie in the slightest. He walked out the door and heard rather than saw Mac settle back in his chair. An unexpected bolt of well-being surged through him. It had everything to do with being there at Pheasant Run, with its shabbiness, and the simple hard work that would have bored or horrified his schoolmates back in New York. They were off being counselors at fancy camps in Vermont or traveling to China to perfect their Mandarin, working at internships or vague jobs with politicians or lawyers. New York boys getting ready to be a certain kind of New York man: polished, armored, private, and invulnerable. Back out in the harsh light, picking out the bottle caps and cigarette butts from the barrel that held the marigolds, Cam felt for a moment that the gash his mother's loss had left in him was manageable here in the weird halo cast by Mac and Pheasant Run. For some reason, out here, his skin coated in dust and grass clippings, he could skirt the hole Laura had torn instead of living deep inside it.

Every two or three days, Cam would practice driving into town. Lucy would engineer a chore: fetching groceries or some bit of equipment from the hardware store. Lucy had turned out to be an easier vehicular presence than his father. She never stamped imaginary brakes or hissed when he took the turn off their driveway and onto the paved road too sharply. She watched him sidelong but said nothing apart from relating details of her reading the evening before. The sure signs of sandstorm in the Empty Quarter: a glaze to the eastern sky and coffee that wouldn't grind fine in the morning. The best times of year and the most useful breed of camel for crossing the sands. "I'm stuck on Arabia these days," she said. "Maybe it's the Osama thing and all." Lucy had theories about landscape and its influence on character. It mattered, she felt, what it was you saw outside your window when you were a small child. She would share these ideas, pass him the shopping list, and seemed to get used to his occasionally asking if Amber could drive him back.

The last time, Lucy looked at him bluntly. Twice she opened her mouth to speak and twice she closed it. He wondered if she was remembering what had happened a few days earlier in the barn, when she was feeding the chickens and he was looking for the ladder. He had asked her where it was and then his hands started to shake. It was the ladder; it was leaving the ground— it brought Laura firmly along. He saw Lucy take in the trembling. The chickens were hot and scratching at their feet. "You've got the shakes, Cam. I'll assume that's not from foolish choices." He had recently learned from Amber that Lucy had testified a few years ago against high school thugs using eighth graders as runners. Her testimony had helped put some boys away for years, Amber said, and her car been smashed in the teachers' lot the next month. "People said all she did was look at the truck, say, 'Well that won't get me home tonight,' and go call Ray Fontaine and AAA." Until the insurance money came in, she'd stayed with Janet and walked to work and when the money did arrive, she bought a used Ford and donated what was left to a drug-use prevention group in town. The story had shocked Cam and he'd immediately told Celia, who hadn't heard it, either. "Do you think she told Dad?" she asked and they agreed that Lucy probably wasn't quite that secretive, though Celia also said, "We probably don't know the half of it about Lucy. We might not want to."

That night in the barn, Cam had not been able to still the tremors. His grandmother had put down her bucket of feed, flipped over his palms, and steered her rough thumbs across them, making the skin travel in a low wave from his knuckles to his wrists. As if his agitation were no more than a wrinkle that required the warmth and pressure of an iron. "Well, that's not working, is it?" she said after a minute. It hadn't, but he still hadn't wanted her to stop.

Today at the supermarket, she decided, again, not to press the subject of Amber and said, as she had before, "That's fine. Home by seven."

Cam tried to see Amber as often as possible, reverent in the face of her power to push Laura back by even a few yards. But her schedule varied or her mother was home, or Mac would tack on chores that kept Cam late at Pheasant Run. When they did manage to spend time with each other, the routine was the same as it had been the first day. They went immediately to Amber's bedroom and had sex, during which she talked and talked and talked. About her brother, who was already at the evangelical college studying to be a missionary. About Len, the boyfriend, whom Cam had glimpsed in a snapshot. He was big as a tractor and had glowering eyes. Cam had edged toward questions about the date and likelihood of Len's return, suspecting Len had a less generous interpretation of their arrangement than Amber.

The light in the room had dimmed and he knew he needed to go. "What are you thinking about?" Amber asked as he pulled her panties down one last time. Pink skin turned from green to blue now in this light, everywhere except between her legs and where the tattoos curled in black rivers along her. She said the needles hurt worse than being kicked by a horse. Cam said he wouldn't know what that meant. "What are you thinking?" she asked again. This was rare. She usually expected no accounting from Cam of how he felt or where his mind wandered. The mattress creaked. Cam thought Amber was a lot older than he was, in a lot of ways. "Nothing," Cam said. "Nothing." He was telling her the truth.

As she drove him home, he asked her, "What would Len or your father do if they found out about . . ." his voice trailed off. He was going to say "us," but he didn't know if there was an "us."

"You and me having sex?" Amber said, solving the problem as she steered around what remained of a skunk in the road. The rich, complicated scent followed them for a few moments. Longer than it took for her to answer, which she did immediately. "Kill you, then kill me, I guess."

Cam froze. He couldn't tell if she was joking. The last time they'd been together, she had asked, "Ever wonder what it would be like to run off to Vegas and get married?" and he had looked at her hard. She admitted that she'd been thinking about it only because a friend of hers had just done it. She went there fast so no one would have time to talk her out of the boy or the marriage. "Five months," Amber said appraisingly. "I give it that long. But she'll be pregnant by then, too."

"I don't really mean it," she said, looking at Cam directly. "I don't think Daddy would like it, but he's harmless." Cam said he doubted that and then regretted his comment. But Amber said no, it was true, he was a pussycat. Besides, he and her mother knew she was really with Len. This stung far more than Cam cared to admit. He heard his own voice ask abruptly, "And Len?"

Amber shrugged. "He cheats on me up in Montana. He says he doesn't, but he'll get these cards or e-mails from these girls named Charlise and Kaylee that he says are colleagues from Bible study. But they're, like, these little girlfriends. Freshmen he strings along."

"It doesn't bother you?" Cam asked.

Amber considered this. She tilted the sun visor so it cut the glare. "Sure it bothers me. But Len and I are going to get married. And after we get married, there won't be any of this. So he better get it out of his system now since I sure won't put up with it later."

Cam didn't mention that she seemed to make room for the same sort of infidelity as Len's. He wondered with a stab of surprising jealousy if the reason Amber couldn't see him on certain evenings was that she had other boys working on her system. Instead he said, "So it's all arranged, you and Len? Does he belong to the same church or something? And the minister chose him for you?" In the rearview mirror, he noticed that the wind was blowing the cottonwoods to tall arches and that forked lightning was flaring over the hills. Ahead of them was only sun and dust, late July light.

"No," Amber said, punching him lightly on the arm. "We love each other. We have since we were twelve." This solved nothing and her certainty made Cam feel unexpectedly worse.

"Bye," Amber said when she dropped him at the edge of the driveway. No one drove up Lucy's driveway unless they had to. Even in trucks with excellent suspension, its washboard surface made your jaws chatter. And Amber didn't want to meet Celia, his father, or Lucy again. This was separate from them. This was separate from everything else in her life. Cam usually started walking as soon as Amber turned around. But tonight he stood there and didn't care if she saw him looking after her. She was heading straight back toward the gray and purple clouds, straight toward what looked like a wide blue sheet of rain. It turned out the storm was farther away than he thought. Rain fell near Cody and left Callendar, as usual, dry.

A few days later Mac invited Cam over for what he called family dinner. "A meal to say thanks for your hard work, Cam." Cam had been eating his lunch on the bench outside the office, watching the cat in Unit 18 try to sneak into the warm bay window. He also saw the little girl's narrow fingers tugging at the cat's back legs. Mac came out and Cam stood, to mask the activity at Unit 18 and because Mac seemed to like it when Cam moved on his behalf. After work, Cam went to find Amber at the Albertsons. She was arranging beets and she looked tired. "Your dad asked me to dinner. Should I come?"

"Stu"—the assistant produce manager and her nemesis— "always says I don't get the pointy ends high enough. He says the beets should look like little red rockets." Amber's beets were certainly droopier than that. Their straggling roots were aiming listlessly at the floor. She sighed. "Vegetables just don't listen to me."

"Amber," Cam said, helping her, in spite of himself, to fan the broad leaves in a more attractive pattern, "what should I do? Should I come?"

"Why not? Daddy says nice things about you. He says you're a hard worker but that he has doubts about your soul." Shania Twain's voice came from the speakers. Cam kept working on the beets, which were starting, under his care, to look much more like little red rockets.

"Your father talks about me?"

"Mmmhmm. Yeah. Every night at dinner." She lifted the edge of a bandage on her inner arm. She had earned a bonus last week for an extra ten-hour shift and had used some of the proceeds to add a few more leaves to a grapevine. Installment tattooing, she called it.

"Does he know? I mean does he have any idea . . ." Cam was almost stuttering.

"No way," Amber said crossly. "And you better get out of here. Thanks for the beets. Stu's about to get back from break."

Clipping hedges the next day, Cam thought he should stop seeing Amber. She told him both too much and not enough, and even though she kept Laura marvelously distant, he was starting to think about her when he wasn't with her, to feel anxious when he couldn't see her—an unnerving feeling he hadn't experienced before. He was starting to find her necessary. He was halfway across the top of a mesquite bush when he heard a voice behind him. "That's not like you. Being careless with a plant." He saw that he'd cut a jagged line in the shrub. It was Nancy Baum, in pale blue shorts and paler blue T-shirt and her usual cigarette. He had squirmed out of her offer of church that first Sunday and several others after that, but she had continued her friendly observance of his tasks around Pheasant Run.

"Girl trouble?" she asked flatly. It was more of a statement than a question.

"No," he said. "Not that." He wondered how she knew. What had his body suggested that made her think instantly of romantic disappointments?

"No cure for those," she said, as if he hadn't spoken, "except more girls." This seemed to make her sad, and she exhaled smoke in a small gray cloud and wandered back to her unit. She moved more slowly than other tenants because she wore those tippy sandals and because she stopped to look at every plant she encountered, even the twists of chamomile that grew stubby and wild between the cracks of the cement walks. He knew it was chamomile because she'd told him.

Nancy's name came up at the Barlows' dinner table two nights later. "She's a fine member of our church, but it would be very nice if she were just a little less cantankerous," Mac said.

Cam accepted another helping of Valerie Barlow's apple-sauce, which came, like the other dishes on the table, in serving bowls the size of radials. Valerie, tall and pale like Amber and Mac, stared at Cam with a mixture of caution and pity. She knew about his sorry, motherless state and, he guessed, more about what was going on between him and Amber than Mac did.

"She just speaks her mind, Daddy. That's what you don't like," Amber said between bites on a chicken thigh.

"It's more than that," Mac answered. He took his hat and his sunglasses off for meals. Like Amber, he had gray-blue eyes that changed color depending on the light. "She seems to be looking for a quarrel."

"Just because she wants to know where the bake-sale and rose-a-thon money went to? Just because she would like to see receipts?" Amber put down the bone she'd cleared of meat and picked up another. The rose-a-thon was something she'd partic-ipated in. You bought a rose for two dollars and got it delivered to someone by a pretty girl. The funds raised were supposed to go to elderly, indigent Christians. Amber had been flattered to be one of the deliverers. "I don't think that's pushy. I think it's smart. She's the treasurer, after all."

"What Nancy Baum treasures isn't going to be found on any receipt," Valerie said as she served herself another ladleful of corn. Mac obviously didn't approve of that comment and asked, a little acidly, if his wife would pass the chicken.

They ate in silence for a while. The meal had started out loudly—the TV on in the kitchen, then Mac's booming, thorough grace—Amber said he seemed to thank every last Christian in the Inner Mountain West—and then the clanking of plates and dishes at the large table. But this last exchange dampened the volume, and all Cam heard was the scrape of teeth on metal, knife on plate, magnified because of the lack of conversation.

Finally Valerie said, "So you're from New York. I've never been there." To please her, Cam had eaten twice as much as he'd wanted to and he sat there, dulled and sweating. He hadn't gotten to a single one of the questions he wanted to ask. How serious were they about Jesus? Would Len really rip him in two? Why did their house smell of melted wax when there wasn't a single candle in evidence? Valerie rose to make coffee.

Mac cleared his throat and asked Cam if he'd been with his grandmother when the horse was shot. No, Cam told him, he hadn't; he'd been working at the Run that night. He didn't add that Lucy hadn't let him help with removing the animal and that Lucy and her neighbor Mr. Flaxman had taken care of the whole thing. Nor did Cam mention that Arthur had left at first light for work and none of them had talked about the incident since. Mac nodded, as if he somehow wasn't surprised that Cam wasn't near the action. Mac himself had been out behind the development when the herd raced through Callendar.

"Not one of your sermons, Daddy, please," Amber said, and got up to clear plates and serving dishes. Since Mac clearly required an audience, Cam stayed at the table instead of helping her. Work was sharply divided down traditional lines in this household. Mac would have no truck with dishes. Mac would preside over after-dinner conversation.

When the horses first came around the bend, he said, he wasn't sure if the sound was drumming or thunder. "I had to hobble my gray or it would have joined the race. But then, Cam, I realized I was lying to myself." Valerie returned with a tray of coffee cups, small and amazingly delicate given the size and heft of everything else. She stood there listening. "I was the one who wanted to get on the back of my horse and run," Mac said, looking at Cam—to spur on his gray and find the herd that spooked pronghorns as it passed, so that the animals, maned and horned, shod and cloven-footed, had briefly mixed, a quilt of wild and nearly wild, treating the land as if they owned it, as if the fences they flew across were only clouds. "They cleared those fences by feet," Mac said. "They shouldn't have been able to. The fences should have worked." They usually did. Each week, he untangled whatever the wire had snared—fur, sinew, bone, whole bodies. The sight of the flying animals had done something to him, he said. Valerie, still standing, went on listening to her husband as she poured out the coffee. "I felt something," Mac said.

"What?" Valerie asked and picked up the cream pitcher. She looked different, somehow. Still a thick-in-the-middle Valkyrie, but filled with something light and dramatic. Cam sensed the enactment of a rite that glued their marriage. They had their kids, their house, the meals they ate together, but they also had this: some kind of call and response in which Mac acted the preacher and Valerie the acolyte. It was weird. It made his skin itch. But he found himself transfixed. Amber was nowhere to be seen. She had left him alone to witness this.

"Longing," Mac said. He was looking not at his wife but at the lumpy wall of his knuckles wrapping her china. "To move that well," he said.

All of this as if Cam were not there and Mac and Valerie were sharing a private moment. "To stretch to the limit of your capacity," she said, and Cam heard her voice puckering. He guessed at her doubts about Mac's capacities. He remembered Mac's failed ranch, the clear demotion that Pheasant Run represented.

"I think I saw them living," Mac said.

Valerie doctored his coffee to tan. "I think you saw what God intends for us," she said, voice unrumpled now. Amber was still not at the table; Cam heard a fierce clanking of cutlery and the swirl of water coming from the kitchen.

"Yes," Mac said, "but not exactly." Cam had seen the recliner in the basement where Amber's father kept an old TV for watching football games and he had a feeling Mac spent a great deal of the weekend in the chair, downing beer and observing the fate of the Broncos. Jesus had no home in that basement. Mac pushed the saucer to the lip of the table, watched the china balance, half on wood, half in air. Valerie did not stop him, though Cam saw she yearned to. "It's not that he wants us to clear high fences," Mac said. "It's that he wants us to exist as if they are not there."

All week Cam thought about this performance. It held a menace he couldn't describe. Amber merely said afterward that he just got on these rants sometimes and her mother indulged him. "Ignore him," she said confidently. But after that dinner, Mac seemed omnipresent.

One afternoon, Cam went to the office to ask Mac if he should mop the laundry room. On the desk, Mac had spread out four reels and an assortment of rods and tackle. "You fish, Cam?" Hooks winked in the light.

"Not really," Cam answered. He didn't know if he should touch anything. But the lines on the reels were tangled and he volunteered to straighten them, knowing his fingers would have an easy time of it.

"Sure thing," Mac said, "I'd appreciate it," and they settled down together. The work required deftness but not much concentration. When they were done, Mac asked Cam if he would like to fish this Saturday. He'd need a license; they'd leave near dawn. Cam agreed instantly, and Mac popped open his rectangular tins of flies. They bristled with feathers and short tufts of sharp thread. The hooks were wickedly sharp. He began to write out the contents of each box on small stickers in tiny letters. To Cam's surprise, his handwriting was womanly. It seemed nearly impossible that fingers so large could shape such delicate strokes.

"Want a beer?" he asked, still writing. Cam paused, not knowing if it was a trick question. Adults were experienced hypocrites about alcohol, but maybe Wyoming was different. It was safer to refuse politely. Mac plucked a Michelob from a small fridge—a new acquisition—and continued to write the names of the flies on the labels.

When the day came, fog still hung in the lower valley, clinging like a blanket to the stream. Mac brought a thermos of coffee and a rod and waders for Cam, but he hadn't mentioned that it would feel like late October so early in the morning. "Rainbow don't wait," was all he said when he picked Cam up.

But the cold wasn't what was making Cam shiver. Memories of Laura had resurfaced when he was in the shower and his hands had begun to shake the moment he stepped into the hot water. His mother coming out of the bathroom when he was five or six—wrapped in a white towel, her hair a tangled mass down her back. "Cammy, pass me my robe," she asked, and folded herself into the terry cloth in one deft motion. Then she twisted the discarded towel into a turban on her head and once again she was sealed off. Always slightly out of reach.

Unlike his sister, who was watching him these days with even fiercer attention than Lucy and Arthur. Celia knew what was going on with Amber, and it made her more caustic than usual. When she heard Mac was picking him up before sunrise, she hooted, "You? Dawn? Do you even know when that is?" His father had looked pleased, then chagrined—another man teaching his son a useful skill that he did not have. Arthur was as bad with fishing line as he was with screwdrivers. He offered, however, to buy a rig for Cam or to call the Barlows and say thank you. Cam quickly rejected both suggestions. "It's just a onetime thing," he said, and for all he knew, that would be true. Really, he didn't care. What he was after was the release from memories about his mother, and those departed the second the truck door slammed and they rumbled off toward Lyon Creek.

Mist curled off the water like pencil shavings of moisture. Mule deer and goldfinches sprang from the willow thickets. They were walking beside a portion of the creek that featured wide pasturage on one side and on the other a steep canyon wall striated with red and black layers of mineral. Mac said nothing, just kept pointing Cam upstream and went on smiling.

The older man finally sat on a log on the meadow side of the water and started to explain what they would do. He put on his waders and showed Cam a reel: it was beautiful—black with mother-of-pearl inlay—and it made satisfying clicks as Mac made sure the line was free of snarls. He was intent now on tying the fly to the line. "Royal Wulff," he said, a little bundle of menace. "The rainbow's favorite meal, except for this," he said, pointing to the barb sparking in the first sun.

Mac stood at the center of the water, feet wide apart, riffling waves well above his ankles. "Watch now, Cam, and then you have a try." His weight appeared to be distributed as evenly as a polar bear's. He had that animal's narrow head and his hair, full and fair, was sleeked back over his ears. He cocked his right shoulder backward. "Just to one o'clock," he called over the hubbub of the creek. He was aiming, Cam saw, for a pool about twenty feet ahead, where the stream had carved a deeper spot for itself and the ripples smoothed out like a rumpled sheet pulled taut. With his left hand, Mac drew back the line. Cam could see the dart and whip of the fly at the end of each of Mac's strokes. Although Cam had never fished like this, he could see that Mac was very good, fluent and practiced, and that he'd achieved mastery in this realm years before.

"Now," Mac said from midstream, his powerful body set squarely between two rocks, "your turn."

Cam pulled on his waders and sloshed out toward Mac. The rod was unexpectedly light. The cork at its base was delicately modeled and slid with ease between Cam's hands. Mac moved aside and said, "Give it a whirl." Cam's feet were cold through the thin rubber of the waders. It would be easy to slip. He shut his eyes briefly, to bring back the image of Mac's right arm and how much line he'd pulled from the reel with his left. Within moments he was making the fly dance on the water at the center of the pool. Something flickered—a fish that he'd interested. His aim was clear and sure, thanks to years of soccer and dart throwing. On the bank, Mac looked on with what he was trying to mask as good humor but was really a clotted sort of rage.

Cam felt the tension in the line increase then retreat. The fly sketched a dimple on the water. Mac was still standing there, smiling that enormous smile.

"This rod belonged to my father," he called out to Cam. "He used it to fish all over Nebraska." There didn't seem to be much need to comment on this information, so Cam kept trying to interest the trout he saw dabbing at the surface of the pool. "He loved fishing, Dad did. We didn't realize why, until after his death, when a woman my mother had never seen before arrived on her doorstep claiming she was John Barlow's wife. Arms on her hips and a Chevrolet in the driveway. I never did find out how she knew where to find my mother."

What were you supposed to say about bigamy? Cam had never heard the topic come up in conversation before. The fish had disappeared. He reeled the line in, looked over at Mac, offered him the rod. It seemed a prudent move. Mac sloshed out to take the rig from Cam and proceeded again to make his expert casts. Cam took his spot on the log. His toes were numb. He warned himself not to rise to the story, but before he could help himself, he asked, "Did she have kids? The second lady?" Cam was trying to imagine the scene.

"Oh yes," said Mac, gazing at the stream ahead. "Three. All about the age of me and my brothers. And so there wasn't a lot to go around. It turned out he'd been a shade nicer to my mother or maybe just more guilty, since she came first. He'd given her a better house and a newer car. When my mother realized she'd been the favored wife, she relented. They send each other Christmas cards and call him 'that old bastard' and include each other in prayer. But it was a shock at the time."

It was impossible to know if this big man was joking. Cam felt it safer to assume he wasn't. He wished Amber were there. Or Valerie, with her frown. Anyone to bring Mac back to normal proportions.

Mac glanced over at Cam. "I take it your parents were not bigamists?" he said.

"Not as far as I know, Mr. Barlow," Cam said, nails scraping the spongy bark of the log he was sitting on. He pulled back a length and saw that the wood below was scored with shallow, lacy grooves, the blind handiwork of insects.

"You should be grateful for that. Though if my father lived in Utah and was a member of the Church of Latter-day Saints, the story would probably have been quite different." Cam thought about fishing with a bigamist's rods. Had they really been used or had they just served as an excuse to go and visit the other wife? Why had he bothered marrying her? Cam wondered. Had he invented a different name? Did Mac know his half siblings? Would he give one of them a kidney if they needed it? This was the kind of story his own father couldn't stand: people behaving irrationally, with dramatic consequences that caused a lot of hurt feelings and unclear loyalties. That was why they'd left New York. Drastic actions. But Cam thought this new territory could prove to be even more treacherous. You had no idea what might be coming. Cold streams with algae-slicked rocks. Bigamists. It was the kind of story his mother loved. He could hear her, her low voice with the breath of southern accent to it. Why do you think he did it? What sort of man was he? What were the two women like? She would have made Mac talk all day. Complicated people interested her.

Cam noticed then that the tip of Mac's rod had bowed. He

had a fish on the line. "Tell me, Cam," he said as he started to reel the trout in, his eyes trained on the glimmer of tail now visible in the stream ahead. "What are your thoughts about matrimony?" He was still smiling.

"That it's very time-consuming," Cam said, his pulse quickening. He had never been around someone so actively dangerous. He had no idea how to behave around a person like that. He wondered if it was odd that the thought of it slightly excited him.

"That's accurate," Mac said with a bark that Cam thought was meant to be a laugh. "That it is." He produced from a pocket in his vest a net to scoop the thrashing creature out of the water. "Ten inches," said Mac. "There's your breakfast." Then he added, "Do the honors," and slid the hook from the fish's narrow lip.

It was remarkable how instinctive it was. Cam pulled a rock from the streambed, grasped the slick fish with grass and made the blunt stone meet the narrow pink-and-silver head again and again until the tail ceased to quiver. He took the knife and inserted it where Mac showed him, low on the belly, felt the tug of the tip on the creamy iridescence of the tiny scales and let its sharpness slide north toward the crisp red gills. Then he watched, numbed now, as Mac's rough thumb took over to scoop out the red, pink, and black organs that had kept the fish alive moments earlier. "Oops. Too bad. A female," he said, and Cam saw a mass of what looked like golden grain spill out next to the skein of intestine on the bank.

They fished for another half hour. Cam hooked his first but let it slide back into the water once Mac's fly had safely been clipped free. Mac kept three others and gutted his catch with the same clinical dexterity as before. They talked little or not at all once the first fish, the only female, had been killed.

Cam kept waiting for the tremor to start up, but it didn't.

The slight, damp weight of the first rainbow Mac had caught, wrapped in want ads, its dappled skin all in shadow, sat on his lap.

"Let's do this again soon, Cam," Mac said as he started up the engine. "You're a natural." That was exactly the problem: it had felt entirely natural to take the stone and connect it to the slender head until the cool silver eye tarnished over. Nothing had come more easily to him, and it made Cam shiver and run to the shower without answering his father when he asked, "How was it? Catch anything?"

That night, Cam watched Lucy and his father from the yard. They did not know he was looking at them. Kinked steam spun upward from their coffee cups. Their faces were still. The silence between them was as worn as Lucy's furniture. As soon as they were in the same room, they looked like chairs that had lived next to each other for years. There wasn't much space for anyone else, Cam thought. They'd been necessary to each other for such a long time. His mother had never quite been able to wedge between them. No one had. Something had happened here, on this land, in this house, that bound them sturdily together. Amber and Mac had that weird solidity, too.

On the kitchen table, where his father and grandmother sat now, he'd carved his name with a nail when he was seven, knowing he was not supposed to, feeling the pleasure of etching the C, examining the scroll of wood that rose from the groove. His grandmother had caught him connecting the two sides of the A. "Your father's is on the other side," she said. "Just the first three letters." He dropped the nail. "Pick it up, Cam," she said. "You might as well finish." She'd come in from the barn with a pail of eggs from her twenty chickens, short white feathers stuck to her dress. She was in her stocking feet, her barn shoes on the porch. That was why he hadn't heard her. He had never noticed his father's name. "There," she said. "Right there, near the place where he always sits." Then she went to the sink and placed the eggs in a colander to rinse away the chicken dirt and straw. The M he'd made had wavered, been smaller than his confident start. His mother was flustered when she found out about the carving, but Lucy said, "I've burned that table dozens of times, Laura. It's not for royalty. Anyway, kids like to mark stuff up."

He settled himself in the dip of the front step, curved from years of sitting, boots, and weather. At supper he'd noticed that the letters of his name were nearly worn away. There'd been so many meals, so many scrubbings. His father's had disappeared altogether. Lucy's house had changed discreetly. New curtains, different doormats. Mugs to replace ones that shattered. But in its essentials, the house with its wide, carefully tended yard and barn, sat unchanged in his memory. Every year, he expected it to show radical signs of aging or even to be there one summer and gone the next. It was so isolated. Fire could inhale it in a moment.

But what had actually changed was something he would never have thought possible. Moonlight bounced off a pair of eyes low to the ground. Close-set, shining disks: neutrally, totally alive. They might belong to raccoon, rabbit, or mink. Animals everywhere here. His mother had hated how the meadowlarks flew straight into the windshield, their round, speckled breasts smacking the glass, necks bent at an impossible angle. "It's not like I try to hit them, Laura," his father had said last summer. "I know," she said, "but it should make you feel worse, Arthur. You shouldn't accept it so easily." That had been her last trip here. Cam wondered if she'd known it at the time.

He walked down the steps, picked up a small rock, chucked it out over the fence toward the eyes—not to hit the creature but just to do something that might chase out pictures like that of his mother in the car, the bird newly dead, her shoulders hunched to prevent vital energy from leaking out. But whatever it was kept watching him. Something scuffled in the brush. Hunting all night long. Instead of walking into the house, Cam turned to go and sleep in the barn. He didn't mind the low, contented clucks of the chickens, the crisp air. He had stashed a couple of blankets there and he liked being high off the ground but protected by the stiff, strong hay. He wrapped himself tighter in the blankets and his hands started to shake when he thought of something Laura said that last summer: everyone liked to believe that the natural world was infinitely forgiving, indefinitely capable of regeneration. "But treat it badly long enough," she said, looking at one of the new gravel roads and the truck lumbering down it, "and it will collapse. That's what no one wants to hear." Her camera was swinging around her neck, but she didn't take a picture.

PART II

. . . we must have

the stubbornness to accept our gladness in the ruthless

furnace of this world. To make injustice the only

measure of our attention is to praise the Devil.

If the locomotive of the Lord runs us down,

We should give thanks that the end had magnitude.

—Jack Gilbert, "A Brief for the Defense"

PART II

ARTHUR

It was Saturday, late July, 8:00 a.m., cloudless, dust on the road, dust in the truck. Dust in his teeth, a film of grimy chalk lining his teeth. Arthur was driving to the office and knew that the six people who passed him would assume that was where he was heading. He'd always been perceived as a worker and he was wearing an ironed shirt. It was amazing what could be sifted for meaning from a vehicle going seventy miles an hour. It was a western specialty. But they would have drawn the wrong conclusion. It was his children who were on their way to their jobs; even his mother was firmly occupied, in the garden killing off weeds that had had the audacity to creep into her soil. He had no one and not much to take care of. He was work-bound for the sole purpose of sleeping. The sky was blue to the point it made your eyes hurt.

He pulled into the lot of Higgins, Crawford, and Echevarria and found it empty of both regular employees and the named partners: Higgins being Dwight Higgins; Crawford being Stanley Crawford, more gecko than man, someone you wanted not in front of a jury but back in the library assembling his meticulous briefs; and Echevarria being Bobby Echevarria, the man you did want in front of a jury, handsome, brassy, Basque, the son of sheep ranchers and compelling to most women. The firm owned an old storefront downtown, next to the Callendar Hotel, a Victorian pile restored to its full, rickety gloom by a pair of former

Californians. The reception area made a stab at preserving the street's historical tone—davenports for clients to sit on, stained glass in a few windows, and a significant newel post stripped to its original oak. But in the annex where the lawyers and paralegals worked, tacked on in the 1970s, no one had even attempted Wyoming authenticity. Out there, it was America as envisioned by Staples, all Xerox buzz and little offices stunned with fluorescence.

Arthur stumped past the waiting room's ferns and beveled mirrors and made his way to the cubicle with a door that Dwight had given him. He knew there was no one else in the place. No lights were on, the scent of coffee was of Friday's, burned and cold. He flicked on the copier as he passed. It came alive like an electronic chicken, all anxious whirs and beeps. He liked to hear it as he was drifting off.

Arthur booted up his computer and knew there'd be e-mail waiting from Dwight, who sent messages with maniacal energy all weekend, but he wasn't going to read them now. The machine's subtle hum had proved to deepen his sleep. He'd discovered the potential of his office as bedroom very early on in the summer. One Saturday he'd been in poring over four different topo maps to figure out where the boundaries of a ranch met those of Cloud Peak Methane's western parcel, when fatigue like a warm cloud enveloped him. He put his head down and woke two hours later, his cheek creased from the edge of the desk but otherwise clearheaded and relaxed, though the furrow in his face looked, in the men's room mirror, like the remnant of a knife fight. Much the same thing happened the next Saturday, although this time he slept with his face on a jacket, and he admitted to himself he now went to the office on weekends primarily to nap. His body was almost trained and he could feel the drowsiness descend the moment he slipped his key into the front door.

He was having trouble sleeping at Lucy's. He didn't know if it was the narrow bed or the heat that lined the low eaves of the attic like invisible fur. It had gotten worse since the episode with the horse. His cheekbone had stung for two days afterward. His mother had apologized but only, he knew, for her loss of composure and not for what the smack had meant. Which was, wake up. Shake yourself alive. You must not be weak.

So his vigilance increased each evening, as if his family needed him patrolling to keep them safe. He became especially conscious of the radical aliveness of the night: the creaks and coughs of birds and animals, wind and horses, the whole high prairie participating in a wild, dark chorus. The house itself sang with noise—stairs, banging window sashes. He grew alert to the patterns of the others—his restless mother, up and down at times in search of books or a bulb if the one in her reading lamp blew. Cam also wandered, mostly in and out of the barn. Not to smoke, Arthur ascertained, both with direct questions and frank sniffing of Cam's clothes. "I just like the hayloft," Cam said when asked. "I sleep better there. It smells good." There seemed no harm in it, and he did seem calm if flecked everywhere with golden lengths of straw. But having Cam in the barn made it inexplicably harder for Arthur to rest well, as if his attention had to draw a larger circle that thinned and threatened to break as it gained in circumference.

He thought doggedly about the children. Cam had developed some kind of relationship with Mac Barlow's daughter, a girl shadowed with tattoos. His son didn't speak much about her but seemed if not happy then pleasantly distracted. Lighter in spirit, less cloistered from the world. Not squinting angrily at the sun quite as much as he usually did in Wyoming. Celia was quiet, too, but also seemed to like her job and being near Lucy, whom she was coming to resemble. Tall women with serious faces.

In some ways the gamble seemed to be working. Lucy had folded them into her routine, a structure that provided firm direction for the day. Arthur allowed himself to think he might have made the right choice, but this reassuring possibility did not provide rest.

The problem was the tick of anger still crackling through his body. Given the slightest opening, it seized the opportunity to flare through him. Once settled in Callendar, he began to realize the extent of the interior damage Laura had wrought. Twisting on his bed in the low heat, he felt that he carried a bombed house inside himself, a ruin that his bones and muscle, still intact, hid from the view of others.

But here at the office, something grew numb. He did his work with rote competence. He fenced off his family at the very edge of thought. He displayed no pictures of them. The only decoration was a framed map of Wyoming and a print, matted in blue, of sailboats. Yet the room's sterile blandness was oddly tonic. He was nothing more than a matrix of cells equipped with some knowledge of the law. He felt without character, like the office itself, and once he was emptied of himself, he could rest. This suspension from himself was quite comfortable. He was more than content to slide past his history for a few hours, awaken, and have forgotten not only exactly where but who he was. He created this ritual of weekend sleep, it seemed, to experience those six floating seconds just after he woke up, when he had no memory of what had happened to him.

People rarely came to work on weekends. Not that they didn't push themselves hard Monday through Friday, but they filled their Saturdays and Sundays with Wyoming life—fishing, family, church. Now and then a big case would pull everyone in around the conference table on a Friday night, but all the lawyers and most of the paralegals had computers at home. Callendar was connected. Along with particles of gold, coal, gas, and diamond, a web of underground cables swam below the surface of the earth, all of it claimed, even when you couldn't see it.

He had just put his head on the desk when he heard a door open. The lights in the main office flicked on. The intruder also activated the air-conditioning. He peered out and saw Carly Anderson, a paralegal, twenty-three, bound, she hoped, to Laramie for law school. She was taking the LSATs in a few weeks and had been querying the attorneys for hints. Arthur hadn't been helpful, she pouted. But they'd reorganized the entire exam since his day; his advice would be out of date. He envied her the newness of her aspirations.

"Yoo-hoo? Anyone here?" she called, and he answered rather than be caught hiding out. Carly came to perch at the threshold of his office. She was in, she said, to finish up on that Wind River Indian case. Carly was blond, with deep curves, and she looked more like a volleyball player than a lawyer. She smiled a lot as she tugged at her hair, which she'd made artfully casual, and he suddenly saw himself from her perspective: the tragic widower, local boy turned New Yorker returning with the ragged remnant of his family. "Aren't you going to make some coffee?" she asked.

"Mine's the worst west or east of the Rockies," Arthur said. "At least that's what my kids say." The thought of sleep evaporated. He followed her to the kitchenette. As he filled the pot, veiled with the oily skin of dozens of gallons of coffee, he felt alert. The coffee brewed quickly. He poured her a cup and added cream and sugar as she asked.

She took a sip and grimaced. "You're right, Arthur. This is terrible," she said and put the mug down. "But you've got some competition at TJ's." TJ's was the truck stop attached to JT's Lube and Filter, where Arthur's grandfather had worked after leaving coal mining. No one went to the garage anymore, but the truck stop, run by sons of the mechanic, was always crowded. Carly probably wouldn't know about JT's. Arthur reached to scratch the scar on the back of his head and calculated that he was exactly twice her age.

It didn't take much. In retrospect, it seemed inevitable, as most disasters did. At first, she tasted of his bad coffee, then of her own sweet, Crest-flavored mouth. She admitted she knew he was in the office, that she'd spotted his truck here one Saturday and found him conked out. "You don't snore, but you sure are a deep sleeper."

He kissed her again, hard, to keep her from saying anything. He kissed her to obliterate her mistaken impressions of him and make her realize that he was nothing but skin and muscle and hair; she should expect nothing more.

He led her to his office. "Arthur, baby, don't you want to go to a hotel?" He shook his head no, his voice too thick for talking. If they had sex here in this bewitched place he wouldn't remember a thing about it, and that was the entire point.

He unbuttoned her flimsy shirt and eased off her shorts. She had long, muscled legs and toenails painted bubblegum pink. She was giggling. The air conditioner rattled, the computer gave off its faint vibration of electric potential. He hadn't touched a woman other than Laura since 1983, and in twenty-one years of faithfulness and attention he had scarcely thought about what it would be like. Lately, shock, grief, and rage had been quite effective at tamping down desire. It was better like this, he thought, cupping Carly's thighs. Not to have even thought about it, to have her arrive like this, so bountifully.

This girl was all pink, pink skin. He had never seen so much skin. Carly proved vibrant enough, different enough, to wipe clean any trace of his wife, or maybe that was simply how it was with bodies. Each was so distinctive, it occupied all your immediate attention. Good sex had no room for flashbacks.

She was slippery, she was clean, she came equipped with a condom. Girls these days. He had to slow down; it had been so long. He pinned her against the wall and in her effort to keep herself upright, she pulled down the Wyoming map. Why, Arthur thought, hadn't it been the goddamn sailboats? But he didn't want her on the featureless wall, Wyoming at a slant on the ground near his feet. He liked her with her ass spreading on the imitation wooden grain of the desk. Her eyes were closed and her fingers moved like a cat's paws on his back. "Open your eyes," he told her, "and quit that with your nails. You'll scratch me." She obeyed instantly. The keyboard came crashing off the desk and swung into his knee. When they were done, she lay with the monitor pressing into her side at an uncomfortable angle. She was breathing hard, her eyes shut again. "That was amazing, baby," she said, breasts pressed close to his chest.

He made no answer. He was fighting an overpowering need to fall deeply and instantly asleep, no matter if the keyboard dented his calf or if he crushed Carly beneath him.

"I just couldn't stop coming." This was out of some magazine. No one had told her she should never talk like that. And she wasn't going to let up.

"You did not, Carly," he said, lifting himself off her and searching in the well of the desk for his pants. He tossed her his T-shirt to daub herself off with, then zipped himself up and buckled his belt. He watched her mop the damp channel between her breasts and he tied a knot in the condom. This was a new situation, too: where to put a used condom? He and Laura had never used them. "Don't tell me lies," he told her quietly and picked up the map, which now had a crack flying across its glass.

She sat up slowly and he could see questions gathering around her. He'd almost forgotten this part of sex, the girls asking about the next time or what it all meant. He replaced the keyboard and shut the computer down. It pulled all its static energy to a central white point at the middle of the screen and clicked to general blankness. "Don't ask me anything," he told her. "If I said something now I couldn't mean it."

She was buttoning her shirt slowly. He left her with a kiss on her temple and her shorts draped over her firm, round thighs. She seemed to be staring at the sailboats. He threw the condom in a trash can in the parking lot. He took the ride home slowly. Meadowlarks were dashing toward his windshield with apparent suicidal intent. Ground squirrels equaled their desperation with ill-timed leaps across the red highway. He should have cared about the emptiness on Carly's face as he left. He should have worried about the consequences of this encounter with a very young person at the law firm that had taken him on out of kindness for his widower state. He did not. "I do not," he said aloud. He felt nothing, in fact, except for an animal relaxation, a deep bodily release free of anything to do with his mind, his past, his future. It reminded him of his old sexual self, the one that fucked and ran as he'd done before he met Laura. He forced himself not to think of her lean profile, her wide, sweet mouth. They had been sufficient unto each other. Would she be the only person with whom that kind of continence was possible? He wanted to smoke but had no cigarettes. An object with the soft density of something alive bounced off his tire rim. A brief glimpse of brown fur, a tail, a paw. A raccoon on the prowl at the wrong time of day. His first large mammal of the summer. It was still living, he saw in the rearview mirror, and limping slowly toward an irrigation ditch.

If he'd had a gun, he would have killed it. Even the thought of having a gun made him feel oddly calm; it was an idea he could have now that Laura, entirely opposed to firearms, was dead. Carly was a girl he could have now that Laura was dead, too. He wished he felt more disloyal: to Laura, his children, his mother, to what he had grown used to thinking of as himself. Instead, he drove faster down the highway. He passed no one. The sky had burned to white. The windows were all down and the seats, his wrists, and face were growing speckled with a fine layer of dust, sparkling, no doubt, with minerals someone would one day want to pull from the earth.

Dwight and his wife, Denise, and their three huge German shepherds roamed around in an outsize house built into the foothills. It was like a log cabin that had clearly been doping, with a lawn the size of a cornfield and two stories' worth of antlers and Navajo blankets. "It's a fucking parody of itself," Dwight liked to say cheerfully. Though the whole family was invited, Lucy had claimed a need to do chores and Cam had said vaguely that he had a date. But Celia had been coaxed into coming by the promise of playing with the shepherds. The dogs bounded up silently, with tails full as foxes'. Celia bent to gather the animals in her arms and Arthur leaned in to kiss Denise and give her a bowl of what he suspected was inedible potato salad, which Celia had made and put into one of Lucy's best bowls. This was sure to irritate his mother, who was getting territorial about small things. If they were going to stay through the fall, he should start looking for a place to live in town, convenient to the high school.

It was a late Saturday afternoon, a week since Arthur had had sex with Carly on his laminate-topped desk. She had e-mailed and left notes and worn short skirts all week. He was dealing with it badly: not just avoiding her but ignoring her entirely. She was sure to be here tonight; it was Dwight's turn to host the barbecue that rotated among the three partners throughout the summer. Of the three, he was the most generous with alcohol. You would have thought Bobby's parties would be the most popular, but his wife didn't drink and their parties were flat. Stanley grilled the best short ribs, but everyone looked forward to

Dwight's gatherings because things seemed to happen at them that oiled office gossip for weeks.

Denise took the bowl and said, "Just what we needed. No one brought any." Unlike Dwight, she was tall and well built. She actually suited the proportions of the house. The dogs followed her everywhere. She was easy to find, with her great sweep of blond hair and the flurry of fur by her knees. Arthur noted that looking at women, even married ones, even one married to his boss, was a newly activated facet of his character.

Dwight saw Arthur watching and said, "Years before Denise or I got married, I was a judge at a county beauty pageant, and I picked Denise to win for the express reason of being able to ask her out. She refused the crown, saying the other girl was better-looking and had worked harder at her baton twirling. And she still wouldn't go out with me. Said I didn't respect her mind. Took me fifteen years to convince her." He laughed and slapped Arthur hard on the shoulder. "Go get yourself a drink."

Arthur fetched a beer at the bar and stood on Dwight's baronial grass and looked at the crowd around him. Twenty-five years ago, Dwight had been living with his first wife on her family's ranch, the Lazy Z. They had tried to breed sheep from Wales and then llamas from Argentina. The ranch and the marriage failed at about the same time, a familiar Callendar duet. The wife was long gone. But Dwight had busily kept himself afloat, going to law school, building his practice, bouncing around town. He was very good, Arthur thought, very thorough. His finest invention had been of himself as civic leader. A man who couldn't sell a llama, but people barely remembered that. In less than a generation Dwight had gone from that scruffy ranch and that scruffy wife—Martha? Ruth? a bare-boned, biblical name—to this: the spectacular Denise, the dogs, the trucks, and water abundant enough to keep the lawn its unnerving shade of green.

The beer was gone. Arthur got another kind: Moose Drool, from Montana. Microbrewed, probably by a bunch of Yale graduates who now wore pointy-toed boots. It tasted like its name and he stopped drinking after two sips. He thought about the changes not just in Dwight's circumstances but in Wyoming's shifting landscape. How directly was Dwight responsible for the surge of acquisition he'd clearly experienced? You didn't see houses like this twenty years ago in Callendar, and now that was all you saw, with more and more men like Dwight, doughy and smart, who understood that ranches and agriculture were untenable in the long term, but you could make a lot of money off those who still tried to stay tied to the land. These men kept horses for riding on weekends. They owned large guns they used in small, violent episodes before retreating to their steroidal houses and fireplaces made of boulders. Men who mixed law with real estate, Wyoming's version of the Molotov cocktail.

If he stayed, Arthur would become one of them. Not so big-hatted. There wouldn't be so much bronze on the shelves. He was Lucy's son, after all, and Laura's husband. If he and his children stayed, they would probably buy one of the old bungalows near the train station and return it, as the real estate ads had it, to its "authentic past." Taken literally, that would mean installing a Chinese railroad man and his twelve kids and a bath in the kitchen, not to mention the pigs. He might become a partner of Dwight's, talk a great deal about football, and tag along on hunting parties. Marry again.

An uneasy feeling that he was floating slightly above the ground started to hum through him. At first he thought the sensation was like one he'd had at parties with his New York colleagues, the impression that those around him were swimming inside a current of talk and connection in which he could only tangentially participate. Those tight eastern laughs, the heavy cotton of their shirts, their polish. It didn't matter that he was the best lawyer among them. He would never have their ease in steering conversation, their relaxation in the flow of talk about golf and tennis. They so rarely got snagged.

In truth, he'd had the same feeling at most parties. Out here, he'd been too cerebral. Back there, New Yorkers would say, "Arthur's from Wyoming," as if he were an Inuit from the Arctic Circle. And in Callendar, people mistrusted the fact he had enough money for Manhattan and a wife delicate enough to require constant sunscreen. A wife who disapproved of guns, a difficult woman.

He glanced around and saw that Celia was still playing with the dogs, and thankfully Carly wasn't in sight. Denise had put out Celia's potato salad, but no one had helped themselves. He went inside the house. In Denise's kitchen, he stood in front of the picture window and looked out at the thronged lawn. The associates were getting very drunk. They'd just won a big case that involved getting an oil company in Casper off the hook for a spill at one of its pumping stations. They were very pleased with themselves, though it seemed to Arthur they'd had an unseemly amount of help from Stanley Crawford. They'd even managed to get the environmental impact statement partially amended, a coup in financial if not ecological terms. Depending on the final net for the firm, one or the other of them might be elevated to partner for the success. Their hats were tipped far back on their heads. Their cheeks were red with sweat and their laughter the laughter of men who have just gotten laid. Their backs were to the spreading blanket of light and highway and beyond it, the twilight gray of Callendar Valley and the desert.

Arthur focused on the window that framed the partygoers. The glass was decorated with black stickers in the shape of crows and meadowlarks to prevent live ones from trying to sail through the glass. "Dwight said we had to have them up. He gets sentimental when he finds the little songbirds with their necks broken." It was Denise. She brought with her, as she opened the door, the tang of barbecue smoke and the high sizzle of meat. The largest of the dogs was at her side. Denise and her pet were so well brushed they looked related. A pale mound of Celia's salad stood untouched on the plate she was holding.

"Is it as bad as it looks?" Arthur asked. He had known Denise since they were children. She was one year older than he was and had been an epic cheerleader. But he was at boarding school during those years and had missed her thrilling jumps.

"She's learning," Denise said. "It's nice she tried." She put the plate on the counter and sat down on the barstool in what Arthur supposed would be called the breakfast nook and stared at her nails.

"You going to stay, Arthur? Dwight says the secretaries are betting six to one you'll be gone by September. Unless, of course, you find a girl out here." She still wasn't looking at him. If he remembered correctly, she had had an early marriage that ended with a moderate bang and had settled down with Dwight some ten years later. Arthur wondered what she had done with those ten single years, if she'd had fun. He envied her that long, untethered span.

"So the Broncos inspire more confidence than I do these days?" he said. He was still eyeing people on the lawn. Now he could see Carly among the associates, though he knew she was flaunting her pinkness for his benefit, hoping he was somewhere watching her. "If I knew, Denise, I'd tell you. We just have to see how it goes. The kids are doing fine. We sure appreciate all your and Dwight's support."

Denise snorted. It startled Arthur. This was not a noise you heard that often from women in New York. It was refreshing and, surprisingly, did nothing to detract from Denise's brown-gold attractiveness. Her nails were awfully long. "Your kids are pretty remarkable, Arthur, though you'd better watch Cam with Amber Barlow. Mac will eventually find something to object to and there's some Neanderthal boyfriend of hers waiting in the wings. Your little girl needs to eat more, too, and get a haircut."

"You getting out much, Denise? I thought grooming those dogs would take all day. Apparently not. Apparently not so much that you can't find time to scrounge gossip at Albertsons." It amazed him how easy it was to talk back to her and also how much she knew and saw and felt comfortable telling him about. It was equally astonishing that she so easily demolished his neat little package of sentiment.

Denise smiled. "Just letting you know, Arthur. You also need to find a graceful way to inform Carly Anderson you're not interested. Dwight's worried about how it will affect her LSATs."

Arthur stiffened. "Oh really? Carly Anderson seems to be doing just fine." He tilted his barely touched beer toward the lawn. The sky was starting to turn the hungry blue of late summer twilight and the torches on the patio had been lit. Inside the ragged circle of fire stood Carly and the associates. She looked like a blend of lifeguard and Greek nymph in disarray. Her blouse had slid off one shoulder to reveal a pale, sturdy bra strap.

He couldn't see Celia anywhere and let himself hope she was playing with the other two shepherds. Or maybe chatting with Dwight, who had understood within seconds of meeting Celia how to talk to her. "Do you know that Sheridan is sitting on one of the deepest reverse-angle faults west of the Mississippi?" he had asked her. Arthur hoped that his daughter and employer were on the other side of the pool discussing unstable geology.

Denise came to stand next to him. The dog clicked its way over. Arthur listened to its steady panting, felt its warm breath on his ankle. "This dog cost five thousand dollars," she said, as if still marveling that she or Dwight had so much money to spend on a mere pet. It would have been different if it had been a bull or a flock of sheep, but the dog was purely ornamental. "Isn't he beautiful? His name is Thor." She leaned into Arthur and kissed him, her hair sweeping across his cheek in a honey-colored veil.

It is odd about kisses that they tell you instantly what you want or don't want. Arthur returned Denise's kiss with quick, deep pleasure. But then he pulled back and said, "Ah, shit. No, no, no, Denise. Can't do that. Can't go there." It was better, wasn't it, at least to seem to resist? Wouldn't that be what a normal person would do? Perhaps he was no longer what would pass as a normal person; it might have had something to do with Laura, but now she was nowhere to be found. All he could think of was Denise and what he really desired, which was to pull her clothes off that instant and make love to her on that clean, hard floor.

Denise leaned back. Thor had settled himself on the tiles at her feet. "That's what they all say," she said. She went to the refrigerator. A wedge of white light caught her as she opened the door. She offered him another beer, which he refused. "Dwight needs you, Arthur."

She had a dizzying ability, this woman, to switch conversational directions. She would not, Arthur felt sure, make kittenish commentary after sex. Denise went on. "Stanley's going to retire in the next couple of years and Dwight wants someone around who can write briefs as good as Stan's. He'd make you partner pretty fast." There'd be the bar to pass, the money wouldn't be great, but he was doing well, Dwight was, and could make it an interesting package. Some of the work would be tricky. He'd have to fight neighbors sometimes; coalbed methane was Dwight's first food group, she said. But he'd be near his mother, of course, and the kids wouldn't have to be back in that city. It might be good for his family.

Most of the notes Arthur received after Laura died had done nothing to console, but Denise had written one of the only letters that even approximated the right thing. There were no words for how awful it was to lose your wife, she wrote, and anyone who said they were sorry should be hanged. They were basically saying they were glad it hadn't happened to them. Suicide was often hard to see coming and the one thing she hoped was that Arthur would not blame himself. She knew it was almost impossible not to, but it was Laura who had made her choice, sad as it was. Reading that letter, Arthur had been aware that she knew what she was talking about. Her father had killed himself, with a shotgun in his pickup, on the first warm day in the spring of 1973.

"Why did your dad do it?" Arthur asked now. He could barely see Denise. They had not turned on the lights and were sitting there in the kitchen. Partly they stayed in the dark because they didn't want anyone to see their bodies so close together. Partly they both seemed to think it was more beautiful that way. She picked up his hand. The oddness of his question seemed not to perturb her. Given her height, her fingers were broad and small.

"Some people said it was money. He owed J.T. Booth alone five hundred bucks and God knows how much to everyone else. He bet too much on rodeo and football. My mother said it was booze." Her voice sounded tired. The sounds of the party were growing more raucous.

Carly was dancing now at the center of her fiery circle, her hips echoing the oval that surrounded her. She is going to be lucky not to get gangbanged tonight, Arthur thought, but felt no urge to save her from her fate—another piece of his character he did not recognize. Helping women in jeopardy had been one of his strengths, even compulsions. He still could not see Celia, and that began to worry him. He needed to go. At least, he thought, my children still move me. But Denise's thumb stroked his with gentle pressure. It was so calming to be touched that simply and consistently.

"What do you think?" he asked her.

"Did you know my father was the only quarterback from Callendar High to take his team to state finals three years in a row and to win twice?" Arthur nodded. It was a significant local accomplishment. Billy Graves had been huge and handsome and even in his mechanic's uniform, which was more grease than cloth, he had been a riveting figure. Denise didn't say any more. Arthur knew what she meant. Her father had gone from golden promise to the underbelly of Chevy trucks, and this loss of status had happened within view of everyone he'd known his entire life.

"And Laura?" Denise said, removing her hand from Arthur's. She could ask him that. Denise had lived through the years after a suicide and emerged as someone distinctly herself. She had survived a bad first marriage and gone on to make her next one highly lucrative. She had her dogs, her hair, and some arrangement with herself about Dwight. She was an interesting woman and she had the prettiest mouth. What could he say? That Laura had never been fully with him, that some part of her was caught in the grip of persistent pain that finally wore her out? That she had promised she would never leave and then had broken the contract in the most absolute way?

Then he remembered Denise's letter. However great her despair, his wife had made a dry, hard choice to get herself to the ledge and to launch herself off. She had wanted that. She sat there, she pushed herself free, she fell. What he really wanted to say—that he was outraged at being forced to live without her, that her death had helped him discover noxious elements of his character that would need to be studied if understood—was not yet something he could confess, even to Denise. He was going to have to mine himself for information. He was too old for this, and too tired.

Light flooded the room then and Denise and Arthur, their

heads close together, close enough to feel each other's breath, sprang apart. It was Celia. Denise is right, Arthur thought, she's too thin and she needs a haircut. He couldn't believe he hadn't noticed. Thor bounded over to her for another round of boisterous affection, but she turned and slammed out of the kitchen.

On the ride back from the party, Celia wouldn't talk. He had raced after his daughter, calling her name; she had merely stalked ahead. He found her by the truck, shining there in the moonlight. "Don't say anything, Dad, just don't say a word."

That morning, Arthur had dropped Celia off a little early at the ranch so she could spend the day sweeping, washing dishes, and mooning after Carson, the skinny cowboy who was not giving her the time of day. To be fair, he also knew that "mooning" was too strong a word for how Celia was behaving. She was too self-possessed. She wasn't giddy. But she arranged herself to be near him, and the desire for proximity often expressed the first layer of longing. She had waved to her father and then headed straight to the corral to position herself among the wranglers spraddled along the bench, long-legged, hats cocked, waiting for the first of the dudes to be saddled up. What was there to say about her hopeless yearning or his own? "It's not what it looks like." But it was exactly what it looked like. "You will understand more when you're older." For Celia, that would have been insulting.

During the long trip back she sat hunched in her seat and he drove with slow, excessive care. Ray Fontaine made a point of being visible on Saturday nights. It had been a bad enough evening without having Ray loom over them with his FBI-big flashlight.

At Lucy's, Celia slammed out of the truck and stomped up the stairs. Cam wasn't due home until midnight, but Lucy was in the living room polishing brass candlesticks. The air smelled of the flatly metallic paste she used. "A rousing success?" Her hands were moving beneath a worn dishcloth.

He sat opposite his mother in the soft green chair that his father had always used. "She caught me with Denise Higgins in the kitchen," he said.

Lucy said only, "What?" and her fingers stilled in their task. Small yellow eyes of brass winked through the gray skin of the polish.

Arthur watched the dog at its licking, and remembered what his mother had said when he won his only ribbon ever at the rodeo. Lucy had wanted to leave right away. She was proud that he had had a triumph, but she was through for the day. She had what she called complicated feelings about rodeo. Arthur had felt the command in her voice and her assumption that he would follow. But he said, in a tone he scarcely recognized, "No, I'm staying here. See you later, Mom."

"What?" Lucy had said, not angry yet, just surprised. "Suit yourself," she added and turned, her braid whipping out behind her. Lucas Howard, one of the timers for the event, said he had never seen anyone stand up to Lucy King before and the last thing he expected was to see it from an eight-year-old boy. Arthur had felt guilt and enjoyment mixed in one: guilt at having been rude to his mother, exhilaration at having proved himself. There was no exhilaration now.

Lucy put down the candlestick. Upstairs, Celia was slamming around. First to her room, then to the bath, where she turned on the tap with a sharp squeal, then flouncing back down the hall and closing her door with a thud just short of the slam that would have brought a reprimand.

"Well, that was foolish of you. From several perspectives." Lucy fiddled with her braid. The dog whimpered in its sleep. "Arthur," his mother asked, "do you want to stay here? Is this going well?"

The floorboards above them settled. "I thought it was. I want it to," he told her. He thought he meant it. He could not have said what he meant exactly by "going well." None of them had died, had they? No one had even gotten sick and he'd been the only one to hurt himself all summer. Wasn't that enough for now?

His mother went back to rubbing at the candlestick and said, "Then you'd better start trying harder." She picked up the brass and stood. "Janet told me last year that Denise Higgins has slept with at least three of the associates at that firm." She said this without apparent judgment. He knew she was fairly embarrassed about her own long-standing relationship, if that was what it was, with Ray Fontaine. She was merely advising him to be careful. Still, Arthur was surprised. He'd heard no gossip about Denise or Dwight among his colleagues. He'd seen no indication of the disrespect that clings to a cuckold.

He knew his mother was right to question him and he told himself testily to shape up. This self-admonishing voice had always worked before, steered him back to his studies, his work, to whatever he needed to pay attention to. Yet he felt rising within him the same floating sensation he'd had at the party. What he had thought was insecurity was transforming into a strange feeling of liberation. He wasn't happy, yet he felt, oddly, unaccountably, free.

Lucy finished the polishing and went to bed. She seemed worn out, leaner. She didn't seem inclined to confide and Arthur knew better than to press. He turned off the lights and leaned into the sofa. The house rang with its nighttime sounds. He was, as always this summer, strung somewhere between exhaustion and sleeplessness. He looked at the chair where his father had always sat. He rarely thought of him, and it was only thanks to the photographs Lucy had around the house that he remembered Sean's face. Tonight he could imagine him in the chair, in the same dim lamplight Lucy had used for polishing the candlesticks: Sean holding a bridle whose noseband needed repair. His hands were quick with the sharp jackknife and brown worms of pared skin lay on the toes of his boots as he worked with silent efficiency. More than that, thought Arthur—he worked with pleasure. He loved the tasks of winter, the repair of the tack, the assessment of rope, the building of fires, as much as he loved the harsh springs, the calving, the pulling of animals through bog. Love was not a word he would have used. That's what Laura would have said. And maybe that was why Arthur didn't miss his father, not now at least. The ache left by his absence had become a low, dark note that had resonated for a time, then gradually faded out. Arthur did not want his son to have such dampened feelings about him. He would wait up for Cam.

But when he woke, all balled up on the sofa, it was already morning and the first frost of late summer had crept in. He found Cam in the kitchen. His son's hair was studded with bits of straw that looked like tiny flames in the sharp morning light. His breath made a cone of steam. Against all expectation and in a direct snubbing of the forecast, temperatures had plummeted and the grass, garden, and hills were crusted with cold silver lace. Cam looked at his father and poured water into the coffeemaker. "Late night, Dad?" he asked.

Arthur remembered a morning in New York. Cam was three and sitting in his bed, his arms around a stuffed dog he hauled with him everywhere, crying and crying, saying something was coming to get him. The hissing radiator shook with the pressure of the steam rising from the boiler room eleven stories below. It was the first cold day of the fall and the heat had just been turned on. He had held his child and comforted him, telling him that the heat was here to soothe.

He wanted nothing more than to go to his son and apologize for not being awake when he came in. He even tried to cough out a few words about the advisability of dating Mac Barlow's daughter. But Cam just looked at him and asked if he had a headache. Absorbed in preventing his father from getting near the coffeemaker, Cam did not notice that Arthur needed to hold the table to keep his hands from shaking.

The cold that had visited the valley was gone, and in its wake arrived days cut of blue and gold. Gold for the strips of wheat and the rounds of hay, the first tinting of the aspens from their summer color to fall. Blue only for the sky, but that was enough: it was miles wide and clouds had been banished as if they were ne'er-do-wells that ought to seek employment elsewhere. Something about the weather sharpened Arthur and the floating feeling had, to his relief, vanished for the time being.

With his solidity regained, he spoke to Celia on one of their drives to the C Bar C. She was stiff-armed and stone-faced as they wound down the driveway, her body pulled entirely to her side of the cab. She had turned on the sole radio station not wreathed in static. A clear statement of contempt: it played only the worst possible contemporary country, which she loathed.

He saw that she had readied herself for lies and equivocations, but Arthur decided to go ahead anyway. "Honey, I am sorry for what you saw the other night." Celia said nothing, just kept glaring at the windshield. "I know I shouldn't have let it happen." As he spoke, he felt the first cut of shame the experience had brought him.

Celia's eyebrows flickered upward at this. That was an understatement, she managed to suggest. He saw her start to speak, then quell herself, then start again in spite of it all. "She's married, Dad, to Mr. Higgins." Moral outrage. The province of the young, who need certainty and are inexperienced with compromise. Unlawyerly in their disregard for nuance and exception. Yet in their clarity, they're often right.

"That's true," he told her. "It's wrong. It shouldn't have happened. And there are no excuses. It won't happen again." He waited to make the turn onto the highway. Three horse trailers and a semi left fans of dust in their wake. As he eased into the pale cloud, he watched her face.

"Lucy told me the other day that she and Mr. Fontaine were . . ." Lucy had probably used the blunt word "lovers," but this was too much to say to her father.

"Involved," Arthur supplied, with his attorney's instinct for euphemism.

Celia nodded. "She said she couldn't help it. It was just something that happened between adults sometimes. She said she thought you and Mrs. Higgins had probably always liked each other." She placed a slight but unmistakable emphasis on the "Mrs." Another flurry of emotion passed across his daughter's face. "Just be careful, Dad," she said, as if she were the parent advising the child on his first tentative steps toward dating, toward love.

He promised he would be, not exactly sure what he was giving his word to, except for the general agreement not to hurt her or Cam or even, surprisingly, himself.

"You're lonely," she said and turned down the radio. Even at a low volume, you could hear the country music with its profusion of minor keys and honeyed accents.

Arthur said nothing. Only because it had been named, he suddenly felt as lonely as he had ever been since Laura died. It was a terrible thing to be noticed so attentively.

To get his voice back to normal, to sound again like the parent he wanted to be, he asked her if she would like to get a haircut. "Do I need one?" she asked, alarmed, her hands flying to her head.

"No, no," he assured her. "Just if you think you'd like one. It might be a good idea. I've got to get one, too."

The next day, he took her to the best place in town. She emerged with inches off the ends and layers gleaming with good shampoo and what Celia proudly called "product." As she emerged from the salon in the brilliant afternoon light, Arthur did not recognize his daughter for a second. She was that delighted with herself. She thanked him for the cut and said shyly that the stylist had suggested she get contacts. Could they stop on the way back to make an appointment at the optometrist? Within a week she was squinting out at the world without the shield of her large, round glasses.

That weekend he took his children to Yellowstone. The trip had the double benefit of providing the satisfying distractions of watching large wild animals and letting him avoid another barbecue. It also made him feel soberly, appropriately paternal. They were exploring the wonders of the natural world.

He still had Carly to deal with, however, and he apologized to her on Monday morning. He said he hadn't been as kind to her as he should have been. Her eyebrows lifted much as Celia's had, but Arthur plowed ahead even so and told her that she should be with someone her own age. He even said, wincing slightly, that she had her whole life in front of her. She sniffled a little, but when Arthur was at the optometrist the next week with Celia, he glimpsed Carly in the parking lot with Mike Taggart, one of the associates for whom she'd gyrated at the barbecue. Even Dwight became more confiding than usual, taking Arthur to long, steak-centered lunches in which he discussed what he called his vision for the firm.

The only ones still looking at him askance were Lucy and her dog. "It's not that I'm judging you, Arthur," his mother said one night. "God knows, you could judge me from here to Seattle and back, and you'd be right every step of the way. I just don't like people laboring under illusions about themselves." She went out back to pull the last of the beans up from the garden. The frost had nipped her vegetables a little early, though she had salvaged an admirable amount for canning.

Yet he was almost fine, and sleeping better, until the Sunday that Celia needed to go the C Bar C for a special last-of-the-season party. "Everyone's going to be there," she said, her spiffy new haircut sailing out from her shoulders, her eyes screwed up against the light. He had gotten her a pair of sunglasses, but they kept falling off her steep nose. "Everyone" meant Carson, Arthur knew. Still, he drove her to the ranch and said he'd go do some errands or work and come and get her a few hours later. Instead, once he'd dropped his daughter off, he realized he could drive right by Dwight and Denise's and pick up the serving dish for Celia's terrible potato salad. As he had foreseen, Lucy had been irritated by Celia's choice of a bowl and was pestering for its return. He forced himself to hope that Dwight would be there and not Denise, though of course when he saw that Dwight's Tahoe was not in the driveway, he could not contain the surge of anxious pleasure that ran through his body.

Thor, Odin, and Frigga barked as you would bark, too, if you were a Norse god trapped in a dog's body. It wasn't hard to imagine the big house as Valhalla. Denise could have passed for a goddess, if goddesses wore jeans and bedroom slippers.

She stood at the threshold and looked at him. "I've got a cold," she said. "I'll go get the bowl." He saw her face through the screen, a haze of mesh cut into thousands of tiny squares, blurring her strong bones, emphasizing her uncertainty.

Then she opened the door and walked into the sunlight. The dogs came tumbling out with her and the lower half of her body was a swirl of tawny fur and the clicking of sharp nails on concrete. Her nose was red and she was indeed holding a Kleenex, but she might just as easily have been crying. She made no move to get the bowl. "Come in, Arthur," with a tone he could recognize for what it was, which was resignation.

Dwight was in Denver, she said, locking the door. They made it to the foot of the stairs before Arthur took off Denise's shirt and bra to reveal full, soft breasts. They had been legendary at the Callendar Grammar School. But he just wanted to touch, feel, and taste her exactly as she was now, not as she had been. "Oh, God, Arthur, I am just too old for this." One of the Navajo rugs slid out from under them.

Upstairs, Denise also had condoms. He remembered what Lucy had told him about Denise's sexual forays, but the condoms were Dwight's, Denise said, for use on his trips to Denver and Cheyenne. Arthur was silent in the middle of the huge bed, a symphony of white sheets and feather pillows, clouds assuming earthly form.

Denise had been leaning on his chest, but she rolled over onto her side. "You didn't know that about Dwight?"

"No idea," Arthur said, turning to face her. "Bobby talks about women all the time, and even Stanley the old lizard mentions them more than Dwight does." He thought about Dwight at restaurants, smiling tolerantly at jokes about the waitresses' tits and asses, but never participating. This was a feature of the lawyer's life that was independent of geography: an underlying ability to see women as slightly inferior, better suited to certain functions than to others, and the blonder the better, even if you did have to hire them as associates. Arthur considered himself lucky to have had Lucy as a mother, which had made it mostly impossible to see women as anything but formidable. Even Laura's frailties were impressive. So he and Dwight were the only two men who never engaged in the lawyers' banter about girls, and Arthur had assumed that Dwight's relative restraint came from the depth of his devotion to Denise.

"That fucker," Denise said calmly, "has been unfaithful to me since the second week we were married. He'd been getting it on with the cleaning lady at the firm and I caught them at it on a Saturday in the supply closet."

Arthur didn't reply at first. The office was apparently a little less sexually sterile than he had thought, given what he and

Dwight, at the very least, were up to there on those quiet week-ends. He propped himself on his elbow. "Charlene?" he said at last, the fact of it finally dawning on him. Charlene was slack-breasted and mousy-haired, but now that he thought about it, sullenly confident, even entitled. If she didn't feel like doing the bathroom, no one could make her do it.

He looked more closely at Denise. When she and Dwight were first married, ten years before, Arthur had been struck with her radiance. She seemed genuinely happy. Laura had said, "She can't believe she got that lucky. He's rich, and in the bargain, she loves him." "How can you know all that?" he had asked. Laura had shrugged and said, "It's obvious." His mother confirmed everything Laura said. "Dwight's a charming man," Lucy added, and again, Laura agreed. "Dwight?" Arthur asked. "Sexy," Laura said. "There's no explaining it."

"There was no sign he was like that before you got married?"

"Not a one," she said. "He pursued me like he might die if we didn't spend the rest of our lives together. He took me on va-cations. He bought me the dogs." She sighed. "He even wrote me poems. Pretty good ones. Did you know Dwight likes poetry?"

Arthur did not. What he wanted to ask even more was how quickly it had taken the couple to reach their apparent compro-mise. And did they still sleep together? Had Denise really made it a habit to poach the lawyers in Dwight's firm? Did Lucy know about this feature of Dwight's personality?

"Is it something he just can't help?" Arthur asked. He thought of Dwight's generally obsessive nature. The barrage of e-mails. The thirst for more clients, then more of them. The need for the largest trucks, the biggest house, the most beauti-ful wife.

Denise sneezed. "God, I feel awful," she said. "Yes, I think that's what it is. He's so ambitious it comes spilling out of him. One woman just isn't enough for him. He would hate this, but he reminds me of Bill Clinton." She blew her nose.

She was so pretty, even with her sadness and her cold. "What are we going to do, Denise?" He pulled the voluminous covers up around her shoulders because she was shivering now.

"Fuck if I know, Arthur," she told him, her teeth chattering. "The thing is, though he can't stop me having, you know, affairs, he's terrified I'm going to fall in love with someone. He'd sniff it out in three seconds." She did not say what would happen then. "I always liked you," she said.

"Same here," he said. "Denise, this could turn out terribly."

She yawned. "That's an understatement. Would you heat up some chicken soup? It's in the fridge."

He pulled on his underwear and shirt. He was, he realized belatedly, still wearing his socks. Clouds were building in the west, where the storms rolled in from the mountains. The temperature was going down again. It could easily turn to snow at the higher elevations. He remembered a late August storm that had come howling down on him and Sean when they'd been out gathering some cows that had strayed into a draw off their own land. The slice of the wind and the abrupt descent and fury of the swirling flakes had been stunning. His father and his father's horse, Roscoe, the one that killed him a year and a half later, turned into a moving statue of crusted ice within minutes. It was one of the few times he hadn't spoiled a moment that required utter physical concentration and precision. He had ridden like a true horseman, perfectly balanced. They had not lost a single heifer. They had not gotten tangled in broken wires, tripped on a stump, or fallen into the creek. No piece of cowboying that they attempted together had ever gone so smoothly.

On his way downstairs, his footsteps muffled on the high pile of the carpet, Arthur was swept with longing for his father—worse, for a man who would have said more than, "Well, sure was cold out there today." Sean had walked away from the shining pride in his son's face, undisguised because so rare, but his father had not noted it. Later that day, the sun had returned and all that was left of the snow were puddles that burned silver in the strange return of the heat.

He found the chicken soup and poured it into a bowl, then searched for the microwave. Another piece of useful machinery that Lucy refused. He set the timer to one minute and thirty seconds and watched the soup spin on the glass turntable. To his horror, grief would not stop rising. Apparently, there was no piece of mourning you were allowed to skip. You could leave out a step, but, ineluctably, it would find you. The sadness expanded from the hollow that Sean had left to the one that Laura had created. He was standing in black socks and a T-shirt and boxers in the kitchen of man he had just cuckolded, and he was crying, filled with the feeling that he was drowning. He had never been much of a swimmer, as his father never failed to tell him.

Arthur felt her before he heard her. Denise stood behind him, wrapped in one of the blankets she had pulled from her bed. It rose above her shoulders like the costume of some alien species on *Star Trek*, where the strange new races have weirdly padded shoulders and high necklines. Her eyes had bags below them and she wheezed. Even so, she looked beautiful. The timer on the microwave sounded, and the rich smell of broth filled the room. She opened her strange robe and folded him close. She was naked below the quilt and sniffling. "Oh, honey," she kept saying. The biggest dog came with her and it looked calmly at him. It was extremely easy to imagine the animal shifting from patient watchfulness to snarling aggression, its ivory teeth around his ankle.

"It's everything," was all he managed to tell her. The dog kept eyeing him.

"I know," she told him.

"I'm lost, Denise," he said, feeling his desire rise, despite it all. Knowing that within minutes they would spread the blanket on the tiles and make love exactly where he had wanted to the first night he kissed her. With the dog watching, although this time the blanket's softness would cushion them. He had had no idea how thin his inner life had become. When you refused to let even the ghosts in, it was torn as easily as gauze. "I miss her so much," he said, stroking Denise's arm.

She brought his fingers to her mouth and kissed them. "At least you know that," she said. "That's a place to start," and she pulled him down to her.

CELIA

That morning, the blinds in Celia's room tapped the sill and made the wooden slats clack. Venetian, she thought—a word propped in her mind next to "palazzo," "gondola," "carnival." Words you didn't much use in Wyoming. Venice with its shimmering canals and elegant decay was as far as you could get from the high desert, mule deer, and trailers that were just plain decaying, nothing artistic about them. Venice was a place her mother admired. It surprised Celia somewhat that she would rather be here than there. All summer at the C Bar C she'd been hearing tales about brothers and sons gone missing, jobs and industries that disappeared, limbs crushed on hillsides under horses or mangled in the guts of tractors. People didn't stand on ceremony about what could happen in a lifetime out here. Celia had forgotten almost all of the lines she'd memorized of the *Aeneid*, but not the struggle of it, how hard Aeneas had worked to found his city. She thought she might take Spanish or even Japanese next September.

The school had a Japanese exchange program, Lucy told her. An odd picture, all those rawboned blonds of Wyoming among the cherry blossoms and the bullet trains, but she, too, would look strange in that setting. Still, Celia could imagine herself walking through the raked gravel of Kyoto's gardens and taking pictures of Mount Fuji's perfectly balanced shape. Japan was orderly, clean, a place of deep cultural precision. She could learn to fold an obi.

Pulling back the covers, she listened, heard birdsong and the smack of wind on the side of the house. She stepped onto the floor, her feet slapped with yellow then ash gray as the light angled through the shade. Although it was still early, she knew that she'd been alone for some time. The quiet was at least half an hour old. No drip of tap water on enamel, doors no longer alive on their hinges. It was almost seven.

Cam had left early for work and had taken Lucy with him; she was having breakfast in town. Arthur was in Boise at a conference on western water rights: the past, the present, the future. Or, as he had said, when we didn't have it but it didn't matter since no one was here; followed by fighting for what little was left; and ending with the bleak realization that the Inner Mountain West was soon to be the northern extension of the Sonoran Desert. Celia loved it when he talked like this, aware of the irritations of his legal life, but doing the work, doing the responsible thing anyway. In truth, she loved him no matter what he did, her clumsy, semi-attentive, guilty father. All he had to do was stay alive. He had no idea how simple it was to guarantee her loyalty. That was almost all she asked of him, though she was still mad that he'd tangled with Denise Higgins. She did not begrudge him affection; no, she thought, I do begrudge him affection. I am jealous of it, of Denise, and I want him to be loyal to my mother. Loyal to a shadow. It makes no sense, but it's how it is. Lucy would have understood, but Celia had told no one but Courtney Van Buren.

She made her bed as she had done all summer, with knife-sharp creases in the sheets and the coverlet. She tidied her pajamas and slid them under the pillow and took the tumbler by her bed downstairs, watering a begonia Lucy was trying to coax back to life with what was left in the glass. Next, she made coffee and toasted bread, using the same knife she always used, a steak knife with a nick in its blade, to spread the butter. It had gotten pretty hideous, this need to keep the borders of the day ferociously consistent. She was hiding it from Lucy and her father; Cam wouldn't have noticed. At the ranch, it passed for a good work ethic and an excuse for a raise. No one polished utensils the way Celia did.

The anxiety ebbed once the first tasks of the day were achieved with the exactitude she demanded. Out of doors, the mania for order subsided a little and her heartbeat settled. On the porch, she sat on the swing, put her feet on the shaggy back of the dog, and enjoyed the ragged pull of air through his ribs, his steady tolerance of her weight. She sipped her coffee and realized the extent of her isolation, even though it was temporary; Carson would be here in a few minutes to take her to work. If she needed to leave, she could go only by foot. Nor was anyone nearby to help her if she hurt herself. No vehicles were available for use, and she didn't drive. She'd managed to avoid that responsibility all summer, though when it came time to go to school, she knew she'd have to learn. But now there were only horses that didn't belong to the family in the pasture and a saddle she barely knew how to slide on an animal's back. She had adopted Lucy's habit of shaking out shoes each morning in case a baby rattlesnake had curled there for the night. They had found five in the house this summer. It was good that Carson would be here soon. He was a person who lived in full consciousness of the potential for accident.

The hills shone gold and tan with late summer light. Rabbits quivered at the edge of the high hay, then dived into it. It would be harvested next week; Ted Flaxman was coming with his big combine. But Celia wasn't thinking about the huge, efficient machine with its great cutting blades. She was thinking about what Carson had told her when she called to arrange a pickup time.

The tire vandal had struck again. Carson sounded bleak as he said it. Celia had already seen the item in the paper. A color picture of a funnel of smoke fronted by a bulky cluster of troopers and firefighters in protective gear. It had cost the town $4,500 to send the pump engine all the way out there to douse the burning rubber, which meant that the fire company had spent most of its budget this year on these destructive, thoughtless pranks. In the same edition, there was a picture of another decorated compressor well. The Poetry Painter had struck again, the sixth time this summer. What, an editorial demanded, was going on with law enforcement in Callendar? Was it time to call in assistance from the federal government? To raise taxes so as to afford another salary and another patrol car? To admit that Callendar wasn't what its inhabitants thought it to be? "Callendar: A Citizen's Choice, a Citizen's Anger," the editorial was called.

Although Celia read every page of the biweekly paper, she found herself especially drawn to the weddings with their consistent attention to color themes—the bride chose plum, white, and daffodil. Navy and pink. Baby blue and lime green. "After a wedding trip to Las Vegas, the couple will make their home in Rawlins, where they will work at the Evans nursing home." Order shone in these stories: the bride's and groom's attendance and graduation from high school, the names of their grandparents, the ages of their flower girls. All the messy, dangling pieces were left out—the boyfriend who had broken the bride's heart, the jobs the groom had been fired from, the baby swelling in the bride's belly. Lucy would glance at the photos and fill in all those glaringly lit details, but Celia wished she wouldn't. Didn't people earn the right at least once in their lives to appear in their local paper for a happy reason, in pure black-and-white? Her mother's suicide had been noted in the *Post* and the *News* in horrible bold print. UPPER EAST SIDE MOM PLUNGES TO HER DEATH, cried the *Post*, followed by a couple of narrow

paragraphs and a blurry photo of the dented canopy. TRAGIC
LEAP, said the *News*. The *Times* hadn't thought Laura mattered
enough for an obituary, much less a story.

Celia's breathing grew faster. She started to count the number of times her feet tapped the dog's side. Irritated with the increased pressure, he rose and ambled to a corner of the porch.
She forced her attention back to the morning. She was wearing a
new blue T-shirt for the first day of her last week at the C Bar C.
It was for Carson, though he probably wouldn't notice. She'd
been slightly encouraged when he'd registered the new haircut
and the contacts. She'd been trying to dislodge her crush on him
for weeks without success. It was stuck like the stubborn end of
a splinter in a heel.

Carson's truck was entering the driveway. She could hear it
these days from the moment it turned off the highway. It had
lost its muffler and Carson was saving for a new one. He had an
appointment next week at the garage and in the meantime the
truck had reached a new level of unrespectableness.

Carson looked sour and Celia wondered if the ramshackle
quality of his vehicle was finally getting to him. He barely said
hello, and she guessed that this wasn't going to be one of his gar-
rulous mornings. When he took a left instead of a right at the
highway, she still didn't say anything. He had a destination
other than the C Bar C in mind. She asked if they could stop at
the Kum and Go so she could call to say she would be late, and
he answered, with a meanness she didn't know he had, that he
didn't think everyone was waiting around for her before they got
started. No one was going to miss her for twenty minutes.

A prickle of tears rose in response to his snappishness, but
there was no question of growling back. She did not want him to
know how vulnerable she was to him. She flicked a peanut shell
off the seat and watched the dark peach curve of a meadowlark's
breast swerve away from the window.

Carson turned on the windshield wipers to peel away a scrim of dead bugs. The smears left behind were almost as hard to see through. "Sorry," he muttered. "Sometimes I wake up and it's just clear I'm going to be an asshole all day." He still didn't explain where they were going or how long it would take.

Celia figured out pretty fast they were heading to Kelso. She was starting to make sense of Callendar's geography, and she realized they were on a circuitous route that did not take them directly through the town. Taking pictures all summer had helped her fix its sprawl in her mind: she knew turns and shortcuts now. For some reason, Carson was adding five miles to their trip to avoid notice.

The eight abandoned houses dipped and rose as they drove the hummocked road. This will be it, Celia thought. He's mad and he's driving carelessly and he'll break something critical this time. But the truck lumbered forward, in and out of the craters.

When she saw the column of smoke before she saw the tires, she didn't care that she was going to be late to work, and by far more than twenty minutes. All summer she had been insistent on the need to break the day into small twigs of time that she could count at sunset. To say I've done this, this, and this. She sliced the lettuce into green fans. Removed sticky buns from the oven and set them like rolls of sweet brown snails on trays lined with waxed paper. She polished wineglasses and inspected knives for crusted bits of food. A hundred small chores, mastered. Exactly as she'd done her homework, as if someone were planning on checking it at the end of the day, though no one had, until her father sprang into action after Laura died. And that was years after Celia had needed someone to congratulate her on her mastery of irregular French verbs.

Her ass started to hurt a little, and she realized it was because her mother's ring was pressing against her flank in her back pocket. Celia had taken to bringing it with her wherever she went, along with the camera. She didn't like to think about

why she did this and willed her brain blank when she found herself at her bureau, groping for the velvet box nestled amid her
socks. Her father and Lucy thought themselves such careful
guardians, but they watched as if with binoculars, from a re-
spectful distance. Now, in the truck, her routine disordered, her
sense of time misplaced, she knew how badly she wanted to be
discovered. She wanted Lucy or her father to walk in and pry
open her fist and see what was shining there. To create a stir and
be called on to explain herself fully.

The only person she had told so far about the ring was
Courtney Van Buren, with whom she was keeping up a steady,
increasingly personal correspondence. Courtney was seeing a
shrink. She wrote that talking to someone and not having them
tell you their lives back made you want to invent things so that
what you'd been through would sound more interesting, but this
counselor wasn't interested in her stories. Instead, he brought
her back, over and over, to her mother. And I keep telling him,
Courtney went on, I must have said it twenty times, that I was
really sad but I wasn't surprised. That my mother cried all the
time. That she took a lot of pills. That she worried about her
weight and she had no friends. My father wasn't that nice to her
and she missed my older brother since he'd gone to college and
she worried I wasn't pretty enough. She was—and I hate to say
this, but it's true and I am not supposed to be lying these days—
a really unhappy person. The week she died, she had gotten her
novel rejected for the fifteenth time. I loved her because she was
my mother, but that doesn't mean I didn't see her for what she
was. Celia thought most adults would be appalled by what their
children really knew.

She wrote back that she wished she had Courtney's clarity
about what had happened. She wanted badly to point to a reason. But her mother had seemed all right. She had been working
on her pictures. She had been quiet, that was all. It wasn't one of
the bad times, when she couldn't get out of bed, when she stood

in the kitchen and couldn't cook. None of them had known she was anywhere close to dying. But Celia, she said to herself, that isn't quite true. You decided not to peer at her anymore, to spend less of your own life watching hers. And there was something else, too, but Celia didn't think she could say what she knew even to Courtney Van Buren.

She was able to think about all this because Carson was entirely silent as he drove. He guided the truck up a last rise and stopped it on what had been Kelso's main street. The smoke from the tires was thicker up here and blowing in their direction, blue and evil-smelling, pure toxin. "Do they know what it spells this time?" Celia asked.

"H-O-M," Carson answered, stepping toward the smoke and the tires. "Someone nearly caught her. Some guy out on the Cody road saw a car heading up here and thought it might be something fishy. Got his gun and his dog and came up and nearly nabbed her."

"Her?" Celia asked and Carson nodded, still walking across the glass-studded grass, past the tractor shot full of holes. Her camera swung on her neck.

"The guy said it was a woman. He saw her running back toward her car, but he didn't see the car itself. She must have parked it in a gully after she dumped the tires."

They reached the smoking mass of rubber. Celia saw the melted base of the M. "She was spelling 'home,'" she said, "and then she heard the guy's truck."

"No shit," Carson answered and ground a wedge of glass into the dirt so hard he looked as if he might lose a bootheel in the process. Then she knew what he knew, and the reason for the extent of his gloom. The paper hadn't mentioned that a woman had been glimpsed or that someone in a truck had spotted her. Not even Lucy knew about those pieces of information. This meant that his mother, Teresa, must have told Carson that she'd been the one hauling tires out here in the dead of night and that she'd doused them in kerosene so they could flash their cryptic signals to the pilots on their way to Denver.

"Come on," Carson said. "Let's go." Celia followed him. She thought about the letters Carson's mom had chosen. CAR, short for Carson. HOM, as close as she could get to home, and MAT, the first three letters of Matthew, the son who died on the pipeline in Alaska. Celia framed a vista of smoke and rubber and snapped the shutter.

They were quiet for a while, and when Carson pulled up at Teresa's house, all Celia asked was if his mother was at home. Carson shook his head. "Nope. Work." Celia didn't bother asking if or when they were going to get to the ranch for their own jobs. Today, those commitments seemed expendable. This was an amazement to her—that routine could be shattered without her heart battering and a film of sweat in her armpits. Today, it seemed that order could be cast aside.

Carson led Celia around the back, where she was surprised to see a generously proportioned corral and inside it a grazing horse. It was Jack, looking as if he'd never lived anywhere else his whole life. "What's he doing here?"

"He was kicking horses in the pasture. Al was scared he was going to bust a leg. They told me to get him out of there." It had been worse than that, as Celia learned when she probed. Al, the head wrangler, had told Carson that Jack was mean to the bone and would never turn into a decent saddle horse, that Carson or his dad should sell him for glue, that Jack was not worth the time or the money or the risk. Celia knew, too, that Carson respected Al and in any other circumstance would have listened to him.

He wouldn't be holding so tightly to this bad horse, Celia guessed, if his brother were still alive. When the worst things happen, you're oddly freed from caring about what other people think. Before the terrible event, you have this notion that if you behave well or do what others ask, that your life will proceed in a normal way. Then something goes wrong, such as your mother's jumping out the window or your brother's being blown to bits in an explosion, and you realize that your good deeds, which you'd seen as insurance, amount to a useless currency. His parents' marriage, his father's lousy employment history, Matthew's death. All of it made it that much more important to hang on to what little he still had to care about. For better or for worse, that terrible horse had got hold of him.

Jack seemed peaceful. He swished his tail at flies, kept his head bent to nibble the yellow-gray grass. She and Carson leaned on the rough rails of the paddock. His father's work, Carson said, the product of some scheme he had about horse training in the backyard. Jack ambled over to Carson and butted his head against the boy's chest. Celia might not have been there for all the attention they paid her. Carson leaned in and let his red hair drift into Jack's forelock so the colors shimmered over each other in a loose braid of black, copper, white.

"She did it, my mother did it," Carson said, his forehead still on the horse's. Jack was stamping his pleasure at his contact with the boy, and a short column of dust rose around his front leg like a dry, cloudy fountain.

"Why?" asked Celia. Carson would have scoffed at her if she feigned surprise. And "why" was the only question worth asking. The how—obtaining all those tires without people knowing, taking them up there in her car—all those were answerable. They were technical. They had an exact response.

Carson lifted his head but kept his hand on Jack's cheek. The horse widened its nostrils and leaned in even closer to the boy. "She said if she hadn't done something like that, she just might have gone and shot somebody. She said she just missed Matt."

She'd lost her mind for a while, it seemed to Celia, and done something entirely out of character as a way to get back to who she thought she needed to be. Like her father with Denise Higgins. People become maddened by grief and their flimsiness in the face of it. Being on the front lines of that kind of sadness made you see the world in very stark terms. You knew just how comfortless a place it was, and it seemed impossible and somehow wrong that other people could move blamelessly forward, assured of their good fortune, their open futures. You needed to let them know they shouldn't count on their easy luck. Knowledge like this made it impossible to be normal, to even accept the idea that there was such a thing as normal, though that seemed to be what everyone around you kept wishing you'd return to.

Celia thought that Carson's mother had taken a less destructive path than a lot of people. Her fiery gesture hadn't hurt anyone. She'd been careful, as the police and firefighters had noted, to make sure the damage wouldn't spread. She'd put the tires on an old road so there was little chance for the wind to catch and push the flames past the tarmac. She'd chosen clear, still nights for her work, so that the pilots the next morning would be sure to see her handiwork. It was nuts, what she had done, but there was something vital to it. A scrap of a crazy poem, toxic and illegal and weird, but a poem in any case, about how much she loved her boys, and wanting in some way to be larger than her circumstances.

"I told her I wished she'd let me know earlier. I'm stronger than her. I could have helped her spell the words out to the end," Carson said. He looked at Celia then. "I wish I knew why I was telling you this. I can't figure out why it's easy to talk to you." Maybe, he said, it was because of Mrs. King; he'd always liked her grandmother. "You look like her," Carson added, and checked to make sure Jack had enough water in his tank.

"Want a Dr Pepper?" and Celia nodded, though she had no taste for the soda. As they went in through the kitchen door,

Celia said, "Your mom wouldn't have wanted your help, Carson." She was unsurprised to notice a shelf full of the rodeo trophies she'd glimpsed in her vision, the electroplating worn off, as she had seen, with titles she could now read. CHAMPION — PEEWEE POLE BENDING. His prizes. "She wanted to be alone."

Carson agreed. "It's just that she's never done anything like this before." He got Celia a can of soda, which was warm, though it had come from the refrigerator. The house was a place of cramped surfaces. Not enough counter space. Low walls. Stingy little carpets. The pictures of the boys on the wall were five-by-eights in black frames. His brother had been blond, like his mother.

Celia said then, "I caught my dad and Mrs. Higgins together." The adults in her life, she wanted to say, were specialists at not behaving as you expected them to. They were prone to spiraling out of control if put under too much pressure, though they always pretended that that wasn't what was happening. "I think that's worse in a way, because of Mr. Higgins. At least your mom didn't hurt anybody. My dad is going to dive straight into this, though he promised he wouldn't."

"I don't know. Maybe it's not so bad. Mrs. Higgins doesn't seem so happy with Dwight, and my mom says he's got girls all over the place. Maybe she'd be better off with your dad." Carson drained his Dr Pepper. He had practice with marriages ending, it seemed. "Pop filed for divorce again," he went on. "Not that it means anything yet, since he's done it three times before, and every time, he goes and stops it just a couple of days before the judge is supposed to rule on it. They think he's a freak down at the courthouse."

Celia looked hard at Carson then. No wonder he was prepared to walk away from a day at work. That was nothing compared with what he'd seen adults do. It also interested her that Dwight Higgins had a bad reputation and that Carson knew about it. People watched each other like TV out here. All of this also added to why he needed Jack: a good, hard project that would require lots of concentration. "Carson," she said, "we've got to go to the ranch."

But instead of getting ready, he reached for her hand. "You look nice in blue, Celia," he said. His skin was hard as a worn bit of soap. He laced his fingers into hers. "Your hands got rougher from all that dishwashing this summer." He said then, "You're getting real pretty," and she nearly leaned in to kiss him out of sheer gratitude—what amazement that such words could be said directly about her—but his voice held her back. He had sounded so sad. Then he sat up and wedged his hat against his skull. He said that since they were three hours late, they should probably make themselves accountable to Mr. Starmer.

At the C Bar C, their boss commented they were the last people he'd have expected to be so irresponsible. Celia felt guilty; living up to expectations was a hard habit to break. Carson didn't seem to mind Mr. Starmer's irritation. He merely apologized, picked up a lariat, and went to saddle a horse. Celia moped for the rest of the day, took on extra work in the kitchen scrubbing pots and ironing napkins, and could not conceal from herself her disappointment at losing face before her employer. The stack of clean linen rose and rose, but not a soul commented on the high piles, like folded wings, on the glistening tables.

All summer her brain had been pushing small forecasts of the future to the surface. Now it revealed a picture of her hand on a letter. It was from Courtney, she knew, and it would not contain good news. It would be about sleeplessness or bouts of tears, and Celia would have to call Courtney's father and tell him that his daughter wasn't managing. There was certain information you had to act on, even if it entailed breaking a promise, even if you got bits wrong.

She didn't see Carson the rest of the day. When she went to look for him at the corral, another wrangler told her he'd left soon after he arrived—not feeling well or something, the cowboy said. Celia suspected he'd gone back to Jack. Some guests came up then, a family of four in clean denim. They wanted gentle horses, they said politely. Their boys were new to riding. Celia saw that the children were scared, but they would let themselves be pressed up and onto the backs of the ponies and jolted along. They trusted their parents not to let them fall. She remembered Laura urging her to give it a whirl. "Try, Celie, just try." The only person to call her that. She made Celia sit on the wide brown back of an animal so placid even walking seemed an affront to him. None of it had made a difference—the endearment, the horse's gentleness—she was still too far off the ground. She had tumbled back into Laura's arms and her carefully masked disappointment. Now, watching the boys eased up on their mounts, their shiny boots groping for the stirrups, she wished she had tried harder. She should have worked harder to make her mother happy. The horses started to amble, tails rasping at flies, the parents at the bridles, urging their family forward.

By the end of August, all of Callendar seemed to quiet below a thick press of heat. No more coalbed methane wells had been vandalized. The new wing to the high school would be ready in time for school the first week in September. The *Post-Tribune* reported on a host of nuptials, and even Lucy couldn't remember much gossip about those particular couples, who looked flattened by the high temperatures under which they began their wedded lives. Carson admitted on one ride back to Lucy's that his mother had been scared by the close call she'd had and decided not to set any more tires on fire. She'd gotten it out of her system. Gray, his father, had retracted the divorce papers and given up his room at the Motel 8. Carson seemed more relaxed with his father around. Arthur was working hard, but coming home each night for supper and keeping their weekends scrupulously full of family activities that did not include the Higginses. Cam fished, saw Amber, and spent an unholy amount of time around the Barlows. He was giving off a strange sheen, which Celia thought could only mean he was happy. Only Lucy and the dog seemed somber.

It was time for the rodeo, which explained some of Lucy's bad mood. She didn't approve of how the horses were handled, how the bulls were often drugged up and the little kids allowed to ride without helmets. She knew all the statistics about how many necks got broken at Cheyenne Frontier Days and she didn't think it was worth it. "Every year," she said, "I am reminded that at heart I come from miners."

But Celia was looking forward to it. She wanted to see Carson in action. Like everyone, she loved watching him round up the animals at the C Bar C, so loose and light on a horse that the creature below him seemed scarcely aware of his presence. A boy you barely noticed when he walked into a room, you couldn't take your eyes off him when he was horseback. Al had lent him a bay gelding named Punch, one of his own, a quarter horse with more than a touch of Arab in him. He had elegant feet and a high curve to his neck that gave his blood away. Carson was entered in seven competitions and might walk away with top honors this year, except in bull and bronc riding, which he did not engage in. "That's for idiots who can't do anything to an animal but fall off him," he said dismissively, but Celia knew that since his brother died, Teresa had forbidden him to ride the wild horses and cattle. Even so, Carson stood to gather prizes tonight. Miss Wyoming Beef, a Norwegian girl named Terri from Laramie, was going to be attending, too, and would be the one to crown him.

The event lasted for three days and the Kings, from tradition, went on the night of the second. Cam had slipped off earlier with Amber, but promised to join them, so Lucy, Celia, and her father drove into town together. Lucy, in spite of herself, was looking forward to the evening. Once they were settled in a central section of the grandstand, she hailed former students in the crowd and summoned them for an accounting of their recent activities. Even the ones in their thirties, children at their sides, were slightly bashful, glancing down at their scuffed boots. She also spotted acquaintances from the Historical Society and her gardening group. Soon she was surrounded by a crush of old friends and local chatter. This is why she's stayed here so long, Celia thought, sitting one row behind her grandmother in the high seats. All these people know it's her just from the way she gets out of a car. Lucy looked less downcast than she had in several weeks, the wrinkles framing her mouth softening from brackets to parentheses. The light was brass beaten to translucent thinness, and the air smelled of diesel, manure, fried food.

Celia noticed that her father looked better, too, his hair now grown in. He was glancing cautiously around the crowd— probably looking for Mrs. Higgins and probably slightly relieved not to see her. Arthur was trying to rope in his worst instincts, Celia knew, a fruitless attempt, but at least he was trying. An hour later, Cam and Amber joined them and Amber, they all noticed, didn't seem as drawn to Cam as he was to her. The glittering skin of indifference with which Cam protected himself was peeling away after contact with this girl, whose own skin was almost entirely masked by tattoos. It was vaguely discomfiting; they weren't used to Cam being generous with himself, to letting himself be seen as openly, unironically engaged.

Celia felt a tight prick of envy travel through her body. That was what love, or at least connection, could do. No one in the family much trusted such a laden word as "love." Laura had used it so easily and torn herself from it just as carelessly. Still, Cam had found a bond where none was expected, and its discovery renewed some trust he had in himself and others. He would want to stay in Wyoming, Celia knew. He'd be willing to make this place as much of a home as any of them now could have. Loneliness as heavy as a musty blanket settled around her. No one at the entire rodeo was looking for her, or wanted her as badly as her father and Cam wanted to hold a woman. Little is more punishing than to feel yourself invisible in the middle of a relaxed crowd. Her mother's ring was pressed into her back pocket, making its small O in her flesh.

At least you could go and distract yourself and stand in line and get Cokes for everyone and then traipse down to the rails and take pictures of the horses being groomed, their tails braided and their hooves polished to the gloss of glazed pottery. You could eat a hamburger and chips and look at the cowboys trying to back up their horse trailers and assess who could cram the largest amount of profanity into the shortest amount of time. Horses were being raced around barrels, children on ponies were running their mounts from one end of a track and back. Little boys tried to wrap a rope around the tail of a bewildered goat. Girls' braids bounced on their backs, their ponies ran so fast. Crackling pronouncements came from the announcers' booth: Casey Varitek could be picked up at the first-aid station, Sam Eggers wouldn't be riding today because of a bum back— good luck, Sam, get better soon. Upcoming events: Bull riding. Bronc riding. And there's Kelly Matlock the Rodeo Queen, and a girl in a green-sequined shirt would gallop around the ring on a gleaming buckskin. Celia and her family settled in. Amber slipped off. Other friends drifted by and away, colleagues from the law firm, former classmates of her father's.

Celia felt herself almost lulled—she'd been to the rodeo al- most every year of her life—except when she saw the flashing lights of the Callendar ambulance, two EMTs posted right at the corral's entrance. Some awful accident took place almost every year, usually during bull riding. "Bulls, seven; cowboys, zero," as the announcer put it. Her mother had often refused to come, and remembering that, Celia felt her despondency deepen. Perhaps that was what the loneliness was finally about. Her mother had sensed the possibility for damage everywhere, and it was the trait she had passed on most conclusively to her daughter. Celia's shoulders were ropy with tension because the crushed skull, compressed vertebrae, or shattered femur had yet to happen this year. She refused to consult the green, electric lining of her brain where the visions lurked. She did not want to know.

Not even watching Carson helped dispel the presentiments, although he looked glorious out there. His horse was as tall and lean as he was, and his hair flashed dark gold above the burnished brown of the animal's glowing curried skin. Punch twitched as if aware of his—the only word was "majesty"—as he and Carson cantered into the ring. The crowd stilled, noting the looseness of Carson's wrists, the ease with which his long legs gripped the horse's body. In a place that venerated democracy as a framework that allowed the sharpest outlines of individuals to emerge, people could still recognize a king when they saw one. Steers walked with seeming deference into the perfect loops of his rope. He anchored every relay team and came away with the banner, racing past the finish line as his competitors breathed the earth Punch's flashing hooves sent sailing toward them. "Carson Novak, wrangler at the C Bar C," the announcer said. "We are getting pretty damn used to hearing that name around here."

It killed him, Celia knew, not to have his own ranch attached to his name, like so many of the other cowboys. But you couldn't sense that disappointment from the way he rode or, later in the evening, with the sun starting to sink: he just kept shining there in the center of the ring. Punch's coat was painted with sweat, yet Carson's hair was still a beacon, his face brighter than that. He was going to win the overall prize, Celia was sure, and all the Kings were staying to watch, not just for Carson, but for her. Because he was her friend. Even Lucy couldn't take her eyes off him. Celia felt pride swell in her like blood.

When the sun was down and the floodlights were glaring, the final results were announced. Carson had won in all seven categories he'd entered and stood there to receive his trophy, a huge tower of gilt, with a grin on his face that Celia had never seen. He looked purely happy holding the enormous trophy, which seemed hard for him to grasp. He had done exactly what he wanted, how he wanted. No one could take away what he managed to achieve. Not one piece of it could be reclaimed.

When the applause died down, he walked to the edge of the ring and let his mother hug him. His father kept sawing at his arm. Photographers and men with video cameras swarmed around him. Al took Punch, who was startled by the flashes, and without the horse by his side, Celia saw how slender and uncertain Carson was. Then even his trophy was taken away; his father was cradling it awkwardly. Ranch owners came to smack his shoulder and whisper in his ear. Offers of employment, Celia guessed, promises to let him train their horses or enter as many rodeos as he liked. Rich men used to buying the best of help. And he would accept some of those offers, work precisely as long as he needed, until he had the money to buy his own place. He wouldn't care whether there was a house on the land. He just wanted fields and fences, pasture, a few head, and horses, horses, horses. He'd described it to her once: he said he didn't even care if there were trees. He said he'd sleep in a tent. He said he was too skinny for the rattlers to want to bite him.

Celia wanted to leave him alone, thinking he'd more likely want company once the crowd around him had died down. But Arthur and Lucy insisted on pressing through the throng to give their congratulations. They bumped first into Gray and Teresa, clinging to each other, their knuckles as pale as the whites of their flashing eyes. Fortune had conclusively turned their way, but they didn't trust it, partly because they hadn't felt it in so long, and partly because they knew how fast it would fade. Carson's gilt tower tilted at their feet. The rectangle where his name would be engraved was still an unblemished yellow, but the announcer said all he had to do was take it down to Bob's Sports and Bob himself would do the honors.

Slowly, Arthur, Lucy, Cam, and Celia pushed forward. Carson stood in the circle of approval, looking happy enough to shout. Celia reached out to punch him on the shoulder. "That was great," she said. "You were amazing." And he smiled at her with what she understood instantly as tenderness—but not attraction or the river of feeling that connected lovers. She knew that because when her brother, beautiful Cam, reached out to shake Carson's hand, the redheaded boy could barely speak, and Celia could tell that Carson would have done anything for that touch not to end.

It broke something in her, brittle and small, like a wind-tossed bone, but something final. She had to leave. In the mass of people surrounding Carson, no one would notice that she was gone. And she knew, too, what she would do. She'd seen Carson's truck parked by the 4-H barns, rustling and warm with the animals spending the night there. She smelled the comforting mix of hay and manure and nearly stopped in to sink her fingers deep into the stiff, high wool of a merino sheep, something she had loved to do since childhood. Her mother had always gone with her, during the day, the part of the rodeo she could tolerate, looking at the beautiful, shining cows and sheep, the ones the children raised before they had to be sold off and slaughtered, Laura had said, making Lucy and Arthur frown. Easterner, they were thinking. Judging without knowing.

Celia understood, though her mother did not, that for most ranchers, these annual killings were sacrifices. It was never easy to part with the animals over whose births they had presided, calves from which they had stripped the caul, whose crooked limbs they had straightened, whose deaths were grievous to them. It wasn't accurate to say that ranchers thought of those animals as nothing but what they could be sold for. Meat was certainly part of the whole enterprise, its red, unruly, passionate core. But Carson had helped her grasp that most ranchers lived with double vision: they knew precisely how heavy a cow had to be to make her worth killing, and at the same time savored with complete and incontrovertible pleasure the way those cows grazed black and red on green strips of pasture. Pleasure with a hierarchy: the humans were always in charge and they didn't feel bad about that. They saw what they did, their very work, the way they saw the cows and sheep and horses they tended, as a living animal. A livelihood based in an old, deep braiding of human to beast to land, inextricable.

Carson was bound to this understanding of ranching, to its contradictions, just as he was bound to men. She'd never had a hope there, and now she knew why. None of the summer's visions had produced truly useful information, but he had been what passed for a friend out here, and now that, too, had changed. He had trusted her with essential knowledge, even if he didn't trust himself with it.

The keys were in his ignition, as she knew they would be. Even people with good trucks often did the same. Cars were being stolen more frequently now that crystal meth was rampant, but no one, not even a crazed addict, would be tempted to take Carson's truck. Celia teased him that he would be relieved if someone walked off with it, but she knew that wasn't true.

She was so used to sitting on the passenger side, it felt like the violation it was to take Carson's place. Still, she did it. And she, unlike the owner, strapped herself in. It took a minute to adjust the seat to the length of her legs, but she had to move it less than she thought. She was nearly as tall as Carson; she just wasn't used to thinking of herself that way. She remembered again the look of pure longing that he had cast at her brother and hurried herself.

It couldn't be too hard to drive this truck. It was an automatic; those were supposed to be easier. She had practiced a few times with her father and her feet vaguely remembered where to put themselves. Left for the brake, right for the gas. She put her mother's camera on the seat and turned the engine on, though finding the headlights was a challenge. She shifted the truck into drive, jerking slowly along. As she passed the barns, her lights caught the reflective surfaces of the animals' eyes.

Carson's house wasn't far from the fairground and it was easy enough to get there without anyone noticing a truck going seven miles an hour, since almost everyone in Callendar was at the rodeo. Celia felt surprisingly at ease as she drove the stolen vehicle. She let the full truth of Carson's inability to be with her sink in. No wonder he never talked about the high school. No wonder he kept to himself. Not one piece of his real self would be safe out here in this town.

She found it was possible to cry and drive simultaneously if you were willing to proceed as slowly as a lawn mower. The truck, though rattletrap, was perfectly sound and took the corners crisply. Braking was tricky, but she didn't hurt anybody, not even the skunk trundling along the edge of the road, a smelly scrap of black-and-white carpet. He looked up at her as she passed, his tail a sudden flag.

The Novaks' little house was dark and so were the windows of the other houses on Princeton Street. Celia parked in the driveway, knowing that maneuvering the truck into the garage was beyond her limited abilities. At first she braked in gear, not remembering that she had to move the shift into park to turn the car off safely, but she figured it out, and then there was silence. The sweet, dark night came down through the open windows. Stars were thrown across the sky as if diamonds were salt.

She could hear Jack's whinny from the corral. He was confused, she guessed, because he'd heard Carson's truck but didn't hear or smell Carson. She had nothing to give him, no carrots or apples. The pinto wouldn't be swayed by such offerings. No humans but Carson were to be trusted, even those bearing treats. Celia got out and felt the wind dry her face. She left the camera on the seat and went out back. "Hi, boy," she said to the horse and leaned against the rough boards of the paddock. The moon had come out and was shining at the full power of its half self, casting enough light for Celia to see that the animal was walking from the water tank toward her, ears pitched forward. He recognizes me, she thought. He's seen me often enough to know I am someone Carson knows. "He did great tonight," she told him. "He won everything." Jack gave a cautious whinny, as if hoping that Celia was concealing Carson behind her. "He's not here," she said. "He's at the rodeo, getting famous. I hope it gets him a good job."

She hadn't quite known what she was going to do once she got there, but she knew now. She climbed over the fence and the horse, startled, wheeled and danced to the far end of the coral. She stood in the grass he'd worn almost to soft dirt and started to walk slowly toward him. "I'm not going to do anything to you," she said, and he nickered, surprised perhaps at her audacity.

When Celia was fifteen feet from Jack, she said, "Carson won on Punch tonight, but it was you he really wanted to ride. He wants a lot of what he can't have. He loves Cam. He loves Cam, not me." She could not keep herself from crying, though she tried to do so quietly. The horse seemed not to mind and went back to grazing.

Hiccuping, moving forward, still not quite believing she was going to do what she was going to do, taking a risk her father would have killed her for, she walked decisively toward Jack, grabbed hold of his mane, and heaved herself onto his back. He was not tall, her legs were long, yet she had no idea how she managed to get her whole body onto his. It ought not to have been physically possible. She hadn't leaped onto him from the fence or a block. She had so little experience with horses. She had nothing but her own cussedness and a desire to depart from what she knew and trusted. It was enough to land her squarely on the pinto's back.

Oh, Jesus, she thought. Oh my God, what am I doing? He is going to kill me. Who the "he" was was unclear: Arthur, Carson, Jack. At first the horse seemed barely to register that he was being ridden. He blew out through his nostrils and shifted forward almost ploddingly, as if bored. She felt his strong shoulders move below her hands, and she wound her fists into the coarse lengths of his mane. He was walking mildly across the corral, as if every night a girl came in to his domain and leaped onto his bare back. "I knew it was going to happen," she said to him. "I saw it, but I didn't know what it was." He pivoted his ears at her voice and walked slightly faster now. It was what she had longed to tell Carson all summer, and what she had never confessed to Courtney Van Buren, the piece of news so wretched she could not imagine an occasion drastic enough to tell anyone. The metal of her mother's ring ground into her skin.

On her way to school the day Laura died, a twist in her vision, the unpleasantly familiar prelude to unsolicited knowledge, had stopped Celia on the street. Inside the eerie gap between one normal moment and the next, she saw a shoe hanging from a tree and another on the hood of a car. City light, thin but penetrating, lined the sharp shapes of the branches as if to make them glow with special intensity at the very limits of their bark. She had learned about that from Laura, a trick of exposure. At the darkest edge of an object, the sun gathers at its brightest; to become aware of light, you need the steady presence of its opposite. Then she had seen the glint of gold that signaled her

mother's ring, though again she hadn't seen that it belonged to
Laura. Afterward, she knew, however, and had stooped to find it
just where she'd seen it in her premonition, inches from a sewer
grating. But when the vision seized her, it happened quickly and
there was nothing to tell her that this omen was more significant
than the others, except the unease gathering in her lungs, squeezing them tight. Then it receded, like a strange-smelling tide. She
adjusted her backpack, started walking again, and nearly col-
lided with a taxi.

I should have known, Celia had told herself a million times
afterward. What happened bothered me enough to stop me on
the street; it quivered somewhere deep and wrong. I will always
feel I could have stopped it. I will never be free from feeling
I was given something useful and I squandered it. The note she
didn't leave us came to me instead as a thought, a picture.

Jack was trotting now. "Slow down," she said to him, "slow
down, boy." But he started to gather speed, and the rough trot,
which bounced her high off his back and rattled her spine,
flowed into the smoothness of a canter. He was letting loose his
own strength. He had no interest in listening to her. She was not
in any kind of control of him. She had no skills or power with
which to cajole him to a gentleness he did not at heart possess.
She knew this should have frightened her. Even an hour earlier,
the thought of being near this dangerous horse would have terrified her. But then everything had changed.

He was galloping now in tight, elegant circles. Carson had
always said he had beautiful gaits. He edged closer to the
boards, then pulled away from them at the last moment, as if re-
gretting his impulse to sweep her from his back. He would give
her one more chance. Celia knew she should be feeling nothing
but the most abject fear. She thought of her grandfather and the
horse he loved that killed him. She thought of her father, and of
how he didn't even need a horse to fall to the ground and wound

himself; he could manage all on his own. She thought of her mother and the way horses freed her. She was feeling it now, what Laura had tried to show her. Pure forward motion. How could her mother have felt that and wanted to die? The worst question now pressed in on her, Jack's mane whipping her arms, the smell of his sweat rising: What if, as she dropped toward the pavement, she had wanted to reverse her decision? What if she died not in freedom and release but in regret and doubt?

Yet along with these questions, a thrilling, complicated delight rose through Celia's bones. The gift of riding. This was why people loved it. This exact sensation: your body connected to an animal's, an essential wildness loaned to you, direct access to an un-self-conscious grace in which you were magically allowed to participate. The horse chose to carry you in a surfeit of untethered, ancient generosity. There was a crazy joy in this animal and a blade of fear. Jack had no idea why she had leaped onto his back; there'd been no agreement reached and its absence freed him of any rules Carson might have taught him. It was night and the moon had risen and nothing was as it seemed in daylight, where he knew exactly how wide the corral was and when Carson would come to feed and stroke him. A banshee had found him, and that allowed him to behave like one himself.

He was going to jump the fence, Celia guessed. She could feel the power gathering in his legs and then he was arching over the top board, hooves clearing the edge with inches to spare, her whole body slammed up against his neck. "Oh, Jesus," she yelled, "oh my God," but even as her legs slewed to the left of his neck and she clung in a panicked knot of fingers and legs and heartbeat, her hands wound so tightly into his mane they were bleeding, a deep river of pleasure ran through her. This was more alive than she'd known she could be and the center of the joy was realizing that she really wanted to be. She wanted to stay whole, a yearning that arose most sharply only when you risked shattering yourself entirely. She might die at any moment.

Jack started to run down the street and his shod hooves sent sparks flying from the cracked macadam. Running. Not just a canter or a gallop, but speed at his full power—airbound, earthbound, she had no idea. He was a streak of need. Yes, she heard a voice calling, and it must have been hers, but it sounded like a wolf howling, not a horseback girl. "Goodbye," she heard herself cry out, "goodbye," but she did not know to whom. The horse stumbled, and she nearly fell with him, then he gathered himself again and the houses and the empty driveways continued to blur past.

She felt then the crackle at the edge of her brain, the hum of an unbidden vision coming into focus. Like a train felt before it is seen, its power intimated only in the ringing of the earth below your feet. She saw her brother, driving through snow, the windshield nearly obscured. Around him were mountains, close and dark as shadows, full of stirring fear. She felt that this was the last time she would see around a corner. Along with her friendship with Carson, the uninvited talent was being swept from her life. She didn't know why.

A car turned into the street then, the headlights a pair of alien eyes. The driver stopped the second he saw the horse and the girl. "Didn't move," he said later. "Not every day you see a girl hanging for dear life on the back of a crazed horse in Callendar."

The engine, the lights, the sudden interruption of their streak toward some version of freedom—it didn't matter what the trigger was. Jack stopped, too, and reared, and Celia could feel her hands loosened from the mane, the strands ripping lines of flesh from her palms. She could not hold on. She felt her body rising, her lungs opened wide in a shout, hands flung above her head, legs tangled. The man in the car remembered later the oddness of the girl's voice. She didn't sound scared. The word he wanted to use was happy, but he was too embarrassed to say it. He never told anyone what he had heard, but it stayed with him a long time, the way she surrendered to her descent. It was strange, but he had witnessed an outbreak of pleasure that consisted of the wild, rearing horse, the tall girl, her arms as skinny as the reins that weren't there, her voice a stalk of rising joy. And then she fell.

LUCY

At first Lucy thought she couldn't find her granddaughter because of all the activity percolating ringside: Carson flashing a smile no one ever suspected he could muster, his father swearing up a small tornado with that outlandish statue in his arms. Horses stamping, boys hollering—it was close to impossible to keep an eye on anyone. They noticed Celia's absence only when the dust and giddiness began to settle and Lucy, Arthur, and Cam thought to get dinner that wasn't a hot dog. No Celia. They split up to look for her, Arthur at their truck, Cam by the restrooms.

As Lucy climbed the grandstand to see if the girl had thought to meet them up there, she was anxious. It wasn't like Celia to take off. Her granddaughter was nothing if not loyal, even persistent. Unlike her mother. Unlike, if Lucy were honest, her brother. If Cam couldn't be found, no one would have worried, because he was a boy and because he was Cam, prone to furtive slipping off. Celia was the one who stayed. Celia the one who minded the garden without being asked, because she had the habit of being helpful. A habit she needed, Lucy thought, a habit we needed of her.

Walking up the stairs to where she'd sat with her family and seen all of Callendar spread below her in big-hatted, chip-eating tiers, Lucy guessed that Celia had seen or heard something that made her bolt. It must have concerned Carson and the dumb love she carried around for him. Something had shifted that set her loose. She wasn't in the grandstand. No one was. Dozens of cast-off programs chattered in the light wind.

In the parking lot, Arthur was starting to get frantic. He got the announcer to broadcast a message that Celia King should meet her family at their truck. Others heard and also started looking. She wasn't in the bathrooms, either, Cam said. "Where is she?" her father kept saying. "Where'd she get to?" Lucy knew they had to find Arthur a task before terror made him useless.

Cold night air was sweeping over the town from the skirts of the mountains. The floodlights gave the illusion of silvery warmth, but they were all shivering. Suddenly they saw Carson striding up, all tattered jeans and mashed hat. He smelled of sweat and horse, strong enough to blunt the odor of fries and meat that rose around them. "My truck is gone. I think Celia took it," he said, and the impression altered again. He had that deep, authoritative voice, steady even when faced with bad news.

"You fool enough to leave the keys in that thing?" Arthur said to him. Stop it, Arthur, Lucy wanted to chide. You know what the truck looks like. You know how Callendar is. He was good to come and tell us, smart enough to figure it out fast.

"Do you know where she'd go, Carson?" Lucy asked. She plucked his shirt away from his arm and, in this small gesture, discovered how eerily bony he was. A glance or a touch would never make you guess he was lithe enough to turn a horse so precisely or hobble steers. His strength came from beyond his body.

"Three possibilities," he said. "She might have gone back to your ranch, ma'am." Lucy did not miss the longing in his voice as he said "ranch." But she could tell he did not think it likely.

"Where else, Carson?" It was urgent. Celia was driving a truck in terrible repair. She had rarely been behind a wheel during the day and never at night. Around them, cars cautiously steered their way toward the exit, headlights casting long, pale cones that illuminated only fragments of bodies: scissoring legs, an adult's hand engulfing a child's, a profile, the flash of an earring. People heading home.

"She might be out near Kelso, where the tires got burned. We went there a couple of times. Or she might be driving to my house. I'll be going there myself." He looked past them then, unwilling to meet their eyes. His expression wasn't shifty; it simply made him sad to mention their private afternoons. He gave them the address.

"Thank you," Arthur had the grace to say, and Carson nodded. "Good luck," he said and raised his hand. Only then did Lucy notice how tired he was. All of a sudden he seemed like someone who might need to leave the fairgrounds on a stretcher, as if he'd been crushed by the day's events instead of their masterful survivor.

"Do you think we should tell Ray?" Arthur asked his mother, already walking toward his truck. He and Cam would go to the ghost town.

Lucy yanked at one of her fingers. It was starting to ache, as it did when the weather changed. "No," she said slowly. "I don't think anyone took her. I don't think she's gone far. Something happened. But she left on her own." She could hear her own indecision. If she didn't have her history with Ray and her misgivings about his abilities as a police officer, she knew she would have run straight to the authorities. "I hope I'm right," she said.

Arthur looked hard at her. "I'll stop in at the troopers' on the way. I'll see what they say." Lucy nodded. She understood. He couldn't risk another loss, another indication of his failure as a parent. They'd try to be back at Lucy's in an hour.

Lucy herself drove toward the Novaks' house on Princeton Street, a part of town she hadn't frequented in a couple of years. It was the neighborhood that produced the boys who made and sold the crystal meth, the boys who left on the Greyhound or in the prison van. She had spent a fair share of time in the living rooms of those houses trying to persuade those boys and their parents that education was a sound investment and bad habits and lawlessness were not. She couldn't quite believe she had offered the bargain with such certainty. What she had to give away for free was seen, over the years, as shopworn goods, a ticket to a dull show, a band long out of date. Sheer naïveté to think everyone was interested in self-improvement. When she realized this, she retired within a year. Pride, she admitted, more than anything. Not wanting to be a figure of fun, the sad remnant of a culture that no longer existed, an outmoded piece of farm equipment.

What finally got her was an hour in the kitchen of a family named Klum over on College Road. Harold, a chess player and a natural writer, had gotten up and left the room when she arrived, gesturing in disgust. His mother's face had echoed that disapproval, though she poured Lucy a cup of coffee and called her Mrs. King. "Harold has a job over at the lumberyard in Gillette," she said, proud to have a wage earner in the house.

"That's a fine job, Mrs. Klum," she had said. "He's lucky to have it and they're lucky to have him. But Harold's a bright boy. He could go to UW. Then he could make even more money." She appealed to what she guessed were the family's more basic worries and who could blame them. Mr. Klum hadn't been on the scene for years. Harold also had two younger brothers, sullen boys who had not looked up from their video games when Lucy came in. A muted roar, as of an ocean or of bombs exploding, rose from the little screens.

Mrs. Klum sipped her coffee and said, slightly louder, as if Lucy's hearing were going, "Harold has a job over at the lumberyard in Gillette."

At that moment Lucy realized she had just made her last visit to a student's home. Mrs. Klum showed her out and stood on the front step, her meaty arms folded one over the other. She

hadn't worn a jacket, though the wind was wintry. She gave Lucy
a prim smile. Harold hadn't reappeared.

Carson had done most of his growing up within two blocks
of that house and Lucy knew she shouldn't have been surprised
by that. He had been one of those boys who was terrified that
someone might find out he loved to read.

Turning her truck quickly down the street that led to Princeton, Lucy recognized that Celia had kept her own secrets. She'd
never said a word about going to Kelso or spending time at Carson's house. She should never have forgotten that Celia was an
adolescent, at the age when children discover the practical necessity of secrets and start to live in daily duplicity. She was at a
moment when she needed to keep some piece of her life entirely
separate from adults so as to cultivate new layers of personality.
But of course, with separation came the risk that she would
make foolish choices. That she could endanger herself or someone else. That she would slip too quickly from a safe purchase
into something desolate or draining.

A car rushed past Lucy, headlights on high. Idiot, she
thought, flicking her own lights angrily at the car racing away.
Where the hell was this girl? Lucy pulled in at number 41.
No lights on in the low ranch, but Carson's truck was in the
driveway. Lucy leaned in the open window and saw the keys
dangling from the ignition and Laura's camera. She grabbed the
Pentax and began to shout her granddaughter's name. Her voice
bounced back at her. The house door was locked and the windows as well. Out back was an empty corral that smelled of fresh
manure, though there was no horse in it. Later, Lucy felt she
should have known immediately. The car that had swerved past
her had been driven by a man, not a boy acting like a fool, a man
with a tight jaw and a jut to his chin. Fear had prevented him
from remembering to turn his headlights down. He was taking a
girl he'd found on the sidewalk, an unconscious girl, to the hos-

pital and he feared she would die. But Lucy had guessed none of that. Where in God's name was Celia? And where was Carson? Shouldn't he be back by now?

She drove around the neighborhood, the truck windows down in spite of the chill and her thin shirt. Right on Harvard, left on Yale. Lights slowly returned to the houses, the doors of pickups slammed, TVs flicked back on the moment people walked in the door. "Have you seen my granddaughter?" she called to people still in their driveways. They knew her, they all knew her. Mrs. King, a familiar relic to some, an obsolete authority to others. No one had seen Celia. No one knew what had happened to her, though everyone she asked said of course they'd call right out to the ranch if they spotted her. Did they know what she looked like? "Sure," one man said, "like you, just young," and then he gave a choked laughed, realizing how it sounded aloud. Another said, "She'll be the only person in Callendar I don't know, so I'll have a pretty clear idea of who she might be." "Don't worry, Mrs. King," they all added. "She'll be back." They said that because they too had looked for lost children, because it was what you said to people looking. It was better to give hope of someone being alive than to live with the certainty of another alternative. Let the cops handle the news, the state trooper, the doctor, the officials in charge of loss. The ones who took their boys away.

Later, Lucy was amazed that no one had seen the pinto. His panic had cut him loose from the road the moment of Celia's fall, and he was long gone by the time people started returning from the rodeo. When Carson and his father found the animal a couple of hours after dawn, he was miles past the creek, six leaped fences between him and the corral. A night runner, able to steer himself without injury in the dark. Almost a reason to keep him.

At last Lucy decided to drive back home, but later she could not remember a moment of the twelve-mile journey. On her way, she let herself hope the house would be blazing with electricity, the dog barking—signs of Celia's joyful, unscathed return. But from the end of the driveway, all she saw was blackness. The light from even a single bulb could send a spark over the long field, but there was nothing. The dog had flattened itself on the porch and did not raise its head as she passed. Sensitive to moods from yards away, he had already decided the situation was bleak. It made her, who had raised the animal from the time he was eight weeks old, want to kick him in the ribs, but all she did was step over his body without a greeting. Who was he to give up so conclusively? She placed the camera so hard on the front table that it slid and fell to the floor. She did not bother to pick it up.

Usually, when waiting for news, she moved about, taking control of anything that allowed her to worry and work at once. Doctors' offices and hospitals brought out sewing. Waiting at home for a banker to call or the accountant to tell her how much she owed for taxes gave her hands broader, more vigorous scope: floor waxing, a scouring of the refrigerator. But tonight she could not bring herself to take on an activity. What was the use of attempting any kind of preservation? Of the people in the photographs all over the house, so few were still part of her life: Lucy, Janet, Arthur, her grandchildren, a couple of sisters and cousins. The rest definitively gone, either dead or moved away. More absent even than the land she had lost—the three thousand acres shrinking to one thousand and now to just over two hundred. It had cost the earth to buy the mineral rights to even that small parcel. The rest had been too expensive and she had been too stubborn to ask for help from Arthur or deepen the debt in which Sean had left them. Even so, she knew she was lucky that the rights on the land below her house hadn't been snapped up by someone else in the 1920s.

She sat in the green chair Sean had preferred and which she

had kept not so much as a tribute to him but as a practical con-
cession to their history together. An admission that someone else
had, at one time, shared this space with her. But tonight she
found herself sunk in its cushions, thinking, how goddamn uncomfortable, I have to get a new one.

This was a thought Lucy rarely had about anything. She
didn't replace sheets or towels until they were torn down their
centers or had inches of ragged fringe at the edges. It wasn't
stinginess, she insisted to Arthur and Janet when they pointed
out a carving knife with its blade worn to a crescent, a length of
old knitting needle used to anchor a hinge. It used to be called
"being frugal." It used to be called "living within your means."
You should have seen what my mother did with a single apple.
Even when the sheets could no longer span a mattress, they
could get shredded into cleaning cloths or wedged below the
crack of a door to keep out drafts. You could wring a solid lifetime from linen. They could tease her all they wanted.

Newness was alien to her, its need a kind of cultural disease.
She distrusted people who got a car every year. Her own lasted
fifteen to twenty, and grew so battered they nearly resembled
Carson's. There was deep comfort in knowing the exact capacities of something you had used often, treated well, and repaired.
It showed respect for the limits of what the world owed you. A
sense that you ought to be cautious about what you pulled and
demanded from it. To feel that the green chair had to be replaced was a shock, an unwelcome awareness come to light at an
awkward, anxious time.

If she wanted a new chair, where would it stop? Was she
really saying something else? Did she want to sell the land, the
house, give them up as lost? Was that the uneasiness that had
swirled around her all summer and pushed her to deface wells
and tear up beans? There was only so much more time before
she would have to relinquish it all, anyway. Perhaps now was as

good a moment as any to start thinking about and acting on this. Her will right now left the house, the land, the life insurance to Arthur and his family. But how much of this did he want? Not asking any of these questions had been a way to postpone an admission that she wouldn't be here to help him sort through all that.

She pulled one of the green cushions to her chest. Its mustiness was the smell of something untouched in a very long time. Maybe it really was time to sell the land. Maybe it was time to leave altogether. Everyone else was doing it and had been for years. The Wyoming way. Dust and underpopulation. No one but prairie dogs and truckers on long hauls to look at the sunsets. Why had she been so stubborn and insisted for so long on solitude? On all this conservation? Even Janet had left. I ache, Lucy realized, and it was the fact of sitting down and doing nothing that brought the pain to her attention. I ache in every single bone of my body.

The phone rang then, and she was so stiff that it seemed impossible she would get to it before the person hung up. It was Arthur, with Cam, calling from a gas station. They hadn't seen Celia at Kelso. He sounds old, Lucy thought. His voice is like Ray Fontaine's, all harsh and phlegmy. She explained about finding Carson's truck in his driveway. She talked about her slow tour through the neighborhood, but not about the people who kept telling her it would be all right. Arthur was beyond believing in that sort of consolation.

"Come back, Arthur, but stop first at the hospital." They both knew that if Celia had been hit, she wouldn't have had ID on her and the doctors might not know who she was.

Lucy went outside and apologized perfunctorily to the dog. She looked at her raked-over garden and went to see if the barn was locked. She checked on the chickens, who seemed restless, disgruntled. Feathers plumped, beaks clacking. Maybe the coyote was around. Then she heard the phone ring again and tore into the house, tripping over the dog, hurting him just when she hadn't wanted to.

It was Carson. "I think she took my horse, Mrs. King. He's missing, too."

"Horse? What horse, Carson?"

"The one I was training," he said. "That pinto horse. Too green for Celia." Lucy remembered now. She'd seen it in the C Bar C's corral. Ugly, mean, though according to Carson, the fastest and surest-footed animal he'd ever seen.

"Why, Carson?" It was the only question she could think of, though she couldn't say what the "why" referred to exactly—why that horse, why had she taken it at all, why was this even possible when she was frightened of riding?

He paused and the line crackled as it did when the wind was blowing, making sounds like tiny detonations trapped in the confines of wire. "I think I know, Mrs. King. I think it's for her to tell you, not me." Lucy was struck by the bareness of his voice and its note of strangled guilt. He was holding himself responsible for what happened, even if it had been Celia's choice to take the horse and her own foolishness if she got hurt. He was that rare person, unafraid to face the worst and to hold a confidence.

She still couldn't speak and didn't try to force herself to. She thought Carson would understand. He cleared his throat and said through the static that he and his father were going out now to look for Celia. They'd found tracks in the shoulder of College Road and were going to follow them. Some neighbors were coming, too. They had told the police. Did she want someone to come and be with her?

"No," she said finally, the word dry as an old root in her throat.

"I expect we'll be calling you directly, Mrs. King. I don't think she'll have gotten far."

"Thanks, Carson," Lucy said. "Thanks to your dad, too," and she hung up. Later, she didn't know how long she had stayed there by the phone. It could have been a minute, it could have been twenty. The next thing she knew was that she was on the porch, talking into the night.

She never prayed. When you saw the amount of bad or good luck that could hit a family in even one Wyoming day, it was hard to feel that anything akin to a deity—whether benevolent or punishing—existed. The world was too unpredictable and neutral the way it dealt out fate. Personal stupidity was clearly involved as well. No one was there to save you from yourself. It was people who made their own untidy nests of trouble, people who solved problems or didn't, without any kind of cloudy interference from numinous forces. Besides, what you had right in front of you was perfectly strange as it was. You didn't need to resort to God for mystery.

"You take secularism to new extremes," said Janet, who was, Lucy felt, a bit of a spiritual dabbler. She sang her hymns so fervently. She had ties to all those monks. They were adorable, and worthy, Lucy admitted, but they were still monks, little pursuers of orthodoxy.

"At least I've 'upset myself with reality,'" Lucy said, quoting Grace Paley, whose stories of New York, politics, and motherhood had strangely not been lost on her students in Callendar. They recognized the writer's gallows humor, the starkness of her characters, and their perverse choices.

Yet there she was—one moment in her house, gripping the rounded plastic of her phone, and the next facing the night, the worn boards of her porch below her feet, her body one long bruise though she hadn't fallen, words streaming from her mouth, years' worth of imprecation. There you have it, she thought as she woke to herself. Feeblemindedness at last. I've taken to beseeching. She heard scratching in the sage beyond the fence, and it could have been anything: restless bird, fox, ground squirrel. She knew why she invested the coyotes with such power. They survived with so little in their favor.

Then the phone rang again and it was Arthur. Her heart was a drum in her chest, making her ribs rattle. "It's me, Mom. She's at the hospital. She fell off a horse. She's unconscious, but it's not a coma." She had broken her arm in two places and might need surgery. It's nothing they hadn't seen before. "Mom," he said, "she's going to be fine."

"Carson called. He said he thought that had happened." She could barely speak.

"Carson? She took Carson's horse? That crazy pinto? Why?"

"Later, Arthur, can we talk it about it later? I want to get to the hospital. I'll be right over." Celia was all right. Celia hadn't died. Lucy flew up the stairs to her granddaughter's room. She stuffed underwear and shirts and pants into a backpack. She remembered her glasses and her toothbrush. She was so focused on her tasks she barely registered the howling. Zipping up the pack, she suddenly heard it, unspooling like the yarn from a skein wound wildly by hand, a fierce, uncharitable oddity of scale to it. A big pack. A pack, Lucy knew with curious certainty, that was not on her land but on Ted Flaxman's, a pack she had never heard before. On her way to the truck, she pushed the dog, alert to the presence of new predators, inside the house.

Again, she remembered nothing of the drive to town. Only the difficulty of finding the ER now that yet another wing was being built and detour signs had popped up like toadstools all over the pavement. Arthur and Cam were bent around a pair of steaming cups of coffee. Another man was with them, and he turned out to be the one who'd brought Celia in, the man who'd seen it happen. She recalled the glint of his jaw. The man with the headlights on too bright.

His name was Luke Masters, and he explained that he'd taken a wrong turn and all of a sudden there was this pinto horse and this girl and the horse reared and threw the girl straight to the ground. Luke was alive to his critical role in the drama. He would not have wanted to hear, as Cam pointed out later, that if he hadn't turned into the street just when he did, the horse might not have startled at all and Celia might have calmed it down eventually.

"I thought, that poor thing. So skinny. I just didn't think a moment about it. I got her right in my backseat and drove her straight here." Despite the blood from her open fracture, he said, as if hinting at future restitution. He gave Lucy his card. Luke Masters, Masters Car and Home Insurance, Cheyenne, up for the day to watch a cousin in the rodeo. She wanted to ask him if he'd ever learned, given his work, that moving a person with a potential spine or head injury could kill her.

His cell phone rang every couple of minutes—the hospital was practically the only place in the county where connections worked—and he kept glancing at its leather holster with a measure of exasperation. Implying how occupied his business kept him, how necessary he was to its smooth operation, though it was more likely some fed-up wife or girlfriend, home alone too long with too many kids. I have no time for this man, was the next thought to cross Lucy's mind. She interrupted a fresh telling of Luke Masters's narrative to ask Arthur, "Who's on duty?"

"Doc Ebersole," he said. That was good. Roger Ebersole was competent and thorough, and he knew who they were. "We can't see her until she's in a room," Arthur said. She had had a bad concussion and they were still putting on her cast. She would be woozy for a few days. "But she's going to be all right," he kept saying. As he spoke, Arthur looked at Cam, who was poking holes with a red straw in the rim of his Styrofoam cup.

"Why was she on Carson's horse?" Cam asked suddenly.

Yes, that was the most pressing question, but they would have to wait for Celia to answer it.

Luke Masters started stroking his cell phone again and launched into the third rendition of how he'd found Celia slouched on the side of the road, of how he'd thought, that little girl is dead and gone. Cam and Arthur glared at him, as if they might rise as a pair and share the throttling. "Mr. Masters," Lucy said, "you have done us a great service. But I think someone on the other end of that phone is looking for you."

He gaped at her, as did the other people slouched in the plastic chairs. She never permitted herself to stoop so low, to be so gratuitously impolite. I don't care, Lucy thought. I just don't give a damn what this dress-up cowboy from Cheyenne thinks about me or what kind of stories he tells or what anyone has to say about me. I just can't see him for one more second. He pulled in a little air, closed his mouth at last, turned on the heel of his shiny boot, and left.

Lucy thought then of the new coyotes and of the threat they posed to the pack already settled on her land. The old ones would be harder to displace than the young ones might think. They knew the terrain so well. They knew exactly where to hide, exactly what the land had to offer in the way of shelter and sustenance. They had history on their side.

Lucy was with Celia when she woke the next morning just past dawn. Cam and Arthur had gone back to the ranch to take care of the animals and get some sleep. Arthur had tried to coax her home as well, but she resisted. She had revealed her true cussedness to Luke, the self-important angel, and found it still the strongest element in her character at the moment. She was going to stay with Celia.

The girl had been so still for so much of the night that all it took for Lucy to know that she was awake was the tiniest of twitchings. A delicate stirring and then her eyes were open. What she saw would be blurred, because someone had carefully slipped her contacts out. She would also, the doctor warned, be in pain. "Her head's going to hurt like that horse sat on it," he said and Lucy could tell that that was so. Celia lifted the arm in the cast tentatively, as if surprised by its weight.

The doctor had also told Lucy to make sure the curtains were closed, because light would hurt. Lucy had followed his advice, but even so, a line of sun slipped past the edges of the cloth and Lucy saw Celia pull back from it as if touched by fire. She went to close the fabric more tightly and when she got back, she slid Celia's glasses onto her nose and over the slight bumps of her ears. She noticed scabs like red claw marks scoring Celia's right hand. Horsehair had shredded it.

"Hi, Lucy," she said, and her voice was raw and low. "Am I in the hospital? Why does my head hurt so much?"

"Yes," Lucy told her. "You are. You got thrown from a horse, from Carson's horse. Do you remember that?" She sheltered her granddaughter's red wrist.

Celia nodded slowly. "That's all I remember," she said. "Riding him and then he reared and I fell. But I don't remember coming here." She swallowed, and it looked as if that hurt, too. "Can you help me to the bathroom?"

Lucy eased her out of bed. Celia tottered, and her heavy cast tilted her whole body to the left. It sobered them both to recognize how much Celia needed to be in a hospital. She kept the door ajar as she went in, and Lucy caught a glimpse of herself in the mirror. The ruffled braid, the lined face. Old: conclusively, definitively old.

Back under the covers, Celia asked for something to drink and Lucy went to the nurses' station to get some juice. Walking back, she spied Cam and Arthur coming down the hall, and noticed, as if for the first time, how dark their faces had become over the summer. Cam seemed worn but oddly solid, more present than usual. As if he might stay in the room with them, right next to Celia's bed, instead of perched close to what schools and hospitals and airlines always called "the nearest exit." But Arthur's eyes were sunken, the skin beneath them almost like a football player's before a game, stripes of greasepaint on the cheekbones. He'd looked like this in the days after Laura died, scooped clean of will and understanding. "She's awake," she told them.

"Hi, baby," Arthur said to Celia when he came to her bedside.

"Hi, Dad," she said. "I didn't die, Dad," she added and her voice seemed to surprise him with its roughness. She rasped, like someone old and ill. A part of herself she was supposed to meet years from now that had somehow nudged its way forward.

Arthur put his head down on her bed. Celia didn't seem to realize she had said exactly the wrong thing. Lucy watched her eyes start to close again. She must have fallen back asleep with the weight of his head on her legs.

"Sorry," he said, stumbling to his feet, pulling himself back from the edge of his fear and relief, trying to behave as he wanted to. If Lucy didn't mind, he and Cam were going to go and talk to Carson, Arthur said. The horse had been found miles from town and it had been shot. Arthur wanted to pay the boy for his loss and to talk to the parents. He asked Lucy not to tell Celia right away.

Lucy nodded and watched the father and the tall son walk almost side by side down the corridor. They were going to leave her here for the vigil. These abidings were women's work, and familiar, no matter whom they concerned: sick cows, neighbors, children. She knew the rhythm, the simple watching. Not naturally still, Lucy always had a book with her in case she was stranded somewhere. Now she was reading about the marsh Arabs of Iraq, the tribes who lived in the south of the country in huts built of reeds on islands of clay that drifted lumpily through the swamps. Most of them were gone now, the people and the reeds, killed off first by Saddam Hussein's water projects, then by his henchmen, and then by other wars. But the writer of this account, fifty years earlier, had had the patience and interest to live among them and drink their tea and learn how they wove their crackling houses.

The light that still insisted on creeping past the edges of the curtain grew paler, the thinned liquid of autumn. Now and then a nurse came in to take Celia's vital signs. Celia slept through it all. A few bouquets arrived—one from Dwight, one from the C Bar C, one from the Historical Society. News traveled like floodwater out here and the flowers stood at stiff attention on the radiator. The sounds of a hospital at its business filtered into the room: phones ringing, nurses' clogs padding along the hall, a cart delivering food or medicine to someone waiting in a room exactly like this one. No one occupied the bed next to Celia's and it stood there severely unrumpled, sheets pulled to military tautness.

Lucy hadn't realized that Celia was awake until she heard her voice asking, "Who are they from?" and saw the girl pointing to the arrangements.

"Family friends," Lucy said.

Celia looked disappointed and Lucy thought she understood. She'd been hoping Carson would send some, that there would be absolution. But flowers wouldn't be his way, in any case.

"How did I get here?" Celia asked, but she couldn't look at Lucy as she said this. Instead, she stared at her cast, which crept north of her elbow. It was terribly confusing that something so significant could happen to a body with barely a memory of the experience lodging somewhere. "I keep trying to remember," Celia said, "but nothing's there." The horse, her body airborne, and that was all.

Lucy explained about Luke Masters and told her the doctors said she had a concussion. At first they had worried about a hairline fracture of the skull. "You were lucky as far as these things go. You've got a tough head." But she should expect to feel pretty rocky for a few days. The arm was a bad break; she'd landed on a stone that had busted through both bones. The cast would be on for at least two months, if not longer. "Might delay the driving for a while," Lucy said, and she folded the corner of the page of her book and set it on the table. She hoped that would be as close to rebuke as she would come. She would restrain herself from saying that Celia didn't have the experience to ride an old nag, much less a barely broken mustang. To have done so at night, without a saddle, was beyond foolhardy. She had not merited the good fortune of not dying from her carelessness. Blessed with a luck that people from Wyoming rarely got wind of.

"Carson?" Celia said, still not looking at her grandmother.

"They're only letting family see you right now," Lucy explained.

"He hasn't called?" Celia said, sitting up slightly. Lucy saw her wince and remembered when she herself had had a concussion after slipping on an icy patch in a parking lot. Moving her head felt as if a jagged piece of metal had disturbed the fluid that suddenly filled her skull.

Celia wanted to know about the horse. Had they caught him?

Lucy shook her head, not wanting to lie but not wanting to break her promise to Arthur. "Gray and Carson went to look for him, but I don't know if they found him or not."

"What will they do to him?" Celia was staring past the curtains, it seemed, toward the mountains.

"Gray will shoot him. Catch him and shoot him." That, at least, it felt fair to say. That it had already happened was almost beside the point. Celia nodded and looked down at her arm in its stiff, podgy cast. She had cost Carson his horse. That was why he hadn't come. She had lost all that with one act of stupidity.

Lucy said, watching her closely, "Honey, if he hadn't hurt you, he would have hurt someone else. Everyone who saw him said so. He was marked."

"Not to Carson," Celia said.

That was true, Lucy allowed, not to Carson. The bad horse had meant the world to him.

"Has it snowed yet?" Celia asked suddenly.

"Not yet," Lucy said, admittedly surprised. "But it's on its way."

"Someone needs to watch Cam. Pay attention to him."

"Why?" Lucy asked, leaning in. "Do you know something?" Celia's abrupt authority rattled her. The low, dark voice from the slender, damaged girl in the white bed.

"No," said Celia, "not exactly. Someone just needs to pay attention."

A nurse came in who had none of the efficiency usually associated with the profession. She seemed barely awake, this one, with lank blond hair and a limp body. "I'm here to take your vitals," she said, but it seemed to Lucy that the time might be better spent measuring her own. The blood pressure cuff swelled on Celia's arm and the nurse asked her if she was in pain. When Celia nodded yes, she checked something off on her pad and wandered out.

"That means you'll get something about twelve hours from now," Carson said from the doorway. "She's a slow one. I've been waiting for five minutes."

His hat was off and he appeared not to have changed clothes or washed since the rodeo. His hair was flattened on one side of his head. His bootheels were full of wedged dirt and he wore roping gloves. "Can I come in?" he asked.

"Sure," said Lucy. "I'm going to go get Celia something to eat. I'll be back in a bit." She watched the boy drag a chair next to Celia's bed and watched, too, as he bent his head and did not speak. No matter how big the chair, he always needed more legroom.

Lucy went downstairs to the cafeteria and tried to find something she thought Celia could manage. Soup and crackers. French fries, which she always loved. She was terribly hungry herself, and didn't care that the food looked wan and bland. Sitting down at a table with a stack of flabby pancakes and a cup of coffee, she observed the other patrons. Some were relaxed and laughing; whoever they were here to see was out of danger, on the mend. Then there were others, in padded jackets, though the room was overheated, heads bent together over the tabletops, whispering and muted, in the midst of their vigil, the outcome still unclear. Lucy felt she was somewhere in between. Not in the grip of immediate panic but not yet relieved. It wasn't that she feared for Celia's physical recovery, but for what had happened to her before she even mounted the horse.

When she finished her food, fatigue descended on her. She felt like one of her tomato plants caught by frost, brittle and sagging, blackened. A few minutes outside would help; she needed to breathe air that hadn't been recirculated. She'd forgotten, however, that smokers had to cluster at the entrances for their fix these days, and had to walk toward the center of the parking lot to avoid the tobacco.

From there, she could see Carson's truck at the far side of the lot and also, glancing at the hospital, the window to Celia's room. Clouds were building over the mountains, a sure sign of weather. The temperature, too, had dropped. A storm was on the way, as Celia had said. Tomorrow it would be September. School would start next Tuesday. Cam a senior, Celia a junior. But Celia would still be at home. There would be snow on the ground when they began, too. Some school years started hazy and achingly hot. Some years started and stayed cold.

She watched her breath hang in the air as if she, too, were one of the people puffing away at the hospital door. People drove in, parked, shuffled off to see a doctor, friend, or relative. She should go back.

Then she saw Carson striding toward his truck. He was easy to spot with that unmistakable copper hair, even flattened and

dirty. He hauled the stiff door back and slid into the driver's seat.
But instead of starting the engine, he leaned his head and arms
on the steering wheel. All she could see was his slumped body,
until the sun shifted and made his windshield a blaze of golden
light and she could no longer see him. A minute later, he started
the car, startling five ravens on a telephone wire so they rose
from their perch into the sky like unbalanced crosses. After re-
covering themselves, the birds reeled off after him, as if expecting
that the truck would soon expire roadside and provide them with a
rusty meal. Lucy looked up then at Celia's window. She had managed to get herself out of bed, pulled aside the curtains, and was
standing there, even though the light must have seared her eyes.

By the time Lucy got upstairs, Celia was back in bed. Lucy
had expected tears, but there were none. Her granddaughter
was silent when Lucy set the cafeteria food on a tray. She
glanced at it and said thank you but touched nothing.

"He came to say goodbye," she said, looking not at Lucy but
out the window, the curtains still slightly parted. Carson was
leaving tomorrow for a job in Colorado. He was going to be a
wrangler on a big ranch down there, for a guy who bred quarter
horses. The pay was good.

Then she blurted, looking straight at her grandmother,
"Carson's gay, Lucy. I figured it out last night, and he knew it."

So that was it. The word always struck her as odd; she'd used
it in such different contexts when she was young. Holiday dances
and certain dresses were gay, girls of a merry temperament. She
didn't understand how Celia had seen this; she'd never suspected it herself, and she couldn't connect it to Jack and the ride
that nearly killed the girl. But she didn't need to figure that out
now. What she needed to acknowledge was an essential change
in Celia and most likely in Carson, too. Carson was probably
choosing to seal himself into a version of his self that would try
to keep him from getting killed, beaten up, or refused in the only

world in which he found peace: horses, ranches, cattle, men to whom he would not tell his secret.

"They found Jack and it was like you said it was going to be. They killed him." Now her voice was breaking. "I made them kill him. It was my fault. He wouldn't be dead if I hadn't been so stupid."

"Stupid or not," Lucy said, "that horse had proved himself unreliable over and over. It wasn't the first time, Celia. That horse wasn't meant for people." Yet she knew it wasn't true. Jack had been meant for one person, at least. Two lies in a day. Once you started, they sprang right to the tongue. Living with them was always more difficult.

"I told him I'd get him a new horse. I have almost all the money I earned this summer." Her voice had eased, but she still wouldn't look at Lucy. "He said he knew that, but a new horse wouldn't change a thing. And then he left."

Celia started to cry, and Lucy could only imagine how much it made her head hurt. She stroked Celia's hair, which smelled of sweat and antiseptic. Heartbreak, decisions without the possibility of reversal. More loss. She was too young for any of it. Inevitably, she'd heal askew, like a rodeo cowboy's skeleton, not a piece of it that hadn't been shaken out of line. The way Lucy had healed after losing babies and Sean. She'd become fiercer, which was nowhere near the same as happier.

"Baby," she said when Celia stopped, "you need to eat. Here's soup and french fries, and tonight I'll bring you anything you want." And I will not leave you until I die, is what she wanted to say but did not. She could not swear to something so far beyond her control, though parents always did that, promising what could never be assured. An essential dishonesty so that you didn't raise a child in fear, even if Celia was well beyond believing that kind of cloudy promise.

Still, she was not beyond comforting. She let herself be held and then let herself be fed. She wolfed down the fries, drank cranberry juice, and fell asleep, a veil of red sugar on her upper lip. She looked no older than nine, despite her length. And pale. The only member of her family untouched by sun this summer.

Arthur came in and sat beside Lucy. He was shaved now and had changed clothes, but looked no more rested. "Cam is back at the house, sleeping," he said. "Has the doctor been in?" He didn't take his eyes from his daughter as Lucy told him what she knew, but not about Carson and why he was leaving. "No doctor yet," she said, "just a bunch of nurses." She was getting better. She was young. Her body would heal quickly.

Arthur nodded and nodded some more. "I should take them back to New York, Mom. This has all been a bad idea. I expected too much of them. Of you. We've been nothing but trouble." He'd involved her, he said, in work that wasn't hers: getting through the terrible first year after a death. Not just a death, they both knew, but a suicide, the kind of ending that puts a family into contact with the darkest sort of wonder, the most intense variety of rage, the harshest of abandonments. "I'm not in my right mind, Mom. The kids aren't, either. We're just in awful shape." Denise Higgins, Cam's sudden involvement with Amber, Celia's terrible fall. The ruin and danger were there for all to see. And they did see, Lucy knew. Callendar was a good place to observe behavior: there was so much sky and the light was piercingly clear. Everything that had happened this summer would affect the way people leaned in to say hello or goodbye, how are you these days or how about those Broncos.

She took up nodding where Arthur had left off. She could see that. She knew what he meant by every word he said. But he should never think that he and the children had been a burden. She loved having them there. Every moment. Lucy stopped short of saying that until they had joined her, she hadn't realized how lonely and peculiar she had become. How much she had calcified inside the shape of an old life, how much she welcomed the shift they had forced her to make. She said nothing about her well defacements or her recent questioning of purpose, or the flare of desire to sell the land. She wrapped her arm around her son's shoulders, holding him close to keep from saying that she would wither if they left now.

"None of what you say is right," she told him. "Not one word. You fill up that old house." But she knew he was feeling that they didn't fit out here and never would. Arthur never had a simple time fitting anywhere in his life; places sat badly on him. He'd wanted to be equal to whatever he encountered—the ranching life, his East Coast dislocation, the marriage to his pretty, unstable wife, the raising of his tall, untrusting children—but none of it had come naturally to him. She had nurtured the most maladroit of men.

"Don't make decisions now," she told him. "You're exhausted. So am I. I'm going to go on home and get some rest. Celia needs to see you, too." He leaned into her then and let her touch his hair. You would never know he'd begun the summer with a gash, just as you'd never know, unless you took his X-ray, that almost every bone in his lower body showed some sign of having fractured. Now it seemed he had a child who shared his propensity for breakage. Lucy left them, Celia still sleeping and Arthur bent over the bed as if to keep his daughter from falling from it to the cold tiles below.

Lucy nearly drove into three ditches on her way home, she was so tired. She switched the radio on to keep herself from dozing off. The forecast predicted a blizzard within twenty-four hours. At least a foot of snow expected, blowing in from the Rockies. Back at the house, Cam was still fast asleep, in his bed for once and not in the barn. She greeted the dog, who was hoping to be reinstated in her affections despite his lapse of confidence. It was getting colder and colder. Automatically, she began preparing a list of what she'd need to do to ready the ranch. Get the storm windows on, make sure nothing was about to give out in the furnace, do a big shop, check the freezer to see if last year's steak was still good. She would need, too, to go to the library and bookstore and make a run on some new titles. How many blizzards have I lived through, she wondered as she made a new pot of coffee.

She could not leave this place. Her hands on a mug webbed with cracks, she looked around, knew that Arthur and his children would return to New York, and understood, with a clarity that sucked the air from her lungs, that she would die in this house. She would not yield one scrap of the acres she had salvaged, not one item of furniture. If Arthur had difficulty finding a place that could tolerate all the experiences he'd known and been shaped by, I've got the opposite problem, Lucy thought. I belong here, retired, cross, and lonely. This is the only land on which I can imagine myself. All that reading about those Arabian deserts and humid jungles was just a way, at heart, to stay convinced about Wyoming, to make me grateful for this state. It was odd to realize that what was essential in her character had nothing to do with how she'd occupied herself all these years—the reading, the teaching, the caring for all those schoolchildren. What she was, at the bone, was that view from her porch, the field behind her house where she had buried horses, dogs, a husband, the body of the baby lost at five months. The sky that arched above what was left of her land with supreme, indifferent beauty. The old coyote and her descendants. The house with its photographs, its curtains, every one of which she had made and hemmed and washed herself. It was where she had unfolded the person she had become. To tear herself from that would be not only to betray the land that had allowed her that discovery, but to step inside a self she would not recognize. The reality she possessed came from walking across that floor and into that yard day after day. Would this awareness channel itself into something more productive? Would she become a member of the Powder River Alliance? Organize protests in Cheyenne? Lucy couldn't say for sure, but she doubted it. Her activist days were probably over. She had spent that energy with children, teaching them the rich, portable gift of thinking.

She knew then that she would use the last canister of spray-paint. The criminal trickiness had been a way to keep herself upright, to prevent herself from falling into numbing doubt, as Laura must have. To anchor herself a little more firmly to this windy place. She wrote a quick note to Cam, telling him she'd be back soon. The dog was thrilled to be allowed back in the cab of the truck. The gold paint was all that was left and it seemed fitting to finish her career as a graffiti artist with a gilded flourish. She had no poems to offer this time. Besides, she couldn't stand seeing anyone else misquoted or misspelled. "Wilfred Blake" had nearly killed her.

Ted Flaxman had sold another chunk of his mineral rights. He'd given up trying to fight them, his son had told Lucy at the rodeo. "Now he's got this notion that he's at least going to get rich off them and use the money to improve the ranch." The young man had gone a dark, mottled red as he spoke. Ted, seized with a greed that had only occasionally despoiled his character, was splitting his family as surely as if he'd taken an ax to them. His son, a geology major at UW, could expect to make his living much the same way, if he wanted to. But he still regretted that their land, one of the biggest parcels left in the county, was going to be sullied like this.

The well was off Owl Creek, which flowed into Coal Creek near its border with Lucy's property. There was nowhere to park the truck where it couldn't be seen from the road. Anyone who knew her would know she was there, and might be bored or curious enough to come and investigate. It was hard to care. Lucy was filled with a strange enthusiasm that made her joints feel fluid. The dog seemed to have caught her mood, too, and behaved, suddenly, like an animal years younger than he was.

The light was getting dim, and the sun was streaked with clouds that looked as if they'd spent time near a city collecting soot—red and black and gray, somber and low. The new well was its usual placid self: squat, the color of yellowed clay, studded with valves, and at its center, a tightly locked door. The dog sniffed it as he always did, but declined to pee.

Lucy paused in front of the well. The indirectness of poetry had been a shield against what she really wanted to say. But the coarseness of swearwords didn't suit her, either. Without quite knowing where the sentence would lead, she started: "Look up this draw. Pronghorn live here." She would have written coyotes, but then her message would have been read as an invitation to kill them. She knew from experience that she had only a few words left. "It is meant for them." The "them" was a little patchy, but still legible. She heard a car slowing on the road. The head-lights were on, and it stopped on the verge. She heard the smack of the door and saw someone walking across the scrub toward her. She knew in an instant that it was Ray Fontaine.

Well, that's that, she thought. She put the canister back in her bag and used her belt to leash Franklin. None of her collies had ever liked Ray. He was letting his enormous flashlight travel across the words glittering on the well.

He said nothing, and for once Lucy couldn't read his face. Not only because of the light but because his expression was blank. When he finally spoke, he surprised her. "Hi, baby. I've been hoping I wouldn't catch you." He turned up the collar of his jacket and tilted his hat at the brim. No one looked more like a cowboy sheriff. He even had a great big tumbleweed right be-hind his left shoulder. He lit a cigarette.

"I thought Jesus told you to leave those sticks of sin behind." When, Lucy said to herself, listening to the muted growl of the dog, will I learn to shut up?

In normal circumstances, she would have expected Ray to

use such a situation—a criminal's vulnerability, his own decided advantage—as a chance to gloat, to establish firmly demarcated zones of power and control. Instead, he looked sad and worn. He seemed to need the cigarette badly.

Lucy experienced an unbidden memory of what it was like to kiss him after he'd been smoking. His firm mouth, his chapped lips, and the thread of smoke laced together in a pleasure no one had come close to matching. She had always hated the smell of tobacco, but in Ray, it was linked to desire. It came to her then that he was one of the reasons she was never going to leave her land. He was one of the people who had shown her, even unwillingly, part of what she consisted of.

"I can't do it," he said now, and rubbed the coal of his cigarette across the bottom of his boot in a short comet of red sparks. "If I had, I'd have done it the first time that damn poetry showed up. Who else knows about that kind of goddamn thing? And now I got you red-handed and I just don't give a flying shit." He turned his flashlight off. All that people would see now as they passed would be their empty cars.

"Gold-handed," Lucy said, walking toward him, holding her fingers up to him. In the last flare of the sun, they might shine like large, lighted matches. But they were still slightly damp. She hadn't expected them to leave traces on Ray's cheeks, as if some fabulous creature had fallen from the sky and singled him out as something sacred. When he kissed her, it seemed that holy. If by holy you meant an abiding awareness of what the densest kind of pleasure could do to you, how it opened something wide inside your body but did not stay there. How it rang from your bones and reached through the layers of muscle and skin and out to the cold air, where it announced itself as reverence for being lucky enough to have a pulse.

"You need to go home," he said as he pulled away from her. Amazingly, the dog had been silent. "And you need to stop this." He turned his flashlight on again. "I been worried about you all summer." They walked back to her truck, she heaved the dog in and then herself. He stood there for a moment and asked her about Celia. "She's going to be fine. They're not going to stay, I don't think," Lucy said.

"Well that's as obvious as piss," Ray said. He'd been in the same class with her and Sean and every student there had permanently adopted that phrase into his lexicon.

"Really?" Lucy asked, her fingers cold on the car keys.

"Arthur's just looking for a way for him and those kids to duck that sadness, and who can blame them?" he said. "What we call in AA 'doing a geographic,'" and he sounded all of sudden like himself again, slightly puffed, wedged inside his own narrowness. But gold-flecked, at least, Lucy thought. He and Nancy Baum would both be startled when he saw her tonight. Still, Lucy felt nothing other than a need to leave instantly, to get back to her house, find Cam.

"Thank you, Ray," she said and left him there in the cold sagebrush. The dog maintained a low growl in its throat the whole way back. "Shut up," she told the animal, but it didn't listen.

At the house, Cam was up and starting supper. Beets, pork chops, and fried potatoes. He'd acquired this competence recently, it seemed to Lucy, but looked natural with a knife and a cutting board. "I thought you'd be back soon," he said. Not only had he gotten tan this summer, he'd kept growing. He filled the kitchen. His father had called and would be home by seven.

"Thanks, honey. That's kind of you," she said. "We're going to have to get the house ready for the blizzard. I usually get the storm windows in before Labor Day, but I haven't done it this year."

The chops were hissing in the pan, the dog lurking at Cam's knees. Her grandson was chopping onions for the potatoes. "I know," he said. "I heard it on TV," which meant he had been at Amber's.

"Cam," Lucy said, abruptly aching for a shower, "do you

want to stay out here? Go to school? Live in town?" Do you want to be from here? she was asking. Do you want this place attached to your history more firmly?

"Yeah, I do," he said and looked up from the cutting board. "I didn't think I would, but I do." He wanted to say more perhaps, and she waited, remembering how hard it was for some boys to summon words. Cam had always treated language as if it might leap up and bite him in the face. He hadn't spoken until he was two and then in complete sentences, but only if holding Laura's hand. Lucy sensed he wanted to tell her something, about Amber, about himself. Instead, he looked more closely at her and asked, "Lucy, what happened to your hands?"

Lucy looked down. The gold paint glowed dully in the kitchen's yellow light. She sighed. "I do not want to lie to you, Cam, but I also do not feel up to the entire truth at the moment. It has been a long day."

The pork chops' sizzling intensified. He leaned down to lower the heat. "I know how that feels." He turned the meat in its juices. "I knew she wasn't dead. I don't know how I knew it, but I did."

"I'll be down in a few minutes," she told him. "Thank you, Cam," and she waved her smeared fingers at the table, the stove. Meaning thank you for your confidence, your competence. He reminded her of Sean, whom he did not physically resemble in any way. There he was, turning into a man who could at least in part be relied upon.

Usually, Lucy took showers that lasted no more than the time it took to soap her body twice, rub some concoction of shampoo and conditioner through her hair, and rinse. They took all of three to four minutes, depending on how good the pressure was. She knew better than to waste either soap or water on oil-based paint, but she tried scrubbing the gold that had settled in the folds of her skin. Steam rose in round clouds around her. The paint would not roll off. Water pounded on her back and the cramp eased from her bones. The steam hid her own body from her, though she could see the skin pinkening. She let the wonderful humid warmth envelop her. Through the heat, she heard Cam's curious, slightly worried voice calling for her up the stairs, "Lucy? You OK?" and she did not answer him.

CAM

Arthur had returned shivering from the hospital, and Cam sat with him and his grandmother, her hair still damp, at the kitchen table. Lucy had been in the shower for what seemed like hours, far longer than she would have allowed anyone else to abuse the privilege of water. Perhaps she was counting on the power of the forecast storm to replenish her spring, but Cam didn't think so. His father talked, and Cam had a hard time listening to him. He was watching the odd pattern that the drops from Lucy's hair were making on the table's scored wood. It was going to take time to incorporate this image of wastefulness and need into Lucy. She looked so small with her hair wet—a dog after a downpour, all her terrier edge diminished. She hadn't sounded happy when he admitted to her that he wanted to stay in Wyoming, that he liked it here. His hands were shaking badly and it was not, for once, because he was thinking of Laura, but because he had seen that, at least for the moment, Lucy was without an anchor. He needed her resolute in the face of danger, it turned out.

None of them was eating the food he had prepared and the meal was slowly cooling in front of them. The crimson juice of the beets had leached into the potatoes and the plates had turned a shiny pink. The dog was pacing, as if eager to go out, but every time Cam rose to open the door, he just stood at the threshold and barked. At first, his father talked about Celia— that she was healing quickly, the doctor was pleased, they had to run a few more tests just to make sure she was ready to leave, but she should be back tomorrow. "It's going to take a few weeks for her to recover," Arthur warned. "She may have headaches. She won't be able to start school on time."

School. The word echoed with abrupt severity in the bright room. Cam had barely thought about it all summer, preoccupied with Amber and the Barlows, their weird power to soothe and frighten him at once. Classes. He had no concrete idea of what the high school was like. He'd driven past the building with Amber, scarcely curious about it—she'd absorbed so much of his attention. The soccer field wasn't evenly graded and tufts of gray grass studded the faded green, he'd noticed, but without judgment or real interest. He had been living fully in real time, the past and future blunted by the meatiness of daily life.

Staying seemed like an even better and better idea. It was, in fact, the best idea, a solution to all kinds of difficulties in spite of everything—his father's courting of danger with Denise Higgins, at least as Celia had described it in pissed-off whispers, Lucy's sudden loss of energy, the unhealthy hold the Barlows had on him. Suddenly he was hungry and began to eat the cooled food. The thick-cut pork was flavorful, hickory-smoked, cured by a neighbor of Lucy's. All year, she got to eat this meat she had raised herself, full of its taste of ash and apples. It seemed a great boon.

Between forkfuls, Cam started to listen more closely to what Arthur was saying. His voice had deepened to the tone he used for difficult patches of fathering. He was, he said, reconsidering the decision to live in Callendar. Now he was thinking that as soon as Celia was ready to travel, they should move back to New York. He was sorry he had made them leave so much behind and been so indecisive, but Wyoming wasn't going to work out in the long run for any of them. He should have known that.

Arthur didn't look at either Lucy or Cam as he spoke. His shoulders were rounded inward. The dog kept pacing by the door and growling. Lucy said, her hair still disordered around her shoulders, "That damn dog. He smells the new coyotes."

The new ones? Cam thought. What is she talking about? She wasn't paying attention to the drama of the moment, and for the first time he saw what Lucy might be like when she was an old, old woman and vagueness settled on her. Her distraction gave him a terrible keenness and desire for sharp detail. "What about the apartment?" Cam protested. He knew it had been sublet until winter. He'd work something out with the tenant, Arthur said coolly, and Cam had no doubt that he could. Arthur was nothing if not a skilled attorney. People who signed contracts with him ought to fear him. He was even more likely to win unwritten agreements, the kind that bound fathers and sons.

Lucy continued to look at the dog and pluck up ridges of brown skin on her bony hands, less gently than she'd touched his own in the barn earlier in the summer. She was sitting, Cam noticed, where he had carved his name about a thousand years ago. Not her usual place. Everything was shifting, again: his father was where Laura always sat. The chair that had been removed at the start of the summer, the gap they all slightly avoided, filled now with Arthur laying down the law. Cam kept eating, his knife and fork scraping the surface of the plate, just another sound in the room along with wind on glass, the dog's claws on wood, his father's low voice.

"I'm sorry," Arthur was saying, but he didn't sound sorry. He sounded determined. For the first time in ages, he was looking undefeated, as he did when he won a case. The only time that expression sat easily on him. He appeared truly purposeful, and his voice had none of the false energy with which he had first tried to sell them on Wyoming last spring. Cam felt a buzzing in his brain that transferred to his ears. He finished every scrap on his plate and moved it firmly to the center where it knocked over a saltcellar shaped like a swan. He did not right it. Lucy observed the sprawl of white crystals that poured from the animal's open back, and Arthur reached over, tilted the bird back up, and swept the tiny grains into his cupped hand. Cam realized what he felt was fury. "This has been an enormous amount to ask of you children. I have put you through too much," Arthur said, tapping his palm on a plate to free the salt.

That's one way to put it, thought Cam. He pushed back his chair and stared at his father and grandmother. Lucy wouldn't look at him, and something like shame cascaded across her face. She didn't like what Arthur was doing, either. There's something weak in this turnaround, she seemed to imply. You should make a choice and stick with it. Cam was sick of responding to the consequences of other people's actions: Laura, who made his hands shake, who stuck to him like skin every moment beyond the orbit of Amber and her family; Celia, who had nearly died; Lucy, even, more human and more fragile than he had ever seen her. "Shut up," he heard himself say to his father. "Just shut up." As if he had said pass the mustard please. Quietly, with bland, offhand politeness. As callous as he had been with the trout out on the stream, the smack of rock on the wedge of the fish's head.

Arthur looked so surprised that for a moment Cam nearly laughed. Then he did laugh, though it didn't sound remotely mirthful, but more like one of Mac's coughing barks. Lucy looked up then, blankness on her face. The dog was quiet at the door.

"Stop right now, Dad. You need to listen." Cam's hands were quaking uncontrollably. His father and grandmother were both transfixed by them, as if they were a symptom of some terrible disorder. He almost wanted to spread them out in front of his body, a first-class exhibit of pathology, but his self-disgust was strong, and he shoved his fingers beneath his thighs, where he felt his knuckles dig into muscle. I'm not going to go back to New York, he wanted to yell. I'm going to stay here and if I can't stay with Lucy, I'll find a place in town. You can't yank me like a dog from one place to the next and expect me to tag along. But he could not marshal the words. Instead, all he said was, "I like

it here. I don't know why, but I like it here." The tics kept pop-
ping through his fingers.

"Is it that girl?" Arthur asked. "Has that girl gotten to you?"
Cam was startled at the menace in his father's tone. He said the
word "girl" as if it sat on his tongue like a morsel of rotten food.

Cam had no way to tell his father what it was like to be with
Amber and her family and how strangely it soothed him. He
could easily have told Laura, who never discounted anyone's experience of anything. People took time, the increments of their
lives and feelings the longest, most nuanced of books. His connection with the Barlows would have surprised or even worried
her, but she would have listened.

"No," Cam said. "It doesn't have anything to do with Amber," though that was not strictly true. "I can't explain why I like
it here. I just do." He sat there, his hands growing gradually
numb with the weight of his body.

"Arthur," Lucy said, clicking suddenly back to her old self,
though her hair was still a ragged wetness on her shoulders, "I'd
be happy to have Cam stay with me. I could use help out here.
Besides, he's the only one Franklin cares about anymore." Cam
looked at his grandmother. What she said wasn't accurate. The
dog slept across the threshold of her room every night, and she
tripped on him and swore every morning on her way to the bathroom. The animal lived for a glance or a touch from Lucy. But at
least Lucy was on Cam's side, and for the time being, she was
someone he recognized completely. Someone willing to stand
up to his father and the only person to whom Arthur reliably listened. Arthur said nothing, pulled his mouth to a small, tight
bud, and jabbed a tiny spoon into the swan of salt.

Cam was in new territory now, not sure to whom it belonged, but he felt oddly free. Maybe, he thought wildly, this was
what his mother experienced when she decided to die. Crazily
invigorated because she'd finally made a choice. Cam rose, not
quite sure what he would do or say. His body felt stronger than

it ever had. He had worked it hard this summer. "No, Lucy. I'd live in town. I want to get a job. I don't want to go back to school." This ambition unfolded in him as if it had lived like a crumpled fan in his chest that now was spread to a full and airy thinness. It was delicate but real. "I'm not good at it. I don't want to be there."

He was still standing, swaying slightly, and his fingers, released now, were caught in a powerful jitter. He wanted to say, but couldn't because his body was so clearly disobeying him, that he was actually good with his hands, that his brain got clearer and firmer when he used them all the time, and that there was something sharp and necessary to his labor when performed outside. "I like it here," he said again, sounding feebler this time, aware of the inelegance of his protest. "I just do."

Lucy made herself busy filling the kettle, relighting the stove. "This is between you and your father. As far as I'm concerned, you can stay. Cam, I've never seen you more settled." He'd seen her searching for a word. She'd tried on "happy," he guessed, but it hadn't quite fit. "Arthur, you should stop being so stubborn and look at what's in front of you." She did not brandish the kettle at them, though her voice was full of scolding. But she's faking it, thought Cam. She's pretending she knows what she feels, and she doesn't really. Her fingers were still glimmering in places.

Arthur hadn't seemed to notice any of this. Somehow he had slipped past his history with Lucy. His expression tightened further, as if his skull were caught in an invisible vise. Cam could see the arguments start to line up in his father's mind—long, clean, legal examples which proved that Cam's ideas weren't sensible. Staying in Wyoming would not do him any permanent good. It was foolish to want to leave school. Something else was also gathering on Arthur's face: a deep concern that Laura's irreparable sadness was floating through Cam, and that without someone there to monitor its level, it would rise, like a toxin in a watershed, and one day pollute his son as well.

Dad, Cam wanted to shout, it wasn't just a disease, it wasn't something that just happened to her. At one awful point, she chose. It was what she wanted. She had wanted a black and final ending more than she wanted to be with them every day, and knowing this would make it hard even to get out of bed ever again. But now Cam had found a place where he could manage, and he wasn't going to give it up. It was too important. He was still on the side that chose the daily smack of feet on a cold floor, a cup of hot coffee, a girl's warm body. These things still mattered to him. He had woken up to the mattering this summer, when he thought it was lost to him.

Lucy was still fussing in the kitchen, apparently waiting for the argument to play itself out. "Think of the future," his father implored. "You won't always feel this way about school. What about soccer? Friends?" Warming to his theme, he even said something about expanded landscapes of opportunity on the East Coast.

That did it. Why hadn't his father discussed those when they were living in New York? What had happened this summer that suddenly tainted Wyoming? "What makes Callendar so bad now, Dad? Is it Denise Higgins?" Cam flashed. "Why wasn't it good enough for you out here to start with? Or was it you, Lucy?" Cam shouted into the kitchen. He couldn't believe his voice could swell to such loudness. He had no memory of yelling like this. He felt something high and piercing release in him, like a narrow line of steam, a bright stripe of fire. "What's so bad about ranching? Getting married when you're young? Would someone fucking please fucking tell me?"

Everything around him froze. The dog, his grandmother at the threshold of the dining room and kitchen, his father at the table, even his own hands. Only the wind kept pressing against the window with a slight metallic rattle. Lucy finally sighed and said, "Nothing, actually, Cam, is wrong with any of those things you just mentioned. It depends what you're born with as a talent." She stared at Arthur then, who was slowly turning back into himself, shocked not so much at his son's rude language as at the volume at which it was delivered.

Cam thought about charging out to the truck and driving off to Amber's, but he remembered she was busy at home—with what, she hadn't said. There was no point in making a surprise visit or even trying to phone her. With Amber, busy was busy. He turned toward the two adults: Arthur bewildered, rigid, angry; Lucy unfocused and disheveled. Below the crust of his rudeness and anger, he wanted to love them both, though he could feel no welling up of an apology for his outburst. Instead, he clomped off to his room. It would be too cold to sleep with any comfort in the barn.

Later on, Lucy came to see him. He had gone to bed but not to sleep, and was tossing under the sheets. The moon was very bright and shone with silver intensity through the curtains. Coyotes were howling, and the clack of the dog's claws along the floor had kept him awake. Arthur and Lucy were fighting in the kitchen, arguing in voices they were trying hard to control, without much success. All he wanted was to be next to Amber, curled in her bed below the canopy in the yellow room, his hands still and firm over her breasts.

When Lucy knocked and asked if she could come in, Cam thought she was nothing if not stubborn. He flicked on a lamp and watched it cast velvety stretches of black shadow across the covers, the floor.

"Sorry to bother you so late, baby, but I wanted to talk to you." She sat on the edge of the bed—her bed, which she had forfeited for his sake this summer—and looked around the room as if she hadn't seen it in some time. He'd been put here so he could go out and prowl around without waking other people early in the morning, but they hadn't expected him to prowl quite so much. Out the French doors in Lucy's room and around her land, yes, but not all the way to town, to a girl, to a streambed, to places and experiences his family didn't approve of. He'd never made it to church, at least. He'd resisted Nancy Baum to the end. But what was the point of providing freedom if they weren't going to let him exercise it? He sat up, his bent legs making a tent below the sheets. "Cam, your dad isn't going to budge." His grandmother's feet were in a pool of darkness, and her body looked oddly unfinished. "You're a minor. He's scared you'll do something foolish out here. I don't agree with him, but he's got the law on his side." Lucy was staring at her bureau as she spoke. She had cleared it of her photos, pincushions, and hairbrushes. When he first moved in, it had made Cam feel lonely to see the empty expanse of wood. He had added nothing but his toothbrush and deodorant.

Lucy took a breath and knitted her fingers together. "So I guess what I'm asking you is to do as he asks. Even though, in my opinion, which I know I should not express in this situation, he is dead wrong. There are some people who are not built for school." She turned to look at him directly now. No longer the teacher, he realized with a certain pang. Her hair was dry now, too, but she hadn't woven it back into its braid and it sprang out in a gray tangle around her shoulders. He had never seen her look wild, but she did tonight. He saw again the gold flecks on her wrists. "What happened, Lucy?"

She peered more closely at her nails. "A piece of idiocy I got up to that Ray Fontaine caught me at. Painting those compressor wells with poetry. Though I would ask you not to talk with your father about that. He might find it embarrassing. Lord knows I do."

The poems he had read about in the paper. Amber had been interested in them. She had wondered if aliens were responsible or Christians from another county. He hadn't thought much about them and certainly hadn't suspected his grandmother. No wonder she was looking a little defeated these days. Cam was suddenly weary. He'd never really known that this need to redefine what it was you could live with in yourself could keep returning. He'd been hoping his identity would just gel at a certain point, become clear and unwavering.

"Why did you do it?" he asked. The mounting evidence that the adults around him were capable of making bad decisions both liberated and frightened him.

"Some notion I had of protesting the whole methane thing. I think I was wrestling with staying here or going myself. Old people don't do well in this weather," she said, and he knew she was thinking of Janet and all the relatives who'd moved away to softer climates. She did look abashed. Even in the dimness, he could see that. It cost her to be found wanting in rationality and judgment. "I never thought I would give in to such foolishness, but there's no limit to what a human can do." She stopped plucking at her skin.

"But he's not going to arrest you or put you in jail?" Cam was seized with the image of Arthur going down to the jail to spring Lucy on bail. He had never been in a jail, so all he saw was a picture of Ray Fontaine walking down a corridor of old-fashioned cells, a clump of large keys on a ring, making his slow, jangling way toward the criminal, his grandmother. His mother, he thought, would have loved the poetry, would have loved the idea of Lucy as a jailbird, would have joined her on the escapades had she been invited, would have spent money to get Lucy out, free to write more poems on whatever wells she wanted. Cam started to shake again, but kept his hands hidden under the sheets.

"Anyway," Lucy continued, staring at her guilty, vandalizing fingers, "what I'm saying is, be patient. Just a few more months. And when you're eighteen, you make a choice. Come back here. Go to college. Whatever you want."

Whatever he wanted. It sounded good. Coming from Lucy, it sounded almost believable. But Cam suspected it was another false offer of freedom, like the lure of Lucy's French doors. He sat up straight. "Whatever I want?" he said. Lucy's face was partly in the shadows. "Like joining the army? Like being a carpenter? Like marrying Amber?" Because that was what he wanted, to have this girl around him all the time. To be tied to her with certainty and never let her leave. He had not let himself imagine this before, but must have been harboring the picture in some quiet corner of his mind since it sprang so readily to his eyes. He could see them, then, in a house he'd buy with his mother's money, a house he could learn to fix up. Amber, redecorating, her belly swollen with their baby, the first of many. So many that you would never have to worry if one of them died. You'd have all the others to replace him. Though when it came to babies, Cam knew, even at seventeen, that one never simply took the spot of another who had gone.

"Do you want that, Cam? To marry that girl? To be part of that family?" Lucy's face grew pointed.

"What's wrong with that?" Cam asked, more loudly than he meant to, capitalizing on her fear, responding to it even as it awakened his own.

Lucy turned to look out the window, staring at the moon, the clouds that were rolling in. "The Barlows have meanness in them. I don't know where it started or what got them that way, but there it is." She held her palm up when he started to protest. "I know they've taken you in this summer. I know you have found"—she cast around for a word—"solace among them. But I also know you well enough to say you will outgrow them. I have nothing against marrying young or even marrying often. God knows it's easier to have kids when you're young. But you should try to marry at least remotely the right person. And Amber Barlow is not that."

At first Cam thought she was being a snob, but that wasn't Lucy's way. Disdain about social origins didn't run in their family, especially given how many people in Wyoming were related—and to all manner of people who had been in jail, wound up as drunks, or filed for bankruptcy. It wasn't the tattoos or the fundamentalism. It wasn't even that Mac's family was originally from Nebraska, which was as close as Lucy got to having a prejudice about someone. No, he saw it himself. Some core surliness in that family, some lack of generosity, some kind of ease in dealing out violence. Yet he had found no other antidote to Laura's haunting. Going back to New York would make all that worse. He would not live again in that apartment, look at the window she had leaped through, or see the tranquil rectangle of blameless air through which she had fallen. He could not live among tall buildings and their temptations. He could not live where he could not see the sky and all of its threats right out there in the open.

"I won't talk about this again," Lucy said. Her gaze was unfocused. "And I know I can't make up your mind about what you plan to do." She had run out of words, yet she stayed on the bed, as if unable to summon the energy to stand, move, leave the room that had been hers. She looked tired enough, too, to fall fast asleep right there.

Cam wanted to reassure her, but she had told him she would not come between him and his father. She was letting him know he was without an absolute ally, which was something you had to admire about Lucy: she played fair.

He finally went to sleep, but startled awake from a dream about New York—skyscrapers and rain, the desolation of wet streets. Cam was filled with panicky shame, yet he'd seen no one, not even himself, walking through the city. Slowly, he sat up and glanced through the windows at the stretch of tan field and a sky only two shades lighter. It was close to dawn, the first day of September, and the air was padded with layered gray clouds, row upon row of malevolent weather. He'd hardly thought about New York this summer, the orange-eyed pigeons, his afternoons on the soccer field in Central Park. New York had become a fantasy, shimmering at the horizon in distant unreality. He had never been in Wyoming during severe cold. He knew it only through heat, aridity, evenings as long as days, the rasp of grasshoppers. Today, after a summer of near-total dryness would come the harsh and steady wetness of a blizzard.

After the shreds of the dream had faded, this was the memory Cam kept thinking of. Lucy frozen on the bed, staring listlessly around her, an unwelcome apparition of frailty and sadness to both of them. He hadn't spoken, and she finally left.

It was so early, he knew he was the only one who was moving in the house, and he was grateful, for the hundredth time, for the French doors. He slipped on jeans, a shirt, sneakers, and a denim jacket and walked out into the harsh air. It was even colder than he'd realized, but he didn't dare linger. He was going to take his father's new truck, and he didn't want to risk conversation, much less discovery of his departure simply to add another layer of clothing. Besides, he was going to have to get used to the cold. He had his keys, his wallet with his license, some papers, and what seemed to him an abundance of money, at least three hundred dollars.

He was careful to start the engine fast and pull directly out onto the driveway. He would call later to let them know where he was and what he was doing. But they would guess, anyway. They might even go to Amber's house and engage in some terrible, solemn talk with her parents. He had to get there quickly.

Cam's chest filled with an uneasy blend of elation and fear as he drove. He was pleased by his general competence in handling this large vehicle, how he knew its rhythms and habits. A skill acquired in only a few short weeks, to which he could proudly add lawn mowing, minor carpentry, fly-fishing, lovemaking. A summer of private but permanent discoveries. For the moment, his hands were steady, but his mood wasn't. It was veering like the sun, alternately hidden by banks of clouds, then revealed in great streaking beams that pierced the sky like the word of God made manifest in a children's Bible. "Jesus rays," Lucy called them sarcastically. Behold, the Lord. No meadowlarks were risking their lives against the windshield today. In fact, all the land that rolled past seemed devoid of birds: they had sensed the strength of the coming storm and found shelter as close to ground as possible. Apart from some deer, which were starting to turn a darker dun now that the season was shifting, he saw no animals at all.

The Barlows' house seemed unfathomably quiet when he reached it, and he was overcome with total indecision. It was folly, what he was proposing to do. Amber didn't love him enough to follow his lead as he hoped she would. She didn't love him at all. She told him so in her usual blunt way, though that hadn't stopped her sleeping with him whenever she could. She'd keep that bored, frozen look on her face until the moment when he touched her, and then she turned to another substance entirely—melting girl. There was no pretending with the body; it just didn't lie. But that was never going to be enough to glue Amber to him. For all he knew, she'd react like this to any pair of hands that belonged to a man. And he didn't know if he loved her or not, either, though she stopped Laura in her tracks. He was protected when he was around her. That could be enough, couldn't it, at least for now? His plan wasn't going to work, but he was here. He had made the step toward her.

The stark light flooding the eastern sky, as if flouting the coming storm, revealed all the raw meanness of the Barlows' house. The dull cream of the vinyl siding. The miserly glint of mica in the tar-paper shingles. Even the low, cropped bushes bought on sale at the Agway that did nothing to hide the concrete foundation, bushes that only drew attention to the flat gray surface they were meant to mask. He saw all this, and it did not stop him from opening the door, after scuffing his sneakers carefully on the mat that said WELCOME FRIENDS AND NEIGHBORS. Nor did it keep him from climbing the stairs as softly as he could.

It was just six o'clock. The house was filled with the weighted feeling of people still asleep. Mac, Valerie, and Amber, tattooed Amber, whose face would hold a golden glow under her high yellow canopy.

But he was wrong. As soon as he opened her door, he knew he was wrong. A long person was lying next to Amber and talking to her in a moderate whisper, a whisper that suggested the man didn't want to wake anyone but wasn't worried if it happened, a whisper that belonged to the house. The individual anchored to that confident sound turned when he heard the door. Although Cam had never seen him, he knew it was Len. He recognized the squinting eyes and beefy cheeks from photographs Amber had shown him.

What Cam couldn't stop staring at was Amber's face. She had seen him a fraction of a second before Len had, and nothing had flicked over her unsurprised features. If anything registered, it was slight irritation, Cam as a minor draft that had snaked through a crack in the window. You bitch, he thought, you cheating bitch. He almost felt a grain of sympathy for Len, who'd also been deceived. A pair of cuckolds—a word he retrieved from some distant memory involving Shakespeare, a New York classroom, boys in loosened ties, another life.

Then he saw that Len was not going to share his sense of outrage. Len was going to exact his vengeance in the way that boys like Len always did. He hadn't moved more than his head, but everything Cam needed to see was spread across his wide red face, as obvious as a smear of jam. His hand was inside Amber's pajama top. Cam knew that pair of pajamas: white flannel scattered with pictures of improbably ripe strawberries. Amber liked to change into them when she got home sometimes. He saw, too, that Len was a lefty, and wondered if that made any difference in his ability to arouse Amber.

Improbably, he felt an untrammeled surge of joy rise inside him. This was going to end badly, and he had sought it out. There would be a vivid, bloody mess when it was over. He turned then to find Mac Barlow, without sunglasses or hat for once—in fact, wearing nothing but boxer shorts and a V-neck T-shirt. His calves were fantastically hairy, and it was that detail—those tight black spirals springing up from the supernatural pallor of his skin—that finally teased out Cam's fear, which, once it announced itself, became the defining emotion of the next few minutes. Cam's hands were still. It was the rest of his body that was shaking.

"Did anyone invite you in here?" Mac asked and took a swaggering step toward Cam.

Cam shook his head but did not speak, not trusting his voice. Len's fingers had slipped from Amber's body and he had swung his wide legs over the edge of the bed. Amber was the only one who hadn't stirred, except to button the gap through which Len's enormous hand had slipped.

"Then what are you doing here?" Mac said, advancing. The room was small and within a moment he would be on top of Cam. Len stood now, a long, thick block of menace.

There was no way to get back to the door, still slightly ajar. On it, Amber had taped a poster of some Christian singer she claimed to like. Cam couldn't remember her name but her voice came back to him suddenly, full and passionate, singing about Jesus as if he were the best boyfriend ever. He saw the woman's glimmering smile the moment before Mac's fist came swinging across his jaw.

Believer, he thought, but as usual could not say. So this is how a believer reacts when he finds the wrong man in his daughter's room. The pain bloomed in a fierce, wide line across his face. Then he felt Len take his elbows, almost tenderly, as if wanting to announce his capacity for gentleness just before he inflicted pain, to let Cam know that he, indeed, was capable of both. "Shitheel," Len said calmly in exactly the voice Cam had known he would have. Only two syllables, but they revealed such a commitment to stupidity. Amber sat up and pulled her knees to her chest. She was watching what was going on with what appeared to be a sullen curiosity. She would look on, say, the dismemberment of a cat with about the same level of detachment. Where was Valerie? Was she still asleep? Would the sound of her husband's fist cracking someone's jaw not wake her? Perhaps she had learned not to let such noises disturb her.

Mac's fist came forward again and Cam ducked instinctively and the blow landed near his temple, which hurt less but caused more damage. The room upended. He felt sick to his stomach. "Pussy," he heard Len say with the same soft intonation he might have used when fondling Amber.

Mac retreated to the center of the carpet each time he hit Cam, as if to examine his handiwork and see what piece of the chore he'd left undone. He was more careful with this project than he had been with any part of his job at Pheasant Run. Cam knew he was being punished for his competence, as well as everything else. For instance, showing Mac up in front of the sexy woman who knew Mac was taking money from the church treasury. Cam missed his grandmother with a passion that astonished him at that moment, but not even Lucy could have stemmed the progress of the brutality. Her presence would mean only that the police would be called, and by the time they came, he might well be dead.

"Are you a bigamist, too?" Cam asked Mac, wondering what else Mac was ashamed of. But by now his lips were so swollen he knew that no one could understand what he was saying.

"Had enough, stupid fuck?" Len said, almost politely.

"Yes," Cam said. This, at least, came out clearly. He had never felt more certain of anything. He hadn't known, either, that clarity of purpose could serve as its own fuel, its own strength, and he wrested himself from Len's grasp without quite believing he could do so. It startled Len as well, who looked at him dumbly. Cam took advantage of the moment to swing as large a punch as he could muster at Len's ear, which, to his delight, spurted blood. Len screamed, the scream of a girl, the scream of a boy who didn't like paper cuts.

Cam started to laugh, though it came out mostly as drool and blood. Some of his teeth were loose in their sockets. He spat on the center of Amber's carpet and was happy to see the strong, bright spot of dark red in the sea of pleasant yellow. Amber had a decorating manual that said that yellow was a good color for kitchens and cheerful bedrooms, instilling a mood of happy reflection.

Cam dashed out the door and into the hallway, where he ran into Valerie, wrapped from neck to pudgy foot in a white terrycloth robe. "What are you doing in my house?" she snapped.

This struck Cam as unbearably funny. "Ha ha ha," he kept sputtering. "Ha ha ha." What does it look like? he tried to say. I'm bleeding all over your house. He sent another wad of spit and blood to the floor, although it hit her foot instead, which was far more satisfying. Cam raced down the stairs as steadily as he could, clutching the banister, the sound of Valerie's appalled gasps in his ears. He lurched outside and over to the meager bushes, where he threw up what little there was in his stomach.

Amber was exactly like her father: people committed to satisfying their own curious definition of pleasure, even or especially when it involved inflicting pain on others. He would not want to be Amber, and he couldn't believe now how fiercely his desire for her had overcome him this long summer. How much safer she would have been with him, who only wanted her in bed. But safety was not what Amber was after. Safety was not what she had signed on for. Cam wiped his mouth, and his hand came away sheathed in red. Standing up from his retching, he leaned over and planted a maroon print on one of the strips of siding.

The neighborhood was just as quiet as it had been when he'd driven up no more than ten minutes ago. When he'd gotten there, he'd had a face. But the houses were just as peaceful, the street just as empty. The only element that had changed was that the cloud bank had advanced and blocked the sun out entirely. The first fat, slow flakes were tumbling from the sky. Cam put his palm out and caught a clump shaped exactly like a bear before it melted to a warm drop of water.

The wind soothed his skin. He didn't want to look at himself, but he would have to, sooner rather than later. There was a split in his lip that reached into the skin at the corner of his mouth, which felt torn and was bleeding as if Mac had turned on a small faucet. He should probably go to the hospital and have his teeth dealt with. But he wasn't going to Callendar Memorial. He wasn't going to visit Celia or go back to Lucy's. He was going to get on the highway and head west to Cody, through the Bighorns. That was as far as he would let himself imagine. If he just bit the journey off in small segments, he might get where he was heading without undue panic.

Inside the car, he mopped himself with a bandanna that Arthur used for a handkerchief, and was surprised but somehow not frightened at how quickly it became soaked. He didn't want to linger at the Barlows' house—he feared Valerie now more than the others, who had already exercised their bloodlust; he could imagine her with a baseball bat or the butt of a rifle, swinging it against the windshield or his head.

The engine turned over and he backed out slowly into the street. To his astonishment, he saw the lean, low, unmistakable shape of a mountain lion lope past his back wheels and dive into the reedy brush across the street. Its head was huge, the paws wide, its grace complete. A ditch that ran off a containment pond for a methane tank provided enough moisture for reeds to flourish, attracting ducks and their natural predators, the lions, to what had once been, as Mac put it, an exclusively residential neighborhood. Amber had told him she'd seen one last year and someone down her street had had three cats eaten. That was when the sign warning people that this was a mountain lion area had gone up. "One sighting and three lost cats?" Cam asked. Amber shrugged. "They're deadly," she answered, as if it were obvious.

From what Cam had glimpsed, even though the cat was on the run, that was true. As blood continued to drip onto the blue upholstery of the Whale, he was glad that the Barlows had not seen the animal. It would surely have drawn them with all their weaponry.

The snow was thickening as Amber's house dwindled to a squat creamy speck in his rearview mirror. He turned on the wipers and saw that the truck needed gas. He chose a Sinclair on the western edge of town, just off the highway, a station he'd never visited, where no one would connect him to the Kings. But he hadn't counted on the fear in the face of the young woman at the counter where he went to pay his thirty bucks for filling the tank. "Holy shit," she said, pulling back from him. "What the fuck happened to you?" Her words were sharp with profanity, but her voice was filled with nothing but the softest wonder, a horrified but unmistakable kindness.

Cam hadn't counted on that. He stumbled away from her to the men's room, which was one large square, adapted for wheelchairs now, and cleaner than any restroom he'd been in all summer. There was even a vase with a stiff spray of artificial flowers in it on the sink. There was also an abundance of hot water. For five minutes, the water streaming off his face was translucent red. Slowly, the bleeding stopped and he steeled himself to look in the mirror. Both eyes were swollen nearly shut, the left worse than the right. His nose was a pulp, as was one of his ears. His mouth had indeed torn, and a wide gash split his lower lip. Several of his teeth rocked unsteadily in his gums and caused more bleeding when he touched them with his tongue. Pain was starting to make his whole body throb. He badly needed water.

When he came out, the girl was waiting for him at the door. It was early enough for her not to worry about other customers.

The name tag on her red polo shirt read HI, YOU CAN CALL ME CINDY. "Hi, Cindy," he said, or tried to. She was holding a steaming dishrag. "I heated it in the microwave," she said and stood there, pressing him back against a recent delivery of Mountain Dew as she daubed his face. She was nearly his height, broad and strong as a well-built cabin.

"Don't tell me who you are, so if anyone asks, I can say I don't know." She was his age, he guessed, plump, blond, and confident. A rancher's daughter? A rodeo rider? A hunter or an EMT? People here were rarely just their job, and being young hardly seemed to matter. Childhood apparently lasted only about five years in Wyoming and then something happened that made almost everyone definitively adult. After cleaning the worst of the cuts, saying nothing, only frowning intently, she sighed, "Wait here." He did. He would do anything this girl told him to. She kept bathrooms so clean. She knew you could microwave a wet towel and turn it into a compress. She brought back a bottle of Advil from which she shook six pills that she made him swallow with a cup of warm, milky coffee. "The caffeine will make it work faster," she said, and again he did not doubt her for a moment. She took out a first-aid kit and taped and bandaged the worst of the gashes with cool, expert fingers.

"I'll be OK," he croaked. This was the first sentence since the beating that was apparently intelligible to both him and a listener.

She looked at him appraisingly, not sharing his optimism. "Sure you will," she said slowly, screwing the cap back on the Neosporin. She put her hands on her hips. A gesture she had learned from her mother, Cam guessed, another woman who was probably formidably competent around wounded men, men in trouble. They made their way carefully back to the cash register.

He told her he wanted to buy some food. His face was stiff under the Band-Aids and he wasn't hungry yet, but knew he would be. And he didn't want to have to stop in places where his appearance would cause comment, even out here, where men got beat up. She shook her head. "I already got you some stuff. Sandwiches, pop, power bars. My treat." She put in the first-aid kit and the Advil.

"Why?" he asked, looking at the bulging shopping bag, then at Cindy. She was suddenly shy, glancing at plastic sheaths of peanuts.

"I do know who you are. Well, I know your grandmother. Mrs. King. She taught me American history the year before she retired." Cindy rotated a gold ring with a tiny garnet in its setting around her middle finger. "She meant the world to me."

Cam realized then he should have gone straight back to Lucy. There was no escaping the net of family, no escaping the hard conversations. Even this girl was aware of who he was and he was in the one place in town where he thought he could avoid detection. She meant the world to me—the words were curiously old-fashioned and alarmingly open, and Cam knew exactly what she meant.

"Please don't let her know I looked this bad," he said and smiled.

She couldn't help wincing as he tried to shift his mouth. "Don't do that for a while," she told him. "It'll hurt too much."

"Thank you," he said and reached out a hand to hold hers. Her fingers were harder than he'd expected, but warm, and his own did not shake. He wished he had met Cindy at the beginning of the summer instead of Amber. The other hand started to tremble where he awkwardly stuck it, in his jeans pocket. "Thank you, Cindy."

"Good luck," she said and started wiping down the counter. He noticed that she had thrown the blood-streaked towel she'd used on his face into the large trash barrel next to the cash register. "God bless you," she said as a seeming afterthought, just as the door was about to close on him. Cindy's sad, careful words actually felt like a balm.

Another truck was pulling up next to his and he ducked his face away from the driver just in time. He would have to stop for a hat and gloves somewhere. Maybe tonight in Cody, if he got that far. The Advils weren't working yet, but he was glad to know they were in his system and would soon numb the first layer of ache.

The flakes were coming down in curtains. He guessed that his father and Lucy would have left the house by now to go and find him. He imagined his grandmother had woken with the first chug of the engine and raced downstairs to see the exhaust trailing down the driveway. She wouldn't stop to wonder what it meant. She would act with decisive confidence, the way Cindy had—the way Laura never could, with one exception.

He steered west, on the narrow length of highway that stretched out toward the Bighorns. When he had come to Wyoming in earlier summers, he and his family spent a lot more time in the mountains, hiking past patches of snow to find a bald rock, warm in the sun, on which to bolt their picnics. They had a picture of Celia and Laura standing below a sign for Crazy Woman Creek, each looking outraged at the designation and pointing mock-accusatory fingers at each other. He was heading straight toward that pass now.

Few other cars were on the road. Weather advisories were surely being broadcast, and the signs that flashed yellow to warn drivers to put on chains would soon be flaring. There was no time to waste if he was going to make it over, but he didn't turn on the radio to learn more. Storms scrambled reception anyway. He passed the state troopers' office, and saw that the cruiser was parked and empty in the small lot. Either no one was in the station or the officer was fast asleep. Cam was actually pleased that the most important law enforcement in the area had not been notified he was missing.

A semi in the other lane hooted at him, whether in fellowship or in warning Cam couldn't tell. He pressed on the gas as the grade of the mountain grew steeper. Even the parts of his body that had not been punched were aching. They'd concentrated on his face, not his ribs or balls or stomach, and for that he was grateful. They hadn't wanted to kill him, just to make him ugly.

The storm was starting to pummel the trees, whipping the great branches of ponderosa left and right with careless strength. He began to feel how solitary his endeavor was, if that's what you'd call it. Driving alone in a blizzard. He heard Lucy's voice. "Foolish," she would say, the harsh word banked by love. He imagined Celia's face, worry spread across it like a tight sheet on a bed, wanting him to come back and stop being headstrong, to stop being so private. She wanted him to admit that they were still there, what was left of his family. His father's face, too, appeared to him, full of anger and love and puzzlement and something that would never understand him.

In going to the Barlows, he had severed ties not only with Amber but with his own family. This seemed obvious. A large, dark shape emerged on the road in front of the truck; he braked and skidded, which frightened him more than anything else had so far. It was only a mule deer, trotting toward its perception of greater safety, but Cam's heart would not stop battering.

As his pulse slowed, he thought about the implications of being beat up by Mac and Len. They wanted it to mean that he'd never come back, but Cam didn't think that was the most important part. They'd cut him loose. What was most significant was that their brutality made him realize how alone he actually was. He was untethered, and the sensation made him feel awful. It took time to build and seemed to come with the deepening of the switchbacks as the road approached the pass. The trees were black under the snow and bending lower with the weight of the wind. He was going more and more slowly. His beams were on high. There was no traffic in the other lane. He hadn't seen a truck or another car in miles. The way you could drive and drive and encounter nothing but land, trees, fences, animals, sky was a feature of Wyoming his mother had openly admired.

His hands started to shake again. He'd known it would happen, of course, because no snowstorm, no beating, no girl could slice him free of her. He felt himself give in at last to the haunting, to the possession. He let himself remember what he had spent the past months trying to stash away, as if it were a key to something precious, a stolen ring, a secret journal. Or maybe it was just pushing its way through, Cam thought, because there was nothing left to block it. Snow almost entirely obscured the windshield. The wipers pushed it back in heavy ridges, the circle of glass through which he could see diminishing. The other windows in the car were sheathed in fantastic whorls of ice.

He had come home early that day from school. The coach was ill and no substitute could be found, so he and the rest of the soccer team had been released from practice. Cam had felt unexpectedly sad that he wouldn't have that sweaty two-hour stretch of muscling the ball from one end of the field to the other. The other players cheered, and he hooted with them, but he felt none of their apparent relief. Time was easier to manage when it was filled.

Some boys went off for pizza. Others drifted off in the park to smoke. He was invited to do both, but instead he went home. He was worried about his mother then, and often found her at her desk or lying on the sofa, and she was always, always tired. She had stopped reading newspapers and they lay in gray stacks on the back elevator landing so his father wouldn't see them going to waste. "All those happenings," Laura would say, waving her hand, "out there." He wanted to see his mother. To be near her. To get her to drink or eat, and to tell her something about his day. To coax her back.

The moment he turned the corner onto his street, he knew something was wrong. He saw a ring of people below the canopy. He saw that something had damaged the canopy itself.

He heard sirens. He ran. He ran as fast as he could toward it, though his entire body wanted to head in the opposite direction. He saw the doorman and his look of horror, his hat off, his knees scuffed. He saw neighbors, women in tidy suit jackets and low-heeled pumps. He saw the dog from 10A. But no one recognized him. In the confusion, he was able to slip inside the building, sprint the length of the lobby, and enter the elevator, jabbing the number for their floor.

The moment he entered their apartment, he knew. It is always possible to tell when a place is occupied. The hum of something human makes its presence felt, disturbs the air in a way that wind or heat cannot. The push of living cells pressing for more air, more life, even when the body is asleep or lying still or sitting, looking out the window at sparrows, pigeons, shadows on brick walls. Life insisting on life. The moment he walked into the hall, he knew there was nothing alive in the apartment. "Mom?" he called. At the wheel of the truck, which was barely moving forward now, his face a throbbing mass of cuts and bandages, he remembered how much hope he had invested in that single word. He would never want anything as much as he wanted to hear her answer, "In here, Cam, in the kitchen. I'm in here." But there wasn't a sound.

Then he saw the note on the dining-room table, anchored by a vase of flowers that needed fresh water. It was on unlined paper from a sketchbook. She used to fill pages with drawing after drawing—him and Celia, their father, the park, Lucy and her garden in Wyoming. She would add features that weren't there in real life: birds, a bow in Celia's hair, funny glasses on his father's nose. Just testing, she would say, to see how it looks.

The note was in his wallet now. He pulled over vaguely to the right and put the truck in park, although it was impossible to tell where the shoulder was. He had no idea where he was, how close the pass was, if he had reached it, if he was on the other side and on his way down. The walls of the storm, white and furious, were closing in. He turned off the windshield wipers. He wasn't sure, but he thought the tires slipped a little. The heat was on high, but he was still cold. His hands were dancing, and he didn't know if it was because they were close to being frozen or because he was letting the memory in as near as he had ever let it come. He pulled his wallet from his pocket and out fell his wad of money. He had no idea how to find a hotel in Cody. The idea to go there had been ridiculous from the beginning, but that didn't mean he wasn't going to pursue it.

He eased out the note, which he kept folded next to his driver's license. He had grabbed it from the table, had dashed to her bedroom, had seen the open window and the curtain billowing, and then he had run down the back stairs, flight after dizzying flight, and had not stopped running until he reached the park and the deserted soccer field. He had stayed there, torn wide, silent, sitting on a bench covered in blistered green paint as the first of the tremors settled into his hands. Children ran past and crunched the curled brown leaves of plane trees below their feet. He couldn't remember how he got back to his building, but the next thing he saw was his father in the lobby. His mother was no longer on the sidewalk. "Cam?" his father said, and started to sob.

He had let himself be held, he had let himself be told the news. But he had been in the apartment when she was not. He had the note and decided the moment he read it that he would never show it to either his father or his sister. Once concealed, it could not be suddenly proffered, the pain it delivered redoubled because of its long sequestration. All she had written was, "This pain is larger than anything I will ever know. But I am so tired. Please forgive me."

He did forgive her, Cam told her, aloud in the cold truck, the wind shoving at its heavy body. He had forgiven her the moment he read the note, because that was what his love for her was: complete acceptance. He knew her. He shook as the cold gathered. He could feel everything and nothing all at once. He could move forward, backward, stay still, walk straight into the woods the way that deer had done. No movement, no choice would console him for what he could not endure, which was the thought of what it must have felt like to go hurtling through that air. To know your wish was coming true but to know as well that it would hurt so badly. She had fallen ten stories. More than a hundred feet. It must have hurt so much to land on that sidewalk. She, whom he would never stop loving, now or later, in the mountains or on a coast, alive or frozen, whole or broken. It must have hurt so much. He opened the door. He walked into the storm.

ACKNOWLEDGMENTS

I would like to thank the Ucross Foundation, which provided me with space, time, and the inspiration to first develop this book. Sharon Dynak in particular deserves my gratitude. I should note here that the town of Callendar is fictional, although coalbed methane mining and the problems that split estate gives rise to are not.

Much of this novel was written during my year at the Dorothy and Lewis B. Cullman Center for Scholars and Writers at the New York Public Library, and I am grateful to everyone there for their kind encouragement.

Elisabeth Sifton, most gifted of editors, is always there, always right, always trusted. I would like to thank as well these talented people at Farrar, Straus and Giroux: Charlotte Strick for the gorgeous cover; Jonathan Lippincott for the book's elegant design; Maxine Bartow for another outstanding job of copyediting; Wah-Ming Chang for all her excellent help with production editing; and Charles Battle for all his kind assistance. Jennifer Rudolph Walsh and Virginia Barber read my work with grace and insight, and I deeply appreciate their support and guidance.

I would also like to acknowledge my treasured family: Edie and Ham Kean, Jim Bacon, Rachel Bacon, and Nick Bacon. And finally, my essential companions, my heart's center—Brad, Tobias, and now, at last, Thea.